Sand & Sutures

L.M. NELSON

Sand & Sutures
Copyright © 2016 L.M. Nelson

ISBN-10: 0-9985135-1-2
ISBN-13: 978-0-9985135-1-5

2 3 4 5 6 7 8 9 10

This is a work of fiction. The events and characters described herein are imaginary and are not intended to refer to specific places or living people.

Cover Design Assistance by: Rachael Ritchey
Photos Courtesy of:
pixabay.com/JuliWatson CC0 (cityscape)
wikimedia/Barry Haynes CC3.0 (beach/surfboard)

Chapter One

The Maternity Ward of University of Washington Medical Center overflowed with patients. Unoccupied delivery rooms were scarce. Nurses, patient technicians, and doctors frantically bounced around from one room to another attempting to dodge the chaos and tremendous influx of people who seemed to swarm the ward today.

Dr. Randal Hanson flipped through yet another patient chart, trying to comprehend the information in front of him. He hadn't had a cup of coffee all day and his energy tank was quickly depleting. "Who opened the flood gate?" he said to one of the on-duty nurses. "Did every single pregnant woman in Seattle go into labor today?"

The nurse gave a bemused smile. "I don't know, Doctor. But the patient in room 213 is crowning."

"Who's her doctor?"

"Dr. Jamison, but he's on vacation this week."

"Who's covering for him?"

"Dr. Drexol, but he's not available right now because he's busy with the patient in room 220."

With a heavy sigh, Dr. Hanson put the chart back and headed to room 213. When he walked into the delivery room, a young woman gripped her hands into her bulging abdomen and pulled her knees up to her chest. Her facial muscles tensed, her teeth clenched, and she screamed in excruciating pain.

The nurse glanced up at the clock on the wall, turned her eyes to the doctor briefly, then focused on the clock again. "Dr. Hanson. Thank goodness you're here."

Calmly, Dr. Hanson headed over to the sink to wash his hands. "How's she doing?"

"Baby's head has crowned."

He pulled a couple of paper towels from the dispenser, dried his hands, then turned the water off. Being a first-year resident doctor, Randy Hanson held a medical degree but could only practice medicine under the supervision of a fully licensed physician. Fully understanding that the attending physician in charge was ultimately held accountable for anything that happened in that delivery room, Randy asked, "Has Dr. Drexol been notified?"

"Yes, Doctor. He said to get started and he'd be in as soon as he could."

Randy tossed the damp paper towels in the trashcan and slipped on a pair of latex gloves. While the nurse filled him in on vitals and other pertinent information, he took position at the end of the hospital bed, helped the patient slide her feet into the stirrups, and prepared to deliver this baby. "Alright, go ahead and have her push."

With the nurse assisting the patient, who had no labor coach of her own, Randy monitored the delivery to ensure that nothing went wrong.

Five minutes into the pushing process, Dr. Drexol shuffled into the room. "How's it going in here?" He picked up the patient's file to check her stats then peered over Randy's shoulder. "Looks like you have things under control." He scrubbed up, slipped on latex gloves, and stood behind Dr. Hanson, looking on while he continued to make the delivery.

Pushing proceeded for another ten minutes before the baby made his grand appearance. Several loud cries followed, as well as tears from the mother when Randy placed the baby on her chest.

"Nice job, Dr. Hanson," Dr. Drexol told his protégé. "Your father would be proud."

"Thank you." Randy's father was a local obstetrician with an impeccable reputation in the Seattle metropolitan area. Once his residency training was complete, Randy planned to fulfill a lifelong dream of joining his father's private practice.

"How is your dad anyway? I haven't spoken to him in a while."

"He's doing well." Randy removed his latex gloves and threw them in the hazardous waste bin. "Stays pretty busy with his practice."

"Does he still fish?"

"Yes he does. In fact, he and I went fishing last weekend."

"Give my regards to your father for me. He's a great man."

"Will do, Doctor. Thank you."

"I have a scheduled Cesarean this afternoon and I'd like you to assist me in the OR."

The first time Randy met Dr. William Drexol was during his residency interview. He was one of UW's upper division clinical teaching physicians. Not only was he a wonderful mentor, he was also one of the few physicians who did his best to get to know his mentees on a personal level.

"Put on some fresh scrubs and meet me in the prep room in fifteen minutes," Dr. Drexol instructed.

"Yes, Sir."

Randy reported to the physician's locker room. As far as hospital locker rooms went, this one was pretty comfortable. Each white locker, labeled with a physician's name, had a small storage compartment underneath. In the corner was a large cabinet, which held several pairs of scrubs folded neatly and sorted by size. A comfortable white oak futon gave physicians a place to take a load off, and two windows allowed natural light to enter the room. Overhead, florescent lamps brightened up the area and several green potted plants added a spark of color. The facility was well-organized and clean. This hospital treated its doctors well.

Randy opened a drawer full of blue disposable non-skid surgical shoe covers. He pulled out a pair and slipped them over his loafers. He locked up his belongings, put on his hospital photo ID badge, which also served as a controlled access card and gave him access to the Pneumatic Tube System, and headed to the OR to scrub up.

The main entrance of the University of Washington Medical Center displayed framed photos and informational plaques of all the attending physicians and resident doctors affiliated with the hospital. Randy's photograph hung among them—J. Randal Hanson, M.D.

Even though Randy walked past this wall daily, he still beamed every time he saw the letters M.D. after his name. The process of getting his medical education had been grueling, with long hours, arduous classes, obnoxious and demeaning physicians and residents, and exhausting tests. For him, even with the difficulties, that journey had been worth it—every long hour, every second of humiliation he was subjected to, every minute of stress. He was a physician now, an obstetrician/gynecologist, and he was ready to take the next step—that long four-year residency.

After a long day of hospital rounds, performing multiple deliveries, pelvic exams, and surgical procedures, Randy went back to the lab to process some samples for testing. Feeling antsy, he glanced at his watch every ten minutes.

A colleague of his questioned his restlessness. "Anxious to get home, Dr. Hanson?"

"I'm looking forward to this weekend so I can spend some time with my wife." Randy and his wife had recently relocated from San Francisco to the Seattle area. They were finally settled into their new home, but now that she was in grad school and Randy was working an average of sixty to seventy hours per week, adjusting to their new schedules had proven to be a bit challenging.

"How long you been married?"

"About three months."

"Still newlyweds. Congratulations." He shook Randy's hand. "I'm Greg Hutchins, second year resident. I've heard about you, but we haven't officially met. Welcome to the UW Residency Program."

"Thank you."

"What's your wife's name?"

"Jane."

"What does she do?"

"She's in grad school, studying psychology." Randy checked the time again. This day seemed to be dragging endlessly.

Randy's watch had the Lakers logo on it, which instantly piqued Greg's curiosity. "Are you a Lakers fan?"

"Yup."

"So am I. Maybe we can catch a game together sometime."

"That would be great." Wanting to learn more about this doctor, Randy asked, "You married?"

Greg blew off this question as if it had little importance in life. "Nah."

"Have a girlfriend?"

"Nope. Not looking for one either."

Greg's tone was a bit hostile. Randy was drawn back by this, wondering why this man was so openly negative.

"My bitch of an ex cleaned out my bank account, stole a bunch of my shit, and left," Greg snarled.

Well, that explained the hostility. "Ouch. Damn, that sucks."

"Yeah, well, shit happens."

A young medical student stepped into the lab, interrupting their conversation. "Excuse me, Dr. Hanson?"

Randy turned his head. "Yes?"

"I'm sorry to bother you, but there's a woman in the waiting room asking for you. She claims to be your wife."

Randy said, "Is she five foot seven with long brown hair, green eyes, and an amazing smile?"

The medical student nodded. "That would be the one."

"Yes, that's my wife." He dropped what he was doing and went out to greet her.

Curiosity led Greg to follow him.

With a wide grin, Randy ambled over to Jane. "Hey, Babe. What are you doing here?"

"I left you a text. You didn't get it?"

"Been busy," he admitted. "Haven't checked my messages in a while. What's up?"

"Aren't you off in twenty minutes?"

"If I get this lab report done I am. Why?"

"Because I thought we might go out for Chinese food tonight."

"Alright," he said cheerfully. "Give me a minute to finish this. You can wait out here if you want."

Randy left Jane in the waiting room while he went back to the lab to finish his report.

"That's your wife?" Greg asked.

"Yes."

Greg turned his head to Jane once more. "Wow. Beautiful."

"I think so."

As soon as Randy finished his report, he grabbed his belongings and reported to the medical student he was working with. "Mr. Allen."

The medical student turned around. "Yes, Sir?"

"Thank you for your help today. When you get a chance Monday morning, check on the lab results and let me know if you find anything unusual."

"Absolutely, Doctor."

"Have a good weekend, and try to get some rest."

The medical student replied, "Thank you, Sir. You too."

Randy swore he would not be the condescending ass so many residents he encountered in medical school seemed to be. He made every effort to be courteous and kind, and because of this, the UW medical students floating around the hospital liked him. As a mentor, Dr. Hanson was well-known for his kind, helpful attitude and friendly personality. He was very understanding and tried to guide the medical students, not put them on the spot. The attending physicians and other residents found him knowledgeable and hardworking. He was thorough in his reports and clear and concise during Grand Round presentations. He quickly became popular in the OB/GYN professional ranks.

Chapter Two

Saturday morning, after a good night's sleep, a refreshing shower, and a shave, Randy slipped on a pair of shorts, a Lakers tee-shirt, and a comfortable pair of sneakers. Feeling reenergized, he trotted down the stairs.

An African Grey Parrot spotted him and squawked frantically, "Hello, Doctor."

"Good morning, Birdbrain." Randy opened the cage and reached inside, allowing the bird to perch on his arm.

The parrot waved its claw and began to sing, "Oh, What a Beautiful Morning…"

Randy's parrot was a high-maintenance pet. He required a good deal of personal attention and many hours each day out of his cage. This bird not only had a high vocabulary of speaking words, but he was also quick to learn and had the talent for being able to imitate things like phones, microwave ovens, alarms, and doorbells. This clever twelve-inch grey parrot learned to mimic these sounds, and he used them to get Randy's attention whenever he wanted it, which annoyed Randy sometimes because the bird would replicate the noises from his cellphone to make him run to answer it. This intelligent bird, whom Randy appropriately named Mr. Fingers because he would often bite strangers, was good at speaking in sentences and responded appropriately to questions. This observant bird noticed everything that went on in the house. He studied every movement and reaction. Sweet and affectionate, he was a dedicated and loyal bird. Randy loved this remarkable creature.

Randy quickly examined the parrot. His grey wing feathers were neatly primped, his beak and nails filed. The brilliant red tail feathers and white around the eyes were well-groomed. His head and neck feathers had their normal scalloped appearance. He was boisterous, vivacious, and playful, screaming bloody murder at his toys—his normal naughty self.

Randy chuckled and said, "Crazy bird." He perched Mr. Fingers on top of his cage and headed for the kitchen to prepare a pot of coffee. While he waited for the pot to brew, his cellphone rang. When the name Dr. James Ryan popped up on his caller ID, Randy's face instantly lit up.

"Well, hello Loverboy," Jim said when Randy answered.

"Hey, Jim."

"How's married life treatin' you, Bro?"

"Amazing," Randy responded, feeling happier and more content than he could ever remember feeling before. "What's up?"

"Jill and I have set a date."

"Oh yeah?"

"Yup. But here's the thing," Jim explained. "We're not gonna have a big shindig, just a small get-together with a few friends and family. I know it's kinda short notice, but the only day we were both able to get off is next Saturday. I need you and Jane there."

"Might be cutting schedules a little tight, but we'll be there." Randy was glad Jim chose Jill. He always liked her.

While on the phone with Jim, Randy poured himself a cup of coffee and stepped outside onto the deck to take in the morning sunshine. They talked for a long time, sharing stories from their various rotations, both grateful to hear the other's voice. They had been apart three months and had some catching up to do.

Around 11:00 A.M. that morning, Jane stepped out on the porch to see Randy sitting in the front yard sipping from a water bottle. "Hi, Sweetie."

Randy turned his head toward her. "Hey, Baby."

She quickly scanned the yard. The grass had been neatly mowed and edged, the front bushes trimmed, and there wasn't a speck of dirt on either the front walk or the driveway. The soil in the flower beds was moist, freshly watered. "You've been busy out here. The yard looks nice."

"Thank you."

She sat in the grass facing him.

He leaned back and supported his weight with his hands. "I called my sister this morning."

"How's she doing?"

"Apparently she's down in L.A. with Bruce." Bruce Buckman and Randy were good friends who graduated from medical school together. Bruce was now in a Neurosurgery Residency Program at UCLA. "She's planning on staying with him for the summer."

This sudden decision was odd. Bruce and Randy's sister had been dating off and on for a while now, but Jane could have sworn she heard Bruce say he didn't want her as a roommate. "I thought he didn't want Stephanie living with him?"

"She says it's only temporary. He wants to be able to see her, but his schedule is crazy. And she's so indecisive and flighty, she makes things difficult for him. He tries to talk to me about it, but I don't want to get involved."

"He's your friend," Jane reminded him. "And friends talk to each other about that kind of stuff."

"I know that, but she's also my sister, and their relationship is complicated. I try to keep my nose out of it. By the way, Jim and Jill finally set a date."

"They did?"

"Yup. We have to be in San Francisco next weekend."

"Yay!" She softly clapped her hands. "I'm so happy for him."

"So am I." Swiftly, he stood up and dusted himself off. "Care to join me for lunch?"

"Yes. I'd love to," she replied. "I'll be in, in a minute."

He winked at her and headed inside.

Lying in bed that night, Randy reclined onto his pillow with one hand behind his head. He wrapped his other arm around Jane. She snuggled in next to him and rested her head on his shoulder, lolled in dreamy contentment.

"I told Daddy we'd be in San Francisco next week," she said.

"I bet he's excited to see you."

He felt her nod against his chest. "He's looking forward to seeing you too."

Randy snickered slightly.

"What?" she asked, wondering why he reacted that way.

"I don't know, Jane. Sometimes I think he'd rather I wasn't around so he can have you all to himself."

"That's not true. Daddy likes you."

"He makes me uncomfortable."

"I know he does, but I appreciate the way you try to bond with him anyway." She cuddled in a bit closer. "I got a call about a part-time job today."

He looked down at her with widened eyes. "Doing what?"

"The YMCA is looking for coaches for their peewee basketball league."

This sparked his interest. "Really? That's cool. What are the hours?"

"2:30 to 6:30 for now," she told him. "It won't interfere with my class schedule."

"That's good," he said. "When do you start?"

"Tuesday."

He gently kissed her forehead then tucked her hair behind her ear. His thumb gently grazed across her cheek as he gazed into her emerald green eyes. Playfully, he reached his hand down and squeezed her butt.

"Hey, Mister."

"Hey what?" he asked innocently.

"No grabbing."

He rubbed his hands across her backside and squeezed again. "What are you gonna do about it?"

She sat up and straddled his lap.

His hands groped her, stripping off the silky nightie she had on. He sat up and kissed her, almost instantly becoming erect. Jane crawled off him long enough to remove her underwear before she stripped him naked and repositioned herself on his lap. She tightly wrapped her legs around him.

He caressed her entire body, taking in every touch. The smell of her skin, the taste of her lips, the painstaking look of ecstasy on her face every time he penetrated roused every sense. Hearing the little noises she made when they made love and knowing he satisfied her made him want her more. He loved the sensual stimulation making love to his wife offered him.

Randy released a long, pleasurable sigh. His body shuddered. Gasping for air, his mouth dropped open; he threw his head back and closed his eyes. His fingertips dug into the flesh of her hips. He pulled her body into him and buried his head between her shoulder and chin. He made no attempt to fight his urge to climax. He wouldn't have been able to fight it anyway; it came with a vengeance.

Not only did he and Jane have a happy, healthy marriage, he was convinced that they had the best sex of any two lovers west of the Rocky Mountains. Great sex, to him, was a result of the extreme emotional connection he had with her, love more powerful than any natural source of strength.

Trying to regain a normal breathing pattern, he took in a few cleansing breaths. He clasped both of her hands in his and gazed at her with adoring eyes. "I love you so much."

"I love you too." Slowly she slid off of him and rolled onto her side.

He spooned in behind her and kissed the soft skin of her shoulder. "You're amazing," he said in his bedroom voice. He reached up and turned off the bedside table lamp and kissed her gently on the lips. "Goodnight, Honey."

"Goodnight."

They nuzzled closer together. Randy reached his arm around her and held her hand. Slowly, they drifted off to sleep to the pitter patter of raindrops on the roof.

Chapter Three

Nighttime traffic in Los Angeles was atrocious. Bumper to bumper, moving slower than tar, and drivers were exhibiting road rage worse than Bruce had ever seen before. When he finally made it home, he came inside his apartment and took a deep breath. "Steph?" he called out. She didn't respond right away so he searched the apartment for her. He found her sitting on the toilet seat staring at something in her hand. He leaned against the doorway watching her. "You ok?"

She looked up at him, tears flooded her eyes.

Stephanie wasn't normally a crier. The fact that she had tears in her eyes concerned him. "What's wrong?"

"It's positive."

"What is?"

"This." She held up a plastic test strip from a home pregnancy test. "I'm pregnant."

Bruce stood up straight and stared at her with giant stunned eyes. His entire body tensed up; his heart rate accelerated. "You told me you were on the pill. How the hell did that happen?"

She admitted, "I might have forgotten to take a few."

Irritated by her irresponsibility, he reprimanded her. "Are you shitting me? How do you forget something like that?"

"You're just as guilty as I am."

"You're the one who didn't take your pills. If you would have told me, I could have taken precautions." Bruce held his hand up to his forehead, feeling a headache coming on. He slowly slid down the wall to the floor, bent his knees, and held his head in his hands. In no way was he prepared for this. "I just started my residency. I can't…" A million questions swirled around in his head, none of which were good. He looked over at her and, in an accusatory tone, asked, "Is this baby mine?"

"I can't believe you asked me that."

But Bruce wasn't ignorant. Stephanie was promiscuous, and they had been separated for a while. He wanted the truth, so he asked again, "Is it?"

"Yes." She buried her face in her hands and sobbed.

Seeing tears stream down her face made him wish he hadn't harangued her. She was right. He was just as much to blame as she was. "I'm sorry. I shouldn't have said that."

She sniffled and wiped her eyes. "Do you know how angry my father is going to be when he hears about this? What am I supposed to tell him?"

Bruce crawled over to her and pulled her into his arms. He wasn't thinking very clearly at the moment but did his best to console her. "First, let's confirm with an OB. Then, since we're flying up to Seattle for Fourth of July weekend, let me talk to Randy."

Stephanie thought that was a stupid idea. "Why? What's that going to solve?"

"For one thing, he's my friend. He'll probably beat the shit out of me when I tell him I got you pregnant, but maybe he can help us find a way to gently break this news to your dad."

She nodded in agreement.

Randy and Jane picked Bruce and Stephanie up from the airport the following morning. Bruce was anxious to see Randy's new home after all the pictures he sent, so Randy gave him the grand tour while the women picked up lunch for everyone.

The two of them retreated into Randy's office space. Now that he and Randy were alone, Bruce used the opportunity to talk to him. Dreading what was about to occur, Bruce toughened up and swallowed his anxiety. "Randy, I need to talk to you."

"What's up?" Randy replied with a smile.

Bruce hesitated, licking his lips. "You might want to sit down."

The look on Bruce's face told Randy he was serious. He sat down.

Bruce wheeled over the computer desk chair and sat face to face with Randy. "I don't blame you if you want to kick my ass and never talk to me again."

Convinced that Bruce was overreacting, Randy sniggered, "Come on, Buckman. What could possibly be that bad?"

"It's about Stephanie."

"What about her?"

Not wanting to prolong this, Bruce broke down and told him. "She's pregnant."

Randy's brows drew together and his jaw tightened. With a hardened expression, he glared at Bruce. "What did you say?"

Bruce remained silent, crushed by the infuriated look on his friend's face.

Randy demanded clarification. "Did you just say my sister is pregnant?"

"It was an accident."

Feeling betrayed, Randy grumbled, "An accident? You fuckin' got my sister pregnant, Jackass."

"She said she was on the pill. I believed her. But as it turned out, she forgot to take them."

"What the hell?" Randy blared, outraged by Bruce's actions. His eyes bored into him, and if they weren't such good friends, he would have beat his ass right on the spot.

"I told you you'd be pissed."

"Pissed?" That was an understatement. "I trusted you."

"She didn't take her pills, Randy."

"You could have worn a damn condom."

"Had I known, I would have." Randy stood up and paced the floor, obviously disturbed by this news. Bruce tried to apologize. "I'm sorry. I take full responsibility for this."

"Damn right, you're going to take responsibility. I can't believe you got my sister pregnant." Randy combed his fingers through his hair, hoping to release some tension.

"Randy, please," Bruce interjected. "I know you're angry, and I'm sorry. I wish I could reverse this, but I can't."

Randy shook his head, disappointed.

Trying anything to gain redemption, Bruce said, "Look." He peered up the ceiling trying to gather his thoughts. "Stephanie needs your support." Hoping this didn't ruin their friendship, he begged, "I need your support."

Randy pursed his lips together and sat back down. He leaned forward, resting his forearms on his knees. "You and I have been friends for a long time, Bruce. I am extremely pissed off at you right now, but I will support you and Stephanie."

Bruce breathed a sigh of relief. "Thank you."

Randy looked up at Bruce, thinking about the horrible wrath he was going to have to face. "Do you have any idea how furious my father is going to be?"

"I know. Stephanie and I were kind of hoping you could help us with that."

"Me?" Randy wasn't about to get involved in this. He shook his head wanting nothing to do with it. "Oh no! I am not getting in the middle of this. He is going to wig all over your ass, and I don't want to be around to see that storm."

"Stephanie is really scared. She doesn't know what to say to him."

Laughing a little at this predicament, Randy said, "You guys are so screwed. My father is going to fly off the handle. Stephanie is going to be on the receiving end of hell, and you'll be right there enduring it with her."

Cracking his knuckles, Bruce leaned back in the chair. "Dammit. I wish your family wasn't involved in this."

"And I was just thinking that if this had to happen to Stephanie, I'm glad it was with you. I know you'll take responsibility for this baby." A smirk slowly crept onto Randy's face. "Forgot to take her pills? What the hell kind of lame excuse is that?"

Bruce gave a lopsided grin, despite the fact that he was terrified and not sure how to handle this situation.

"Does anyone else know about this?" Randy asked.

"No."

Randy heard the girls come in. He and Bruce stood up and skirted into the kitchen where Jane and Stephanie each carried a bag of groceries. Feeling sympathy for his sister, Randy took the bag from her and gave her a hug.

Stephanie knew Bruce had told him. She buried her head in her brother's shoulder and cried.

"It's ok." Randy gently rubbed her back offering comfort. "It'll be ok."

"How am I supposed to tell Dad?" Stephanie asked, sounding desperate.

"We'll figure it out."

Jane set her bag on the counter. "What's going on?"

Randy looked down at his sister. "You want to tell her, Steph, or do you want me to?"

With a sniffle, Stephanie replied, "You tell her."

Randy turned his eyes to Jane. "Stephanie's pregnant."

Jane's jaw dropped. "Bruce Buckman!"

Bruce tried to defend himself. "Why is everyone blaming this on me? I'm not the only one in this room who was responsible."

The guilt-ridden look on Bruce's face made Randy laugh. "It's no one's fault," Randy said, trying to ease the tension. Redirecting the conversation to his sister, he said, "We'll find a way to tell Dad. Don't worry." Randy kissed the top of Stephanie's head.

Stephanie's face tensed up. "I don't want to."

Randy knew how she felt. Giving their father bad news was never a fun time. That horrible look their father got on his face when he was upset about something had the ability to make a person feel like the lowest lifeform on Earth. He was glad he wasn't going to be on the receiving end of it. "You can't hide this from him. It's better to tell him now than have him find out when you start to show."

"I know. But the last time I had to give him bad news...I don't want to see that look on his face again."

Randy completely understood. "Neither do I.

After lunch, they all went over to Randy's parents' house trying to act as normal as possible. Casual conversation ensued. Two hours into the discussion, Jane took Randy's mother into the kitchen. Randy signaled to Bruce that it was time to drop the bombshell. Bruce acknowledged and took Stephanie's hand. Randy joined Jane and his mother while Bruce and Stephanie boldly confronted her father.

"Daddy," Stephanie said, getting his attention. "I need to tell you something." She quickly looked over at Bruce. "We need to tell you something."

Dr. Mark Hanson eyeballed Bruce then turned his eyes to his daughter. "What is it?"

Stephanie panicked, not sure if she could do it. Bruce squeezed her hand to help her regain some confidence. She inhaled quickly and looked her father in the eye. "I'm pregnant."

Dr. Hanson stared at her, but didn't say a word.

While this was happening in the living room, Randy's mother questioned what was going on. "Randal, why did you drag me in here?"

"Stephanie and Bruce are giving Dad some news he's not going to like."

"Oh come now. It can't be that bad."

"She found out she's pregnant."

Ellen Hanson covered her mouth. "Your father is going to lose it."

Upon hearing this news, Dr. Hanson stood up, towering over his daughter and her boyfriend with an infuriated scowl on his face. "Stephanie Lynn," he scolded. "If I'm not mistaken, I wrote you a prescription for birth control pills, did I not?"

"Yes, Sir," she replied.

"Did you or did you not fill it?"

"Yes, Daddy, I did."

"Did you take them?" he asked, implying that she had not.

"Most of the time."

His stance grew more intimidating and his lips drew back in a snarl. "Didn't I warn you about the possible consequences if you skipped a day?"

Her faced reddened. "Yes, you did."

"Then I'm confused as to how this happened. That was irresponsible, and you know how I feel about irresponsible behavior." He turned his attention to Bruce, who dreaded this moment the second he walked in the house. "And you," Dr. Hanson raged. "You are a doctor, and I know damn well you learned about the female reproductive system and the possible effects intercourse can have on an ovulating female."

Mark Hanson's voice became ugly and belittling. Bruce didn't like being on the receiving end of it. This ridicule made him feel about the size of a pea. Bruce understood now what Stephanie and Randy were talking about. This man had a way of making him feel small without ever raising his voice. This kind of quiet rage frightened him. And that ice-piercing glare on Dr. Hanson's face was the most awful look Bruce had ever seen. Feeling degraded, Bruce replied, "Yes, Sir. I did."

"Then how could you let this happen?" Mark lectured. "You are just as irresponsible and just as much to blame for this as she is."

"I'm not denying that, Dr. Hanson. I take full responsibility for this."

"That's a good thing. Because you are responsible for this. You and Stephanie both." He waved a finger at them. "And you damn well better be responsible about it." Mark turned his back to both of them and slipped away into his bedroom, closing the door behind him.

Randy peeked out and saw that his father had left, so he, Jane, and Ellen came back into the room. Trying to get her daughter to calm down, Ellen held Stephanie and let her cry.

The minute they all returned to Randy's house for the night, Ellen came into the bedroom and sat on the bed next to her husband, who was propped up on the headboard reading a medical journal with a very cross expression on his face. "Mark, Honey."

"I am not in the mood, Ellen."

"At least she had the courage to tell you."

He did not look up.

"She's young," Ellen said, trying to support her daughter.

"She's irresponsible and careless. And Dr. Buckman...I'm disappointed in that young man. He seemed so bright and so together. How could he let my Stephanie get pregnant?"

"You know how passion gets the best of young people."

He couldn't believe she tried to justify this irresponsible behavior. "To the expense of being unwed and pregnant? To the expense of breaking my trust and sacrificing her youth and her future to care for an infant? Did she think about those things when she allowed him into her bed?"

"Probably not. Did you think about those things at her age?"

"I was in medical school at her age," he snapped.

"Stephanie has always been flighty, Mark. You know that."

"This has nothing to do with her flightiness. It has to do with the fact that she has never been able to tell a man no. Our daughter has always been overly promiscuous even though she tried to hide it from me. I'm not ignorant, Ellie. I know my daughter."

"I know you do. But do you really think she planned this?" Ellen asked him.

"Of course she didn't plan it, and that's the problem." Mark shook his head in disbelief. "I will love this baby, as it is my grandchild, and I love Stephanie. But I hope both of them make the right choices regarding this and don't do anything without fully considering the consequences."

When Bruce and Stephanie retired for the night, Randy and Jane retreated to their bedroom. Randy pulled his polo shirt off and said, "Man, what a crazy day. I can't believe Buckman got my sister pregnant." He sat on the bed and kicked off his shoes. "Stupid ass. I never thought he would let this happen."

"He didn't do it on purpose, Randy."

"That's not the point, Jane." He leaned back and rested his head on his pillow. "I'm going to be an uncle," he smirked. "Does that make Bruce and me related somehow?"

Jane slipped her jeans over her hips and removed her tee-shirt and bra then pulled a silk nightgown over her head. "Do you think Bruce and Stephanie will get married?"

"I don't know. I'm not sure I want them getting married if the only reason they're doing it is because of this baby. Marriages like that don't usually last."

She rolled onto the bed, lying on her tummy with her chin resting in her hands. "Your dad handled the news better than I thought he would."

Randy explained, "Dad was always more subtle when it came to discipline, at least he was when I was a kid. He'd glare at me and make me feel smaller than a flea. That's why I hated it when he found out I did something wrong. All he had to do was give me that disappointed look and I'd feel guilty as hell."

She grimaced. "I hate those looks."

"Me too. They really suck," Randy agreed. "And my father is the master of them. Every time my dad got upset with me I wanted to crawl under a rock and hide. But Robby was a yeller, so Dad had a harder time dealing with him. Dad's evil glares didn't seem to work with Rob. Sure worked with me, though. I hate that damn look he gets when he's angry."

"Did you get that look a lot?"

"Got my fair share. Tried to avoid getting them though. I hate disappointing my father. That, to me, is worse than any punishment he ever dished out."

"And your mom? What kind of a disciplinarian was she?" Jane asked.

"Mom was more the nurturing kind," Randy explained. "She baked us cookies if we felt like crap and brought us hot cocoa when we were sad. She was the calming figure in the house and always knew if something was bothering us. We could never hide our feelings from Mom. She insisted we talk about them. But she supported Dad's decisions when it came to discipline and enforced the rules he made. So if you fessed up to Mom or did something she knew about, Dad would find out about it. She never kept secrets from him, and we all knew that. He usually got angry when he found out that way though. It was better to tell him face to face than have Mom tell him."

"Everyone was an open book in your house."

Randy nodded. "Yup. Which is why we are all so close now. We know each other well. All of our strengths as well as our weaknesses were always exposed. And forgiveness was big in my house. We all made mistakes, but we learned from them, were honest about them, and forgave each other for them. That's what I want for us, Jane. Open communication, honesty, forgiveness."

She scooted closer so she could kiss him. "I want that too."

"Good." He kissed her back.

Bruce felt uncomfortable spending another afternoon at Dr. Hanson's house. He knew the man was angry, and he felt like he had let the family down. But he respected Dr. Hanson and was determined to prove that he was going to take care of Stephanie.

Mark Hanson didn't say much to Bruce all day. He wasn't rude to him, but he didn't make a conscious effort to talk to him either. A few times, he shot Bruce an evil eye.

Bruce kept his distance. He didn't want to make matters worse.

Perturbed about his father's attitude toward Bruce, Randy said, "I'm not trying to sound disrespectful here, Dad, but I really think you're being unfair to Bruce."

Mark looked his son in the eye. "Oh you do, do you?"

"This wasn't solely his fault, you know. Stephanie is guilty too."

"I'm fully aware of that, Randal," Mark replied, somewhat annoyed that his son suggested his actions were unmerited.

"Don't you think you're being a bit harsh with him?" Randy asked. "He's terrified to come near you, and he's convinced you hate him."

Mark denied this statement. "I like Bruce. I always have. But he needs to realize that what he and Stephanie chose to do has consequences. It's those consequences he's going to have to live with."

"He could have just walked away and left Stephanie to deal with this alone. He could have denied that the child was his. He could have tried to keep this from you and not admitted that he screwed up, but he didn't. He fessed up, took responsibility, and is willing to support her through this. That should account for something."

"I'm not saying it doesn't," Mark said. "And I'm sure having a baby in the house while he's trying to keep up with residency is going to be consequence enough, as well as offer him plenty of time to reflect on all of this."

"He's a good guy. One of the best men I know. Don't be so hard on him."

Mark Hanson looked over at Bruce. Maybe Randy was right. Maybe he was being too coarse.

Chapter Four

Tuesday evening, Jane sprang through the door anxious to see her husband. His car was parked in the garage and his stethoscope was lying on the table, but she couldn't find Randy anywhere. His keys and cellphone were missing, as was his basketball. She figured he probably went over to the basketball court by the school, so she headed that direction hoping Randy would be there.

Indeed he was.

He fired several shots into the basket, missing almost every one. "Dammit," he said aloud, obviously frustrated.

She stepped onto the concrete court. "Hi, Sweetie. Whatcha doing?"

Randy turned around, panting. "Just shootin' some hoops." He picked up a bottle of Gatorade and sat on the ground, leaning against the pole under the basket. Little beads of sweat streamed down his forehead. He wiped them off with his shirt and took a big gulp to rehydrate. With the bottle in his hand, he rested his arms on his bent knees.

He wasn't smiling, and he didn't have much to say. Jane knew something was bothering him. "What's wrong?"

"I hate this," he confessed.

She sat down next to him. "Hate what?"

Randy ran his fingers through his hair. "On the way home, when I stopped to put gas in my car, I popped into the convenience store and bought a Gatorade and a package of Oreos. Jim and I used to eat those together all the time." His voice became shaky. "A guy in a Hawaiian shirt strolled through the hospital today. I only saw him from the back, but he was blonde like Jim, built like Jim, he even walked like Jim." With a heavy sigh, he said, "I miss him."

"I know you do. You and Jim have been friends for a long time. It's ok to miss him. But you can't keep dwelling on this. At some point you need to get out and make some new friends."

Randy turned his head and stared at her. "I really don't need your psychoanalytical insights right now, Jane."

Annoyed by his attitude, she started to get up.

"Honey, wait." Randy grabbed her hand. "I'm sorry. Please, stay."

She sat back down.

"You know, there is this doctor I've been working with. He's a second year OB/GYN resident. His name's Greg Hutchins. He's originally from Baker, Oregon but earned his M.D. from Oregon Health & Science University in Portland. And he's a Lakers fan, like me. He's a good guy. We have great conversation and I consider him my friend, but he's not Jim. Don't get me wrong, I mean, I like Greg, but no one will ever replace Jim."

"And you shouldn't try to replace him." She gently touched his shoulder with her hand. "Did you try calling him?"

"I did, but he didn't answer his phone."

"He's probably busy in the ER," she assumed.

"Probably." He picked up his basketball and handed it to her. "You wanna play a game with me?"

"Sure." She took the ball from him and dribbled it across the court.

Around one o'clock the next day, Randy grabbed some lunch from the hospital cafeteria. He saw Greg Hutchins sitting alone and decided to join him. "Afternoon, Dr. Hutchins." He pulled a chair up to the table and sat down.

"Hey, Randy. Did you have a good weekend?"

"Actually, I did. My sister and her boyfriend came up from L.A. for a couple days, and I went fishing with my dad."

"Where?"

"Lake Washington."

"Catch anything?"

"Got a nice sized trout. You fish?" Randy asked.

"I do."

"Maybe we can take the boat out and toss in a few lines."

"I'd like that."

Randy's cellphone chimed. When he looked down and saw Jane's name, his face beamed.

"The wife?" Greg asked when he saw the distinctive look of love on Randy's face.

"Yup."

"How'd you meet her?"

Randy loved talking about his wife. He lit up every time the topic came up. "Playing volleyball on the beach in Santa Cruz. She challenged me to a game."

"She plays volleyball?"

"Basketball too. She played starting point guard for Cal."

"No kidding? A former NCAA player?"

"Yup," Randy boasted.

"Lucky you. Not too often you find a woman into sports like that." Greg unwrapped his sandwich and took a bite. "Nice job during rounds this morning. The medical students seem to like you."

"I remember all too well some of those belittling jerks who used to give me a hard time during med school. I refuse to be that guy."

Greg completely agreed. "I never did understand why attending physicians and higher level residents felt it necessary to treat their fellow colleagues that way."

"Neither did I," Randy said, sipping from his steaming coffee cup. "Which is why I won't do it. It doesn't accomplish anything."

"But I bet it sure makes some insecure guy feel better about himself when he puts a lowbie on the spot like that."

"Sadly enough, it probably does."

"Speaking of which," Greg said. "I saw Dr. Whittleworth do that to a medical student the other day, getting all up in his face about some lab results. The hospital director happened to be standing there at the time and heard the entire conversation. Needless to say, the director was not impressed with the doctor's egotism or condescension, and the family involved personally asked for the medical student to attend to them and refused to let Whittleworth anywhere near the patient."

"Can't say that I blame them," Randy concurred. "Personally, I find Dr. Whittleworth to be an insufferable egotist with delusions of supremacy."

Greg found Randy's comment amusing. "Totally with you on that."

Greg was a cool guy, and he and Randy had similar interests. Randy offered, "So, are you available to go angling sometime?"

"Absolutely. How about this weekend?"

"I can't this weekend. My wife and I are going out of town."

"What about next weekend?" Greg countered.

"Next weekend is good. I want to get out on the water early, though, while the fish are biting. Is Saturday around 6:00 ok?"

"Sounds great. I'm looking forward to it."

That evening, Randy prepared dinner so Jane could study. In the middle of washing his hands, his cellphone rang. Unable to answer it, he called out, "Honey, can you get that?"

Jane reached over and grabbed Randy's phone. She immediately recognized the voice on the other end. "Hi, Jim."

When Randy realized who she was talking to, he quickly rinsed and dried his hands.

"Hang on a second. He's washing his hands." She brought the phone over to Randy. "It's Jim."

"Thanks." He hung the towel up and took the phone from her. "Hey, Bud."

"Hanson, my man. How's life treatin' ya?"

"Can't complain," Randy remarked. "Been busier than hell."

"I hear ya. The ER's been crazy. I've been runnin' around like a madman. Spent my day dodging projectile vomit, plucking shards of glass from someone's arm, and trying to preserve a severed penis. You know how that goes. Typical day of savin' lives."

Jim's passion and obsession for the ER was definitely not Randy's kettle of fish. People on the verge of death never gave him the excitement it always seemed to give James Ryan. "You go ahead and save lives. I'll bring in new ones."

"Deal. I'm so stoked about this weekend. Can't wait to see you."

Spending time with Jim was something Randy was very much looking forward to. This was going to be great weekend. "Me too, believe me." Laughing with his best friend, Randy said, "Bruce and Stephanie came up last weekend."

"Yeah, I know. He mentioned something to me about that."

"You'll never guess what they told me while they were here."

"Do tell."

"I'm going to be an uncle."

Jim hesitated for a moment before he said, "Stephanie's pregnant? Are you shittin' me?"

"Nope, and Buckman is the father."

"Dude, that is seriously fucked up."

Randy couldn't have agreed more. "Tell me about it."

"Hey, but at least with daddy bein' a doctor you know the baby will be taken care of."

"This is true."

"When are you gonna get Jane pregnant?" Jim teased, trying to get a rise out of his friend.

But having a baby was the furthest thing from Randy's mind. "Not for a long time. I want to get through my residency first. Besides, we're enjoying the spontaneity we have right now. We can go out whenever we want, have sex when the urge hits, and stay in bed 'til noon if we feel like it. We want to soak this in for a while before we think about making babies."

"Makes sense."

"But when it happens, you'll be the first to know," Randy promised.

"I hope so." Jim heard a child's voice call for him. "Hey, I gotta go. Chris just woke up."

"Alright. I'll give you a call later. And I'll see you in a few days," Randy said joyfully.

"Countin' down, Dude."

"Me too."

Over dinner, Randy and Jane talked about graduate school, which Jane was far from enthusiastic about. Concerned about her apathetic attitude, Randy asked, "What's the problem?"

"I'm always busy with school. I never have time for myself."

"No one said grad school was going to be easy, Babe."

"I know, but I feel like all I do is study. I'd like to hang out with friends once in a while."

Although Randy was glad she was adjusting and making new friends, he found this statement amusing. "My social butterfly."

She poked him in the chest with her fingertip. "When are you going to quit moping around and get out of the house?"

"Actually, I invited Greg to go fishing with me next weekend."

Proud that he was making an effort to form a friendship with Greg, she said, "Really? That's great, Sweetie."

"It won't be the same."

"At least you're trying."

Randy gently rubbed his hand across hers. "I picked up a bottle of wine that's been chilling in the fridge. Thought maybe we could pop the cork and take a soak in the jet tub. What do you think? Wanna shut the phones off and get cozy tonight?"

The parrot suddenly squawked, "Naughty boy."

"I think he likes the idea," Jane said.

"I'll fill up the tub and grab that bottle." He kissed her and headed upstairs while she cleared the dinner dishes and put them in the dishwasher.

To get away from the hectic noise pollution of Los Angeles, Bruce and Stephanie strolled along the beach. Bruce kept sneaking glances over at her trying to figure out why she hadn't spoken to him all day. He tried to get her to look at him, but she wouldn't do it. "Steph, why won't you talk to me?"

She held a deadpan expression.

"This isn't about you and me anymore. We have a child to think about now."

"I'm the one carrying this baby. You really think I don't know that?"

"I'm honestly not sure what you think," he retorted, "because you won't tell me. One minute you seem cool with the way things are and the next, you're biting my head off. When I'm exhausted from a long week, you get all huffy and don't understand why I'd rather not go out. You call me when I'm in the middle of a procedure, but when I don't answer my phone you think I'm ignoring you. There are days when you won't talk to me, won't look at me, and lately it seems like everything I do and everything I say is wrong. Honestly, I don't know if any of this even matters to you, but it matters to me." He looked her in the eye, begging for an explanation. "What do you want from me?"

In a harsh tone, she told him what was on her mind. "Having a baby with a neurosurgeon at the age of twenty-four was not what I planned to do with my life."

"I didn't plan this either, but you can't keep pushing me away. I want to be involved in my baby's life and yours. At some point you are going to have to face the reality of this."

"And what reality is that?"

"You're pregnant with my child. Don't you get it?"

"Don't you?" She stared at him, clouded with fear and uncertainty. "I'm not ready for this. I don't want to be pregnant with your baby."

Your baby? She said that as if carrying his child was some sort of curse or disease. Her harsh, wounding words cut right through him. "Is it this baby you don't want or the fact that it's my baby you don't want? If it was someone else's baby would you want it then?" Outraged, he walked away from her.

"Bruce, that's not what I meant," she called out to him.

He tightened his jaw, tired of her indecisiveness and the fact that she was constantly stringing him along. "I can't play this game."

"I'm not playing games."

"The hell you're not. I am very willing to commit to caring for this baby with you. But I cannot be the only one willing to try. This relationship is never going to work if I'm the only one who cares."

"You think I don't care about you?" she asked.

"I don't know. Do you?" he demanded to know. "I think you're playing some kind of twisted mind game with me, and I don't like it."

"I am not."

"Then why won't you commit to this? We need to be in this all the way, together, or not at all," Bruce insisted. "I don't want to exhaust my energy and waste my time with you only to have our relationship plummet into the ground. If you're not willing to go all in and give one-hundred percent, no proviso, then I can't do this." He stared at her, wishing there was some way he could make this situation easier on both of them. "I will commit myself to you and our child all the way, but I won't do it alone. You can't blow this off like you do everything else."

She retorted, "That's not fair."

"Why isn't it? Because it's true?" he questioned. "You are fighting me tooth and nail on this, and I think it's because you'd have to put others above yourself if you committed to me and this baby, and you're not capable of doing that." He shook his head in disgust. "I am a doctor with a busy schedule. I don't have time for this crap." He turned away and trekked down the beach. Why did he always seem to get involved with women who caused him pain? And now it was even worse because a baby was involved, a baby he fathered, his flesh and blood. His head was about to explode.

Stephanie ran after him. "Bruce, wait."

He stopped and turned around.

She threw her arms around him and cried, "This isn't something I'm prepared for. I don't know how to care for an infant. I have no idea what to do."

"You think I know the first thing about being a father?" He lifted her chin. "I'm feeling what you're feeling. I'm scared, I'm nervous, I'm worried, and I have my doubts and fears like you do. But together, we can do this, Steph."

"What if we mess it all up?" Stephanie asked. "What if we ruin this child's life?"

He held her in his arms and tried to convince her. "We can make this work, if we both try. It's going to take commitment, and it's going to require a lot of responsibility from both of us, but we can do it."

She nodded her head. "I want to have this baby with you, Bruce."

He was glad she decided to carry this out with him, but in the back of his mind he wondered if she was truly sincere. The fact that she might not be weighed him down. He wasn't sure if Stephanie was capable of the kind of commitment raising a child together would require. Only time would tell.

Chapter Five

Jane woke up at 2:00 A.M. to the smell of brewing coffee. She saw a light on in the living room so she crept downstairs. To her surprise, Randy was on all fours on the floor pumping out pushups. "What in the world are you doing?"

"Can't sleep."

She narrowed her eyes at him. "How much coffee have you had?"

"Just started brewing a second pot."

"You've had an entire pot of coffee?"

"Yup." He bounded off the floor and jumped up and down a few times, wired beyond belief.

His overzealousness made her laugh. "Are you ok?"

"Never been better."

"It's two o'clock in the morning. Why are you up doing pushups and drinking coffee?"

"I told you. I can't sleep."

"And a pot of coffee and exercise will help?"

"Probably not." He pranced into the kitchen to refill his cup.

Jane followed him. "You do not need more caffeine, Dr. Hanson." She took the cup out of his hand and set it on the counter.

"Give that back," he protested.

"Look at you. You are wound up tighter than a spring." Trying to entice him, she seductively rubbed her finger down his chest. "Maybe I can interest you in something else."

He squinted his caffeine-dazed eyes. "I'm intrigued. What did you have in mind?"

She moved her lips to his ear and whispered, "Come upstairs with me and I'll show you." She took his hand and led him toward the staircase.

They didn't make it far before Randy grabbed her into his arms and kissed all over her neck and shoulders. Slowly, he slid the silky robe off her arms.

Trying to entice him further, she caressed his leg with her foot.

"Ooh," he groaned with a lustful tone as he arched his eyebrows seductively. "On the stairs? Kinky."

She helped him remove his shorts and repositioned herself to give him easier access to her. Willingly, and with much enthusiasm, he slid inside. The position was a bit awkward, but the newness of it excited him. Jane wrapped her legs around him and he supported her weight by pressing her body against the wall. She clung on tightly, enjoying the intenseness of his high energy level.

After letting him exert some sexual energy, Jane said to her husband, "Will you come to bed now?"

"I have so much caffeine in my system. I don't think I'll be able to sleep."

"And whose fault is that?" she teased.

"Mine."

Randy had all of his model Matchbook cars lined up neatly in rows on the coffee table. "What have you been doing down here?" Jane slipped her robe back on and sat on the stairs watching him.

40

"I read an article about Bugattis and polished all my sports cars." He stepped back into his shorts.

"You polished all of those?"

"Yup."

"With what?"

"The car wax in the garage. They look good, don't they?" he grinned slyly.

She thought he had lost his mind. "You are totally insane. You really should try to get some sleep."

With a chuckle, he said, "Let me turn off all the lights. I'll be up in a minute." He kissed her and she proceeded up the stairs. Randy followed close behind.

At the airport, after yet another cup of coffee, Randy and Jane took a seat by their gate. While Jane went to use the ladies' room, Randy peeked over at the man sitting next to him. He was reading an article about medical schools.

The man closed the magazine and stated, "For the life of me, I don't see what's so appealing about being a doctor. Only a fool would go into that profession. Smart people can make between 100 and 300K while working nine to five weekday hours, without having to take the ridiculous medical school and residency journey. Doctors are fools for undertaking that feat simply to gain a reputation of high status."

This inconsiderate comment made Randy's face tense up. "Doctors don't care about status. They care about their patients. They save lives and help people every day."

"See, that's the problem," this man remarked. "Everybody thinks doctors are heroes. But every doctor I've ever known is an arrogant know-it-all who really doesn't care about people at all. Doctors only care about making more money than the average Joe, and they think they are better and smarter than everyone else. I certainly don't have that much respect for doctors."

Was that so? What an unappreciative ass. This man pushed every button he could possibly push, and Randy found him insulting. "So if you were to go into cardiac arrest right now and a doctor saved your life, you mean to tell me you wouldn't have respect for him?"

"It wouldn't change my opinion of him, no. I'd still think he was a status-seeking wealth monger who had an inflated superhero image of himself."

"That is idiotic."

Randy's abrupt comment took this man by surprise. "Excuse me?"

"Doctors do everything they can to help people. Not one of them would have put up with all the bullshit they had to endure in medical school if they didn't care. It's not at all about being a hero or gaining status or wanting to make a buck. It's about making a difference in people's lives and improving the overall health of the world. Maybe you should show a little respect."

The man stared at Randy, wondering why he was so offended. "Who are you, and why do you care so much?"

"I'm a doctor," Randy replied. "And I really don't appreciate your disrespectful attitude."

In an attempt to avoid further confrontation with Randy, the man grabbed his magazine and his bag and moved to the opposite side of the room.

Jane returned and sat next to her husband, who had a very cross expression on his face. "What's the matter with you?"

"That asshole who was sitting here," Randy said out loud.

Jane was surprised to hear this foul accusation come out of her husband's mouth. Obviously Randy held resentment toward this man, and he didn't even know him. "Why? What did he do?"

"You should have heard the crap he was saying about doctors, until he found out I was one, then he shut up and left in one hell of a hurry. Not so smart now, are ya Bud?" Randy stared the guy down. "He better not sit by me on the plane."

Much to Randy's relief, their flight left on time. He took his seat by the aisle and waited to take off. "Are you sure your dad's ok housing us for the weekend?" Randy asked Jane. "We can get a hotel." He kind of hoped she'd agree to a hotel. Staying under his father-in-law's roof for two nights wasn't something he was particularly thrilled about.

"I told you he gladly offered. He even said we could use the car if we need to."

"Why is he being so nice?"

"Because we're family."

Although Randy felt uncomfortable about this decision, for Jane he would grit his teeth and bear the torture. Besides, this would give his wife the opportunity to spend some much needed time with her father.

As the fasten seatbelt sign came on and the aircraft began its descent into San Francisco, some commotion occurred at the back of the plane. The flight attendants appeared to be in a state of disorder. Trying to see what was happening, Randy stood up.

"Sit down," Jane instructed him. "The seatbelt sign is on."

"There's something going on back there."

Over the public address system, one of the flight attendants announced, "Attention ladies and gentlemen, if there are any doctors on board the airplane, please make yourselves known to the cabin crew."

Randy immediately flagged down a flight attendant and informed her that he was a doctor. He confirmed this by presenting his medical ID badge.

The flight attendant handed him a medical kit and led him to the back of the plane, where he quickly discovered what the problem was. A young pregnant woman gripped her hands on her abdomen, breathing erratically. Randy knelt down beside her. "Ma'am," he said in a soothing voice. "I'm a doctor. I'm here to help you." Hoping to gain some information from her, he asked, "Can you tell me what's going on?"

"My water just broke, and I'm having contractions."

"Were you having contraction before you boarded?"

"No. I'm not due for another eight weeks." She screamed in pain.

Randy tried to prepare himself for the possibility that this might not go well. Being eight weeks premature, under these circumstances, this delivery had the potential of being loaded with complications. This could be detrimental considering he didn't have necessary equipment or the capability of performing a surgical procedure if needed. All he could do was hope for the best.

Randy washed his hands and opened the medical kit. He reached inside and pulled out a stethoscope and portable blood pressure monitor to check her vitals. Her pulse and blood pressure were a bit high, but she was within normal range considering the stress involved.

With the help of the cabin crew, Randy moved her to a more private area. He had her lie down on the floor while a flight attendant retrieved a blanket and pillow to make her more comfortable. He slipped on a pair of latex gloves and checked for dilation, but the baby's head had already crowned. The show was about to start whether they were prepared for it or not.

Randy instructed one of flight attendants to have the pilot radio the San Francisco airport to have an ambulance on standby. While the plane made its descent, Randy did his best to guide this woman through delivery. Many passengers, including Jane, turned their heads to watch.

Seven minutes later, the entire airplane cheered when the infant's cry echoed throughout the cabin. Randy and the attendants helped wrap the tiny infant in a blanket and handed the baby to the mother right as the plane touched down.

Their flight was immediately sent to a gate. Randy remained by the woman's side to monitor her and the infant until they docked. When paramedics came on board, he turned the woman and her newborn over to emergency personnel. She was wheeled off the plane on a stretcher.

While the other passengers disembarked, Randy removed his latex gloves and washed his hands before he finally returned to Jane. "Well, that was something I've never done before."

"Nice job, Doctor," Jane said, giving him a kiss.

"I need a cup of coffee."

"You always need coffee."

All the people leaving Randy and Jane's flight had huge smiles painted on their faces, and talk about the doctor who saved the day seemed to flood the airport.

A blonde man wearing Bermuda shorts, flip-flops, and an Aloha State of Mind tee-shirt met them at the bottom of the ramp. Seeing him made Randy's entire face light up. "Hey, Jim."

"What the hell is goin' on?" Jim asked. "EMT's are buzzin' around all over the place and everyone from your flight is talkin' about some woman who was lucky to have a doctor on board."

"A woman on our flight went into premature labor, and I had to deliver her baby."

Jim's eyes widened. "On the airplane?"

"Yup."

"Damn, Dude. Are you serious?"

"Being eight weeks premature, we could have run into a ton of complications. I'm glad everything went smoothly and the baby is ok."

Jim and Randy reunited with a hug. "It's good to see you, Bro."

"Good to see you too."

When Randy entered Jim's apartment, two children instantly mauled him. "Uncle Randy!"

Randy pulled two five-dollar bills out of his wallet and squatted down to the children's level. He handed one to Sabrina and one to Christopher. "Here. Get some ice cream or candy with it."

They both grasped the money in their hands and ran off to their rooms.

"You old softy," Jim said. "Bribin' the kids with dead presidents."

"Christopher has gotten big," Randy remarked as he stood up.

"He's three now. Started preschool in September."

"Damn."

Jim grabbed two Coronas out of the fridge then he and Randy retreated to the balcony. He pulled up a couple lawn chairs and the two of them sat down to talk. "Looks like married life has been good to you," Jim remarked. "You look happier and healthier than I've ever seen you."

Randy popped the cap off his beer and took a sip. "I love being married. Jane keeps me in check. She's patient, supportive, understanding. She's a good wife." He put his feet up on the balcony railing and leaned back to relax.

"You used to wearin' a ring yet?"

Randy held up his left hand and admired the gold band on his finger. "Hardly notice it. Work in it, sleep in it, proudly wear it 24/7."

"That's awesome."

While Jim and Randy sat together on the balcony, Jill turned to Jane and asked, "Has Randy been moping around since you guys left?"

"Yes, as a matter of fact he has."

"Jim has been too. It's driving me nuts. He refuses to go out with any of the doctors he works with and gets all bummed out when he sees anything that has the Lakers logo on it."

"Oh my god," Jane declared. "Randy's been doing that too. He bought a package of Oreos last week and has yet to open it."

"Jim won't even look at Oreos. I bought some for the kids the other day and you would have thought I brought a snake into the house."

"We definitely need to get them together more often." Out on the balcony, Randy and Jim were joking around together and having a great time, a sight Jane hadn't seen in months.

Jim flicked a pebble over the balcony. "Jill's been off the pill for about a month now."

"Really? Didn't even wait 'til you got married, huh?" Randy teased.

"Nope. Figured the sooner we started the better."

"You're serious about this baby thing, aren't you?"

"We each have a child. We want one together now. Speakin' of which," Jim said with a smirk on his face. "I can't get over this whole thing with Bruce and Stephanie. How'd your parents take the news?"

"Mom took it a lot better than Dad did. She's excited about being a grandma. In fact, she's been out buying baby stuff for them. But my dad...all I have to say is I'm glad it was Stephanie and not me."

"He was pissed, wasn't he?"

"You could say that."

"You think they'll get married?"

Randy raised his shoulders. "I don't know. Bruce is willing, but the last time I talked to Steph she had her doubts."

"About what?" Jim asked.

"Being married to a neurosurgeon. It's not the fact that he's a doctor that bothers her. She likes that aspect—it offers her status and stability. But she doesn't like his schedule. He works a lot of hours and the work is demanding, so basically Bruce has no life outside residency right now."

"He must have had a little spare time on his hands if he got your sister pregnant."

Randy actually found Jim's comment funny. "Technically, you can get a woman pregnant in five minutes."

"Yeah, if the sex isn't that good."

"True," Randy chuckled. "But with his schedule, he won't be around much, which will force Stephanie to handle the baby on her own. And you and I both know how irresponsible she is."

"How many hours does he work?"

"Right now, eighty minimum, sometimes as many as a hundred a week."

"That's ridiculous."

Randy tipped his Corona bottle up and took another sip. "I read on the medical forums that in the field of neurosurgery, academic big names have enough influence to ruin residents' careers if they don't comply and put in the hours. It can go as far as not allowing the resident to take the boards or trying to get him fired, among other things. It isn't always pretty, that's for sure. It's grueling beyond belief. Ninety-eight percent of neurosurgery residents sleep, on average over the course of their residency, less than six hours a night. And advancing years in residency doesn't mean shorter hours, it simply means the responsibilities grow."

Jim didn't see what was so appealing about that. "That sucks. And Buckman is into that shit?"

"Apparently. I asked him what he thought, and he told me the system is inefficient. He has too much paperwork, not enough PA's, and no one to do the grunt work for him. As a result, he's running after lab results when he should be operating or managing patients. That seems to be his biggest problem. He flat out doesn't have help."

"Bogus," Jim said, thinking all of this sounded unfair.

"I agree. I'd much rather have 24-hour on-call status than deal with that crap," Randy claimed. "It's definitely not a specialty to choose if you don't absolutely love it. When he's finished, he'll make at least 500K annually, but it's not worth it, I wouldn't think."

"Oh, hell no," Jim concurred. "That's bullshit."

"With the demands and hours placed on him, he won't be able to get up in the middle of the night to help with feedings and won't be available at the drop of a hat. According to Stephanie, that is the underlying issue."

"But you don't believe that, do you?"

"It doesn't matter what I believe," Randy replied. "In all honestly, I think she's with him for the convenience of it all, the lifestyle."

"Doctor's dinero?"

Randy couldn't argue with Jim's conclusion. He never thought Bruce and Stephanie were right for each other anyway. "Unfortunately I think so. Despite all of that, I trust him. And if they do wind up getting married, I know Stephanie will be taken care of. My dad wasn't too happy about her quitting school, but with a new baby, it will probably be easier for both of them if she doesn't have classes to contend with. Stephanie was aimlessly attending school with no apparent career goal in mind anyway. And since my parents aren't paying tuition right now, they'll be able to use their money on themselves for a change."

Jim flicked his bottle cap onto the concrete. "That'll be nice."

"So, why did you and Jill opt out of a traditional wedding?" Randy asked.

"Jill didn't wanna go through the elaborateness of a formal get-together, and you know I'm not into all that romantic shit. We just want to exchange vows and make it legal. A few witnesses, a signed document, and we're good to go."

"Sounds simple."

"Besides, I saw all the hassle and stress you went through tryin' to pull your wedding together. It was a beautiful ceremony, but damn, all that prep work. With our ER schedules, there was no way either of us had time to plan out somethin' like that."

Randy shifted in his chair, turning so he was face to face with Jim. "How does that work, being in the ER with Jill all day? Doesn't that make you uncomfortable? I don't know how I'd feel if Jane was a nurse in the OB/GYN wing. Think I'd have a hard time staying focused."

"We met at the hospital, and we work together in trauma situations all the time. She knows my body language and I can communicate with her easily. That comes in handy in an emergency situation."

"That's true, I guess."

"And you know what? Now that I'm a resident in charge of medical students, I kinda feel sorry for them," Jim claimed. "I totally ragdolled one of them the other day though."

"Why?"

"Fuckin' moron walked into the Emergency Room with an open Coke bottle and a half eaten sandwich in his hand. I told him never to come into my ER with any kind of food whatsoever. I then proceeded to tell him that he needed to either get the hell out of the way or put on some clean scrubs and make himself useful."

Randy gawked at his friend. "Damn, Dude. You're ruthless."

"He was contaminating my area, and he was a smartass who needed to be knocked down a notch. Some of them get cocky and think they know everything."

"But most of them are really on the ball and eager to learn. You shouldn't be so harsh with them." Randy checked the time on his watch. It was almost 5:00 P.M. "We should probably go. We promised Jane's dad we'd have dinner with him tonight."

"Then let's roll."

Jim chauffeured then over to Dale Davine's house. Before Randy stepped out of the car, he said, "Guess I'll see you in the morning."

"Yup. We exchange vows at eleven o'clock."

"We'll be there."

The two men knuckle bumped and Jim flashed a thumb and pinky wave out the car window before he drove off.

Randy wheeled their suitcase up to the house. With a heavy sigh, he turned to his wife and said, "You know I'm uncomfortable about this."

"I know you are, but I appreciate you doing it anyway." She gently kissed him on the lips.

"He's going to make me sleep on the couch. Just watch."

"Why would he do that?"

"This is the same man who thought you were a 21-year-old virgin, Jane. He used to glare at me every time I tried to touch you, remember?"

"You're my husband now. It's different."

"I hope so."

She grabbed Randy's hand and stood by his side on the front porch. "You ready?"

"Not really." He stared at the door for a minute before he knocked.

Dale Davine answered with a hug for his daughter and son-in-law. He showed them inside to a tiny room with a double bed. The room was a bit cramped, but at least he didn't make them sleep in separate beds.

When Jim said "I do" and gave his new wife a kiss, Randy couldn't help but grin. The image of his own wedding and the excitement he felt when Jane paraded down the aisle in her gorgeous gown flashed through his mind. He could still smell the aroma of roses and hear the sound of waves lapping on the beach. As this picture filled his head, his eyes met Jane's briefly. He smiled at her, and for a moment he was certain they shared the same thought.

Following the ceremony, they all headed to Jim and Jill's apartment to partake in post-nuptial refreshments. With beers in hand, the men retreated to the living room.

Randy grinned at Jim snidely. "Somehow all of this seems unbalanced to me."

Jim fiddled with the new addition on his finger. "What are you talking about, Bro?"

"At my bachelor's party, you totally embarrassed me in front of our friends with that stupid pig. And you followed it up with that bullshit toast you made at my wedding. But I didn't get the honor of embarrassing you. That isn't fair."

Jim smirked. "Just proves I'm better than you."

"Shut up, Jackass."

Jill's daughter, Sabrina, came out to the living room and climbed onto Randy's lap, eyeballing him with her forehead creased. "Uncle Randy?"

"Yes, Sweetheart?"

"Is Auntie Jane having a baby?"

Randy stared at Jim, thinking he had deviously put this idea into the girl's head. "Why do you ask?"

"Grammy told me people have babies after they get married."

"Well, yes, that's true, but Aunt Jane and I are going to wait a while before we have a baby."

"Why? Don't you like children?"

Knowing how uncomfortable Randy felt about this particular topic, Jim fought to keep a straight face. He couldn't wait to hear how his best friend was going to respond.

Randy replied, "We like children, but sometimes after people get married they want to spend some time together before they decide to have children."

"Daddy says you take care of mommies with babies in their tummies. Is that true?" she asked him.

"Yes, it is. I'm a doctor called an obstetrician," he explained to her.

"Do you see a lot of babies?"

"I see quite a few, yes."

"You and Auntie Jane should have a baby."

Dumbfounded, Randy watched this little girl climb off his lap and stroll out of the room. Unsure what to think, he turned to Jim for answers. "Where did that come from?"

Jim thought this was hysterical.

"Did you have something to do with this?"

"No. That was all her, Bro."

"Why would she even bring that up?"

Jim explained, "She's been fascinated by pregnant women and babies lately. Her friend's mother had a baby recently, so she's been askin' a lot of questions about it."

"How much have you told her?"

"We haven't gotten into details with her. She wouldn't understand it anyway. Jill's parents told her that people have babies once they get married, which is probably why she thinks Jane is havin' a baby. She associates marriage with babies. Which also explains why she keeps tellin' everyone we know that we're havin' a baby, even though Jill's not pregnant, at least I don't think she is," Jim said. "Although she might be."

Randy shook his head. "Glad it's you. I am not ready for that."

"Aw, come on, havin' kids is great," Jim tried to convince him.

"I'm sure it is, but Jane and I are our enjoying our freedom and spontaneity too much. We're not ready to make that kind of commitment."

Jim and Randy were the fuel that kept each other going. Being able to spend time together recharged them both and allowed them some much needed bonding time. As a result, their parting was much easier on them this time. "We really need to do this more often," Randy suggested. "Next time you're coming to Seattle."

Jim concurred, "Alright. I have a few days off next month. I'll see what I can do."

"That would be awesome." They parted with a hug and a handshake.

When Randy took his seat on the plane, a huge grin decorated his face. He turned to Jane and said, "This weekend was fun. I really enjoyed hanging out with Jim. It'll be cool when he comes up to Seattle next month."

"Are you finally going to open that package of Oreos you bought?"

Randy laughed, "I might even eat a few."

Chapter Six

After a long, stressful day of surgical procedures and office calls, Randy was very ready to go home. He hopped in the Corvette and, since the sun was out, he put the top down. He slipped on his sunglasses, popped in a CD, and peeled out of the hospital parking garage. Once he hit the freeway, he weaved in and out of traffic, driving well over the speed limit. When he checked his rearview mirror, he saw red and blue lights flashing behind him. He slowed down and moved over to the right lane allowing the officer to pass. With its siren blaring, the police car tailed him. Randy tightened his jaw, realizing the lights were for him. "Shit." He flipped on his right turn signal and pulled over to the shoulder. The cop pulled up behind him.

Randy turned off the engine and removed his sunglasses. He checked his rearview mirror again and saw two police officers sitting in the squad car, one of them on the radio, most likely calling in his plates. "Dammit." He tapped his fingers on the steering wheel and waited for the officer to approach.

One of the uniformed officers stepped out of his squad car with his hand on the butt of his gun. He eased up to Randy's window. "License and registration, please."

"Yes, Officer." Randy reached into his glovebox and pulled out his registration card and proof of insurance then dug through his wallet for his driver's license. He handed all three to the police officer.

The officer clipped these onto his clipboard. He spotted Randy's lab coat and stethoscope lying on the passenger's seat. "Is there some medical emergency, Dr..." he read the name on Randy's license, "Hanson?"

"No, Sir," Randy replied, trying to be respectful and not do anything to upset the officer.

The officer gave Randy a cold, hard stare. "Stay here. I'll be right back."

He held a blank expression. "Yes, Sir."

The officer returned to his squad car.

The only thing Randy could think about at that moment was Jane. She always told him he drove too fast and would get pulled over someday. Well, she was right. No doubt he was going to receive a hefty ticket for driving like a lunatic on the freeway, or even worse, a reckless driving citation. He hoped it wasn't the latter.

Randy received a green copy of a speeding ticket, which was a non-criminal offense but would still be tagged onto his driving record and cost him over four-hundred dollars.

"This is a busy freeway," the officer lectured. "You are in the business of saving lives and helping those who are involved in accidents, but with the way you were driving, you'll be the cause of one instead. Slow down, Doctor."

"Yes, Sir. I will do that."

As soon as he was cleared, Randy pulled out and drove away, grateful he wasn't cited for a more serious offense. He drove home much slower and actually obeyed speed zones.

He pulled into the driveway, much later than he wanted to, and opened the garage door with his remote. He put the top up on the Corvette and turned off the ignition. He sat there for a minute, not moving, staring at the green traffic ticket. Realizing he could no longer put this off, he leaned over and grabbed his lab coat and stethoscope. He pulled his keys out of the ignition and carried them, along with the traffic citation, into the house.

The minute Randy walked in the door, Jane pulled him close and greeted him with a kiss. "Hope your day was better than mine."

Was she kidding? There was no way her day could have been worse than his. "Did you have a bad day?" Randy draped his lab coat over the back of a chair, set his stethoscope on the table, and placed his keys in a decorative glass bowl.

"There's this new guy at work, and you won't believe what he said to me today."

"Do I dare ask?"

"He told me that women shouldn't be coaching sports. He said there was no way a woman could possibly know anything about the fundamentals of basketball."

Although Randy found this horribly funny, he tried to maintain a straight face. "Oh man. I bet that pissed you off."

Her voice grew tauter as she spoke. "Talk about your Tarzan syndrome. He's a pompous ass who thinks he knows everything. What an egotistical son-of-a-bitch. You know what he did? He handed me his coffee cup and demanded that I do my womanly duties and fill it for him." She growled in aggravation. "I wouldn't do a damn thing for him. I hope he gets castrated by a lawnmower."

"That's not a kind thing to say, Honey."

"He's an asshole. He does this all the time too. I got him back though."

He hoped she didn't do anything rash. "Uh oh. What did you do?"

"I placed the coffee pot on his desk and told him he had two arms, he could get his own damn coffee."

"Good for you."

"My boss saw all of this, and before the guy left, she called him into her office and fired him."

"Sounds like he got what he deserved." The angry scowl on Jane's face made him laugh. "You're cute when you're mad."

"I am not," she pouted.

"Yes you are. I love that little wrinkle you get on your nose when you're angry." He touched the tip of her nose with his fingertip. "If it makes you feel any better, my day wasn't so hot either."

"Why?"

Randy flashed the ticket in front of her. "Don't say a damn word, Jane."

Jane took the green paper from him. When she realized what it was, she said, "You got a speeding ticket?"

"Hush."

"I told you," she teased him.

Not at all amused, he brushed his bangs off his forehead.

"Didn't I tell you that you were going to get a ticket for being a speed demon one of these days?"

"Yes, Dear," he scorned. "You did. Let's rub it in my face now, shall we?" He snatched the ticket back from her. "Four hundred and eighteen bucks."

"How fast were you driving?"

Not wanting to admit his flaw, he hesitated. "Eighty in a sixty-five."

She gasped, "Randy, you're lucky they didn't arrest you for reckless driving."

"Yes, I realize that."

"Just because your car can go that fast doesn't mean you should. The freeway is not a racetrack."

He smiled at her adoringly. "Are you finished now?"

"Yes." She wrapped her arms around his neck.

He placed his hands on her hips and pulled her closer. "What do you say we put this day behind us and go out and do something fun."

"I think that sounds fabulous. I'll get my purse."

Meanwhile, down in L.A., Bruce came home late to find Stephanie stuffing clothes into a suitcase. He stared at her, perplexed. "What are you doing?"

"Packing."

"Why?"

"Because I need to go back to school."

Bruce dropped his menacing eyebrows. "But you said you were going to stay here with me so we could take care of this baby together."

"Well, I changed my mind."

Bruce leaned against the wall. "So in other words, you lied to me."

"I did not."

"Then what the hell would you call it?"

She continued to pack, ignoring his question.

"Was that your intention all along?"

She tossed more clothes in her suitcase, but refused to answer him.

"Dammit, Steph, don't ignore me."

She stopped packing long enough to acknowledge him. "I'm not allowed to change my mind?"

Annoyed with her attitude, he boldly stated what was on his mind. "You told me you were going to stay here so we could raise this baby together, now you're telling me otherwise. Why did tell me you were going to stay if you didn't mean it? Just to appease me and get me to shut up?"

"No."

"Then why?"

She grabbed a pile of tee-shirts and shoved them into her suitcase.

He squeezed his hand into a fist, quickly losing patience with her. "I don't want to keep you here if this isn't where you want to be, but dammit, you can't keep running away from your problems like this." He took her hand and forced her to look at him. "What do you want?"

"I don't know what I want."

Fed up with her indecisiveness, he demanded, "Well you better decide pretty damn quickly because I don't have time for this bullshit."

She watched him walk away. "Bruce."

Bruce turned around, hurt by her impulsivity that always seemed to be at his expense. "You need to decide how important this is to you, because you deciding to up and leave to go gallivanting about whenever the hell you please is not something I am willing to put up with." He left the apartment and roamed around the UCLA campus to clear his head. No matter how hard he tried, he felt like nothing he did was good enough for her. He wanted to make this work, if for no other reason than for the sake of his unborn child. But he was beginning to doubt the value of their relationship. He grabbed himself a bite to eat before he returned home.

He figured Stephanie would be long gone when he got there, but she wasn't. Instead she was curled up in a ball on the couch hugging her knees. Her eyes were glossy, as if she'd been crying. Knowing they needed to come up with some kind of mutual understanding, he sat down beside her. "Stephanie, I don't want to argue about this anymore. I feel like I'm fighting a losing battle here. I want to make this work, but I feel like I'm the only one who's trying."

She refused to look at him and didn't say a word.

Her silence spoke volumes. "Obviously I'm keeping you in a place you don't want to be."

"But I do want to be with you."

He didn't believe her. With pain in his eyes he said, "I'll be here for you through this pregnancy, and I'll be responsible for my child. But I want the truth." He looked her in the eye and asked, "What do you want?"

She wasn't sure if she was ready for all of this, but she didn't want to be alone and try to raise this baby by herself. To appease him she said, "I want us raise our baby together."

He took her hand in his. Even though he feared their relationship was destined to be filled with lies and heartache, he didn't want Stephanie to go through this alone. "Then stay with me."

Bruce Buckman cared for his child and was willing to take responsibility. That alone was enough to make her stay.

Chapter Seven

In the wee hours of the morning, Randy's cellphone went off. Snuggled comfortably under the blankets, still half asleep, he groaned and reached over to answer it. "Dr. Hanson." Almost instantly, the color drained from his face. He flipped on the bedside table lamp and frantically hopped out of bed. "Where are you?" He stumbled around to find some clothes and quickly got dressed. "Alright. I'll be right there."

"What's wrong?" Jane mumbled.

"I need to get to the hospital."

"You're not on-call tonight," she reminded him.

"It's Robby."

Abruptly, she sat up. "What's wrong with Robby?"

"He's been in an accident."

Jane covered her mouth with her hand. "Is he alright?"

"I don't know. Dad says they haven't talked to the receiving doctor yet, so they don't know how bad it is." He shoved his cellphone in his pocket. "I have to go."

"I'm coming with you." She crawled out of bed.

"Honey, we don't know what kind of condition he's in."

"Which is why I'm coming with you."

She wasn't taking no for an answer, so Randy gave in. "Alright, but hurry."

Randy and Jane ran into the Emergency Room to find his mother nervously fidgeting with her hands and father pacing the floor. "How is he? Have you heard anything?"

"They're running a CAT scan on him now," Ellen Hanson replied.

Mark stopped pacing and turned to his oldest son. "Thank god no one else was in the car with him."

Four uniformed police officers stood in the waiting room and three squad cars were parked outside. "What are the police doing here?"

"DUI," his father bluntly stated. "And this is Robby's second offense. As soon as he receives medical clearance, they're taking him into custody."

"Jesus." Randy suddenly felt sick to his stomach. He couldn't stand to see what his brother's reckless behavior was doing to his parents. "That damn kid. What the hell was he thinking?"

"That's the problem, Randal. He doesn't think."

Randy closed his eyes trying to take in all of this. Robby's actions were horribly embarrassing for the family and potentially harmful to his father's career. But Robby was never one to think about those kinds of things. He was always egocentric and unwilling to see things from anyone's point of view other than his own. Troubled by this entire incident, Randy plopped down on a waiting room chair.

Many hours passed before Robby was released from the hospital. He had several lacerations on his forehead and face, a blackened eye, and his arm was wrapped in a sling.

Randy tried to make eye contact with his brother, but Robby wouldn't look at him; he kept his head hung down. All the family could do was watch as the police escorted him out of the hospital in handcuffs and drove him away in a squad car.

Randy and Jane went over to his parents' house for breakfast that morning. Trying to ease some tension, Randy took his dad out in the boat to cast out a few lines.

Mark was quiet throughout angling, a sure sign he was upset. In an attempt to break the silence, Randy said, "Dad, I'm sorry. I know how hard this must be for you and Mom with all the added stress Robby has placed on you. I want you to know that you are wonderful parents, and Robby's problems are in no way a reflection of you."

Even though Randy's words were an amiable sentiment, Mark knew his oldest son didn't know the entire story behind Robert's behavior. "There are many things about Robert you are unaware of, things that occurred while you were in medical school we didn't want to burden you with."

"What are you talking about?"

Mark tossed his line into the lake. It landed with a splash. "He has a lot of problems, most of which he blames on me."

"That's ridiculous. Why would he think that?"

"He's convinced I favor you and Stephanie over him. He says I don't support him and feels cheated because he thinks you had more privileges than he did, but the reality of the situation is that your brother lost a lot of privileges because of his poor choices. When he was in high school, he got written up for fighting and was suspended from school for a week. The police knew him quite well. He was constantly getting in trouble for vandalism, possession of alcohol, underage drinking, disturbing the peace. He even received an assault charge for beating the crap out of someone when he was drunk. Sent the guy to the hospital."

Randy found this appalling, and he was a bit offended that his parents had kept this information from him. He wanted to be informed about family events, especially if his little brother was involved. "He was in trouble with the law and you didn't mention any of this to me? How come you never told me?"

"You had enough to think about with medical school. I wasn't about to let Robby's recklessness distract you."

"Maybe I could have talked to him or tried to help him."

"It wasn't your responsibility. You needed to stay focused on school," Mark insisted. "Your brother was, and still is, a trouble maker. But trouble maker or not, he's still my son, and I love him."

Randy sat in disbelief, disgusted that his younger brother acted that way. "It kills me to see the hell he's put you through. I know you've tried to help him, but apparently he's done nothing but defy you and reject the help."

Mark reeled in his line and cast a glance at his son. "I'm sorry Jane had to see that last night."

"She insisted on coming. She wanted to be there to offer support. That's how she is."

Robert Hanson was sentence to thirty days in jail, which his parents posted bail on, plus sixty days Electronic Home Detention. He had to pay $3,436 in fines and had a twelve-month license revocation. He was ordered to five years of probation, had to install an ignition interlock system in his car for five years, and was ordered alcohol evaluation and treatment for two years. The family hoped this incident would get him to clean up his act.

Several weeks passed. Now on a night rotation, Randy made his rounds through the Maternity Ward. All was quiet that night, so he headed to the cafeteria to grab a quick cup of coffee. On his way there, the hospital's intercom system announced, "Dr. Hanson, report to the ER, STAT. Dr. Hanson, to the ER, STAT." He rushed downstairs where his expertise was needed.

The attending ER physician hollered, "Step aside!" The ER crew hustled down the hall with the ambulance gurney. "Hanson!"

Randy ran to the doctor's side.

"We have a 26-year-old female, twelve weeks pregnant, struck broadside by a drunk driver. Unconscious, vitals fluctuating, heavy vaginal hemorrhaging."

"I'm on it." Randy knew exactly what to do. Trained to do so in under a minute, he slipped on a pair of scrubs and latex gloves. While the ER staff worked to stabilize vitals, he attempted to control blood loss.

Upon further examination of this patient, Randy came to the frightening realization that this woman was most likely miscarrying her pregnancy. He performed a pelvic exam and a quick ultrasound test to confirm. Unfortunately, his diagnosis was correct. The accident proved to be too stressful for the fetus and the heartbeat had ceased. He was able to stop the bleeding but unable to save the baby.

Once the patient was stabilized, Randy removed his blood-covered gloves and stepped over to the sink to wash his hands.

The attending physician approached him and said, "When you're done here, I'd like you to come with me."

"Yes, Sir." Randy finished washing up, changed out of his bloodied scrubs, and followed the attending physician out to the waiting room.

"Mr. Jensen?" the ER doctor said.

A young man with a fade-style haircut stood up and acknowledged them. Fear clouded his features. "How is she?"

"Your wife is going to be fine," the doctor reassured. "She's still unconscious, but she's stable."

He breathed a sigh of relief. "Thank god."

The attending physician introduced Randy. "Mr. Jensen, this is Dr. Hanson. He's the obstetrical resident doctor who worked to stabilize your wife."

Mr. Jensen shook Randy's hand.

Randy realized the ER doctor wanted him to tell this man that his wife had miscarried. In no way was he prepared for this. "Mr. Jensen, please have a seat." Randy directed him to a chair. In a sympathetic voice, he explained, "Sir, your wife was hit directly in the abdomen, the placenta separated, which caused severe hemorrhaging. We were able to stop the bleeding and get her stabilized." He put his hand on Mr. Jensen's arm. "Unfortunately, the accident caused extreme trauma to the fetus. I'm sorry, Sir. We lost the baby."

The man sat in shock for a moment before the painful reality of Randy's words finally struck him. He held his head in his hands and wept.

These types of situations illustrated the downside of medicine. Randy's heart ached, and even though he felt like crying with this man, he couldn't do that. Doctors were expected to be superhuman and taught to let go of human emotions when it came to dealing with patients and their families. But Randy always had a hard time doing that. He couldn't distance himself from his human side. "Let us know if there's anything we can do, Mr. Jensen."

Following this unpleasant experience, Randy stepped outside to get some air. He leaned against the wall and placed his hands in his pockets, trying to regain his composure. He looked up at the stars, and the first thought that came to him was Jane. What would he have done if she would have been lying on that gurney? What if that was his child?

The ER physician peeked around the corner to check on Randy. "You ok?"

Randy liked this man, not only because of the caring way he dealt with patients and their families, but also for the respect he always displayed toward interns, resident doctors, and medical students. Randy stood tall, trying not to let this man see the emotional state he was in. "Yes, I'm fine. Just getting some air."

"Unfortunately that's the harsh reality of medicine, Hanson, the humanness and vulnerability of it all. As upsetting as it is, I'm glad you had the opportunity to experience that. Many in that situation would have faltered, but you handled that well. Very professionally done, Dr. Hanson."

Randy took a cleansing breath, seriously questioning this statement. "Thank you, I guess."

The attending physician checked the time on his watch. "What time does your shift end?"

"In about an hour."

"Good. Go home. Spend some time with your wife."

As soon as Randy's shift was over that night, he gathered up his belongings, including the bloody scrubs, and sped toward Robby's apartment.

He pounded on his brother's door.

Robby answered sleepy-eyed, wondering what Randy was doing there at four o'clock in the morning. "What the hell?"

Randy barged inside and threw a plastic bag full of blood-soaked scrubs at his brother. "You son-of-a-bitch!" he shouted. "Do you see those? Take a good hard look! That is the blood of a woman who was wheeled into my ER tonight. She almost bled to death. She was pregnant, Robby, and she lost her baby. And why? Because a drunk ass driver hit her and caused her to miscarry. I had to go into that room and tell her husband that their baby didn't make it. I had to see the anguish on his face and hear the pain in his voice. That could have been my wife, my child!" Randy's voice grew louder. "You insensitive, cold-hearted bastard! You could have killed someone!" He pointed to the bloody scrubs. "Look at them, Rob. That is blood you are responsible for. A baby, an innocent victim who never had a chance at life because of drunken assholes like you! I hope you are proud of yourself." Randy stormed out of the apartment and slammed the door.

When Randy got home, he felt numb, both physically and emotionally. Trying to be as quiet as possible, he sat at the dining room table and buried his head in his arms.

Jane heard him come in. She slipped on a robe and headed downstairs to greet him. When she saw Randy sitting at the table with his head down, she knew something was wrong. "Randy?" She sat next to him and gently placed her hand on his back. "Sweetie, what is it?"

He looked up at her, his face full of anguish.

"What happened?"

"Jim is crazy. How the hell can he do that day after day and not go completely insane? I was in the ER for a total of forty-five minutes today and I'm about to lose my mind." He swallowed to clear the knot in his throat. "I received an emergency call tonight. A pregnant woman had been in an accident. She was t-boned by a drunk driver and knocked unconscious. She was bleeding and..." Randy closed his eyes trying to get the horrid vision out of his head. "There was nothing I could do. She lost her baby right in front of me, and I had to tell this woman's husband that their baby didn't survive. I had to witness that dreadful look on his face."

She squeezed his hand in comfort. "I'm so sorry."

"And to make matters worse, I totally wailed on Robby tonight."

"Robby?" She wondered what Robby had to do with this.

"I was so angry, I don't even remember what I said to him. You know, people always say you shouldn't bring your work home with you, but dammit, how can I not bring my work home with me? I deal with people's lives, Jane. I've witnessed death." He looked into her eyes. "You never really realize how precious life is until you experience death firsthand. I've seen enough death to last a lifetime."

She reached around and hugged him.

"Honey, I love you. I don't know what I'd ever do if I lost you." He kissed her forehead and focused on her eyes again. "This world is full of crazy people who make my job much more difficult than it should be. I'm in the profession of saving lives, and there are people out there who kill, who recklessly disregard human existence, who show no compassion or sensitivity and completely lack any regard for efforts I make to save the very lives they try to take away. Has the human race really become that uncaring?"

She sympathized with his plight, but wasn't sure what to say to him. "Some people act that way because they've never experienced a caring environment. How can you care about anything if no one has ever shown you how to care?"

He loved her positive outlook on life, but in this case it wasn't that simple. Some things in life were just downright awful. Randy flopped his head back on the table. He could barely keep his eyes open.

"You look exhausted," Jane told him.

"It's been a very long day."

She held out her hands to help him out of the chair. "Come on, Mister. Bedtime for you."

He trudged upstairs, removed his clothes, and was asleep as soon as his head hit the pillow.

Randy saw his brother a few weeks later during a family get together at his parents' house. The two of them spent the entire afternoon staring at one another, but neither one initiated conversation.

Mark Hanson wasn't going to tolerate this cold shoulder treatment between his children, so he intervened by talking to his oldest son. "Randal, exactly how long are you planning on ignoring your brother?"

Randy blew out his cheeks in exasperation. "I'm not ignoring him. I'm just not sure what to say. I feel like an ass for yelling at him the way I did the other night."

"He looks up to you, you know."

"He does not."

"Yes he does. He talks about you all the time. He was so excited about you moving back up here, yet you've hardly acknowledged him since you arrived."

Randy looked over at his little brother, feeling guilty. Robby wasn't a bad kid, he was simply misunderstood. "I've been a little busy rotating through my residency."

"You're making excuses, Son. We are a family here, and we do not treat each other this way. You need take some time to shoot a few baskets with him or go out for burgers. He thinks you hate him."

"I don't hate him. I was just angry the last time I saw him."

"And that's ok, but you can't stay mad forever."

"I know." Randy focused his eyes on his brother, who wallowed about with a sad expression on his face. "He's my brother. I love him."

"Did you ever tell him that?"

"No," Randy sighed.

"Maybe he needs to hear that from you," Mark advised. "Fix this, Randy."

Randy loped over to his brother. "Shoot some hoops with me." He grabbed a basketball and carried it out to the driveway.

Robby went with him.

They dribbled around for a while, not talking to each other. Feeling uncomfortable about the tension, Randy broke the silence. "I'm sorry I reacted the way I did. It wasn't your fault, and I shouldn't have yelled at you like that."

"You were right." Robert's voice was brittle. "I could have killed someone. I know that now."

Randy felt sorry for his misunderstood younger sibling. Robby always tried to fit in but never seemed to succeed at it. He was a loner who kept to himself; he spent most of his time playing videogames or working on the engines of cars. And he didn't have many friends. He struggled with girls and always felt inadequate. Trying to make amends, Randy suggested, "I'm off tomorrow. Why don't you and I grab some lunch, catch a movie, and check out some sports cars?"

"Why the hell would a prestigious doctor want to hang out with a loser like me?" Robby said rather dejectedly.

Robby's depressive state had Randy worried. "Stop that. You're not a loser. You're my brother, and I love you. Nothing will ever change that. The fact that I'm a doctor has no relevance on anything. We're still brothers and we always will be. I might not have as much time to spend with you as I did when we were kids because I have responsibilities with my job, my house, and my marriage, but that doesn't mean we can't hang out once in a while. You have my cell number. You can call any time you want."

"Yeah," Robby moped.

"And I would love to beat your ass at Burnout. I love that game," Randy suggested, knowing how much his brother loved video games. "I need someone to eat greasy burgers and fries with because my wife won't do it."

The corners of Robby's mouth slowly curved upward. "Bro, I've seen her eat pizza. She dabs off all the grease and picks half the toppings off before she eats it."

Randy chuckled. "Depends on what kind of pizza it is. If it's veggie pizza or Canadian bacon and pineapple, she'll chow down the whole thing. But she doesn't like greasy or fried food. Never has."

"Guess she wouldn't like Dick's Drive-In then."

"Oh, hell no. She wouldn't be caught dead eating there."

Robby openly laughed. Even though he never expressed it to Randy before, Robby always thought his brother's job was fascinating. In a way, he was kind of jealous of the excitement Randy saw on a daily basis and the expertise the procedures he did required. "How many babies have you delivered?" Robby asked.

"A bunch."

Robby grimaced, "They made us watch a childbirth video in health class. It totally grossed me out."

Randy got a kick out at his brother's reaction. "It's not that bad. Some of the stuff I saw in med school or the trauma wing of the ER was far worse than anything I'll ever see on a delivery table."

"Like what?"

"My Anatomy class. The class itself was interesting, but when we had to go back to lab after eating lunch, that was pretty bad. That vinegary fume of death that clung to the cadavers, not at all for the weak of stomach."

Although he totally admired and respected his brother, Robby didn't understand the excitement his brother found in medicine. "I bet not."

Randy put his arm around Robby and locked him in a playful chokehold. "Come on. Let's set up the volleyball net. You can be on my team." He playfully gave his brother a noogie before joining the rest of the family.

Chapter Eight

Randy anxiously stood at the bottom of the airport ramp awaiting the arrival of his best friend. When he spotted a blonde-haired man wearing baggy jeans, a bright orange flowered Hawaiian shirt, and green Vans, he approached him with open arms. "Man, it's good to see you." Jim had a carryon bag over his shoulder, a pair of sunglasses propped up on the top of his head, and a jacket in his hand. "Do you have other bags?"

"Nope. This is it."

"Sweet, then we're outta here." Randy escorted him across the sky bridge to a thirteen-thousand car parking garage. It wasn't raining, but because it was slightly overcast and cool, they chose to leave the top up on the convertible.

As they drove through the city, Jim peered out the window taking in the new scenery. The monochromatic grey skies in Seattle could get ominous at times to those who didn't favor rain, but the result was a bright green landscape that earned the Emerald City its nickname. In October, Seattle was vivid. Trees turned to shades of orange, red, and yellow, and the waters throughout the city reflected the glittering hues. The majestic view of Mt. Rainier and endless waterways throughout the city made Seattle sparkle.

Jim flipped through the CD's Randy had in the car and popped one in the CD player while Randy drove across the 520 bridge, up Lake Washington Boulevard past Marsh Park, and down to his street. He typed in the code on the security gate allowing them access into the gated community where he lived.

"Wow, nice place you've got here. Great scenery. Fresh air. I'm impressed," Jim commented.

"It's comfortable. Jane and I like it."

"This is a beautiful city. Seems a helluva lot more relaxed than San Francisco. I gotta get the hell outta there. After my residency I'm gonna look into goin' somewhere a little less bizarre."

Randy doubled up in laughter.

"I'm serious, Dude. The other day this chick came into the ER sniffin' amyl nitrate and asked me if I wanted some. I'm tellin' ya, San Francisco is seriously deranged."

"I don't think it's San Francisco. I think it's the ER."

With the daily demands of the ER, sometimes the blood and life-threatening trauma got to be too much. As much as Jim loved the action in the Emergency Room, he was glad to get away from it all for a while. "The ER was nuts yesterday."

"Why? What happened?" Randy asked.

"What the hell didn't happen? We had seven code blues, four broken appendages, a case of heat exhaustion, excessive vomiting, thirteen automobile accidents, a major gunshot wound, three asthma attacks, a near diabetic coma, and a burn victim all within a two-hour time frame. I've never been so damn busy in my life."

"I have to do a four week ER rotation in January," Randy complained. "I am not looking forward to that. I hate the damn ER. It is painstakingly exhausting. You must be shy a few brain cells to work there day in and day out. I don't see how you do it."

"I can't help it. The rush is addictive."

"You're crazy.

"Bruce is the one who's crazy," Jim claimed. "I talked to him the other day. I see he and Stephanie are still a thing."

"Yes they are."

"I don't get those two. They have nothin' in common and they don't get along that well."

"In all honesty, I never expected it to last this long," Randy admitted. "It's been pretty up and down for them. I'm convinced they're only staying together because of this baby."

"Speaking of which," Jim declared. "We found out Jill's pregnant."

"No shit?"

Jim grinned smugly. "Yup. She's due the end of May."

"Congratulations. That's exciting."

While Jim and Randy enjoyed their bonding time together in Seattle, down in Los Angeles Bruce sat on the sofa and read the paper, happy to have a day off so he could relax. Stephanie, still sleepy from a nap, came out to the living room and sat next to him. Her hair was tousled and her cheeks flushed.

Bruce chuckled when he saw her. "Nice hair. You going for a new look?"

"Shut up," she snapped.

He found the scornful frown on her face funny. "What's wrong with you?"

"Besides the fact I just puked up everything I ate yesterday, my boobs hurt, and I feel like a beached whale?"

"Goes with the territory."

Her eyes zeroed in on her pregnant belly. "Look at me. I'm huge. My clothes don't fit anymore."

"Buy bigger ones."

She glared at him, unimpressed with his lack of sympathy. "And I've been craving the strangest things lately."

"Like what?"

"I actually want a bologna and cheese sandwich. I hate bologna." She rested her head on the back of the couch and groaned. "Think I'll get sterilized after this or have my uterus removed."

"You're too young to have that done." Bruce stood up and walked into the kitchen. "I'd like to go up to Seattle with you for Christmas, if you don't mind."

Bruce's schedule rarely allowed him time to do anything, let alone take a week to go up to Seattle with her. "You would?"

"I have some vacation time so I took a week off. I'd like to spend it with you and your family." He chugged down a glass of water. "Besides, it will give me a chance to hang out with Randy."

"How come you never visit your parents?" she wondered.

The smile instantly left his face. "I have no desire to go to San Diego." He returned to the living room and sat in the chair across from her. "There's a lot about my family that you wouldn't understand. My dreams of becoming a doctor were quickly shot down by my father. He thought college was a waste of time and money. Likewise, I got no support from him. He acted like it was a crime to want more out of life than mediocrity. I remember what he said to me the day I told him I wanted to go to medical school. He looked me in the eye and insisted that I take a job instead of going into debt over a dream I had no hope of ever achieving."

Stephanie didn't understand why a father wouldn't want his son to pursue avenues that would lead to success. "He said that to you?"

"Yes, he did," Bruce claimed. "But I wasn't about to be stuck in a job I hated or settle for less than what I was capable of. I wanted more than that. I wanted to make a difference in people's lives."

Stephanie and Bruce never really had a heart to heart talk like this before. Bruce Buckman truly was an amazing, giving man. The dedication and determination he demonstrated made Stephanie realize his reasons for putting up with the apparent hell he seemed to endure in his neurosurgery training. He was the paradigm of perseverance.

Bruce got up and rubbed Stephanie's pregnant belly. "I'm gonna head to bed. I have to go in early tomorrow." He leaned over and gave her a kiss. "I'll see you in the morning, Steph."

Chapter Nine

Randy and Jane planned to spend Thanksgiving in San Francisco. The day they were scheduled to leave, a huge cold front swept through the Puget Sound area. Ice blanketed the telephone poles. Water lines froze solid. Icicles hung from electrical wires, and blinding snow made the roads treacherously slippery. Trying to get to the airport was a chore and took much longer than anticipated.

Randy checked the flight board. Delayed. Every flight was delayed. "Damn!" he said, frustrated by the weather. Knowing they were running late, he pulled out his cellphone and called Jim. "Hey, Buddy."

"Hanson. What's up, Bro? I thought you were on an airplane headin' down here?"

"Unfortunately, we're stuck here. With all this damn snow and ice, the flights have been delayed. They have to scrape the plane's windows and wings and put de-icer on the runway so flights can take off. It's crazy."

Jim offered his insights. "If it keeps snowin', maybe you can jump on a sled and head down. San Francisco is downhill from Seattle, right?"

"That's not a bad idea. We'd probably get there faster."

"How delayed are ya?" Jim asked.

"About an hour right now. Still haven't boarded yet. The runway is backed up."

"It's a little foggy and cold here, but nothin' like the crap you guys are gettin'. Bet you miss California now, don't ya?" Jim asked.

"When I'm stuck in this crap, yes. It'll be nice to get out of this weather, if we ever get off the ground."

When they finally landed in San Francisco, Jim greeted both Randy and Jane with a hug. "Here." He handed Randy a cup of coffee. "Thought after all the travel stress, you might need this."

"You read my mind." Randy took a sip and felt the warmth of the caffeine flow through his system. "Thank you very much."

Jim dropped them off at Dale Davine's house, where he popped the trunk so Randy could grab their luggage. He stepped out of the car and accompanied them up to the door. "Guess you're with the family all day tomorrow?"

"Yup," Randy said. "We're gonna watch Brian's game while we gluttonously guzzle down turkey and pie."

"That's right. Your brother-in-law plays for USC," Jim remembered.

"Apparently some NFL recruiters are scoping him."

"Professional football?" Jim had never known a professional athlete before. "That's wicked cool."

"I'm proud of him." They knuckle bumped and did their secret handshake. "Friday then," Randy said, looking forward to spending a day with Jim.

"I'll be here bearing doughnuts and coffee."

"Cool," Randy replied. "I can't wait."

Jim flashed Randy the shaka sign. "Later, Bro."

"Later."

Randy and Jane had a pleasant conversation with her father over dinner, discussing happenings in the life of OB/GYN, which Dale found fascinating. Jane talked about school, her job, and the new friends they had made. Dale was pleased with how happy his daughter was and how well her needs were being met.

In an attempt to build a tighter bond with his father-in-law, Randy stepped into the kitchen to see if he could offer some assistance. "Need some help?" he asked Dale.

"Sure."

They rinsed the dishes together and loaded them in the dishwasher. While Randy dried off his hands, Dale went over to a shelf in the living room and pulled down a book. "Here, you might enjoy this."

Randy read the title, Sports Cars of Yesteryear. He flipped through the pictures admiring the classics. "Cool."

"Come with me for a minute."

Randy wondered why. Curiously, he followed his father-in-law into the garage. Dale dug behind a box on a shelf and pulled out a model car. He blew the dust off and handed it to Randy.

Randy carefully examined it, admiring the intricate details. "This is a 1969 Chevy Camaro Z-28. V-8 engine, 290-horsepower, razor-sharp handling, classic muscle car."

Dale pulled down another one. "This is one of the first cars I ever got. My parents gave it to me when I was twelve."

Randy set the Camaro down and carefully took this car in his hand. "1955 Porsche Spyder. James Dean's car."

"That's right," Dale said.

"This car is a legend."

Dale set a large box on the floor in the garage. "I have a bunch more in this box." Dale and Randy sat on milk crates and rummaged through this box together, pulling out miniature replicas, pictures, old Matchbook cars, and unbuilt model racecars while they discussed their shared love of sports cars.

Jane peeked her head into the garage to see what her father and husband were doing. Observing them together, she witnessed a side of her father she hadn't seen in years—that playful, boyish side. Jane forgot her father had that car collection and was glad to see the common interest her father and husband shared was bringing them closer together. Randy had always been so apprehensive around her father. Witnessing this connection was a pleasant transformation.

She wrapped her arms around Randy's shoulders. "I see you guys found some toys."

"These are not toys, Babe," Randy corrected. "These are classic collector's items of extreme historical significance." He held one up to show her. "See? This is a 1966 Ferrari 365 California Convertible. Very rare vehicle. Only fourteen of these were ever built." He drove it up her arm and made a revving sound.

She laughed at his playful antics. "You guys want some eggnog?"

"Sure, I'll take some." Randy picked up another model and used a rag to dust it.

Jane looked at her father. "Daddy?"

"Yes, I'll take some too. Thank you, Sweetheart."

On Friday, Randy spent the afternoon with Jim. Jill had to work, which left Jim to take care of the kids. He and Randy packed a bag with snacks and drinks then bundled up the kids and took them to the park. Sabrina climbed on the monkey bars and swung on the swings while Christopher stayed engrossed in the sandbox playing with the big Tonka truck his dad brought for him. Jim and Randy sat on the grass supervising the kids, sipping on coffee, and munching on Oreos.

Randy watched Jim's children, paying particular attention to Christopher. "I can't believe how big he's gotten."

"Growin' like a weed," Jim replied.

"And Jill's really taken on the job of being a mother to him."

"Jill is his mother. She's taken on Chris as her own," Jim declared. "Trina pisses me off. She doesn't even acknowledge her own son. As far as I'm concerned, she has lost all access to him, and I'm not sendin' her pictures anymore. She doesn't give a rat's ass about him."

"Does Chris even know who she is?" Randy wondered.

"No, which is fine with me."

"In all honesty, I think having Trina around would do more harm than good anyway. You and Christopher definitely got the better end of this deal. You gained a daughter and a wife, and Christopher gained a loving mother and siblings."

Jim nodded in satisfaction. "That's true."

They took the kids to get cheeseburgers for lunch. Randy was amazed at how similar Christopher and Jim were. They looked alike and had the same mannerisms. The chatterbox child talked about everything under the sun, and he was kind of obnoxious, like his dad. Jim even dressed him in a pair of sunglasses and a Hawaiian shirt. Randy enjoyed the cute personality of the 'mini Jim' who sat in a booster seat sharing lunch with him.

Sabrina was one of the most intelligent little girls Randy had ever seen. At six years old, she read quite well. She tried to teach Christopher letters, sounds, and numbers, but became frustrated when her younger sibling lost interest. She was fascinated by Jim's medical books and loved looking at the pictures of body parts. She constantly doctored up her dolls and pretended to be a doctor, wearing her mother's scrubs and the old stethoscope Randy gave her years ago. She was quite a sight to see.

When Jill came home from work, she took over childcare duties so Jim could drive Randy back to his father-in-law's house. The men said their goodbyes and agreed to get together again for Jim's birthday in January. But for now, Jim had to work a double shift in the morning and needed to get some rest.

When Randy entered the Davine house, a heavenly aroma instantly caught his attention. "It smells amazing in here." Jane had dozens of various types of cookies spread out all over the kitchen counter. Chocolate chip, peanut butter, snickerdoodles, oatmeal raisin, and even some chocolate brownies. Randy's eyes grew wide, staring at the scrumptious confectionary sight in front of him. "You've been busy."

"I've been baking."

"I can see that." Randy drew closer and gave her a kiss. "My wife, Mrs. Betty Crocker."

Jane placed a mixing bowl in the sink and rinsed it. "Did you have fun with Jim?"

"Oh yeah. Christopher is getting so big. Jim bought him a little basketball hoop and a ball and taught him how to slam dunk. And Chris wears sunglasses and Hawaiian shirts just like his dad."

"Aww, how cute," Jane said. "Daddy's out back starting the grill if you want to go out and help him."

"What are you gonna do?" Randy asked.

"Clean up then finish making dinner."

"Don't overdo it, Honey. You're supposed to be on vacation, remember?"

"You know I love to cook. I'm happy." She smiled contently.

"Good. That's what I want, for my Janey to be happy. May I go outside and play now?"

"Yes. But play nicely," she teased.

Randy grabbed a cookie on the way out.

Cuddled up together in the double-bed guestroom, Randy kissed Jane's head. "I had fun on this trip. Your dad and I talked a lot over the last three days."

"About what?" she wondered.

"He told me about your mom. She sounds a lot like you."

She drew her bottom lip between her teeth. "I've been watching you and Daddy together. I haven't seen him get excited about his cars in a long time. You seem to bring out the side of him that hasn't been present since before Mom got sick. He's like a different person."

"Coming down here for Thanksgiving was the best thing we could have done. For years I felt so uncomfortable around your father, but I don't feel that way anymore. Our first Thanksgiving together as husband and wife has been incredible."

"It has."

Chapter Ten

Upon returning home to Seattle, Randy decided to pay his brother a visit. With a Tupperware container full of Jane's cookies, Randy moseyed into Robby's apartment. "I brought you some cookies."

Robby sat at the table and nibbled on one. He had dark circles under his eyes, and he appeared underweight.

"You look like hell," Randy remarked.

"I've had better days."

Concerned about his brother's health, Randy asked, "You alright?"

"My life sucks."

"Why do you say that?"

He shrugged unenergetically. "My boss is a dick and this apartment complex blows."

"Find a new place to live."

"I can't afford to live anywhere else," Robby griped. "I work for minimum wage."

"Then look for a better job."

"The Lake Washington Institute of Technology offers a specialized auto technician program. I'd really like to take some classes and open my own shop, but the program requires fees I can't afford and tools I don't have."

"Did you talk to Dad about it?" Randy asked.

"He's pretty pissed at Stephanie right now for dropping out of school after he paid all those years for her to go to college. I don't think he's going to risk spending that kind of money on me."

"You're not Stephanie," Randy reminded.

"I know that. But he doesn't trust me."

"How serious are you about this?"

"Serious. I really want to do this."

By the look on his brother's face, Randy could tell he was sincere. "I believe you, but Dad has to be convinced. Present him with all the facts and information about this program and be honest. It's all about how you talk to him. You have to stay calm and listen to him without getting defensive. Do that, and I guarantee he'll support you. I can go with you when you talk to him if you want."

"I might take you up on that."

Randy snagged a cookie from the container. "What are you doing next weekend?"

"Nothing that I know of. Why?"

"Come over on Sunday. Jane and I are shopping for Christmas décor and I need you to help me hang up Christmas lights."

Robby shoved the rest of the cookie in his mouth. "You going to get me more of these cookies?"

"If you come over and help me, I'll give you a whole plateful of cookies."

Robby gave his brother a crooked grin. "Deal."

When Randy returned home, he found Jane curled up on the couch reading a book. "Hello, Beautiful."

"Hi, Sweetie."

He gave her a kiss then stepped into the kitchen to wash his hands. When he walked past the dining room, he noticed a box sitting on the table. "What's in the box?"

"I don't know. It has your name on it."

"I didn't order anything." Randy dried his hands then proceeded to examine the box. The word FRAGILE was written on it in very large red letters but no return address was indicated. Curious now, he brought the box over to the living room floor, sat down, and opened it. On top of a pile of Styrofoam popcorn, Randy found a note. *Randy, All these will do is collect dust in my garage, so I'm giving them to you. Enjoy. Dad.* He handed Jane the note then dug into the box. He pried around with his hands until he felt several small metal objects. He grabbed one and pulled it out. It was his father-in-law's mini replica of a 1966 Ferrari 365 California. "What the hell?" He dug in further, dumping popcorn all over the floor. Dale's entire sports car collection was hidden within the packaging material of this box. The books and pictures he had, Matchbook cars, sports car replicas, and all the models he'd painstakingly put together. "Your dad's entire collection is in here, thirty years' worth. And some of these are rare and worth a lot of money. Why did he send these to me?" Unsure what to think about all of this, Randy turned to Jane for answers. "Are you responsible for this?"

"I had nothing to do with it," Jane explained. "I haven't seen Daddy touch his cars in years, until he was with you."

Randy hesitated for a minute. "How can he give all this away?"

Jane didn't know how to respond, but she enjoyed the excitement in Randy's eye as she watched him pull out each item, one by one, and line them up neatly on the coffee table.

"I have to get a display case for all of these. This is awesome!" Carefully, he pulled out the last model and set the box aside. "I will definitely have to give him a call and thank him."

This year marked Randy and Jane's first Christmas together as husband and wife. They spent the morning buying ornaments, lights, yard decorations, and other Christmas décor. They borrowed his father's truck and traveled to a Christmas tree farm to cut down their own Christmas tree. It was chilly outside, so upon returning home, Randy started a fire in the fireplace. Once the living room was set aglow by the flicker of flames, he put on some Christmas music and together, he and Jane sorted through all of the bags and boxes of Christmas decorations.

They diligently worked together to set the freshly cut Douglas Fir in the tree stand then began decorating it with dangling ornaments and glittery garlands. They hung a shiny string of glowing lights around the fireplace mantle. Two red stockings, one with Jane's name and one with Randy's, dangled below. Several red Christmas candles of varying sizes were displayed on the mantle surrounding a large poinsettia. The stairwell railing was draped with a garland, and a sprig of mistletoe hung on the ceiling at the bottom of the stairs. A hand towel decorated with green and red patterned needlework hung over the stove handle, and a large stuffed Santa Claus leisurely sat on one of the barstools at the kitchen island. The house definitely had a festive holiday aura.

Around three o'clock that afternoon, Randy grabbed a ladder from the garage and started to work on decorating the outside.

Wearing a black jacket and a Seahawks baseball cap, Robby approached the house. He looked up at his brother, who stood on the roof holding a string of lights in his hand. "Yo, Randy. I wouldn't stand too close to that edge if I were you. I'd hate to see you fall off the roof."

Randy peeked over the edge. "If you're so concerned about my safety, why don't you climb up here and help me."

Three hours, thirty-four strings of lights, and five heavy duty extension cords later, the outside of the house was illuminated in reds, greens, blues, and yellows. Santa and his reindeer glowed brightly in the yard, two large plastic light-up candy canes stood upright in the grass on either side of the mailbox, and a big red ribbon wrapped around each porch column. A decorative wreath with a big red bow hung in the center of the front door.

Robby stood back and looked at their creative masterpiece. "Wow," he said. "Not quite National Lampoon's Christmas house, but it's definitely the brightest on your street."

Randy joined his brother at the curb. "It looks good. Thank you." He patted his brother's shoulder. Robby had lost a significant amount of weight, in fact, his arm felt bony. "When's the last time you had a decent meal? You need to eat more; you're too skinny. Stay and have dinner with us."

Robby gladly accepted.

The entire house smelled of freshly baked cookies.

"Smells great in here, Babe," Randy remarked.

"Thank you."

Jane made homemade chicken tortilla soup for all of them, then Randy and Robby munched on a few cookies. Shortly afterwards, the two men headed into Randy's home office.

"USC beat UW," Robby remarked.

"I know. My brother-in-law played in that game. I'm disappointed Washington didn't win, but happy for Brian. Since USC won, that means he's going to the Rose Bowl." Randy handed his brother a legal-sized white envelope. "Here."

"What is it?"

"Something for you. Open it."

Inside the envelope was a Rose Bowl admission ticket and round trip airfare to Los Angeles.

"Jane and I are flying down to L.A. to watch her brother play. Thought you might want to tag along with us."

Robby's eyes widened with excitement. He flashed the biggest smile Randy had ever seen. "I can't believe this. This is awesome, Bro!"

"And we'll be staying with Steph so you won't have to worry about a hotel or food expenses."

Robby hugged his brother. "This is the coolest thing anyone has ever done for me. Thank you."

"You're welcome."

Robby sat down in the rolling chair and twisted it back and forth "I talked to Dad last night about those mechanics classes."

"What was the verdict?"

"He agreed to pay for it. He and I are going shopping next weekend to get the tools I need."

"That's great, Rob. When do you start?"

"January third, spring semester."

Randy grinned, thrilled that his brother took initiative to make this positive change in his life. "I'm proud of you."

"Thanks."

Chapter Eleven

LAX on December 31st was extremely busy and overly crowded. Randy clasped Jane's hand tightly while they zigzagged between hordes of people. He peered over heads searching for Bruce and Stephanie. He finally caught sight of his sister and led his wife that direction.

When his petite sister with a big pregnant belly waddled to greet them, Randy grinned devilishly.

Before Randy could utter any teasing words to her, Stephanie said, "Shut up."

"I didn't say a word," he replied with a smirk.

"I know what you're thinking, Brat. Don't say it."

Randy shook Bruce's hand. "Hey, Buckman."

"Hey, Randy. Good to see you."

People wildly ran around the airport. Check-in and security lines piled around corners. The whole airport was a mass of confusion. "Jesus, what a mess. This place is mayhem," Randy remarked.

"Tell me about it. Everywhere you go in L.A. it's like this. And with the Rose Bowl going on, it's worse than usual. I'm far from impressed with L.A. It's a rat race down here."

"Didn't you grow up in Thousand Oaks?"

"Yes," Bruce declared. "But I don't remember L.A. being like this when I was a kid."

Bruce and Randy stepped up to the baggage claim carousel together. "So…Daddy huh?" Randy teased.

"Yup. Getting close. Stephanie's not particularly comfortable at the moment, and these crowds make her irritable. She doesn't like being pregnant."

"No, I bet not. Doesn't look like it would be very comfortable. Definitely not something I would want to endure."

"Nor me," Bruce admitted.

"How you feeling about all this?"

Bruce was blatantly honest. "Nervous, but excited. The baby's room is full of frilly pink shit, and I'm not sure how I feel about that. But hey, it is what it is."

Randy remembered the time, shortly after Jane moved in with him, when Bruce harped on him because female paraphernalia was scattered throughout his apartment. "I find it funny that you gave me such a hard time about Jane's flowered towels hanging in my bathroom, yet now, ironically, you're having a girl."

"I thought about that the other day too."

Bruce and Stephanie's three-bedroom apartment was located in one of the more prominent neighborhoods around UCLA. The apartment itself wasn't overly large, but the size didn't hinder the charm and elegance of it. It was comfortable, and Bruce had it decorated in a sophisticated style.

"This is a cute place."

"It's expensive as hell," Bruce complained. "But I refuse to live in the ghettos, so I'll cough up the rent if it will keep us in a safe neighborhood."

"Don't blame ya."

"Robby, you get the couch," Bruce said.

"Aye, aye." Robby bounded into the living room, staking claim to his spot.

"Let me show you your room." Bruce led Jane and Randy to a quaint little room with a double bed and small chest of drawers. The room was cramped, but the comfortable shade of blue on the walls and the antique furnishings—perhaps family heirlooms—gave the room a certain charming appeal. "I know it's not much, but the bed's comfortable."

"Je ne sais quoi," Randy said. "They say love grows best in small spaces." He winked suggestively at his wife. "It's perfect."

"Good. Have you guys eaten?" Bruce asked.

"Nothing of substance."

"There's a place right down the street that makes awesome Belgian waffles if you're interested."

"That sounds good."

"Alright. Then let's go."

Later that morning, Randy was able to catch Stephanie alone. She held her hand on her lower back with a scowl on her face. Concerned about her, he asked, "How you feeling?"

"My back hurts, my boobs are sore, and my feet are swollen."

"That's normal."

She grabbed his hand and placed it on her tummy.

When Randy felt the baby kick, the corners of his mouth raised. "Have you guys picked out a name yet?"

"Emily Lorraine."

"What last name are you going to give her?"

"We talked about hyphenating her name." She sat on the sofa and put her feet up.

"Emily Lorraine Hanson-Buckman? Seriously? You're going to do that to the poor child?" Randy held a cup of coffee in his hand and sat next to her. "Bruce told me he's asked you about marriage but you haven't given him an answer. Are you planning on making a commitment to him?"

"I'm considering it."

"You say that as if you have doubts."

She gave a lazy half shrug.

"He's a good man, Steph, and he cares about you. A lot of guys would have run away from this responsibility, but he's stuck around. That must mean something to you."

"It does."

Her tone was indifferent, which made Randy doubt her sincerity. "Let me ask you something, and be honest. Do you love him?"

"He's the father of my child, Randy."

"That's insignificant. And that's not what I asked you."

"I'm not going to take care of this baby alone. Bruce wants to be a father. He's stable and can support us."

"But do you love him?"

She hesitated for a moment before she said, "I don't know."

Just as Randy feared. "Even though you're not sure if you love him, you'd marry him anyway?"

"If it will help me gain stability for my daughter, then yes."

"A marriage of convenience in other words." Randy didn't like this arrangement. "That's not fair to Bruce, Steph. Consider everything and everyone involved before you make a commitment like that. Make sure you're doing this for the right reasons."

Chapter Twelve

Randy started his ER rotation the following week. Aside from normal ER duties, his gynecologic and obstetrical expertise would be utilized when such cases came in through the Emergency Room. Few obstetricians wanted to serve on-call for hospital Emergency Rooms, therefore the ER staff loved having Randy there.

Women with no prenatal care came in ready to deliver. These were Randy's most high-risk patients. One morning an intoxicated, suicidal pregnant patient in labor checked herself into the ER. The staff placed her in the Isolation Room, and, after arguing with the nursing staff, she left the hospital three minutes later. When Randy requested the hospital guard's assistance, the insolent woman had the temerity to fight off security. Unable to tolerate the pain any longer, she returned to the ER fifty-two minutes later on her own accord.

By noon the Emergency Room was packed. It was not uncommon for several patients to arrive at the ER almost simultaneously, virtually on their deathbeds. Each of these people often required extensive interventions in addition to intensive medical therapy. As the physicians ran from patient to patient, they were often besieged by requests from various hospital staff, medical students, relatives of patients, paramedics, police officers, and local media. To say the ER was a busy place was an understatement.

About thirty seconds after suturing a gouged arm, a nurse came up to Randy and said, "The lady in room two is seizing, and we can't get an IV in her. The IV team tried and they said you'd have to do it."

How difficult was it to put in an IV? "Alright. I'll be there in a minute."

It was commonly accepted that a human could not be in more than one place at a time, but ER physicians were expected to be immune to this limitation. Things were hectic enough in the ER without efficiency being impeded by a number of factors. Among these snafus was trouble with the phone systems, which kept randomly disconnecting. They were also experimenting with 'new and improved' technology. Rather than allowing the doctors to read x-rays directly, they scanned them in the radiology department and read them in the ER by viewing the images on a monitor. This posed a problem because the inherent degradation in the resolution of the image made the x-rays hard to read. As a consequence, subtle findings—often crucial—were blurry. And to make matters worse, it was raining cats and dogs outside.

A gynecological case came in and Randy was beckoned, but the case was so complex, involving shattered pelvic bones, that he had to call a consultant. The orthopedic consultant, from the background sounds, was evidently having sex. Must have been good stuff, because every few seconds he asked Randy to "hold on a minute" then continued to go at it.

"Dr. Grey?" Randy called to him, trying to get him to return to the phone. "Dr. Grey, I have an emergency situation here. Please advise."

Every time the orthopedic surgeon returned to the phone, he panted and said, "Sorry about that, Hanson. Can you repeat the case again?"

Was he for real? This was more than an annoyance, since anything that wasted Randy's time limited the time he could devote to patients.

ER doctors found themselves enmeshed in the same predicament every day—the ER was inevitably swamped with critically ill patients. You couldn't simply make them stand in line and wait their turn. Some patients could not wait. A patient who wasn't breathing couldn't be scheduled for an appointment next Tuesday. Through this experience in the ER, Randy became more and more aware that his best friend was insane.

After a hectic day in the ER, Randy came home tired, hungry, and glad he didn't choose emergency medicine as his specialty. "Brr," he said to his wife. "It's cold outside. Weather report says possible snow." He laid his stethoscope on the table and gave Jane a kiss.

"How was your day?" she asked him.

"Long, busy, and full of weirdos. How was yours?"

Randy's cheerful disposition, yet opposing commentary, made her laugh.

"I'm exhausted. This ER rotation is killer, and being on-call is a joke," Randy scoffed. "When they say on-call in the Emergency Room they really mean stay all day and all night at the hospital. We know you're not scheduled to come in today, but we really need your expertise. And since you're a first year resident and the grunt of the flock, we'll force you to work a double so you can suffer from sleep deprivation, get covered in blood, listen to patients scream, and watch people die."

"You don't sound very impressed."

"The ER sucks," he said. "I'm learning a lot, but damn. The crappy shifts, the constant inflow of patients, and the hospital coffee in the middle of the night is either watered down or tastes like sludge. How the hell do they expect doctors to stay alert when we drink that crap? And the food in the cafeteria is terrible. Nothing compares to your cooking, Babe. I can see why they can't get OB's to offer their services on-call in the damn ER. That work is awful. I think Jim has a screw loose. He actually enjoys this shit."

"It's a good thing he does because someone has to take the ER."

"And he can have it. That madness is not for me."

After a nourishing meal, homemade by his wife, and stimulating conversation that did not involve blood, broken bones, or respirators, Randy called Jim. He'd seen enough weird medical cases in the last week to keep his imagination running wild for a long time. He couldn't wait to tell Jim all about it.

When Jim answered the phone, Randy blurted out, "You are a crazy son-of-a-bitch, you know that? How the hell do you handle the ER day after day?"

"Dude, you ask me that all the time."

"I have never worked so hard or been so damn tired in my life. Between the lack of sleep, lack of nourishment, shitty ass coffee, idiot consulting physicians, and the complete and total chaos that seems to steadily flow into the ER, I almost went nuts. How many weird things can happen in the ER during one 24-hour period? I sewed up 367 sutures in one day."

"You counted them?" Jim asked, amused by his best friend's comment.

"Yes. Now this is the same day I splinted seven fractures, had a patient with major head trauma, one methadone overdose, one DOA, a sigmoid colon infection, a man with all the symptoms of a cardiac aneurysm, helped put in seven chest tubes, performed CPR three times, had a patient hit on me, and had to find exit wounds for a gunshot victim. Then I watched a drunk man walk into the street and get himself hit by a bus right in front of the ER. And, being the OB/GYN specialist on duty, I had two deliveries from women who had received no prenatal care whatsoever. One was a psychopathic drunk woman who left the ER in the middle of labor then fought off hospital security only to return in an hour with the baby's head emerging. The other was a breech baby whose foot was sticking out and I ended up performing a C-section. I treated severe abdominal cramping which resulted in a miscarriage, dealt with violent family members, and had one hypoglycemic pregnant woman come in convulsing. The orthopedic surgeon I called for consultation was having sex while I was on the phone with him, and some moron seemed to think that he could ride his skateboard behind a car that was traveling forty-five miles an hour; in doing so he broke almost every bone in his body. A bunch of medical students couldn't figure out how to put in a damn IV. An IV for Christ sake, simple procedure that any medical student should be able to perform, but no, they asked me to do it."

Jim busted a gut in the background while Randy griped. "Yeah, it's great, isn't it?"

"Seriously fucked up is more like it."

"No way, Dude," Jim disagreed. "I love the ER."

"So blood and dismemberment is a turn on to you?"

"Hell yeah. It's great," Jim boasted.

Randy shook his head, not seeing Jim's obsession with it. "You are insane, James Ryan. Fucking insane."

Chapter Thirteen

Snow came as predicted, heaps of it. Randy opened his eyes and peeked out the window to huge snowflakes falling from the sky. He bounded out of bed. As soon as he got dressed, he rushed downstairs, plopped a pile of random items on the couch, and put on his insulated boots, Gore-Tex gloves, and North Face jacket. "Going outside, Babe," he called to Jane.

"What?"

Randy grabbed the pile of objects off the couch. "I'm going outside."

"I don't even get a good morning kiss?"

"Of course you do." He entered the kitchen and greeted Jane with a kiss. "Good morning."

"What is all this stuff?" she asked.

"You'll see."

Randy pranced out to the front yard and dropped all the items on the snow-covered ground. He crawled on his hands and knees and formed a snowball, pushing it around the yard to make it bigger. When it reached the size he wanted, he rolled it to the middle of the yard and packed some snow around it to hold it in place. He made two more snowballs and stacked them one on top of the other. Once balanced, he carried the pile of objects over to the snowman. He wrapped a surgical gown around the snowman's torso then found two twigs for arms and poked them through the sleeves into the sides of the middle snowball. He tied a pair of latex examining gloves on the end of each stick making hands and placed a surgical mask over the snowman's face. He strategically placed two rocks in for eyes. To top off the look, he draped an old stethoscope around the snowman's neck.

Satisfied with his snow doctor, Randy retrieved a scrap of plywood and a two-inch dowel from the garage. He screwed them together then, with a big black permanent marker, wrote Healthy Holidays on the sign and hammered it into the yard right next to the snowman.

Jane came out in the yard and spotted the snowman Randy made. "Who's this handsome doctor standing in our front yard?"

"This is Dr. Frosty. You like him?"

"I do. Pretty creative there, Dr. Hanson." She bent down, picked up a handful of snow, and threw it at him. It hit his leg.

"You're gonna get it." He retaliated by throwing a snowball back at her. After several tosses back and forth, Randy grabbed her by the waist and pulled her into the snow with him.

"It's cold lying here," she said, giggling a bit.

"It is," he teased. "But that's what you get. Next time, maybe you'll think twice before you start a battle with me." He leaned over and kissed her then hopped off the ground and held his hands out to her. "Come on. Let's stoke up the fire and try some of that cocoa my mom gave us."

They stood on their feet, dusted snow off each other, and headed back inside to warm up.

To Randy, there was no better site than looking down and seeing his wife lying naked on the bed. He loved the glow on her face, the steady rise and fall of her chest, and the slight sheen of sweat on her body that told him how much she enjoyed what they were doing. He held off as long as he could, but the sights, sounds, and smells in that bedroom drove him to climax pretty quickly. When it finally came, neither of them said anything for a few minutes. They just stared at each other, lightly caressing one another's bodies.

Randy began to roll off of her, but before he could, Jane held him there. Her beautiful face gazed up at him. "Don't go yet."

"We have things to do today."

"Just a few minutes longer."

They slowly rolled over so they were face to face but side by side, still intimately joined together. His eyes moved to her lips; he leaned in to kiss her, but this wasn't a quick kiss, this was a deep, tongue in every part of your mouth kiss. They were interrupted when Randy's cellphone rang. With a smirk on his face, Randy said, "No respect for privacy." He reached over to answer the call. "Dr. Hanson."

"Hey, Randy. Hope I wasn't interrupting anything."

When he recognized the voice on the other end, he flashed a crooked smile and slowly drew away from Jane. "No, not at all. What's up, Buckman?"

"Stephanie's in labor."

Randy raised an eyebrow. "Is she?"

"Yup. Brought her in about thirty minutes ago."

He held the phone between his shoulder and chin while he fumbled to slip on a pair of sweats. "Contractions?"

"Running about three minutes apart at the moment. Pretty strong ones though. She's making good progress. Won't be too much longer."

"How's she doing?" Randy asked, hoping his sister was able to manage her labor pain.

"She's doing great. She's focused and in good spirits."

"How are you doing?" Randy sat on the bed facing Jane.

"Excited to see my baby."

"Good. Did you call my parents?" Randy reminded him.

"Yes. Your mom is looking at airline tickets so she can take the first flight out."

"Cool. Jane and I will try to head down this weekend."

Randy and Jane booked a flight to L.A. that weekend to meet the new addition to the family. They rented a car, checked into a hotel, then acquired directions to Bruce's place. When Randy knocked on Bruce and Stephanie's door, Ellen Hanson answered. Randy hugged his mother then he and Jane entered the apartment. "Hey," he whispered.

"Hey, Randy." Bruce cradled the baby in his arms. "Meet your niece, Emily Lorraine Buckman."

Randy sat down and took the baby from Bruce. Her hazel eyes stared at him. "She's beautiful."

When Stephanie heard her brother's voice, she came out of hiding. "Hey, Brat."

His eyes swept over her. "Hey, Sis. You look good. How you feeling?"

"Better, now that I'm not pregnant anymore."

He gazed down at the baby again. She had Bruce's eyes, Stephanie's feminine features, and the most adorable patch of light brown fuzz on top of her head. "Hi, Emily. It's Uncle Randy." He gently rubbed her hand and kissed her forehead. "She's absolutely beautiful." He was so proud to be an uncle.

Many visitors came to see Emily that weekend, including Randy's dad and brother. Jim flew in from San Francisco. Their dear friend, Dr. Amanda Stevens, came down from Stanford. And Sarah Chan, a friend of theirs from medical school, visited from San Jose. Amanda, Sarah, Bruce, Jim, and Randy hadn't been together since Randy's wedding, where they celebrated two lives joining together. Today, they were celebrating the birth of a new one.

The five friends went out to lunch together to reminisce, share residency experiences, and talk about new happenings in their lives. Turns out Amanda was dating a surgeon from the hospital where she worked. Sarah taught CPR and first aid classes to the local community and had recently been promoted to EMT crew lead. Jim shared pictures of his growing kids, as well as his wife's pregnant belly. Randy talked about Seattle and showed everyone pictures of his new house. Bruce simply sat there, taking in the entire conversation with a grin on his face.

"Two of you men wear wedding bands," Amanda said when she noticed Randy fidgeting with his wedding ring. "When is it your turn, Dr. Buckman? You're doing this backwards."

Bruce chuckled. "Yeah. I know."

"And," Amanda added. "Two of you have children." She focused her attention on Randy. "When are you going to be a daddy?"

Randy's eyes widened at this terrifying thought. "Oh no. No way. We are not ready for that. Not for a long time."

Jim teased, "You don't want a little bambino runnin' around?"

"Not right now," Randy retorted, quickly negating that idea. "Several years down the road and I'll consider it."

"The fact that there's a baby in this world with both Hanson and Buckman blood is frightening."

"Hey," Randy said. "That's my niece, Ryan. She's brilliant and beautiful. And when she gets older, she'll make significant contributions to the world. Then you will bite your tongue for saying that." He redirected the conversation to Amanda. "I don't see you with a wedding band or babies either."

"No, not yet," she replied. "Still waiting for the right man."

"Maybe this surgeon of yours?"

Mandy shrugged, not sure she liked that prospect. "I don't know."

After lunch, the five of them exited the restaurant with arms around each other. Even though they didn't see each other all the time, they communicated often via e-mail and text messaging. They vowed to stay in touch and get together at least once a year to talk and share lunch like they did in medical school. Randy had a wonderful weekend, surrounded by all the people he loved—his family, his closest friends, and his wife.

Stephanie and Emily napped while Bruce tidied up the kitchen. In the middle of unloading the dishwasher, a knock resonated through the apartment. Not wanting Stephanie or the baby to wake up, Bruce hurried to answer the door. His mood quickly shifted when he saw his father standing on his doorstep. "What are you doing here?"

"Heard I had a granddaughter. I'd like to see her."

"She's sleeping." Bruce didn't want to talk to this man or even be in his presence. And he certainly didn't want him in his apartment or anywhere near his daughter. Even though this man was his father, Bruce had no respect for him.

"You didn't return my call," his father complained.

Bruce scoffed, "That's because I didn't want to talk to you. The last time we spoke, you insulted me and told me I was the worst mistake you ever made."

Bruce tried to close the door, but his father stuck his hand out to stop him. "Bruce."

"Get away from me."

"I have a right to see my granddaughter."

"You don't have a right to anything. You're selfish and uncaring and never gave a crap about anyone but yourself." Bruce knew that was a harsh thing to say, but he didn't care. It was the truth, and the irrefutable bastard needed to hear it years ago. "All I ever wanted was for you to be proud of me. But no matter how hard I tried, nothing I did was ever good enough. You've never supported anything I've done and never said a kind word to me in your life. What makes you think I'm going to let you barge into Emily's life and allow you to rub your twisted influence on my precious daughter?"

"I raised you, and I have a right to see my granddaughter. You owe me that."

"I don't owe you anything. You can't just waltz into my life and expect everything to be ok after spending my entire life not caring one ounce about me. All Lewis and I ever wanted was a little of your time and attention, but you were so busy working late and screwing your secretary that you completely blew us off. You treated Mom like shit and your blatant infidelity pushed her over the edge and drove her to alcoholism. I don't blame her for leaving you."

"How dare you say that to me!" his father fumed. "What kind disrespectful brat speaks to his father that way?"

"You lost my respect years ago. I want nothing to do with you." Bruce closed the door in his father's face and refused to talk to him any longer.

After dinner, Bruce rocked the baby to sleep then gently laid her down in the cradle. As soon as she was snuggled in, he sat on the sofa next to Stephanie. "She finally fell asleep."

"Good."

He stared at Stephanie with an impish expression on his face. "I'm still waiting for an answer, you know." Bruce presented her with an open felt box. A gorgeous diamond solitaire ring glistened inside. "Maybe this will entice you."

Stephanie's mouth gaped open. The ring in front of her sparkled in dollar signs. She considered the implications of marrying Bruce Buckman. He was a neurosurgeon. He brought home a decent salary that would only get larger as he progressed through residency and began to practice on his own. With Bruce's income, their daughter would be able to get everything she needed. Aside from Emily's needs, Stephanie thought about herself. Her high-maintenance lifestyle would easily be maintained with Bruce Buckman as her husband. A doctor's salary, to her, meant a large house, lavish possessions, shopping sprees, and fancy cars. She certainly wouldn't have to worry about money with him.

Bruce took her hand and pulled the ring out of the box. "So what do you say?"

In a barely audible voice, she replied, "Ok."

He softly kissed her. Then, very carefully, he slipped the ring on Stephanie's left hand. "I want to get married as soon as possible."

"I don't want to rush it though. We need time to plan."

"We don't need anything fancy, Steph. An civil service will suffice. I just want to exchange vows and call it good."

Stephanie's face turned downcast. "I've always wanted an elaborate wedding. I see no reason why I can't have one."

It was painfully obvious he and Stephanie didn't see eye to eye on this. Trying to meet her halfway, he offered, "We can have a traditional wedding, but I don't want anything fancy or over the top. Let's keep it simple. And I don't want to wait too long. We need to set a date that's not far off."

The gears in her head turned. He could see she was disappointed, but he didn't want to make a fuss with a huge ceremony. A small family affair was more than enough for him.

"Are we in agreement?" he asked.

Her mouth curved upward, indicating she agreed.

Chapter Fourteen

A woman admitted to the hospital complained that the over the last twenty-four hours her baby's movements had decreased. Randy thoroughly examined the patient's file and noticed several things. Prior to pregnancy, the patient had been diagnosed with type-1 diabetes, which had remained untreated for years. Even now, at twenty-six weeks gestation, she admitted she was inconsistent about taking her insulin. She was not gaining weight and a recent ultrasound indicated fetal measurements were smaller than should be expected for the gestational age—less than the tenth percentile. All of these symptoms were indicators of a possible problem with the baby. "Dr. Givens, can you come over here for a minute please?" Randy asked his attending physician.

The doctor plodded over to see how he could be of assistance to his apprentice.

Randy handed him a patient file. "Take a look at this."

Dr. Givens examined the file. "I don't like these numbers."

"Neither do I," Randy said. "This baby isn't growing like it should, and her diabetes is out of control. We need to monitor this closely. I'd like to run an ultrasound and CTG on her."

The attending physician agreed. "Go ahead."

Randy examined the baby's head and abdomen and compared those measurements to growth charts to estimate the baby's weight. The ultrasound indicated reduced-sized internal organs and low weight. Ultrasound also determined a low amount of amniotic fluid in the uterus, which signified possible Intrauterine Growth Restriction. Next, he placed sensitive electrodes on the mother's abdomen and held them in place with a lightweight stretchable band. Electrode sensors connected to a fetal monitor measured the rate and pattern of the baby's heartbeat. This test indicated the baby's heartrate was below normal.

Once data was recorded, Randy showed the chart to Dr. Givens. "This baby is under intense stress. I think we need to order an amnio to check for chromosomal abnormalities and put Mom on bedrest. Educate her on proper nutrition and up her caloric intake to increase baby's weight. If her symptoms don't alleviate, we might want to consider inducing her."

"That's risky and can put baby's health in serious jeopardy," Dr. Givens advised.

"Baby's health is already in jeopardy."

"Yes, but if we deliver too early and the baby is too weak for the stresses of labor and delivery, it could lead to severe complications."

Randy hadn't considered this. "That's true. I didn't think about that."

"And be mindful that babies born prior to thirty-four weeks usually end up in the NICU."

"What about cesarean?" Randy suggested.

"Less risky, but still dangerous. Let's go with your original plan of amniotic testing and bedrest. See if we can get to her thirty-four weeks. We'll go from there."

"Yes, Sir." Randy wrote a referral for an amniocentesis and counseled the patient about treating her diabetes, proper nutrition during pregnancy, and bedrest. He hoped that would be enough to get her through the next eight weeks.

San Francisco was foggy, but the temperature was quite warm for February. Jim wished he could be out enjoying the sun instead of being stuck in the hospital all day. Midway through his lunch break, the intercom system announced, "Dr. Ryan, please report to the ER. Dr. Ryan, to the ER please."

"Dammit." He quickly shoved another bite into his mouth and threw his tray in the trash. He rushed down the hall to the ER, scrubbed up, and slipped on a pair of latex gloves. A young girl, around Sabrina's age, sat on an exam table holding her right arm. Jim picked up her chart and studied it. "Hi, Carrie." He wheeled a stool up to her and sat down. "I'm Dr. Ryan."

"Hi," she sniveled.

Trying to get her to relax, he talked to her as he examined her arm, which was swollen and bruised. "I have a little girl about your age."

"You do?"

"Yes I do. She likes gymnastics and dolls. Do you like dolls?"

She nodded. "Uh huh."

"How'd you hurt your arm?"

"Rollerblading," she said sadly.

He checked her x-ray. She had a fractured radius—the most common forearm fracture, usually caused by a fall onto an outstretched hand. Jim showed the x-rays to the girl's mother, pointing out the injured area. "You'll have to take her to an orthopedic pediatrician to have it looked at. We'll get her a splint and a sling to keep it stabilized until you can get her an appointment. Be right back."

He left the examination room to get materials to splint her up only to be stopped by another physician. "Ryan, we need you over here."

"I have a little girl over here who needs her wrist splinted," Jim stated.

"And I need you here," the attending physician insisted. He led Jim to a blood-covered gurney where a young man, bleeding profoundly, screamed in pain.

Every time Jim tried to help a patient, some attending physician or higher level resident pulled him away. He found this extremely aggravating. Jill was on shift that day and sensed his frustration. To offer support, she gently placed her hand on his shoulder. He drew in a long breath to release some tension then tightened his upper lip and carried on with his duties.

His shift ended at two o'clock that afternoon. Feeling run down, he went to his parents' house to pick up his son.

"You look awful, James," his mother said when she saw him.

Jim sneered at her comment. "Gee, thanks."

"You ok?" she asked.

"The ER ran nonstop all day. Had to work a double because one of the physicians called in sick."

"You need to take better care of yourself. You're not getting enough sleep."

"Mom, please. I'm too tired to discuss this right now." He sat down for a minute.

His father abruptly uttered, "Have you heard anything from Trina?"

Why did his father insist on bringing up that topic? "No, Dad, I haven't, and I probably never will, which is fine with me. Chris doesn't even know who she is."

His father shook his head. "Trina should be involved in his life."

"We've discussed this already. Trina is a selfish bitch and doesn't give a crap about Chris."

"She's still the boy's mother."

"Jill is his mother."

"Not his biological mother."

Jim raked his fingers through his hair, trying not to get upset over his father's belittling comment. "What the hell difference does it make if Jill gave birth to him or not? His biological mother is a fuckin' junkie. Do you really want Christopher around someone like that? I sure as hell don't. Jill has taken him in from day one and cares for him like her own son. Why isn't that good enough for you?"

"Are you swearing at me?" his father asked, bothered by his son's tone.

Jim's mother interjected, "Anthony, leave him alone. You didn't like Trina anyway."

Christopher ran into his father's arms. "Daddy!"

Jim lifted his son off the ground. "Hey, Buddy."

"Where's Mommy?"

"Mommy is still at work," Jim explained. "We have to get Sissy then we'll head home and eat dinner."

Christopher screeched in excitement.

Jim set him down and said, "Go get your stuff, Chris."

The child ran off. Jim stared at his father. "This is my family, Dad. Trina is not and will not be a part of it, ever. You're gonna have to accept that." When Christopher came back with his bag, Jim stood up. "Thanks for watchin' him for me." He kissed his mother on the cheek.

"Anytime, Honey." She waved at her grandson. "Bye, Christopher."

Jim and his young son left the house holding hands.

Jim's mother glared at her husband, appalled that he had treated Jim that way. "Why do you do that to him?"

Defensively, Mr. Ryan replied, "The boy needs his mother."

"Jill is his mother. Why is that such a problem for you?"

"Because that woman should have taken responsibility for her son instead of dumping him off on James."

"You can't get after Jim because of Trina's irresponsibility. That is not fair. None of this was his fault," Jim's mother defended. "James is doing a good job with Chris. He's a good father. He's happy and he loves that little boy. Support him, please. He's been through enough. All he's ever tried to do is make you proud."

"And I am proud of him," Anthony Ryan said.

"Then maybe you should tell him that once in a while."

After Jim picked up Sabrina from school, he brought the kids home and made them macaroni and cheese. Exhausted, he gulped down a giant cup of coffee and sat on the couch watching his children play. He wished he could go to sleep, but couldn't until Jill came home. Hoping to stay awake, he picked up his phone and called Randy.

"Hey, Jim. How's it going?"

"Just got off a double shift," Jim wearily replied. "What are you up to?"

"Was about to mow the grass and wash my car before it rains."

"If you wash your car it's bound to rain."

"Living in Seattle makes rain pretty much inevitable," Randy retorted.

"My dad pisses me off," Jim remarked, changing the subject.

"Why?"

"He insists that Trina be involved in Chris's life."

"But she's a heroin addict who abandoned him and hasn't had any contact with him."

"I tried to tell my dad that, but you know how he is. The man walks around with blinders and earmuffs on. He really has no damn clue," Jim complained. "It fumes me that he brings her up all the damn time. Christopher doesn't know who she is and I would really like to keep it that way. She is a blast from my past I really want to nix."

"Don't blame you."

"How's Jane?" Jim asked.

"Working on a research paper at the moment. Spring break is coming up soon. She's looking forward to that."

"You guys doin' anything?"

"Going to Puerto Rico with my family. I took the week off."

Jim thought that was an excellent idea. "Sweet."

"Hey, guess what we found out?"

"Jane's pregnant?" Jim teased, trying to get a rise out of Randy.

"No, Jackass. Why do you keep saying that?"

"Because I'm anxiously awaiting the day it actually happens."

"Well, you'll have to wait a long time," he replied. "You know how I told you Jane's brother was in the NFL draft?"

"Yeah."

"He got picked up by the 49ers in the first round," Randy bragged. "We have a professional football player in the family now."

"That's kickass." Jim returned to the subject of babies, giving Randy a hard time. "Jill and I were checkin' out baby names the other day. You do know what your name means, don't you?"

"Randal? It's an English name. Lots of knights had that name. It's noble."

Jim corrected him. "Randy is English slang. It means havin' a strong desire for sex. How fitting is that for you, Horn Dog?"

Randy was able to keep Jim awake until Jill got home. He went out like a light that night. Luckily he was off for the next two days so he'd be able to rest.

Chapter Fifteen

Jill went into labor earlier than expected. In fact, she was three weeks early. Her contractions hit hard and she was in serious pain. Her usual obstetrician was out of town that week, so the 'back up' doctor had to take the call. This man was new to the hospital, and he kept disappearing without telling anyone where he was going. The one time he did step into the delivery room to check on Jill, he fumbled around with his latex gloves as if he'd never worn a pair before. He stared at the fetal monitor, confused by the information on it, and when Jill asked for pain medication, the doctor ignored her request. He didn't appear to know the first damn thing about obstetrics. Based on first impressions, Jim did not like this man.

Demanding answers, Jim pulled the doctor into the hallway. "What the hell is going on? My wife has been asking for pain medication for the last forty-five minutes. Will you please do something about these contractions? Why you won't call anesthesia up here is far beyond me."

"Sir, please calm down," the doctor advised.

"No, I will not calm down," Jim snapped. "Do your job, dammit." Jim was about to get on the phone and call the anesthesiologist himself.

"Sir, I really don't appreciate your tone."

"Then get off your lazy ass and be a doctor." Jim stepped back into Jill's labor room, pissed at this snot-nosed brat. He tried to comfort his wife and begged the nurses to call anesthesia, but they told him they weren't authorized to do that. He said he was a doctor and was authorizing it, but they ignored him.

When it was time for Jill to push, suddenly the doctor was nowhere to be found. "Did you page him?" Jim asked the nurse.

"Yes, Sir. He's not answering."

"Then do an all call for him."

"We did. He's not responding."

"You have got to be kidding me." Jim stepped over to the sink and scrubbed up.

"What are you doing?" the nurse asked.

Jim laid it on the line. "If the doctor who's supposed to be making this delivery isn't going to be here to do his job then I will." He slipped on a pair of latex gloves and took position. He didn't have a whole lot of obstetrical experience, other than what he learned in medical school and practiced during his residency, but in this situation he had no choice.

"Sir, you can't…"

"Please, Miss," he read her nametag, "Klauson. My wife is ready to push. Her doctor isn't here. I am a licensed physician. Will you please step aside and let me do this?"

Jim was familiar with the procedures and motions of the ward and could scrub up in under a minute. That, and the fact that knew medical vocabulary and could easily read a fetal monitor, made her realize he was serious. "You really are a doctor, aren't you?"

Aggravated by this nurse's lack of reasoning, Jim replied, "I've been trying to tell you that all afternoon. But for some reason people in this ward don't listen. Now either help me or move out of the way."

She chose to help him. Jim did the best he could, considering the situation. Jill was in pain, but she did her part and pushed. Eighteen minutes later, his daughter was born. He went through the motions of cutting the cord and assisted with the placental delivery. After which, he removed his latex gloves, washed his hands, and let the nurses and pediatricians take over. He stood by Jill's side and held her hand. "Honey, I am so sorry."

"Don't be," she said. "I'm glad you were here."

"That incompetent prick is gonna get an earful from me."

When the doctor finally decided to grace them with his presence, Jim exclaimed, "I want to talk to you."

"Sir, I'm a little busy to be…"

Jim didn't let him finish. He pulled the doctor into the hall and let him have it. "You are in some serious trouble. Where the hell were you? "

"Look, Sir, I don't know who you think you are, but you have done nothing but insult me all day. What gives you the right to speak to me with such condescension?"

Jim whipped out his UCSF Medical Center identification badge and flashed it in this doctor's face. "James Ryan, M.D. I told you I'm a doctor and it's a damn good thing I am because I had to deliver my baby because you were too busy doing who the hell knows what when you should have been with your patient."

"I was on my lunch break."

"Was your pager on?"

"I shut it off."

This angered Jim even more. "I sure as hell hope you have job opportunities in another hospital and have good malpractice insurance, Dr. Morrison, because what I witnessed from you today was the most unprofessional attitude and crappiest medical care I have ever seen in my life. First year Anatomy students take better care of their formaldehyde-soaked cadavers than you did with your patient, you incompetent ass."

"Doctors are human and make occasional errors, especially when under immense pressure."

"Pressure? How hard is it to sit on your ass while my wife is in labor? You deliberately ignored the situation. Gross negligence is inexcusable, and I will not let you get away with this."

"I had a lapse in concentration."

Ok. This guy was getting on his nerves. Jim wanted to punch him. Maybe that would knock some sense into him. "A lapse in concentration? What kind of lame excuse is that? Your lapse in concentration is far more disastrous than for an accountant or a baker. We're not balancing books or baking cookies here for Christ sake."

"Come on, Dr. Ryan. You're a physician. I'm sure you understand. I'm having some personal problems and wasn't on my game."

Oh, this was rich. "Do I look like I give a shit about your personal problems?"

"You've never had your personal life occasionally slip into your professional life?"

Jim had heard enough. He eyeballed this guy and firmly stated, "When people's lives are at stake, no. If you had a good explanation that would be one thing, but you don't. You were grossly incompetent."

"No conclusive harm was done. It was an inconsequential mistake. Your wife is fine. The baby is fine," he tried to defend himself.

"Is that all you care about? You had a duty to act and you failed to exercise due care. I have every intention of speaking to the hospital director in regards to your actions, and this incident will go to the complaints manager of the health authority."

This doctor was in trouble, and he knew it. Jim could see the fear in his eyes. "You can't talk to the director."

"Give me one good reason why not."

"What do you want me to do?" the doctor begged.

"An admittance and an apology would be a good place for you to start." Jim turned away and returned to his wife and new daughter.

Jim called Randy that evening with a range of emotions running though his head. Needing to get this incident off his chest, he told Randy all about it. "The cocksucker didn't even have his pager on because he said he was on his lunch break."

Randy found his completely unacceptable. How could a fellow obstetrician be so inconsiderate? "I can't believe he did that."

Venting, Jim said, "Then he had the nerve to beg me not to tell anyone, tryin' to justify it by sayin' he was havin' personal problems. Like I give a fuck."

"What a douchebag."

Jim agreed. "No shit. OB is not my specialty, especially when my wife is the one lyin' there screamin' because that son-of-a-bitch wouldn't call anesthesia. Damn, Dude, I needed you today."

"Are you going to report him?" Randy asked, hoping Jim wouldn't let this incident slide.

"I already did. I'm sure as hell not gonna ignore somethin' like that. That qualifies as medical negligence. The OB nurses backed up my story and they're reporting him to the medical board too."

"Good," Randy said. "How's Jill doing now?"

"She's fine. A little sore. Luckily we didn't have any complications."

"How's the baby?"

Jim's voice shined. "She's great. Seven pounds, four ounces. Little blondie, and she has blue eyes."

"Uh oh. A blonde, blue-eyed cutie, huh? Lock her in a closet and get the shotgun."

"Man, I hope your first child is a girl so I can pester you," Jim said. "If she looks anything like Jane, you're gonna be in trouble."

Randy couldn't argue. "What'd you guys name her?"

"Jalene."

"That's a pretty name."

"Jill and I have been talkin' about havin' me adopt Sabrina an gettin' her last name legally changed to Ryan."

"Can you do that?" Randy wondered.

Jim explained, "Under the right circumstances. Jill hasn't heard a word from Sabina's father and doesn't even know where he is. She knows he won't contest it because he hasn't had any contact with Sabrina. We'll have to petition it in court, but legal step-parent adoption changes the legal identity of the father. I would become her legal father. It won't change her name on the birth certificate, but legally she'll be known as Sabrina Ryan, my daughter."

"That's cool," Randy said.

"We have to wait though, because in California we have to be married at least one year before we can proceed. It's a process, but we are definitely lookin' into it."

Chapter Sixteen

"Dr. Randal Hanson?" a man in a tailored suit beckoned while Randy was on duty in the Maternity Ward.

"Yes?"

He handed Randy a sealed envelope. "Sign here, please."

Randy's eyebrows dropped and his stance tightened. "I'd like to know what I'm signing."

"I'm sorry, Doctor, I cannot reveal that information. Details are in the enclosed documents. If you'll please sign here that you've received them."

Hesitantly, Randy endorsed the document.

"Thank you, Sir."

Randy stood there staring at the sealed manila envelope. Curious, he stepped into an empty room and pulled out the contents—a bunch of legal mumbo jumbo and a document indicating that he'd been named in a malpractice suit for medical negligence. Stunned, he raised his hand to his forehead and almost collapsed. "Shit."

A nurse barged in and summoned him. "Dr. Hanson?" She could tell he was rattled. "Are you ok?"

He quickly slid the letter back in the envelope. "Yes." He cleared his throat. "I'm fine." But he wasn't fine. He was devastated. This document told him that what he did with all his heart and soul had harmed someone.

"The patient in room 413 is asking for you."

"Thank you. I'll be right there." He folded the envelope and slipped it in his lab coat pocket.

He tried to focus on his daily tasks, but this lawsuit hung over his head like a dark cloud all afternoon. This entire situation was a serious blow to his confidence and he began to doubt his worth as a physician. The first opportunity he had to take a break, he stepped into a private room and called Jane. "This is the worst day of my life."

Jane immediately noticed the tenseness in his voice. "What's wrong?"

"A process server handed me legal paperwork at ten o'clock this morning. I'm being sued for malpractice."

Jane sat silent on the other end for a moment before she responded. "Oh my god."

Randy wasn't sure how to react to this situation. His first instinct was to get defensive. "Apparently a patient I worked with for a total of two hours went into premature labor and gave birth to a stillborn. I wasn't even in the delivery room. How can my involvement in this possibly be justified?"

"Did the paperwork name you specifically?"

"Yes." His hands felt tight and his stomach lurched. "This could ruin my career. I've worked too hard to have everything crumble beneath me over some stupid, unjustified claim."

"Have you talked to your dad? Maybe he'll know what to do."

"That's a good idea. I'll stop by on the way home."

"I think you should." Knowing Randy was seriously distressed, Jane said, "Randy, no matter what happens, I'll be by your side to support you. You know I believe in you."

"I know you do, Baby. And knowing that means more to me than you can possibly imagine."

Unable to shake the emotionally devastating effects of this, Randy turned to his father for advice. "What the hell am I supposed to do? This could be detrimental to my career and seriously damaging to my reputation, Dad."

"First off, don't panic."

"Don't panic? How can you say that? Being a physician isn't just a job, it's part of who I am. This is my life, my livelihood. I've barely started my career and already someone is out to ruin it." Randy sat on the sofa and leaned his elbows on his knees. He hung his head down in despair. "I can't believe this is happening."

"Let me see the paperwork."

Randy showed his father the summons. Mark Hanson read through it thoroughly, trying to make sense out of it. "You're not the only doctor listed on this. Who's Dr. Givens?"

"He's the attending physician I was working with during an OB call."

"What do you remember about this patient, Pricilla Walkens?"

"Priscilla Walkens was a patient who came in at twenty-six weeks gestation with no prior prenatal care and untreated pre-pregnancy diabetes. She had low fetal activity, exceedingly high blood sugar, and an under-developed fetus," Randy explained. "But we took immediate steps to monitor baby. We ran a nonstress test on her, took an ultrasound, and ran a Doppler to check fetal heart rate. I counseled her on proper nutrition and treated her for hyperglycemia. We ordered an amnio to check for abnormalities and put her on bed rest. I knew the baby was under stress and suggested we induce her, but Dr. Givens suggested we wait. I did everything I was supposed to do. I don't understand this."

"A stillbirth is not necessarily a result of negligence, Son. No matter how good you are or how hard you try, there will be bad outcomes under your care. That doesn't mean it's your fault. But if a bad outcome occurs, you might be blamed for it."

"But I didn't do anything wrong."

"A lawsuit doesn't mean you're a bad doctor or a bad person, Randal. It means someone's angry and needs someone to blame. You need to try to depersonalize this. This is not a personal attack against you."

"It sure feels like one."

Mark put his hand on Randy's shoulder. "The first thing you need to do is go to risk management. They'll look over the case and offer you legal counsel. Those lawyers are equipped to deal with such cases."

Randy took his father's advice and made an appointment with risk management. The attorney looked over the details and stated, "The facts of this case are murky. Your name is listed merely as a resident M.D. who provided care. You are not listed as the primary physician. It's rare that a resident is targeted in a malpractice suit, and because you're still learning, there's a high probability your name will dropped from this case."

"Really?"

"Yes. We have great success in getting residents dismissed."

This was encouraging. "That's good news."

"The plantiff's attorney must prove you breached the standard of care and has to determine causation." He skimmed through the file again. "The fact that you kept concise and accurate records will most likely get you dropped from the suit. You recorded every conversation you had with Dr. Givens, noting what treatment plans were discussed at length and why you chose specific treatment routes. And looking through this file, I can see that you addressed indicated issues and took immediate steps to monitor the unborn baby. Signs of fetal distress were dealt with, risks and structural abnormalities prior to birth were identified and tested. The data indicates you did nothing egregious. Your strengths in documentation will help your defense."

"What happens now?" Randy asked.

"The investigation process. All parties involved will be called in for deposition. You state your case and the judge will decide what's admissible and what's not. Most likely during this process, he'll see that no medical malpractice was found and the case will be dismissed. Often these cases are settled out of court." He closed the file and looked Randy in the eye. "Were you present during this birth?"

"No."

"That's definitely a bonus." The attorney sat up in his chair. "This looks really good for you, Dr. Hanson. I feel confident. On the downside, sometimes these cases can take months to resolve. Until the investigation is complete, seek a support system, but don't talk to anyone about the case. Don't answer any question about it if anyone asks you."

Randy nodded, indicating he understood. "Alright."

"Carry on with your duties. I'll keep you updated."

Randy shook the attorney's hand. "Thank you. I look forward to hearing from you soon."

When Randy strode through the door that night, Jane greeted him with a kiss. "How did your meeting go?"

"Very well, actually. The attorney seems to think there's a pretty high probability that my name will be dismissed from the case."

"That's great!"

He sat on the sofa, took Jane's hand, and pulled her onto his lap. "Thank you for supporting me through this."

"You know I'll always be here to support you, Randy. For better or worse, remember?"

He drew his lips a bit closer to hers. "For better or worse." He tipped his head slightly and moved in to kiss her. "I love you, Babe."

"I love you too."

Chapter Seventeen

With this malpractice suit hanging over him, and his first year of his residency nearing completion, Randy looked forward to spending a week with his family at the Rio Mar Beach Resort and Spa in Puerto Rico.

Randy and Jane's flight to Puerto Rico had a seven hour layover in Miami, enough time to check out some of the sights and eat lunch before they had to catch their connecting flight. Randy had never been to Puerto Rico before so he was excited about this new adventure. They arrived at San Juan's International Airport where a Meet & Greet team met them at the gate and offered the family complimentary airport transportation to their resort.

Randy reclined on the king-sized bed and clasped his hands behind his head. "This is going to be so relaxing."

Jane pranced around the room checking out the amenities. "Look, a hot tub."

"And coffee." He sat up. "Speaking of which, I could use a cup."

Jane giggled as Randy got up to make himself a cup.

Basking on a somewhat deserted beach, Randy tied a hammock between two palm trees. Jane snuggled up with him and they took a nap in the shade under the

Caribbean sun. About an hour later, Randy woke up with his arm slightly numb. His fingers tingled and Jane's hair flowed all over him. He carefully removed his arm trying not to disturb her, but she stirred and opened her eyes anyway. He leaned in to kiss her. "Hello, Baby."

She stretched and bent her leg slightly. "Hi."

The ocean waves lapped onto the shore and the sun glistened down on the beach. A soft breeze blew across their bodies. "You feel like a drink?"

"Yes, but I want something islandy, something Caribbean."

Randy chuckled, wondering what she meant by that. "Like what?"

"I don't know. Surprise me."

He crawled off the hammock and roamed over to the bar by the beach. For Jane, he ordered a drink made with vodka, sloe gin, orange juice, and Southern Comfort peach liqueur. It was served in a Collins glass filled with ice and garnished with an orange slice and a dash of Galliano with a cherry on top. For himself he requested a mix of vodka, Bailey's Irish Cream, and Kahlua coffee liqueur poured into a cocktail glass served over crushed ice.

When Randy retuned, Jane eyed her concoction curiously. "What is this?"

"It's called A Long Slow Comfortable Screw."

She squinted her eyes, not believing him. "It is not."

"Yes it is," he said. "It's a great drink, and it goes very well with mine."

She focused her eyes to his glass. "And what is that?"

"A Screaming Orgasm." He winked suggestively as he took a sip of his cocktail.

"Oh, I see. Are you trying to suggest something, Doctor?"

"Perhaps," he replied. "You should give it a try. You might like it."

In the evening, Randy and Jane sat on their balcony. Holding a cup of coffee in his hand, Randy stretched his legs out in front of him and crossed his feet. He leaned back in his chair and took in the ocean scene while he watched the sun go down.

Jane curled her legs up in her chair, hugging her knees. "Brian starts practice with the 49ers next week," she said excitedly.

"Does he? That's cool."

"His first pre-season game is August sixth."

"In San Francisco?" Randy asked.

"No, in Pittsburg."

"Bummer. Guess we won't be going to that one." Randy took a sip of his steaming coffee. "I need to get fingerprinted and sign up to take my Licensing Exam when we get back."

"Have you studied for it?" she asked, hoping he was prepared.

"A little. I found this book called Strong Medicine that's been helpful. But I'm a bit worried."

"Why?"

"This lawsuit hanging over me. If this case isn't resolved before my scheduled exam day, the medical board will prevent me from taking the test, which means I won't be able to get my license."

"Have you heard back from the lawyer yet?"

"No. I was hoping to hear from him before we left." Randy rubbed the palm of his hand nervously. "You know, Honey, this might not turn out in my favor. There is the possibility that I may be found at fault here."

"But you told me you didn't do anything wrong."

"That doesn't matter. It's up to the judge and jury. If they find evidence that indicated I was negligent, I'm pretty much screwed." For the first time in his medical career, Randy doubted his abilities as a physician. He was always confident when it came to medicine, but right now he didn't feel worthy of the title M.D. "I feel so vulnerable right now. Every medical decision I make is being scrutinized. The prosecuting attorneys are looking for anything they can to prove that I'm a lousy doctor."

"You're not a lousy doctor. You're a compassionate man who cares about his patients."

"Apparently this patient doesn't think so."

Jane had never seen Randy so full of self-doubt. She reached over to touch his hand. "You can't judge your entire worth based on the opinion of one person."

"If this person ruins my career, I most certainly can." With fear in his eyes, Randy shifted in his chair. "What are we going to do if I lose this case? My medical career will be over."

"Sweetie, it's going to be ok."

He raised his hand to his chin, rubbing his knuckle over his lips. "I wish I shared your confidence."

Jane turned to face him. She held both his hands in hers, offering reassurance. "Randy, I believe in you, and regardless of what anyone says, I know in my heart you are a wonderful doctor." She pulled him out of his chair.

Randy leered at her wondering what she was doing. "What are you up to?"

"You came here to relax and get your mind off of all this, and that's exactly what you're going to do." She dragged him into the room. The innocent smile on her face was anything but innocent.

"Uh oh. I know that look."

She led him to the hot tub where she pulled off her clothes, causing Randy's eyes to widen in excitement. She enticed him further by saying, "Come in with me." She carefully stepped into the steamy tub. Her breasts barely peeked out from under the water's surface.

Without hesitation, he stripped naked and climbed in with her, blanketing her with his arms. He looked into her beautiful green eyes. "You're amazing, you know that?"

"Am I?"

"Yes. In so many ways."

She straddled his lap; he put his hands on her hips, pulling her body closer to his. She wrapped her arms around his neck and kissed him. His heart rate elevated; he yearned for more. It wasn't long before their bodies intertwined in a lovers' embrace.

They were interrupted when someone pounded on their door. Randy tried to ignore it, but whoever was out there remained persistent and knocked again. "Randy!"

Between gasps, Randy bellowed, "Go away, Rob!"

"We're waiting for you, Man. Hurry up so we can eat."

The heat of passion remained unbreakable. Randy closed his eyes taking in every sensation, refusing to separate himself from Jane.

Robby beat on the door once more. "Randy, let's go."

Annoyed that his brother would not leave them alone, Randy restated his command. "Go away! I'm busy!"

Jane put her finger over Randy's lip to shush him then moved in deeper, causing him to moan in pure ecstasy.

The carnal sounds of pleasure coming from behind the door made it obvious they weren't leaving any time soon. Robby tightened his lips and went back to his suite.

When Robby stepped inside the room, Mark asked his youngest son, "Are they coming?"

"Doubt it. Based on the noises they were making, it sounds like they'll be occupied for a while."

Ellen couldn't believe that blunt comment came out of her youngest son's mouth. "Robert!" she scolded. "You shouldn't be listening to them."

"Kinda hard to ignore. The whole floor can hear them goin' at it."

"Well, at least you're not deaf," Mark teased. "But damn, Son, you are nosey."

About thirty minutes later, Randy traipsed over to his parents' suite and knocked on the door.

Mark answered with an ornery smirk. "You finally decided to join us. Did you get that urge taken care of?"

Randy's face flushed slightly, flustered by his father's bold statement. "Worked up an appetite."

"I bet," Mark said. "Is Jane ready?"

"She's combing her hair. She'll be out in a minute."

When Robby stepped out to the corridor, Randy clenched his fist and punched him in the arm. "You little shit."

Robby rubbed his arm. "Ow! Damn, Dude, that hurts."

"Good. Maybe you'll learn to stop eavesdropping and mind your own business."

Randy and his brother spent the following day together. Their first stop was the Caribbean Raceway Park where they watched cars scream around a racetrack at amazing speeds. For lunch they ate carne guisada then headed to the Tibes Indian Ceremonial Center to check out the old burial grounds. The Ceremonial Center featured a fifteen-hundred year old Taino village, much of which remained more or less intact and had skeletons dating back to A.D. 700. Randy was fascinated by the history, but Robby was more interested in the morbidity of the skeletons and skulls.

In the evening, they joined their dad and tried their hand at Caribbean charter fishing, where Randy tackled a 180 pound Marlin.

For the remainder of their vacation, Randy and Jane admired the beauty of Puerto Rico. They visited the unspoiled natural beauty of Caja de Muerto Beach and enjoyed snorkeling the shallow reefs around Culebra Island. This island was known for its world-class snorkeling. It had many caves and reefs that housed a plethora of sea life, creating an underwater experience that was not easily forgotten. They spotted parrotfish, trumpet fish, stingrays, barracudas, and even sea turtles. They also spent a day together at the Luis A. Ferré Science Park, a massive forty-two acres of museums, a zoo, and an observation deck. Being the science person Randy was, he relished this opportunity.

The whole family went to Guánica beach where millions of luminescent dinoflagellates lit up the Phosphorescent Bay. The beach had a wildlife refuge nearby that was perfect for bird watching. Fifty species of birds could be found amongst the stunning foliage.

The refuge was also home to several species of endangered animals and plant life. They found the hawksbill, leatherback, loggerhead, and green sea turtles as well as the Antillean manatee and the brown pelican. A path led right to the beachfront from the reserve. Ojo del Buey, otherwise known as The Ox's Eye, was a wonderful family recreation spot. It was so named because a huge rock formation in the area took the shape of an ox's head.

Overall their Puerto Rican vacation was relaxing and gave Randy a chance to recharge, which he desperately needed. Knowing what he was up against when he returned—four weeks of night rotations, a legal dispute, and prepping for his MLE—he was glad he had the opportunity to rest up. No doubt the next few months were going to be exhausting.

Waiting at the airport between flights, Randy received an incoming call from the attorney at risk management. Trying to stay positive, he answered, "Dr. Hanson."

"Hello, Doctor. This is Richard Kinkaid. How are you this afternoon?"

"Waiting to catch a flight in a crowded airport at the moment, but I can't complain."

"I have an update for you," the man said. "The judge overseeing this case has looked through your file. You're scheduled to come in for deliberations next week."

Randy sighed, "Is that good or bad?"

"It simply means he wants more information and wants to hear your side. Are you available next Tuesday?"

"I can be. What time?" Randy asked.

"Deliberations are scheduled for 9:00 A.M."

"Alright. I'll talk to my Residency Director."

"Perfect. Look for an e-mail tonight with more information. Have a safe flight, Dr. Hanson. I'll see you next Tuesday."

Randy hung up his phone and slid it back in his pocket.

"Who was that?" Jane asked.

"Richard Kinkaid. He's the attorney from risk management who's representing me."

Jane bit her lip, hoping Randy had good news. "What did he say?"

"Looks like I have to appear in court." Randy tightened his jaw and nervously twirled his wedding ring around his finger. "I was hoping to avoid this."

She gently placed her hand on his shoulder. "You'll do fine, Sweetie. Try not to worry about it."

If only it was that easy. "I wish I could."

Chapter Eighteen

Another Hanson was about to get married, and another doctor was about to join the family. With catering complete and the reception hall decked out in various shades of pink, the minister was ready to begin the ceremony. Eighty guests filled the seats. Dressed in his tux, Bruce nervously paced the room while Randy and Jim tried to calm him. Bruce kept checking the time and constantly fiddled with his watch. Five minutes until show time and no word from Stephanie. After pacing for several minutes, Bruce finally sat down. "Son-of-a-bitch. Not again. Not fucking again."

Trying to ease Bruce's worry, Randy offered reassurance. "She'll be here. Calm down. Stephanie is always late. You know that."

"Where is she?"

"Let me call Jane. Hold on." Randy whipped out his cellphone and called his wife. It rang four times before she answered. "Is Stephanie with you?"

"She was about ten minutes ago," Jane replied. "But we stopped at a gas station because she had to go to the bathroom."

Randy stepped into the hall so Bruce wouldn't hear. Wondering what was going on, he questioned, "Ten minutes ago? She hasn't come back yet?"

"No."

"Why didn't you go in with her?"

"To the bathroom, Randy? I think Stephanie can handle that by herself."

"Shit," Randy said.

"What's the matter?"

"We are starting this in five minutes. Bruce is freaking out and about to have a panic attack. Go get her and bring her here now," he demanded.

"Alright. Calm down. We're on our way."

When Randy stepped back into the room, Bruce immediately looked at him with pleading eyes. "Well?"

"They're on their way. She had to go to the bathroom."

Bruce checked his watch again. "Now?"

Being involved in a wedding from this point of view wasn't nearly as nerve wracking as it was when he was trapped in the dreaded 'room' waiting to see his bride. Randy felt sorry for Bruce, especially since Stephanie hadn't shown up yet. At least when Randy went through this, his wife was already at the resort and he didn't have to wonder where she was. This predicament, especially since Bruce had been left on the altar before, must have been exceedingly stressful.

Ten more minutes went by. Bruce paced around frantically. Wanting to ease the tension, Randy turned to Jim. "Stay with him for a sec. I'll be right back."

"Alrighty," Jim agreed.

Randy left the room and searched for his sister. She was just stepping out of the car when Randy spotted her. "Jesus, Stephanie. Where have you been? Bruce is in there freaking out."

She stood up with a bouquet in her hand. "My shoe broke. We had to stop to get another pair."

"You could have called. What the hell were you thinking?"

"I'm sorry," she replied, not seeing this a big deal. "Geez, Randy, both of you need to chill."

Jane stepped out of the car dressed in her pink bridesmaid gown. Randy marched over to her with tension written all over his face. Staring at his wife, he said, "What the hell happened? Why didn't you get her here on time?"

"I tried," Jane explained. "The whole shoe incident and the vomiting. That's why she was in the bathroom for so long."

Concerned about his sister, Randy asked, "Why was she throwing up?"

"Her stomach has been bothering her all day, and she started to feel nauseous in the car."

Randy rolled his eyes. "Oh, lovely."

"Then we hit every red light on the way here."

"For Christ sake, Jane."

"This isn't my fault," she defended. "All kinds of situations popped up that were out of my control."

"Bruce is about to have a panic attack in there."

"Then maybe you should be with him instead of out here. That is your job as his Best Man, you know." She gently skimmed her fingers across his chest. "She's here now. Let it go."

He gave her a kiss and went back inside. Bruce immediately rose to his feet, wondering what was going on. Randy smiled reassuringly. "The girls just got here. Evidently they ran into some problems."

"What kind of problems?" Bruce asked.

"You know, red lights, broken shoes, vomiting."

"Vomiting?" This made Bruce turn his head. "Who was?"

"Stephanie."

"What? Is she ok?" Fear crossed Bruce's face. He looked like he'd seen a ghost.

Randy tried to ease his tension. "She's fine." Patting him on the arm, he said, "Come on. Let's go."

Randy and Jim stood at the altar with Bruce. Randy had his sister's wedding ring in his pocket and Jane had Bruce's tied onto her bouquet. It was an interesting change to be witness to a wedding from this viewpoint. The last time Randy stood on the altar at a wedding was when he watched Jane walk down the aisle dressed in white. Now he would witness his sister do the same thing.

When Randy started medical school, Bruce Buckman becoming his brother-in-law was something he never imagined would happen. And seeing Stephanie dressed in a white wedding dress somehow seemed surreal. He grew up watching her serve imaginary tea to dolls. He thought back to the times he and his little sister went to the park and he pushed her on the swings, or the day he taught her how to swim. Many times he had scared her or grossed her out with worms and fish heads. But as he and Jane handed the minister the rings and heard Stephanie and Bruce exchange vows, Randy realized his sister was not the little girl in pigtails he used to tease as a child. She was a grown woman who was a mother and now a wife. For a minute his eyes grew glossy, and he had to fight to hold back tears. In a way, he understood how Dale Davine must have felt the day Jane wore white and took the name Hanson, and he identified with the unspoken meaning of the tear rolling down his father's cheek.

When Stephanie and Bruce kissed to seal their union, Randy looked at his wife, who turned her head at that same moment. Their eyes met and Randy smiled. He had so many memories of his wedding day, and they had hundreds of photographs. He remembered how he felt moments after Jane became his wife, and the way he felt when he kissed her on the altar. The sensations and emotions that memory evoked would forever be embedded in his mind. He would never be able to look at a wedding the same way again.

As soon as everyone filed into in reception hall, Jim couldn't suppress a smile.

"What are you grinning about?" Randy asked.

"Seein' your sister in white. We both know damn well she is probably the most impure bride ever. Maybe she should be wearin' red."

Unimpressed with Jim's blatant crudeness, Randy asked, "What the fuck is wrong with you? You're ruining this moment for me. My sister just got married and I want to enjoy this. Show some class."

Jill walked up to Jim with a diaper bag over her shoulder. "I just changed her," she said, handing Jalene to him.

Jim lovingly held the child, supporting her with his arm.

Christopher ran over and yanked on the bottom of his dad's tux. "Daddy? Can I go play now?"

Jim looked down at his son. "Yes, just clean up when you're done."

Christopher had a small bag with cars, color books, and other toys to play with. Jill picked up the bag and helped him get situated at a table.

Dressed in a pretty pink dress with flowers all over it, and carrying a doll in her arms, Sabrina wandered over to Jim. "Hi, Daddy."

"Hey, Baby." Jalene started to fuss a little. "Could you be Daddy's helper and get a bottle out of the diaper bag for me?"

"Uh huh."

Randy watched the little girl skip away to retrieve a bottle for her sister. "Wow, busy life, this daddy business."

"Never a dull moment, that's for sure." He bounced Jalene on his knee.

"Never a private moment either."

Jim disagreed. "That's not true. Jill and I get alone time after the kids go to bed."

"Man, I see you and Bruce with babies and little kids running around. That kind of responsibility scares me."

"Parenting isn't that tough," Jim remarked. "Having an infant is draining because they're so needy, but Chris and Sabrina can do a lot of things for themselves now. It's fun to watch them grow and see their personalities blossom."

"That's true…I guess. I'm glad Jane hasn't expressed an interest in having babies yet."

"She's gonna get that itch sooner or later, you know," Jim warned.

"I know." Randy fixed his eyes on his wife, who was mingling with the crowd. "I hope she waits until I finish my residency. I can't imagine having a baby right now. Between studying for MLE's, working seventy hours a week, attending seminars and conferences, and keeping up on the latest treatment options, I stay pretty busy. I don't see how you and Bruce do it."

"It gets tough sometimes, but we manage."

"I enjoy hanging out with my wife and doing what we want whenever we feel like it. Doesn't having children take the spontaneity out of your relationship?"

"Jill and I had the kids from the start so our relationship has always involved them. Our schedule's a bit tighter with the kids because we have to get them to their respective places on time before we get to where we need to be. But Jill and I still have fun together. We go out, cuddle on the couch watching movies, and munch on nachos at midnight if the urge hits us."

"But what about your sex life?"

Jim shrugged. "It's good. We have to make sure the bedroom door is locked and the kids are either asleep or not home, but there's still spontaneity there. It's not like we schedule it ahead of time. And I bet Bruce would say the same thing."

Randy cringed. "I'm going to pretend you didn't say that."

Sabrina returned with a baby bottle for her sister and a toy one for her doll. She sat in a chair feeding her baby while Jim fed his. This was a sight that really touched Randy's heart. Perhaps the joys of fatherhood outweighed the uncertainties.

Chapter Nineteen

Randy reported to the King County Courthouse promptly at 8:45 Tuesday morning. His muscles were tense, and with the added stress of not knowing what to expect as far as the procedural aspects of a lawsuit were concerned, his nerves were shot. Dressed in a suit and tie, he walked through the main doors of the courthouse, where he ran into Mr. Kinkaid.

"Good morning, Dr. Hanson," the man said cheerfully, extending his palm to shake Randy's hand.

Randy didn't share his excitement level. "Good morning."

"You ready for this?"

"As ready as I'm going to be."

The discovery investigation process, in which depositions were taken from all parties, was bound to get brutal. Randy's attorney warned him about the ruthlessness of malpractice cases, so he was prepared to take a beating.

"Remember that the plaintiff's attorney must prove that you breached the standard of care, that you did something wrong or didn't do something that any other reasonable physician would have done in the same circumstance. Points will be argued back and forth on both sides. Our expert witness will say one thing and the plaintiff's expert witness will say another.

Answer all questions in the deposition. Don't hesitate. Stand your ground and state your case."

"I'll do my best."

Since Randy was an OB/GYN, he expected to be sued at some point during the course of his career. That didn't alleviate the shock when it actually happened. His confidence was shaken and he began to question whether he could have done something differently. Was he negligent? Did he fail to exercise due care? Thinking about this formed a knot in the pit of his stomach.

The plaintiff's attorney went first. He tried to exploit any shortcomings in medical documentation, nitpicking tiny details and questioning every procedure and prescription ordered, comparing it to what was written in the patient's file. Even though Randy performed the examination and counseled the patient, the procedure orders were countersigned by his attending physician, Dr. Givens. Generally in cases like this, legal liability fell upon the doctor who signed the orders and the hospital where the event took place. But the supervising physician refused to accept any responsibility whatsoever and the hospital denied involvement in the case.

The defense stated its argument and the parties cross-examined each other for several hours.

When they broke for lunch, Randy tried to wrap his head around all of this, but doing so made him dizzy. He couldn't believe his career and reputation were on the line over petty paperwork issues. He approached Mr. Kinkaid with his concerns. "That was the worst three hours of my life. Even after I clearly validated my decision and proved that my actions were justified, that guy refused to back down."

"Things did get a bit hairy."

"This is ridiculous. What did they do, sue the entire hospital? I can't believe they dragged a medical student into this."

"Personally, I wouldn't sue a medical student. I wouldn't sue a resident doctor either, but attorneys representing patients are sometimes forced to if they're going to fulfill their obligation of representing their client. Right or wrong, being sued could happen to anyone involved in a medical case. In this particular case, the patient is trying to blame someone for what happened, and the plaintiff is using any means necessary to find fault."

Randy shook his head, appalled by the nature of this case. "So, where do we go from here?"

"If the judge suspects that negligence occurred, the supervising physician will answer the charges, not the resident or medical student. But from what I gather, in an attempt to cut losses, it sounds like this will settle out of court."

"What does that mean for me?" Randy wondered.

"Nothing, most likely. Quite honestly, I have never heard of a single instance in which a medical resident paid a dime to resolve a medical malpractice suit."

"That doesn't make this any easier. Merely being involved in a malpractice case will follow me everywhere I go and potentially make obtaining malpractice insurance much more difficult."

"We're doing everything we can to get your name dropped from this suit, Dr. Hanson. Give us time do our job."

Chapter Twenty

Randy dropped Jane's car off at Robby's place to get an oil change and a tune-up. Since Jane didn't have access to her car, Randy insisted she take the Corvette to run necessary errands. While she was gone, he went fishing with his dad.

In the middle of cleaning his fish, Jane's cellphone number flashed on Randy's touchscreen. He quickly rinsed off his hands and answered. "Hey, Babe." As he spoke to her, a horrified expression darkened his face. "Honey, slow down. I can't understand you. What did you say?"

From the tone of his voice, it was clear Randy was worried. Mark wondered what was going on.

"Where are you?" Randy frantically rushed to get a piece of paper and a pen. "Do you have an address or the name of the crossroad?" Holding the phone between his chin and shoulder, he listened attentively while he wrote something on a notepad. "It's alright. Calm down." When he was done writing, he tore the note off and shoved it in his pocket. "Hang tight. I'm on my way." He hung up and immediately grabbed the keys to his dad's truck.

"Is everything alright?" Mark asked.

"Jane's been in a car accident." Randy rushed toward the door.

"Is she ok?"

"She's says she is, but she doesn't remember much about it. She says her forehead is bleeding."

That didn't sound ok at all. "Oh no."

"I gotta go." Randy dashed out the door, leaving his fish behind.

He sped to the accident scene. A police car, firetruck, EMS, and two tow trucks were on site, as well as several bystanders. Randy pulled over to the shoulder and ran to his wife, who sat on the back of the EMS truck with her purse on the ground at her feet and a gauze-wrapped icepack on her forehead. Concerned that she had head trauma, he hurried to her side. "Jane."

She dropped her ice pack and sobbed.

Trying to get her to calm down, he held her in his arms and gently caressed her back. "It's alright."

"I'm so sorry, Randy."

"Don't apologize. I'm just thankful you're ok." He inspected the cut on her head. It was a small laceration; the bleeding had mostly stopped. "Does your head hurt?"

"A little."

"You whacked it pretty good. You've got a decent-sized gash. Probably going to need stitches." His father had a small pen light attached to the truck keys. Randy used it to check her pupils to make sure she didn't have a concussion. Her pupils dilated normally, she didn't complain of a headache, and she was completely coherent. No concussion suspected. Randy examined her bruised arm. It was swollen, but didn't appear to be broken. Her foot had a decent sized cut on the top which was bleeding pretty badly, but other than that, she seemed to be ok. He picked up her icepack and held it on her head.

The EMT came over to them and said, "Sir? Do you know this woman?"

"Yes, she's my wife," Randy answered.

"She took a pretty big hit. You should have a doctor check out that cut on her head."

"I am a doctor."

"Even better," the EMT said.

Randy surveyed the scene and almost cried when he saw his mangled Corvette in pieces on the back of a tow truck. He couldn't get a very good view of it, but from what he did see, it looked like it had been run over by a train. With his car in that condition, he was thankful Jane's injuries weren't more severe. "Holy shit," he said. "Look at my car."

Jane sniffled, feeling guilty for destroying his Corvette. "I'm sorry."

"Baby, you have no reason to be sorry." He looked into her eyes. "Cars can be replaced. I'm much more concerned about you. You could have been seriously hurt or even killed." He pulled her close to him, not wanting to let her go. "I almost lost you today." His heart raced as he thought about how close he actually came to that scenario. Losing Jane was something he would not be able to handle. He kissed her tenderly on the lips. "I love you so much." With gentle hands, he doctored up the laceration on her foot and forehead. When he was finished, he picked up her purse and escorted her to his father's truck. "Come on. Let's get you home."

She limped alongside him.

As a precaution, Randy took her to the ER anyway. They gave her a CAT scan and took some neck x-rays to ensure she didn't have a concussion or other brain and spinal injuries. She checked out fine, but was bruised pretty badly, sore, and very shaken up.

They stitched up her forehead, prescribed her some anti-inflammatories and pain medication, and had her rest for a while.

The insurance company assessed the damage and called it a loss, as Randy suspected. He was home from work that day so he hopped in the car, with Robby tagging along, to clean his personal belongings out of the mangled vehicle.

"Where are we going?" Robby asked.

"Jane totaled my car yesterday. I need to clean it out."

"Is she alright?"

"She's a little banged up, but she's ok. Apparently some guy ran a red light, t-boned her, and smashed the hell out of it."

At the collision repair center, Randy retrieved the keys from the front desk attendant then journeyed out to the back lot with his brother. His Corvette was unrecognizable. The entire passenger's side was completely smashed in. The front bumper had fallen off and was lying on the ground, bent in half. The hood was twisted sideways and the engine block was out of place. A portion of the windshield was cracked, radiator crumpled, headlights shattered, front wheels totally out of alignment. Both front air bags had deployed and the dashboard and entire steering column had been violently shoved forward. Shocked by the horridness of this mess, Randy declared, "Jesus. What the hell hit her? Look at my car."

Randy unlocked the bent driver's side door, moved the seat back, then sat down stroking the steering wheel, which was only about an inch from his chest. Seeing this made Randy realize the seriousness of this accident. If the steering column had moved another centimeter or two, it would have crushed Jane's chest. "Holy shit. It's a good thing no one was in the passenger's seat."

After examining the dashboard gauges, he clenched his jaw and opened the glove compartment. He pulled his CD's out of the central console and removed the garage door opener from the visor. He popped the trunk and removed his first aid kit, a set of jumper cables, and a few other things he had back there. He placed them all in a box. Giving one final glance at his sports car, as if saying goodbye, he took a long, sorrowful breath and returned the keys to the attendant. With his box in his hands, Randy vacated the premises, not saying a word.

Robby had never seen his brother so sad. He almost seemed to be mourning the loss of this car. "You ok, Bro?"

Randy sighed. "Did you see my Corvette?"

"It's fucked up."

He set the box in the back seat. "Let's grab some lunch."

On the way home, they drove past a Porsche dealership. Randy slowed down, pulled into the lot, and parked the car.

"What are you doing?" Robby asked.

"Looking at cars." Randy immediately spotted a beautiful metallic red Porsche 911 Carrera Convertible. He peeked through the window at the black leather interior.

"Uh, Randy," Robby said. "That's a Porsche."

Randy smirked at his brother snidely. "I know. It's beautiful, isn't it?" He caressed the side panel then peered under the hood, which the dealership had open so potential buyers could peek at the engine. He read through the specs on the window sticker and carefully inspected every detail. "This is a sweet car."

Randy talked details with a salesman, who let him take it for a test drive. This had to be the coolest car he had ever driven. It was fast, it handled nicely, and it was comfortable. This particular car was not only his favorite color, it also had black leather interior. The dynamic look of the vehicle, topped off with electric softtop convertible roof, projector beam lens Bi-Xenon headlights, and luxury alloy trim made this a sports car lovers' dream. It was cool, it was fast, and it handled great. Randy was sold. He'd always wanted a Porsche. After negotiating with the salesman, who retreated into his office to get some paperwork started, Randy turned to his brother and said, "Oh yeah. The marriage of body and engine."

"I can't believe you're buying a Porsche."

"You know I've always loved sports cars, and since mine got mangled, I have to replace it."

When everything was finalized, he happily drove off the lot in a brand new shiny red Porsche.

It was almost sundown by the time Randy returned home. He left the Porsche parked in the driveway and went inside to see Jane. She was up and moving around and seemed to be feeling better. He walked closer and kissed her. "Hello, Gorgeous."

"Hey."

"My Corvette's totaled."

She frowned as if she was going to cry again. "I am so sorry."

Randy offered reassurance. "It wasn't your fault. Accidents happen."

"You and Robby were gone a long time."

He held her hand and led her toward the front door. "And I'm going to show you why."

Seeing the shiny red Porsche parked in the driveway made Jane gasp. "Oh god, Randy. What did you do?"

"Had to replace my car. And that, my dear, is a badass sports car."

Her eyebrows dropped. "I don't want to know how much you paid for this, do I?"

"No, you probably don't. But for the sweet satisfaction of driving a Porsche, it's totally worth it to me."

Chapter Twenty-One

"Ms. Turner," Randy called out to a medical student under his supervision.

"Yes, Dr. Hanson?"

He handed her a chart. "I need blood drawn and a sonogram done on this patient."

"Yes, Sir. Right away." She happily complied to his request.

On the way to the Maternity Ward to do postpartum rounds, a nurse confronted Randy in the hallway.

"Excuse me, Dr. Hanson. I know you're busy, but we need you. The patient in room 418 keeps trying to take her IV out, and she's screaming to see a doctor."

"I'll be right there." He quickly skimmed this patient's chart then stepped inside the delivery room. "Ms. Quanbeck?" Randy said.

With his white lab coat and name badge, she knew right away he was a doctor. "Tell these nurses I don't want this needle in my arm."

Randy proceeded to explain the seriousness of her situation. "Ma'am, according to your chart you are being induced because you have developed preeclampsia. This is a serious condition. It can endanger your health and restrict the blood flow to your baby. You can't get the required medication into your system without an IV line."

She fiddled with the belt on the fetal monitor around her belly. "And what is this thing?"

"While we induce your labor it is important to continuously monitor your contractions and keep tabs on your baby's wellbeing."

Her face tightened and her lips drew a hard line.

Trying to calm her, he said, "We are only trying to help you and your baby."

After a bit of coaxing, she allowed the nurses to reinsert her IV. Randy stepped out of the room and wrote a few notes on her medical chart, being careful to document everything.

"Dr. Hanson?" one of the nurses called to him.

He looked up. "Yes?"

"Thank you for stepping in. She was starting to get violent with the staff."

"No problem." He placed her chart back in its proper slot and continued his postpartum rounds.

As soon as he finished, he snuck down to the cafeteria to snag a quick cup of coffee. Before he took a sip, he heard his name announced over the hospital PA system. "Dr. Hanson to the ER, STAT. Dr. Hanson to the ER."

He gave a mirthless laugh and grumbled. Guess coffee would have to wait. He rushed down to the Emergency Room.

"Dr. Hanson. I'm so glad you're here," the on-call resident said, handing Randy a chart. "We have a 15-year-old pregnant female complaining of severe abdominal cramping."

"Fifteen?" Randy asked.

"Yes," the doctor confirmed.

Because of her age, she was already high-risk. Randy hated cases like this. They were dangerous and almost always lead to complications. He rubbed his hand across his forehead. "Where is she?"

"Room five."

Randy browsed over her chart then headed toward the room. A young girl gripped her abdomen, screaming. He pulled up a seat next to her. "Hi, Cheryl. I'm Dr. Hanson. Do you know how far along you are?"

She seemed to have no idea what was happening to her.

"Can I see what's going on?"

Terrified, she panted and nodded.

He checked her heart rate and blood pressure then put on latex gloves and checked dilation and effacement. The baby was in a head down position and had moved into the birth canal. "You are about to have this baby. Is anyone here with you?"

"No." Tears streamed from her eyes and her lips quivered.

Randy removed his gloves and held her hand. "It'll be alright," he said reassuringly. "I'll guide you through it."

She gritted her teeth and screamed through another contraction.

As part of his OB training, Randy learned Lamaze breathing and relaxation techniques. He was able to use this knowledge to guide his patients who had no coaching or prenatal care through labor and delivery. "Focus on me and breathe," he instructed. "Next contraction I want you to push."

She bobbed her head.

He stood in a position where he was able to perform his duties, but she could still see him. When another contraction came, he said, "Push." She did. He stopped periodically to let her breathe and refocus. This continued for several minutes. By now two nurses and an ER physician came into the room to assist him.

Twenty minutes into the pushing/ breathing cycle, she gave birth to a beautiful baby boy.

"Call pediatrics and wheel her up to postpartum as quickly as possible," Randy instructed. He and the ER physician signed off on her chart before he headed back to the cafeteria.

That evening, Randy draped his lab coat over the couch and laid his stethoscope on the coffee table. Jane wasn't in the living room or anywhere downstairs. "Janey?"

Before he headed upstairs to change out of his professional attire, his cellphone rang. "Dr. Hanson," he answered.

"Good evening, Doctor. This is Richard Kinkaid. How are you this evening?"

"I'm doing alright. It's been kind of a crazy day."

"I have some good news. The judge reviewed all the deliberations. He informed me that he found no evidence to suggest you acted negligently. Your name has been dropped from the case."

Randy felt a tremendous weight lifted off his shoulders. "Thank you. I've been so worried about this. I haven't had a good night's sleep in months."

"I know the feeling," Mr. Kinkaid remarked. "I'll send you the official paperwork tomorrow. Let me know if there's anything else I can do for you."

"You've done more than enough. Thank you so much, Mr. Kinkaid."

Randy climbed upstairs and heard water running. Trying to be sneaky, he stripped out of his clothes and crawled in the shower with Jane.

She was rinsing her hair and didn't notice right away that he was standing there. When she finally opened her eyes, she flinched. "Dammit, Randy, don't do that."

"I love it when you jump like that." He leaned his arm against the shower wall and watched the water flow between her breasts, down her tummy, and to her legs.

Jane handed him a bottle of lilac scented shower gel. "Will you wash me?"

"Of course." Randy poured some in his palm and rubbed his hands together. He lathered her arms, back, tummy, and breasts then poured a bit more onto his hands. He squatted down and rubbed it all over her legs, kissing her tummy as he did. Moving his hands up to her buttocks, he looked up at her and squeezed. She gazed down at him and threaded her fingers through the thickness of his wet hair.

He stood up, embraced her with both of his hands, and drew her closer to him. "We're all slippery."

"Uh huh."

He closed his eyes and moved his mouth to hers, engrossed in every luscious taste of her lips. The lilac aroma in the air, the sound of water flowing onto them, her slippery skin touching his, the sight of her magnificent curves, and the way her sweet lips tasted stirred every sense.

Her soft lips grazed his ear. "Make love to me," she whispered

His eyes opened.

"Make love to me now."

Randy gladly fulfilled her request.

Jane stood in front of the bathroom mirror in only a tight tee-shirt and underwear while she combed her hair.

Randy jammed his hands in his front pockets and leaned against the doorframe watching her. "I had kind of a weird day. Released one patient from the hospital this afternoon then right after that, four others checked in. A hostile patient refused to keep her IV in and started swearing at the nurses. They called me in to intervene."

Jane found this amusing. It seemed like every day something unusual happened to him. Gazing at him through the reflection in the mirror she asked, "You certainly don't have many dull days, do you?"

"Not lately, no. Then in the middle of a cup of coffee, I got called to the ER to deliver a baby. The mother was a fifteen year old girl."

Jane stopped what she was doing and pivoted her body toward him. "Fifteen?"

"Yup. She had no one there with her and had no idea what was happening."

"I bet she was scared to death."

"She was, but I coached her along and got her to calm down long enough to focus on pushing. She was lucky. No complications and the baby was fine."

"That's good." Jane continued to comb her hair. "Fifteen with a baby. Can you imagine? Poor girl. I wonder if she even knows how she got pregnant."

"On a positive note, I received a phone call from Richard Kinkaid earlier. My name's been dropped from the case."

"That's fabulous news." She hugged him tightly. "See? I told you not to worry."

"My involvement is still on record."

"Yes, but they found you at no fault. I'm sure that will be taken into consideration."

"Hopefully. With my name cleared, I can finally register for my licensing exam, and maybe I'll sleep tonight."

She set her comb on the bathroom counter. "I talked to Brian today. The 49ers are playing in Seattle in December."

"Oh, cool. We'll have to get tickets for that."

"Daddy will want to come see that. And since Brian will be in town, and it's around Christmastime…"

He knew what she was thinking. "You want to invite your dad and Brian for Christmas."

She nodded.

"Go ahead. We have plenty of room."

She stepped into the bedroom to finish getting dressed.

Randy trailed behind her. "Didn't you have midterms last week?"

"Yes."

"How'd you do?"

"I did ok."

Randy cocked his head at her. "What do you mean you did ok?"

"Got a 80 on one exam, and a 77 and 63 on the others.

These grades were much lower than she was capable of. "Are you taking time to study?"

"I'm fine," she argued.

He tried to offer advice without sounding pushy. "I know how challenging graduate school can be with classes, papers to write, research, plus you're working part time right now. You have to reserve time in your schedule to study. I rarely see you open a textbook.

Surely you remember the endless hours I had my face buried in a medical textbook."

"Yes, I do."

He grabbed her hand to get her to stop and look at him. "Honey, you have to schedule study time into your schedule."

She turned her eyes to him. "I study while you're at work."

"And when I'm not at work?"

She dodged the question.

"I know exactly what you're doing. You're making dinner or doing laundry or taking on some other household chore."

"It's my house, Randy. I want to take care of it."

"It's my house too," he reminded her.

"But you're busy with your residency," she claimed. "And this lawsuit has been dragging you down. I didn't want to add more to your plate."

"When we shared an apartment in Berkeley, we shared the chores that went with it. But now, every time I try to help you with household tasks, you shoo me away. We're married. We need to work together as a team." He pulled her over to the bed with him. "I'm going to tell you the same thing you told me when I was in med school. If you need time to study, you need to tell me immediately. We are in this together."

She pulled back slightly, surprised that he mentioned that. "You remember that?"

"Of course I remember that. Those words meant a lot to me. And it applies to you right now. You only have a few years of grad school. Make them count." He kissed her softly on the lips. "Now I'm going to make dinner and you are going to hit the books, Mrs. Hanson."

When Jane rose to her feet, Randy smacked her on the butt. She giggled at his orneriness and went to get her psychology books out of her bag so she could study.

The first day of Randy's Medical Licensing Exam was mundane and horribly long. This two-day assessment was the final examination leading to a license to practice medicine without supervision. The exam assessed his ability to apply medical knowledge and understanding in ambulatory settings. This test focused on basic medical and scientific principles essential for effective health care, including communication and interpersonal skills, medical ethics, systems-based practice, and patient safety. His day included 356 multiple-choice items divided into six blocks of 42 items. Sixty minutes were allotted for completion of each block.

After Randy finished his first day of testing, he decided to stop at the YMCA to catch Jane before she left. He entered the gym and sat on the bleachers. Jane was teaching a group of children how to dribble and control a basketball. Randy leaned back, enjoying this entertaining show. With a whistle around her neck, Jane circulated around to each team and guided them through modified ball drills. Randy admired the way she interacted with the kids. They responded to her and had improved their skills tremendously from the last time he stopped by to watch them. A few of them were quite proficient at running and dribbling at the same time. Randy got a kick out of watching them jump up to the net, which was quite a bit taller than they were, to make a basket.

One girl really grabbed his attention. She was a brunette who couldn't have been more than seven or eight years old. She wore a ponytail like Jane did. She was quick on her feet, dribbling all over the court, and made quite a few baskets. Her shooting style was similar to Jane's and she was rather competitive.

A man sat on the bleachers next to Randy. "You here to pick up your child?" he asked.

Randy turned his head. "No, my wife is the coach."

"Coach Hanson is your wife?"

Coach Hanson—that was new. Randy never heard anyone refer to Jane that way before. "Yes, she is."

The man commented on the University of Washington School of Medicine tee-shirt Randy was wearing. "You're a medical student?"

A basketball rolled Randy's direction. He bent down and handed it back to the child. "Second year resident. Dr. Randal Hanson." He held out his hand.

This man gladly reciprocated. "It's a pleasure, Dr. Hanson. Your wife is wonderful with these kids. My daughter has learned so much from her, and ever since she started on this team, we can't keep her off a basketball court."

"Which one's your daughter?"

The man pointed to the brunette. "The one with the ponytail."

"She handles the ball really well. Reminds me of Jane."

"Jane?" the man asked, not knowing who he was talking about.

"My wife," Randy explained. "Jane Hanson."

"Oh, I didn't know that was her name. The kids just call her Coach."

Of course they did. "She used to play for UC Berkeley," Randy said. "Damn good player."

"I bet, if her coaching is any indication."

Jane blew her whistle and all the kids gathered around her. She drew them together in a huddle and talked to them, but Randy couldn't make out what she was saying. When she was finished, all the kids ran to greet their parents.

The man stood up and shook Randy's hand. "Nice to meet you, Dr. Hanson."

Randy stood up respectfully and replied, "Pleasure to meet you as well."

Once the kids cleared out, Jane rolled a basketball cart off the court.

Randy joined her. "Good evening, Coach Hanson."

Jane turned her head. "Hey you."

"The kids are getting a lot better."

"Yes, they are," she said proudly. "Some more so than others."

"That little girl with the ponytail reminds me of you."

"That's Mariah," Jane said. "She's grown a lot over the last few months."

"She's good. You have a potential college player on your hands with that one, Babe."

"Maybe." Jane wrapped her arms around him. "So, Dr. Hanson, what brings you over here?"

"Just finished my exam."

Her expression hardened. "How was it?"

"Think I did well," he replied. "Was hoping you had some time to grab dinner with me tonight."

"I would love to." She gave him a kiss. "Let me clock out first."

Randy's second day of testing, which lasted nine hours, involved computer-based case simulations. This test focused on his ability to apply comprehensive knowledge of health and disease in the context of patient management. Areas covered included diagnosis and management, with particular focus on prognosis and outcome, health maintenance and screening, therapeutics, and medical decision-making.

Exactly fourteen days after completing the second day of testing, MLE results were posted online. Randy logged in and clicked on his score report. The corners of his mouth quirked up. "Jane," he called out to his wife.

She sauntered into the room and saw him eyeing something on the computer screen. "What?"

"Look," he said, pointing to his score. "Passed my first try. I'm fully licensed now."

She gave him a hug. "I never doubted you."

"We'll have to get another frame so I can hang my license on the wall with the others."

"We will." She kissed him. "Congratulations, Sweetie."

"Thanks." As Jane was about to leave the room, Randy stopped her. "Jane?"

She turned around. "Yes?"

"I know the last few months have been rough. Thank you for your patience and your constant encouragement. I never could have done this without you."

"You're welcome, Dr. Hanson. I have enjoyed every minute of it."

Randy said goodbye to the Medical Licensing Exam. With medical license obtained and a threat of malpractice behind him, he could now relax and enjoy the weekend with his family.

Chapter Twenty-Two

This Christmas, Jane and Randy were hosting the entire family at their house. Jane woke up early Saturday morning and began baking Christmas cookies, which left the house smelling of chocolate, mint, and vanilla. Drooling over the aroma, Randy stepped into the kitchen to check on her. "You need help?"

"No. I'm fine."

"Are you sure?"

"I'm baking, Randy. Baking makes me happy."

Jane loved being in the kitchen. Cooking, baking, and creating culinary concoctions were among her favorite things to do. "Alright." He set his empty coffee cup in the sink. "Hand me the grocery list. I'll pick up what we need for Christmas dinner."

"That would be great, Sweetie. Thank you."

When Randy returned, he stocked cupboards and filled the refrigerator with sodas, Coronas, and a half-gallon of eggnog. Sparkling apple cider and a bottle of champagne chilled on the shelf. A juicy ham wrapped in parchment paper awaited preparation. He opened a bag of foil-wrapped Hershey's Kisses and dumped them in a bowl.

"We'll finally get to use the China we got for our wedding," he said, popping a chocolate kiss in his mouth.

"I know. I can't wait to see Daddy tomorrow."

Trudging across the hospital parking lot, Bruce answered a call on his cellphone. "Hello?"

"Hello, Dr. Buckman."

The voice on the other end instantly boosted his spirits. "Hey, Mandy."

"What are you doing this weekend?"

"Why do you want to know?"

"Because I'll be in Santa Monica for a few days and would love to see you."

He replied, "Steph and I are leaving for Seattle tomorrow. We need to pack this afternoon, but I can spare a few hours this morning. Are you in town right now?"

"Yes."

"Meet me at the Starbucks on Olympic Boulevard," he suggested. "I'll be there in about fifteen minutes."

The minute Bruce saw Mandy, his entire face lit up. He greeted her with a hug. "It's good to see you. How have you been?"

"I've been in the Pediatric ICU all week." She crinkled her nose and added, "Not a fun place to be."

"No, definitely not. Being around sick kids is never a good time."

They ordered coffee and pastries then claimed a nearby table. "How are you?" Mandy asked.

Bruce shook his head, exasperated by his schedule. "Busy beyond belief. I worked an eighteen-hour shift last night, and right as I was about to leave the hospital, they called me back for an emergency. I was on my way home when you called. And with a baby in the house...well, let's put it this way, I'm not sleeping much."

She reached out and touched his hand. "I'm so sorry."

He shrugged it off. "It is what it is. I can't do much about my schedule."

"How's the baby?"

"She eats nonstop. She gets up on her hands and knees now and shakes her bottom in the air. It's the funniest thing," he chuckled at his own narrative. "I was playing with her the other day and she bit down on my finger. She'll be teething soon."

Bruce spoke of his daughter with so much pride. Mandy could tell by the look in his eyes that he loved that baby girl more than life itself. "Better watch it there, Daddy. She'll be after your pumpkin bread before too much longer."

"Wouldn't surprise me." He pulled his hand away and reached into his pocket for his phone. "Want to see a picture?"

"Of course."

Hoping to sneak in a short nap, Bruce walked into his apartment about two hours later. He didn't get far before Stephanie harped on him. "Where have you been?"

"Mandy was in town. I met her for coffee."

Stephanie sneered at him. "You should have been here helping me."

"All I did was meet a friend for a cup of coffee. I don't get to see Mandy very often, so we took a few hours to catch up."

"We were supposed to be packing today."

"And we will," he told her. "We have the rest of the day to do that. But when Amanda goes out of her way to meet me, I'm going to take her up on the offer. Mandy and I have been friends for a long time,

Stephanie. I don't understand why you are so upset about this."

"Because you'd rather hang out with her than spend time with your family."

He furrowed his brow, confused by her harsh statement. "I'm going to be spending the entirety of next week with you and your family. Taking a few hours out of my schedule to hang out with Mandy is not a big deal. You are taking a petty issue and blowing it way out of proportion."

"I don't want you hanging out with her."

Bruce seethed at Stephanie's officious attitude. "Don't tell me what to do."

"I'm your wife."

"That doesn't mean you can boss me around." He turned away from her and headed toward the bedroom.

Stephanie glared at him, irritated that he wasn't listening to her. "I'm talking to you."

Bruce stopped dead in his tracks. "You don't control my life, Stephanie, and you can't keep me from my friends. As far as I'm concerned, this conversation is over." He slogged into the other room and refused to argue with her any longer.

Dale Davine's flight arrived early Sunday morning. This was his first trip to Seattle, and he was anxious to see the life his daughter had made for herself.

When Jane saw her father coming down the escalator, she ran to hug him. "Hi, Daddy."

He kissed her cheek. "Hello, Sweetheart. Where's your husband?"

"He went to get a cup of coffee."

"Of course he did."

On their way to the baggage carousel, they ran into Randy, who held a Starbucks cup in his hand. "Hey,

Dad. Welcome to Seattle." He graciously shook his father-in-law's hand.

"Thank you. I'm excited to be here."

They gave Jane's father a tour of Seattle Center, showed him the Space Needle, and drove over the floating bridge across Lake Washington to their house. Dale was impressed with the way his daughter was living. She and Randy had an immaculate home, finely decorated and elaborately furnished, with both of their personal touches throughout. Randy's home office showcased his love of sports cars, and the cute bear décor in the kitchen, obviously chosen by Jane, made their home cozy and inviting. The pictures displayed throughout the house—wedding photographs, graduation pictures, and still shots of them in Paris, Bermuda, and Mexico—expressed their love for one another in many ways.

The guestroom, painted in a light shade of beige, was relaxing and calming. Venetian blinds covered the window and a beautiful green potted plant on a mahogany pedestal table soaked up the natural light that flowed into the room. The mocha and cream-colored comforter on the double bed accentuated the natural colors in the room. A small glass table lamp on the nightstand offered a warm touch to the already restful atmosphere.

Jane joined her father in the guestroom. "Randy and I want to take you out to lunch before we head to the game," Jane offered.

"You don't have to do that."

"We want to," she insisted. "About an hour or so. Is that ok?"

"Sure. I'll be ready."

The San Francisco 49ers played the Seattle Seahawks that evening. Being a Seattle fan, Randy felt out of place sitting in the stands wearing a Seahawks jersey while Jane and Dale rooted for the 49ers. Even though he cheered for his hometown team, Randy supported his brother-in-law. Brian went in on several plays, including a blitz defensive maneuver in which he was sent across the line of scrimmage to the offensive side to tackle the quarterback and disrupt the pass attempt. The game was wet and muddy from the rain Century Link Field received, and it was a loss for San Francisco.

Instead of flying home with his team, Brian stayed in Seattle to spend Christmas with his sister and her husband. As a professional football player, Brian Davine was making more money than Randy and didn't have to spend hundreds of thousands of dollars on schooling to get there. Randy thought it was incredibly cool that Jane's brother played football for the 49ers, yet somehow he found it unjust that he had spent so much money and dedicated so much time to his profession to be making pocket change compared to his brother-in-law.

Randy awoke Christmas morning surrounded by Jane. Sprawled out in blissful comfort, she had taken over the entire bed. Careful not to wake her, he eased out of bed and padded to the dresser. He slipped on a pair of sweats and a sweatshirt, and, in urgent need of caffeine, trotted down the stairs to the kitchen. Brian was asleep on the sofa nearby, so Randy did his best to be as quiet as possible. He turned on the coffeemaker and, midway through the brewing cycle, siphoned a cup. He poured creamer and spooned sugar into his cup and took a sip. Caffeine seeped through his body giving him an instant boost of energy. Gripping the handle, he took his mug out to the porch with him.

The lake, in all its eerie early morning glory, was beautiful. A fine mist hung over the strands of the tall evergreen trees. Trailing fingers of fog sprinkled dew across the pinecones then dripped off the ends of the branches to the water below. The water was still, breaking into ripples only when an occasional water bird or distant fishing boat slipped quietly by. The air swelled with the tang of cedar and pine, overlaid by the scent of balsam.

Content to sit on the stairs, Randy sipped on coffee and thought about the blessings in his life. He had a job he loved, friends who had his back, family that offered unconditional support, and a happy marriage. Jane was a supportive and loving wife. She made him feel wanted, needed, loved. They laughed together then turned around the next instance and shared painful moments. And she always offered undying encouragement, because she believed in what being a doctor meant.

Randy slowly rose to his feet and strolled back inside. He glanced into the kitchen to see Jane standing at the sink in a red silk robe sipping cocoa from a steaming mug. His mouth went dry as his gaze wandered from the curves of her breasts, over her waist, hips, and bare legs, all the way down to her cute feet with brightly painted toenails. When she flashed her hypnotic smile at him, his heart tumbled.

"You're up awfully early on Christmas morning," she whispered so she wouldn't wake her brother. "Deep thoughts?"

"No. Not really." He cupped his hand around his coffee mug and lifted it to his mouth. "Still half asleep." His eyes met hers and he stared at her as if struck by a thought. "I wish I wasn't on-call today."

She set her mug down, put her hand over his, and squeezed. "I do too."

He laced his fingers through hers and brought her hand to his lips. "Maybe we'll get lucky and no babies will come."

"Maybe."

He placed his cup on the counter and cradled her face between his hands, planting a lingering kiss on her lips.

"Thank you for letting Brian and Daddy spend Christmas here."

"Of course. They're family. It's great to see all of you together like this."

She wrapped her arms around his waist and rested her cheek against his chest. "Merry Christmas."

He lovingly caressed his hand down the silky material of her robe. "Merry Christmas, Baby."

When the houseguests began to stir, Randy plugged in all the Christmas lights to get the festive mood flowing then lit a cinnamon scented candle to unleash the aroma of the holidays. He quickly checked the messages on his cellphone then shoved it back in his pocket. "This is one of those days when I wish I didn't have my phone glued to my side." He shuffled into the kitchen to prepare another cup of coffee.

Brian turned his head. "You're on-call today?"

"Unfortunately, yes." Despite the complaining he did, Randy loved his job. Adrenaline careened through his body every time he delivered a baby, and tears were hard to hide when he handed a newborn to its mother. He loved hearing an infant's first cries and watching it take its first breath. Being witness to it all was a miracle.

Jane stood at the stove making scrambled eggs and toast for everyone. Randy winked at her then checked the time on the microwave. 8:00 A.M. "My parents want to come over this morning to open presents with us. They said to call when everyone was awake. Is your dad up?"

She nodded. "Yes. He's getting dressed."

"Alright. I'll call after breakfast."

Randy's family came over carrying a large Rubbermaid tub full of gifts to add to the already enormous heap of glittering paper and bows under the tree. Once everyone was settled, they took turns tearing off paper and opening boxes.

Emily happily stacked blocks on the floor. Watching the joy and excitement on his niece's face made Randy's favorite holiday that much brighter. When he first learned he was going to be an uncle, he never realized how much that child would touch his heart. He loved that little girl. He reached down and handed her a box wrapped in blue snowman paper with a big white bow. "Here, sweet girl. This is from Uncle Randy."

With his help, she tore off the paper to reveal a lifelike baby doll. Amazement filled her eyes. She hugged the baby doll and kissed it. Along with her doll, she had a Minnie Mouse board book gripped in her hand. He picked her up and sat her on his lap. While she snuggled with her doll, he read the book to her.

Emily was the most precious thing in Bruce's life, and at this moment she was surrounded by all the people who loved her—the caring and supportive family he married into.

But to Bruce, Randy Hanson was more than family. He and Randy suffered through Anatomy class dissecting a cadaver, side by side, with perfect precision. They pained the strains of medical school, celebrated successes, suffered losses, and walked the stage together as new doctors. They drank Corona and watched basketball while they talked about women. Bruce witnessed Randy drunk, and sometimes helped him get that way. He saw the tears in Randy's eyes the day their friend Sarah quit medical school, and would never forget the look of pure love on Randy's face when he and Jane exchanged wedding vows. Memories of Randy digging through a fishbowl of cherry flavored condoms and joking with friends about the orgasm of pigs during his bachelor's party would forever be implanted in his mind. Randy Hanson was one of the most incredible people Bruce had ever known. He loved the man.

Randy kissed Emily's cheek and sat her back down on the floor. He turned his eyes to Bruce, nodding his head in approval. "Who wants eggnog?" he asked.

"I do," Bruce said, and followed him into the kitchen.

Randy pulled a set of Irish coffee glasses from the cupboard and grabbed the eggnog carton out of the refrigerator. "How's life in Neurosurgery Land?" he asked Bruce.

"It's going alright. I worked an eighteen-hour shift the other night, and right as I was about to go home, my director called me in for an emergency meeting."

"That sucks."

"That's normal. It's rare when I work less than twelve hours a day."

Randy didn't see the joy Bruce seemed to find in that kind of work. "That has to be exhausting. I don't know how you keep that up day after day, especially with a baby in the house. I think I'd go nuts."

"Some days are better than others."

Randy poured eggnog into a glass and stuck a cinnamon stick in it to spice it up.

"I saw Mandy on Saturday," Bruce said.

"How's she doing?"

"She's doing well. She loves her current placement. She's definitely found her niche in pediatrics."

"That's good."

"Stephanie wasn't happy that I chose to have coffee with Mandy."

Randy set the carton down. "Why would she care?"

"She seems to think I should have spent that time with her instead. In fact, she told me she didn't want me around Mandy."

"That's like telling you to stay away from me."

"I know. But she threw one hell of a fit, and we ended up getting into an argument over it." Bruce looked over at Stephanie, who refused to look at him.

"Yeah, I noticed some tension there."

Bruce picked up the glass of eggnog and took a drink. "I don't know what it is. She's been overly irritated lately, and everything I do seems to piss her off. She tried to call me in the middle of a surgical procedure the other day and I didn't answer, but boy did I get the third degree when I got home."

"Because you didn't answer your phone during surgery?"

"Yup."

Randy huffed, "She knows you can't talk to her during a procedure."

"You would think, but she acted like I was ignoring her on purpose."

Randy shook his head, appalled by his sister's immaturity. "That's stupid."

"Tell me about it."

During Christmas dinner that night, as the family was finishing their meal, Randy's cellphone went off. He looked down at it and grumbled. "Dammit."

"Delivery?" Mark asked.

"Yes. Why on Christmas?"

"Get used to it. Babies come when they are ready."

He slipped his phone back in his pocket and reached for his car keys. "I'm sorry, Honey."

Jane shook her head, not wanting or accepting an apology from him. "Don't. Just go."

He gave her a kiss. "Be back as soon as I can."

"I love you. Be careful."

"I will. I love you too." And he slipped out the door.

Spending Christmas at the hospital was not an ideal way to celebrate the holiday. But obstetricians had obligations to their patients to be readily available at all times of the day, any day necessary, to deliver babies. This was his job, a job he loved. This was why he spent all those years in medical school.

Randy went up to the Maternity Ward to see his patient. He scanned the chart, checked in with the attending physician, then stepped into the room with a cheerful smile on his face. "Merry Christmas, Mrs. Rosenthal."

"Merry Christmas, Doctor."

Chapter Twenty-Three

Following another day of rotations, Randy pranced through the door whistling a cheerful tune. He set his stethoscope on the dining room table and cleaned out the pockets of his lab coat. "Jane," he called to his wife. A printout of her semester grades openly sat on the table. He picked it up and read through it. She had failed one class and barely passed the other three. This alarmed him. Jane was usually an A/B student, but this report did not at all reflect what she was capable of. He wondered why she hadn't said anything to him about her grades. He took the printout upstairs, assuming that's where she was, to question her about this. "Honey, are you up here?"

"I'm in here," her voice trailed from the bedroom.

When he walked into the room, Jane was hanging clothes in the closet. He wrinkled his forehead and handed her the printout. "What's going on with your grades?"

She snatched the paper out of his hand. "You snooped at my grades?"

"They were sitting on the table. Kinda hard not to notice." He folded his arms across his chest. "What happened?"

"My grades dropped a little."

"They dropped more than a little."

Jane ignored him.

But Randy kept on her. "You have to focus on school."

With her hands on her hips, she turned and snarled at him. "I don't need a lecture, Randy."

"I'm not lecturing you. I'm just concerned. You're capable of better grades than this."

"I wasn't aware I had to justify myself to you."

Despite the fact that she was getting snippy with him, he remained calm. "You don't. But you do have to study and take time to do research. Papers won't write themselves and you can't expect to do well on an exam if you don't prepare for it. Graduate school requires time and dedication. Believe me, I was in a professional grad school, Jane. I know."

Trying to dodge the conversation, she retreated into the kitchen.

He trailed right behind her. "Honey, what happened?"

"Why do you care?"

"What do you mean, why do I care? You're my wife. We are investing money into your education and I hate to see you waste it."

"Is that why you care so much?" she retorted. "Because of the money?"

"I don't give a damn about the money. I care about you."

"If you care about me so much then leave me alone." She turned her back to him and marched out of the room.

Her attitude was certainly shining through tonight, and her tone was far from pleasant. "Would you stop and talk to me please."

She jerked her head his direction. "What do you want, Randy?"

"I want to know how this happened. Did you need help? Did you need more study time? Talk to me and explain what's going on so we can fix this."

Her eyes pierced through him. "I don't owe you an explanation."

"I never said you did. I want to help you here, but I can't if I don't know what the problem is. And I won't know what the problem is if you don't talk to me."

"You're the one who made me go to graduate school."

"What?" Randy tried to dissect this conversation, which had shifted into a place he didn't want to go. He feared they were heading toward an argument, and he did not want to deal with that tonight. "I didn't make you do anything. You said you wanted to go. What the hell are you talking about?"

Defensively, she replied, "I was perfectly happy graduating with my Bachelor's Degree, but no, you said a higher education would be better."

"I never forced you go to grad school. I merely suggested it as an option. If you didn't want to then why did you go through the trouble of taking the GRE and filling out all the paperwork?"

"Because you brought all the paperwork home."

"I was trying to help you," he argued. "You said you were considering it, so I brought home the information you needed. You should have stopped me if you weren't interested."

"Why, so you'd get uppity and in my face about it?" she accused.

His jaw tightened and his entire body tensed up. "I have never done that to you. Jesus, Jane, did you forget who you're talking to? You don't really think I'm a demanding, controlling, two-faced asshole do you, because if you do, then we have some serious issues to work through."

Her eyes teared up. "Why are you getting so angry?"

"Because you are accusing me of crap I have never done. When have I ever demanded anything of you or gotten upset because you chose not to do something I suggested? I would never do that to you. After being with me for five years you should know that."

They both stared at each other for a minute without saying a word. Jane stood stiffly with her arms folded across her chest. Randy shoved his hands in his pockets trying to back away from this confrontation. The uncomfortable silence between them lingered. This was their first argument since they exchanged vows, and Randy couldn't stand the silence any longer.

"Look, Honey, I don't want to argue," he said.

"I don't want to either."

In an attempt to end the dispute, he offered a solution. "If you don't want to be in grad school, that's fine. No one is forcing you to stay, least of all me. Take some time off or cut back your class load if you want to. Do whatever you need to do to be happy. I'll support you."

She dropped her arms. "Really?"

"Of course. You're my wife. I'll always support you. Did you really think I wouldn't?"

"No."

"Ok then." He sat on the barstool by the kitchen island and exhaled heavily. His eyes met hers. "What do you want to do?"

She sat on the stool beside him. "I want to focus on my kids and coaching. That's what I love to do. I've also been given an opportunity to do some consultation work as a sports psychologist for a place called Get Your Head in the Game."

Randy probed for more information. "What's that?"

"It's a private practice service, helping a wide range of athletes from promising high school or college athletes to triathletes and professional sports players. They have golfers, tennis players, marathon runners, Olympic athletes, members of the Seattle Dance Theatre, and equestrians as clients. Pro football, baseball, and basketball players use their services too. The owner, Harvey Brown, divides his time among the athletes he serves and other professionals with high-pressure jobs."

"Who's Harvey Brown?" Randy wondered.

"The father of one of my basketball kiddos. He's looking for another person to help him with his caseload. He found out I hold a psychology degree and specialize in sports psychology so he offered me some part-time consultation work."

This opportunity sounded promising. "That's great. Is that what you want?"

"Yes."

"Then I'll support your decision."

Randy was always so understanding. That's one of the things Jane always loved about him. "Thank you."

"Why didn't you just tell me about this?"

She shrugged. "I don't know. I thought you wouldn't understand. I'm sorry."

"It's ok," he claimed. "But please talk to me about things like this, alright? I'll always be here to listen."

"I know." She leaned forward and gave him a hug. "I love you."

"I love you too, Babe." They joined together in a kiss.

Chapter Twenty-Four

Jane and Randy took advantage of a rainy Saturday by doing some spring cleaning. Randy reorganized closets and threw out unnecessary clutter while Jane banged cupboards, rattled glasses, and sorted through pots and pans. Taking a momentary break, Randy scampered downstairs.

Jane was standing on a stepladder stretching to change a lightbulb on the chandelier above the dining room table.

"Hey, what's up?" he said with a smartass grin.

"Hush," she insisted, unamused by his wisecrack. She wondered what her butt looked like from his point of view and hoped the laugh he interjected wasn't directed toward the view he had of her backside.

"When you're done, do you think you can come down here for a second and talk to me?"

She finished screwing in the lightbulb then stepped off the ladder.

Taking both of her hands in his, Randy led her to the couch, pulling her down beside him. Dropping her hands, he rubbed his thumb back and forth across her pulse. "I just got off the phone with Jim. He has a three-day weekend next week, same days I do. We were hoping to get together for a few days."

She knew what Randy was thinking. "Him coming here or you going there?"

"Actually, we talked about meeting in Kentucky."

This seemed like an unusual meeting place. "Kentucky? Why Kentucky?"

"There's a Corvette Museum in Bowling Green we wanted to check out. But I wanted to talk to you before we made any plans."

"I don't care if you go to Kentucky with Jim."

"Thank you." He noticed her nose was a little pink. "You been working outside?"

"I was yesterday. Pulled up weeds and planted some flowers."

"You should have put on sunscreen. You're a little sunburned." He drew his finger down her nose. "Did I ever tell you that turns me on?"

"Oh, I'm sure it's amazingly sexy."

"On you it is." He kissed the tip of her nose then trailed his lips across her cheek. "How would you feel about taking a break for lunch? Johnny Rockets by University Village has a great lunch menu, and there are some shops over there you might like. Sound good?"

"Lunch and shopping?" She cocked her head slightly, intrigued by his offer. "That sounds fun."

"How soon can you be ready?" he asked her.

"How about now?"

"Fabulous," he said. "Let's go."

Johnny Rockets was a retro diner-style restaurant chain that provided the food and friendliness reminiscent of the 1950's, complete with a nostalgic atmosphere and authentic décor. The menu offered all-American favorites including juicy hamburgers, hand-dipped shakes and malts, and freshly-baked apple pie. The diner served ketchup out of the bottle and had tabletop jukeboxes that belted out tunes for a nickel.

Randy ordered the biggest hamburger he could find, stacked high with two fresh quarter-pound ground beef patties, hand-pressed and grilled to perfection, two slices of Tillamook cheddar cheese, lettuce, ripe tomato, an onion slice, and special sauce.

Jane's eyes widened at the size of his burger. "You're gonna give yourself a coronary eating that."

His mouth watered. "Looks mighty tasty to me."

She shook her head at his appetite. "How can you eat that?"

"I'm starving." He held his burger up ready to take a bite. "You want some?"

All the grease, cholesterol, and calories made her cringe. "No thanks. You enjoy."

He took a bite and enjoyed every morsel.

After lunch, they went shopping. Among Jane's favorite stores was Zovo's Lingerie Shop, where she purchased a black lace-up satin slip to sleep in. Randy loved lingerie shopping with his wife. He helped her pick out items that he would take off of her later that night. Always a bonus for him.

Randy hadn't seen his brother in a while, so Sunday afternoon he stopped by to check on him. When Robby opened the door, the first thing Randy noticed was how scrawny he looked. His body was skeletal-like and his hair was scraggly. "You look like crap. Don't you ever eat?" Dirty clothes and empty pizza boxes were scattered all over the living room. The kitchen sink was piled with dishes and the apartment smelled like a combination of rotting food and sweaty gym socks. Randy cringed at the sight. "You need to clean this place. It smells awful in here."

Robby didn't seem to care. He pushed a pile of clothes off the sofa and sat down.

"Where have you been hiding? I left you a message the other day and you never called me back."

"I've had things on my mind.

"What kind of things?"

Robby wiped his nose and sniffled. "My landlord gave me an eviction notice last week. I have ten days to get out."

Randy wrinkled his forehead. "What did you do to piss him off?"

"Haven't paid my rent in two months."

"That'll do it." Although Robby's pigsty made Randy uncomfortable, he forced himself to sit on the couch. "I thought you were making good money with your new job?"

"I was, but apparently my boss didn't like my attitude, so he fired me." His fingers twitched and he couldn't seem to sit still.

Concerned about his brother's physical state, Randy asked, "You alright?"

"Just tired. Haven't been sleeping well."

"What can I do to help you?" Randy offered.

"I might need a place to stay for a while until I can get another apartment."

"That shouldn't be a problem. Let me talk to Jane first, but I think she'll be ok with it."

Robby managed to crack a smile. "Thanks, Bro."

The conversation Randy had with his brother bothered him. On the way home, he stopped by his parents' house to discuss this with his father.

His mother greeted him at the door. "Is your wife pregnant yet?"

Randy rolled his eyes. "Would you please stop bringing that up? We are not trying to get pregnant."

"But babies bring so much joy to a family."

"We have enough joy."

"The Hanson name will continue through you," she hinted.

"Robby can carry on the Hanson name too. Bug him." Randy wanted to get away from this discussion as quickly as possible, so he changed the subject. "Is Dad home?"

"Yes. He's out back."

"Thank you."

Mark Hanson stood on the edge of the lake staring out at the water. The lake was calm that evening, almost eerily so. Randy moseyed over to the shoreline and joined him. "Hey, Dad."

Mark turned his head. "Hello, Randal. Beautiful evening."

"Yes it is." Randy cut the small talk and went straight to the point. "When's the last time you saw Robby?"

"Several months ago. Why do you ask?"

"Because I'm worried about him. He's lost a lot of weight, and he looks like he hasn't slept in weeks."

"Your brother avoids us. The only time he talks to us is when he wants money."

Robby was always a troubled kid, but recently he'd become reclusive. "He told me he lost his job and is being kicked out of his apartment."

"I'm not surprised," Mark Hanson said. "He went off on a violent rampage and took a swing at one of his customers."

Randy drew his head back, shocked by this news. "What?"

"He's lucky the man didn't press charges against him. His boss fired him on the spot."

"I probably would have too."

"You brother has to learn to face the consequences of his actions. I refuse to bail him out."

Mark Hanson had dealt with Robby's reckless, self-destructive behavior for years. Randy wasn't surprised his father was finally fed up with it.

When Jane heard Randy jingle his car keys, she called to him, "Randy, is that you?"

"Who else would it be?"

"Could you come up here and help me for a second?"

He set his keys on the table and traipsed up the stairs. He poked his head into the bedroom to see Jane stretching up to a shelf in the closet. She couldn't quite reach the box she was trying to pull down, so he pulled it off the shelf for her. "Here you go."

"Thank you."

He softly kissed her then drifted into the bathroom to wash his hands. "What is that?"

"It's for my friend, Andrea. Tomorrow's her birthday. I'm having a cake delivered to her at work."

He lathered his hands then ran water over them to remove the soapy residue. "You gonna save me a piece?"

"If you want."

He shut the faucet off, dried his hands with a hand towel, and hung the towel back on the towel rack. When he stepped into the room, Jane was sorting through the box she had. It was full of baby clothes, pacifiers, and other infant needs. "That's an odd birthday present."

"She found out she's pregnant."

Randy feared this conversation was headed down a path he didn't want to tread—the dreaded baby conversation. He knew it was bound to happen sooner or later, but hoped he could put it off as long as possible. "Did she?"

"Uh huh. She asked about the possibility of you being her obstetrician."

"And what did you tell her?"

"I told her you were doing rotations and didn't have a stationary office location right now. I gave her your dad's number instead."

"He'll appreciate that." He grinned sheepishly, feeling foolish for assuming his wife was going to pressure him into pregnancy. "I stopped to visit Robby on the way home. He's being kicked out of his apartment and needs a place to stay for a while. Do you mind if he crashes in the guest room until he can get back on his feet?"

"Not at all."

"Thank you, Honey." He pulled her hand up to his lips. "What are you doing for lunch tomorrow?"

"No plans."

"Want to meet me somewhere?"

She drew her lip between her teeth. "I would love to."

"Great. I'll call you after my rounds. Decide where you want to go, but pick a place fairly close to the hospital."

"Alright."

Chapter Twenty-Five

"Dr. Ryan?"

Jim turned around to see who was calling him. "Yes?"

"Doctor, there's a woman in the waiting room requesting to speak to you."

"Thank you." When Jim saw who it was, he tightened his jaw and scowled. He didn't want to see this woman, let alone talk to her. He hadn't seen her in years, yet for some reason she sought him out. Hesitantly, he walked out to greet her.

The moment this woman saw him, she rose to her feet. "Jimmy." She inched a bit closer and stared at his name badge. "Dr. James Ryan. I like the way that sounds."

Jim backed away from her. "What are you doing here, Trina?"

"I've missed you," she said. "You look great. How have you been?" When he draped his stethoscope around his neck, she noticed the gold band on his finger. "Is that a wedding ring?"

"Yes."

"You're married?" She tried to get a better look at the ring, but he pulled his hand away. "When did this happen?"

"That is none of your damn business."

"To who?" she demanded to know.

Wishing she'd go away, he said, "What the hell do you want, Trina? Why are you in my ER?"

"I've called this hospital five times looking for you. I've left messages."

"I know," he said. "And you need to stop doing that. I'm busy tryin' to save lives and don't have the time nor the desire to talk to you. This is not a messenger service. It's an Emergency Room."

Trina crept closer. "I want to see my son."

He knew she didn't really mean that. Trina had shown no interest in Christopher at all since she abandoned him as an infant. "Bullshit. You haven't had anything to do with him since the day you left him at my door. He doesn't even know who you are."

In a derisive tone, she stated, "I'm his mother."

"No, you gave birth to him, but you are not his mother," Jim argued. "You know nothing about him and haven't been around to witness any of the milestones in his life. You never even sent the child a birthday card or Christmas present, so what makes you think you have any rights to him at all?"

"Because he's my son," she argued.

"No way in hell, Trina. I am not gonna let you destroy that little boy's life or disrupt my family."

"Your family?" She shot him and evil sneer.

"Yes, my family. My wife and our children." Why was he wasting his breath on this bitch? He had nothing to say to her and wanted nothing to do with her. "I don't have time for this. I have patients to attend to. Please leave."

"This is a public hospital. I have every right to be here." She stood firm and refused to leave.

"You are upsetting my patients by being here. Get out."

"You can't make me."

That's what she thought. Jim sneered at her pathetic childishness and turned away. He pointed Trina out to a security guard and asked him to escort her out of the building. Security removed her, with a fight, and Jim went back to work.

After a long ER shift, Jim plodded into his bedroom without saying a word. He always acknowledged the children and greeted Jill with a kiss when he came home from work, so this behavior was unusual.

Jill saw the indignant mood he carried and followed him into the bedroom. "James. What's wrong?"

He rubbed the tension from his forehead. "Katrina came into the ER today."

Jill sat on the bed and watched him. "What did she want?"

"She said she wanted to see Chris." Jim removed his professional attire, getting more comfortable in his Hawaiian shirt and a pair of baggy Bermuda shorts.

"But she hasn't had any contact with him at all."

"I know that."

"You didn't tell her she could see him, did you?"

Jim curled his lip. "No. I told her to get out and had security remove her."

"Good."

"And I didn't get lunch today because as soon as I sat down to eat, I got a damn STAT call. Turns out it was over some stupid medical student who was fuckin' around with the buttons on the EKG so it looked like the patient V-fibbed."

"They called you for that?" Jill asked, sensing Jim's irritability.

"They thought the guy was goin' into cardiac arrest or some shit and they panicked. That assmunch got a piece of my mind."

Obviously he had a bad day, which put him in a foul mood, and he tended to bite people's heads off when he got like that. "You weren't too hard on him, I hope."

"He was touchin' shit he shouldn't have been fuckin' with. So yes, he got an ass rippin' from me."

That's what she was afraid of. "James. Be nice to the medical students. Remember, you were in their shoes once."

"But I wasn't a dumbass who touched crap I wasn't supposed to. And do you know what some jerkoff did on the way home today?"

"I'm afraid to ask."

Jim ranted, "I'm drivin' through a construction zone and this dude decides he's gonna stop right in the middle of the road. Cars are pilin' up, and since I'm right behind him, I try lookin' through his back window to see what the fuck he's doin'. Turns out some girl was givin' him a blowjob. Right in the middle of the damn street. I'm tellin' you, Jill, we need to get the hell out of San Francisco. This city is fucked up and I am so fed up with morons in this place who do stupid shit."

"Ok," she agreed. "I'm all for leaving San Francisco. You are in your last years of residency. I see no reason why we can't start looking to relocate."

He was surprised she said that. "Seriously?"

"Yes."

Jill was so supportive and so willing to work with him in life decisions. Why couldn't she have been Chris's biological mother instead of that psycho she-bitch ex of his?

"Where would you like to go?" she asked.

"What about Seattle?" He stared at her waiting for a response.

She knew what he was thinking. He wanted to be closer to Randy, and Seattle wasn't a bad idea. "I could live in Seattle."

"For real?" he asked.

"Sure. We know people there. We should look into it."

Jim lifted her into his arms. "You would really be willin' to go to Seattle?"

"Yes."

"Sweet." With a content sigh, he kissed her. "You're awesome. I love you." Jim winked at her and left the room, anxious to get started with his Seattle relocation search.

Chapter Twenty-Six

Monday morning, Randy reported to Harborview Women's Clinic, where he started an eight week rotation in gynecology. During this rotation, he would provide primary and specialty medical care to women of all ages and receive training in specialized skills he'd need later in his career. He would also be required to supervise medical student patient teams, teaching them medical fundamentals, and provide junior residents with adequate supervision and assistance.

"This is a big responsibility, Dr. Hanson," the residency director said. "But we wouldn't have chosen you if we didn't think you could handle the challenge. Congratulations and good luck."

"Thank you, Dr. Embler."

Randy shook the director's hand then slipped out of his office. At the first available opportunity, he pulled out his cellphone to share this news with Jane. "Guess what?" he said. "I had a meeting with the residency director this morning. He made me Chief Resident."

She gasped in excitement. "That's wonderful."

"Along with the promotion, I got a raise. An extra five-hundred dollars every week. To celebrate, you and I are going out to dinner tonight."

"Where are we going?" she asked.

"You decide, but right now I have to go." Before returning to his duties, he told her, "I love you, Baby. I'll see you tonight."

"I love you too."

Randy's friend, Greg, was also chosen to be Chief Resident. Over the last two years, they had become quite close on a personal level, but their individual rotation schedules rarely gave them the opportunity to work together. Both were hopeful that sharing this duty would give them a chance to bond as professionals.

Over coffee and clam chowder, Randy said, "I did a laparoscopic tubal yesterday and the medical student I've been working with came in and…"

Showing no interest in the conversation, Greg interjected, "I met an amazing girl. She works at the coffee shop down the street from my house. She makes the most incredible lattes. You'd love them."

Curious now, Randy asked, "What's her name?"

"Raquel." Greg's entire face lit up when he talked about her. "She's a beautiful woman. Gorgeous red hair, sexy smile, and the sweetest voice I've ever heard."

"Sounds like someone's got a love interest," Randy teased.

"I would love to go out with her."

"What's holding you back?"

Greg shook his head. "She's pretty young."

"How old is she?"

"Twenty-one," Greg said. "I don't know if I'd feel right going out with a girl nine years younger than me. It'd feel like I was robbing the cradle or something."

"Age is irrelevant."

"But nine years, Randy?"

"A lot of women like older guys."

Greg sighed, "I guess."

"Do you think she likes you?"

"Maybe. She and I talk all the time. We seem to have similar interests, but whether she feels any kind of a romantic thing, I can't say."

"The only way to know for sure is to ask her out," Randy advised.

"I don't know. Women and I…relationships don't ever seem to work out for me."

"Maybe it will with her. Never know if you don't try, Greg." Randy casually took a sip of his coffee.

That weekend, Greg came over to Randy's house to play basketball. Fighting hard to score some points, Randy attempted a three pointer, but Greg blocked him. The ball bounced off the rim and Greg snagged it. He dribbled across the driveway and jumped up to make a layup. When the ball went through the hoop, he said, "I asked Raquel out."

Randy retrieved the basketball and held it under his arm. "And?"

"We had brunch together yesterday then spent the afternoon at the Aquarium."

"Sounds fun. How'd it go?"

Dreamy-eyed, Greg replied, "Amazingly well. We had a pleasant conversation, and turns out the Aquarium is one of her favorite places."

"Lucky for you."

"After the Aquarium, we went for a walk down by the waterfront, and you know how amazing the lake looks at sundown."

Randy nodded. "Yup. I know it well."

"Anyway, we're walking along the lake and the sun is about to set. We turn to each other. Our eyes meet."

"Uh oh," Randy teased. "You kissed her, didn't you?"

Greg simply smiled. "No one has ever kissed me like that. So intense."

"Nothing beats a kiss like that."

"She gave me her number. I called her this morning, and in the midst of the conversation she invited me over to her place for dinner tonight."

"Does she live alone?" Randy asked.

"Yes."

Randy chuckled under his breath. "I'd bring some condoms if I were you."

Greg's face reddened slightly. "It's too soon. I doubt anything will happen."

"I don't. Why else would she invite you over to her place when she lives alone? You're an experienced older man, Greg. You said when you kissed her it was pretty intense. Was it a French kiss?"

Greg wondered where Randy was going with this. "Yeah. Why?"

"She wants you," Randy said. "Most definitely."

But Greg had doubts.

Following Monday morning rounds, Greg and Randy sat in the conference room and reviewed patient files. Focusing his attention on an ultrasound, Randy found something unusual—an abnormality between the head and body that looked like a large fluid pocket on the baby's neck. "Hey, Greg, take a look at this."

Dr. Hutchins examined the ultrasound image.

"You see that, right?" Randy asked.

"Yes, I do."

Randy examined the image again. Asking for Greg's medical advice, he said, "I've never seen that before. Chromosomal abnormality?"

"Could be," Greg hypothesized. "Could be nothing though. Monitor and see if it resolves around eighteen to twenty weeks. If it doesn't resolve then I'd look into amnio or CVS just to be safe."

"Alright. Thanks." Randy made a few notes on the chart and closed the file.

"You wanna grab some lunch later?" Greg asked.

"Can't. I'm having lunch with my wife today."

Randy's simple act of devotion made an impression on Greg. "Very cool. Enjoy."

"Oh, I intend to."

Randy sauntered across the parking lot with a stethoscope in his hand, his fancy internet-connected smartphone with pager app in his pocket, and his UWMC name badge attached to his shirt. Even before he officially earned the title M.D., he always played the part well. He presented himself in a professional manner no matter what he was doing.

Smiling at the image he portrayed, Jane said, "You look like a doctor, Randy."

"Well, I would hope so, considering I am one." He rested his hands on her hips and gave her a kiss. "But for the next forty-five minutes, I'm all yours."

Jane eyed the Lakers watch on Randy's wrist. "The high school you went to has purple and white as their school colors, University of Washington's colors are purple and gold, and your favorite basketball team's uniforms are purple. You have an obsession with purple."

Randy found this remark amusing. "No I don't. Quite honestly, I never paid that much attention to the colors before. Funny you say that though, because my favorite color is red. Yours is blue. Blue and red make purple when you mix them together."

"Thank you, Picasso," she teased.

Randy clasped her hand and escorted her to the physician's parking lot. "What made you think of that?" he asked.

"I noticed this morning how much purple we have in our house. Purple represents royalty, spirituality, wisdom, and wealth. It's also considered sensuous and romantic."

Gawking at her, he said, "Where'd you hear that?"

"It's color psychology."

"Oh really?"

"Medically, there's a reason doctor's scrubs are blue. It cools the nerves and is considered antiseptic. Blue is a healing color."

"Is that right?" He found her medical insights hilariously cute. "And Doctor Jane Hanson has found the miracle cure for cancer."

She playfully whacked him on the arm. "Hush."

Randy returned to the Maternity Ward loaded with an excessive amount of energy. Greg was convinced he was on a permanent caffeine high from all the lattes and cappuccinos he drank. He didn't seem to have an off switch, and Greg was certain he had an overdrive button hidden on him somewhere.

"How was lunch?" Greg asked.

"God, I love that woman," Randy remarked. "She and I had the most stimulating conversation."

"About?"

"Colors. She started flashing a bunch of color psychology at me, and my wife was actually lecturing me about the medical benefits of specific colors. Did you know scrubs are blue and green for psychological reasons?"

Greg had never thought about this before. "They are?"

"Blue and green have soothing qualities that calm patients, and both have great healing power. That's why they're often worn in operating rooms by surgeons." Randy twirled his wedding ring around his finger. He couldn't stop smiling. "She has the most interesting psychological information about things. It's quite fascinating."

"I'm sure it is," Greg stated, thinking Randy was nuts.

After work, Randy stopped by the YMCA. Jane was in the middle of a practice session with her eight and nine year-olds. During practices, she would dazzle the kids with some of her quick and accurate crosscourt three-point jumpshots, demonstrate the athleticism involved in making a powerful floating two-handed underhand layup, or show them the skillful moves of her back-to-the-basket offensive weapon—the turn-around jumper. Currently she was showing them the proper form for a free-throw—the forward action of the wrists and fingers, sudden extension of the arm, rising to the balls of the feet. She demonstrated a few times, explaining the technique, then had the kids take turns going up to the line to try it themselves.

She had them stand in a circle and close their eyes, trying to touch their nose with their forefinger. The next minute, they were all pointing at the wall. Randy wondered what they were doing and how this had anything to do with basketball. He never performed drills like this when he played basketball.

When Jane dismissed the kids, they all gathered around Randy. Every time Randy came to watch them, he would let the kids listen to their heartbeats with his stethoscope and give them all a basketball sticker before they reported to their parents. The girls in particular seemed especially drawn to him.

As soon as the last child left, Jane said, "Hey, Doctor. You're popular with the girls."

"It's a gift." He rose to his feet and hopped onto the court to help put basketballs away. "What's up with the nose thing and pointing to the wall?"

She explained, "It demonstrates the brain's ability to determine a trajectory to a known location. When you focus your eyes on a nearby object and point your finger at the object, there is a strong tendency for your attention to shift from the object to your finger. Considerable concentration is required to remain focused on the object. We're working on sighting points and a lot of them watch the ball when they shoot and don't stay focused on the basket. I'm trying to teach them to stay focused on the target."

"Does that technique work?"

"Their accuracy is improving." She picked up a ball and placed it on the cart. "Being a great shooter requires concentration. Knowing when to shoot and being able to do it effectively under pressure distinguishes the great shooter from the ordinary. Good shooters develop their concentration and are oblivious to every distraction. To win games, shooting must be perfected."

"But even the best shooters miss occasionally," he reminded her.

"Yes they do. Every player experiences off nights."

"Off nights used to piss you off."

"I don't like to lose."

"I know." He picked up a ball, but instead of placing it on the ball cart, he dribbled and aimed for the basket. It banked off the backboard and went in.

"Score." He recovered the ball and gave it to Jane. "You hungry?"

"Starving."

"Good. You want to share dinner with me?"

She put her arms around his neck. "I would love to have dinner with you."

"Awesome. It's a date then."

Randy and Jane's lives became a bit more hectic with another person living in the house. Randy wanted to do what he could to help his brother get back on his feet, but made it clear to Robby that living with them was not a permanent arrangement. He agreed to feed him and provide shelter but fully expected his brother to actively seek employment. Robby agreed, and the arrangement worked out well for the first few weeks.

Randy came home from work Friday looking forward to relaxing on his sofa with a Corona in one hand and the TV remote in the other. He changed into more comfortable clothes, turned on the Discovery Channel, then strode into the kitchen to grab himself a beer. He searched the shelf they were stored on but didn't find a single bottle. He moved the milk carton aside, thinking maybe they were hiding back there. No Corona bottles there either. "Honey?" he called to Jane. "Did you move my Coronas?"

Jane came into the kitchen wondering what he was talking about. "No. Why would I do that?"

He opened the refrigerator door further to show her. "Then where did they go?"

She peeked into the fridge. Indeed they were missing. "That's weird. You had a whole six pack in here."

"I know."

Jane stood up and they both stared at each other. In perfect sync, they said, "Robby."

Robby always had a problem refraining from alcohol, but Randy never imagined his brother would steal to satisfy this craving. "He drank that entire six pack?" He opened the pantry to make sure the bottle of wine he had stashed in there hadn't disappeared. It too was missing. Randy's jaw tensed. "Dammit." He snarled and closed the refrigerator. "Guess we're keeping all the alcohol locked up from now on."

Robby didn't return until around two o'clock that morning. He stumbled in the door, tripping over his own feet, and had to hold onto the wall to say upright.

Randy was still awake, and when he saw his brother in this condition, he berated him. "Did you drive home like that?"

"Yeah."

Robby's speech was garbled and he reeked of cigarette smoke. The fact that he chose to drive home drunk, recklessly forsaking the safety of others, forced Randy to assert his authority. "What the hell is wrong with you? It's bad enough that you go out on a drinking binge and risk people's lives with your stupidity, but you also had the nerve to steal alcohol from me."

"I didn't steal nothin'," Robby slurred.

"That six pack of Corona didn't disappear on its own, and I know damn well neither Jane nor I drank it. You're the only other person in this house."

He staggered toward the stairs, completely ignoring Randy's comment.

Randy grabbed him by the arm and turned him around. "If you ever come into this house drunk or steal anything from me again, I will throw your ass out on the street. Jane and I have gone out of our way to help you, and I'll be damned if I'm going to let you take advantage of that." He released his brother's arm, locked up the house, and marched up to the bedroom.

In the morning, Randy found Robby passed out on the couch with the light still on in the living room. Not sure if he should feel pity or anger towards his brother, Randy turned off the table lamp and headed to the kitchen to put on a pot of coffee. "Rob, get up."

Robby groaned and buried his face in a throw pillow.

"Get up," Randy insisted. "You're getting off your lazy ass and helping me today."

"My fuckin' head hurts."

"And whose fault is that?" Randy pulled a coffee mug out of the cupboard and set it on the counter. "Where the hell were you all night?"

"You're not my father."

"No, but when you come traipsing into my house at two o'clock in the morning drunker than a skunk, I think I have a right to know."

Robby raised his middle finger.

"You can grumble and whine all you want, but you're going to make yourself useful today. Get up." Randy filled his cup with coffee, stirred in sugar and creamer, and took a sip.

Chapter Twenty-Seven

Between working as Chief Resident, keeping his house in tiptop shape, and tending to his husbandly duties, Randy barely had time to breathe. Wearing aviator sunglasses, he pulled into the hospital parking lot with the top down on his car and the stereo blasting. He parked in his designated space, placed his aviators in the storage console next to the driver's seat, and reached for his lab coat and stethoscope.

When Randy stepped out of the car, he spotted the gynecologic oncologist he had been working with over the last month. "Good morning, Dr. Evans."

"Good morning, Dr. Hanson. I'm glad you're here early. I'm going to need your help this morning."

"What's up?"

"Mr. Travers called me last night."

"Fiona Travers' husband?" Randy asked for clarification.

"Yes. After reviewing his wife's CT and going over all of her test results yesterday, he and I sat down and had a chat. The chemo we've been using isn't working and the tumors have spread. The one pushing on her diaphragm has grown considerably."

"I saw the scan before I left last night."

"She's on ventilation because her lungs are so weak she can't maintain air by herself. We can't operate on the tumors with her in this weakened condition, and she's not responding to the lung therapy we've tried," he summarized. "She was pretty incoherent yesterday and had no idea where she was or what was going on. There's nothing else we can do for her. Mr. Travers informed me, and Fiona told me before we started all this, that she did not want to be kept alive by artificial means."

"Meaning what, exactly?"

"Mr. Travers signed a DNR last night. He wants to take her off the ventilator this morning."

"But the tumor pushing on her diaphragm is hindering her breathing."

"He knows that," Dr. Evans clarified.

Randy realized the implications of this. His heart sank to the ground. "Oh man."

"Meet me at the nurse's station in ten minutes."

"Yes, Sir." Randy exhaled with a heavy heart. He did not want to be a part of what he was about to do. He had spent the last four weeks treating this patient, who was diagnosed with Clear Cell Carcinoma. His attending physician had been working with her for months. They called in a lung specialist, tried various chemotherapy options, operated and removed the tumors they could get to, prescribed medications, and counseled on holistic approaches. Despite this, throughout her four weeks in the hospital, she grew weaker and weaker every day. Randy and Dr. Evans used every treatment option they could think of to rid her of this wicked disease, and she fought right along with them, strong and stubborn and determined to win. Apparently all of their effort was in vain. Although he didn't like exposing his patients to unnecessary treatments and forcing them to endure procedures that would have no effect, Randy didn't like giving up. Removing this patient from the ventilator was their way of admitting their failure to treat her.

Cancer was not Randy's favorite thing to deal with. If caught early, treatment was often effective, but if diagnosed in stage three or four, the outcome was almost always bad. He knew all too well what to look for early on—uncontrolled growth of cells, invasion on and destruction of adjacent tissues, and spread to other locations in the body. He knew how to administer blood tests, x-rays, CT scans, and other diagnostic procedures and had done several histological examinations in the diagnosis of cancer. Tissue suspected to be malignant was obtained from a biopsy or surgery, both of which he knew how to perform and had done before. Although he didn't like it, he was definitely well-versed in the disease.

Death, on the other hand, was something with which he was not as experienced. OB/GYNs didn't experience death much. However gynecologic oncologists dealt with it often. This was one reason why Randy chose not to consider oncology as a sub-specialty. He liked the healthy aspects of medicine, the success stories, the joyful events like birth of a new life. Death was a topic he didn't like to deal with and certainly not something he looked forward to talking to families about. This particular situation was heartbreaking. Randy couldn't even begin to fathom the turmoil and pain this man felt knowing his wife was going to die in a matter of hours.

Clearing the lump in his throat, Randy took a cleansing breath and went into the building to report to his duties.

As Randy completed his rounds, he thought about what he would do if he was in Mr. Travers' shoes. He honestly didn't know how he would handle it, or if he could handle it. This thought plagued him all morning.

A few minutes before 10:00 A.M., Randy saw Mr. Travers exit his wife's hospital room and fall to his knees, sobbing. Immediately, an RN rushed to his side and another went to get Dr. Evans. In an attempt to comfort him, Randy put his hand on this man's shoulder. "Mr. Travers?"

He glanced up at Randy. His face sagged, and his eyes were heavy with grief.

"I'm so sorry."

To Randy's surprise, this man stood up and hugged him. "Thank you, Dr. Hanson. Thank you so much for fighting for her. She's at peace now," he said. "Finally at peace."

"Please let us know if we can do anything for you, Sir."

While Dr. Evans checked vitals to confirm death and had the nurses and other hospital staff prepare the body for mortuary pickup, Randy spoke to family members and counseled Mr. Travers. He offered hospital chaplain services and gave him a business card for a nearby mortuary.

When Mr. Travers got off the phone with the mortuary, his expression hardened and his eyes became glossy.

"Is everything alright?" Randy asked.

"The mortician says he won't talk to me or help me until three o'clock tomorrow afternoon."

Randy took charge of this situation. "Hold on," he said. He left the room and called the mortuary himself. A very rude man answered the phone. Randy professionally and calmly tried to talk to this man, explaining the situation. "Have a little sympathy here. The man just lost his wife. I'm sure you can spare some time in your busy schedule to speak with him today, man to man, and help him out." Randy handed the phone to Mr. Travers. "He wants to set up an appointment with you."

Once an appointment was confirmed, Mr. Travers again thanked Randy. "You have done more than you needed to, Dr. Hanson. Doctors like you are rare indeed. Thank you so much for everything."

"My pleasure. Let us know if you need anything else."

The man shook Randy's hand, gathered up his wife's belongings, and staggered down the hallway to the elevator.

Not unlike other doctors who had patients die, Randy was plagued with feelings of loss. Throughout the day, images of this patient's face popped into his head. By 5:00 P.M., he was emotionally drained. All he wanted to do was go home and veg on his couch.

When Randy came home, Jane was buzzing around the house watering plants. She set her watering can down and took three big strides toward him, greeting him with a warm hug and a soft kiss on the lips. "How was your day?"

He shrugged.

His downcast face and tired eyes told her something was wrong. "You ok?"

"Had a bad day."

"Why? What happened?"

He drew in a long breath. "I lost a patient."

"Oh, Sweetie. I'm sorry."

Randy closed his eyes trying to clear his mind. "I wish there was more I could have done. I hate giving up."

"You did everything you could."

"Apparently it wasn't enough." He released her and headed upstairs.

She followed him. "It's not your fault. You told me yourself that you won't save everybody."

"Well, that's not good enough. There must have been other angles, things we didn't think about, remedies we didn't try."

"Randy," she said, trying to get him to calm down. "Sometimes the disease is too powerful for human limitations. Don't beat yourself up over this."

He unbuttoned his shirt and slumped down on the bed. "I'm not beating myself up over it. I just feel sorry for that poor man who had to go through hell today. What a horrible thing to deal with, to make a decision like that, to know the decision you make will lead to the death of someone you love, to sit and watch your wife slowly die right in front of your eyes." Tears formed in his eye. "I don't know if I would have had the strength to do what he did. I think that's what bothers me the most. Because there is no way in hell I would want you to suffer, and I wouldn't want to keep you lingering hooked up to life-prolonging machines if there was no hope at all of treatment and recovery. But I wouldn't want to lose you either. Jesus, to have to make that kind of decision." A tear rolled down his cheek.

Jane sat on the bed next to him and gently touched his arm. "Sweetie, look at me."

He lifted his chin.

"There's nothing you could have done."

"I know. But these are people's lives I deal with, Jane. I can't be a heartless bastard and pretend it doesn't affect me when it does."

"Which is why you are such a good doctor. You care about people."

One corner of his mouth slowly raised. "You always make me feel better, no matter how bad my day is. I love that about you."

"I'm your wife. That's my job."

He removed his shirt and tossed it in the hamper. "How was your day?"

Jane positioned herself on his lap, face to face with him.

She rubbed her hands across his chest and slowly trailed them down to the button on his slacks. "Been thinking about you all day."

"Oh really?" He rested his hands on her hips and drew her body a bit closer. Soft kisses traced her neck. Her hair tickled his nose; it smelled like honeysuckle.

Carefully, she unbuttoned his pants and pulled the zipper down. "Your brother asked where you were tonight. When I told him you wouldn't be home 'til late, he ranted and raved and stormed out of the house."

"He needs to realize my life doesn't revolve around him." His hands roamed to her buttocks; he squeezed with the firmness of his fingers. His lips slowly worked their way up her jawline while he fondled for her bra strap, trying to unlatch it.

Jane leaned forward and forced him to lie back on the bed. Her lips interlocked with his. With her tongue, she forced his mouth open, delving in deep.

He made no effort to resist her. Her intoxicating strawberry-flavored lips drove him mad with desire. He closed his eyes and absorbed every taste.

Jane reached her hand down and felt the bulge in his pants. His breath quickened at her touch. She stripped off her shirt, removing her bra right along with it. They lay side by side, bare-chested, caressing each other's fleshy skin.

Randy snuck his hands into her underwear, feeling soft flesh under his fingers. She helped him out by unbuttoning her shorts and sliding them over her hips so he could have more access to her. Taking advantage of this, he moved his hand between her legs and began exploring with his finger. She squirmed a bit. He gawked at her lustfully, indicating his desire to please her.

She badly wanted him to enter her. Her body burned.

He heard her release a pleasurable sigh, her signal indicating she was ready. Randy sat up on his knees and pulled his pants off. As soon as he was naked, he repositioned himself between her legs. Their bodies entwined as one.

The sun shone through the bedroom window, warming the sheets and bringing a beam of light into the room. The parrot squawked in his cage downstairs.

"Alright, alright, I'm up," Randy whispered, trying not to wake Jane. He rolled out of bed, slipped on a pair of athletic shorts, and quietly crept downstairs to put on a pot of coffee. While the pot brewed, he set his parrot free and grabbed his cellphone to call Jim.

Jim's phone blared. Still groggy, he groaned and rolled over to answer it. Seeing Randy's number on his screen, he pushed the talk button. "Dammit, Hanson. You better have a good reason for callin' me this early on my day off."

"You left me a voicemail last night. I'm returning your call."

"You could have called last night instead of wakin' me up at seven thirty in the morning."

"I could have," Randy replied, "But I was busy last night."

"Well, I'm busy now." His loud voice disturbed Jill, who in turn covered her head with a pillow to drown out the noise. "See, now you woke up my wife."

"Then step out of the room so I can talk to you."

Still half asleep, Jim rolled out of bed and stumbled into the kitchen to get a cup of coffee. "What were you so damn busy doin' last night?"

"An interview dinner for a potential resident."

"Well, aren't you special?"

"Someone's a cranky ass this morning," Randy teased.

"You woke me up, Bro. I was havin' the sweetest dream too." Jim siphoned his coffee cup underneath the stream to get a fresh sample.

"Ooh," Randy teased him. "A wet dream?"

"Fuck you," Jim retorted.

"Hey, I'm glad you called. Brian is playing at Levi Stadium next weekend for their pre-season opener. I have a four-day weekend and four tickets. Thought you might want to go."

This perked Jim up. "You're comin' down to San Francisco next weekend?"

"Yup. Flying out Thursday night, but Brian's game isn't 'til Sunday, so I have two days to hang out if you're interested," Randy suggested.

"Hell yeah, I'm interested."

"Alright, then quit your griping and show some gratitude."

Chapter Twenty-Eight

It had been a while since Randy and Jim saw each other. They both found that the last year of their residency was by far the busiest one they'd had. Jim picked up Randy from his father-in-law's house Friday morning and they grabbed lunch together.

Over Baja fish tacos and salsa, Jim said, "We got a new ED director a few months ago. The guy's probably in his fifties. He prances around the ER in safari pants, a casual sports coat, and Birkenstocks with his hair in a ponytail. He looks like his last job may have been a freelance gig for an African Serengeti expedition huntin' lions or some shit."

Randy's face crinkled at this image.

"A few weeks ago he was goin' around the ER with this really pissed off look on his face because we were burstin' at the seams with patients, and the waiting room was standin' room only. We couldn't find any IV pumps or nebulizers because they were all in use. ICU, DOU, and Med Surg were packed. Stretchers lined the hall, ambulances were backed up in the driveway, and the staff all looked like zombies from the long ass hours he'd been workin' everyone. It was a genuine clusterfuck, Dude."

"Sounds like it."

"Now, none of this is anyone's fault; we were just busy, but he's the kind of guy who has to blame someone. So he starts wiggin' out and screamin' at everyone. He fired a tech and two nurses on the spot simply because they disagreed with somethin' he said, leaving us backed up and shorthanded."

"Damn. That sucks."

"The guy's a fuckin' dictator sleaze ball. He finds any reason he can to write people up. He pissed me off the other day," Jim declared. "He totally came on to Jill tellin' her she would look hot in a skimpy nurse's outfit. She stood her ground and told him to back off. He, in turn, threatened to fire her."

Randy cringed in disgust. "What a dick. Not only is that professionally unethical, it also classifies as sexual harassment."

"Exactly, and I wasn't about to put up with him sayin' shit like that to my wife, so I got in his face and went all feral on his ass."

Randy would have done the same thing.

"Then he started gettin' all huffy and bureaucratic with me and threatened to write me up. I told him to go ahead, but there was no way he was gonna disrespect my wife." Jim chuckled a bit. "Jill turned the tides by filing a complaint against him for sexual harassment."

"Good for her," Randy said.

"The dude hates me. He gives me really nasty looks now, but he hasn't been buggin' Jill. He received some kind of written warning, and the hospital director has him under investigation for inappropriate behavior. I hope they can his ass. He's a total douchebag."

Randy held the same opinion.

"I'm telling you, San Francisco is whacked," Jim complained.

"It's not San Francisco. Seattle has its share of weirdos too. A few months ago, a woman in the latent stages of labor was wheeled up to L&D. This 18-year-old kid was walking down the hallway and out of nowhere she grabs him by the shirt and screams in his face. I'm trying to talk her down and get her to let go of this kid's neck while he's trying to pry her fingers off of him. Scared the hell out of the poor kid and he'll probably be scarred for life."

"Dude," Jim chortled. "That is funny."

Randy looked at his watch. "Hey, let's stop by Ghirardelli's."

"Why?"

"Janey. She loves those raspberry dark chocolate squares."

"Ooh, that does sound good."

"There's this place in Seattle—See's Candies. They have awesome Café Latté lollipops made from Columbian coffee. I love those things. Good stuff."

"A lollipop?" Jim chuckled. "My kids suck on lollipops, Dude."

"These aren't ordinary lollipops, my friend. They are gourmet candy on a stick. That place is wonderful. Every time you walk in the door, they hand you a piece of chocolate."

"You're makin' me want chocolate now."

"Then let's go."

At Levi's Stadium, they had to dodge crowds and squeeze through hordes of people to get to their seats. Randy sat between Jane and Jim. Once settled, he remarked, "This place is packed."

"This game is gonna get loud," Jim said. "It's totally righteous that you have a professional football player in your family, Dude."

"It is pretty cool, I have to admit."

"Bet he's seein' a lot more play time this year," Jim assumed.

"Yes he has."

Jane leaned a bit closer to Randy and said, "I knew we should have eaten before we left."

"Grab something from a food vendor."

"Hotdogs?" she sneered.

"What's wrong with hotdogs?"

"Yuck."

The repulsed expression on her face made Randy fall about laughing. "If you're hungry enough, you'll eat one."

"No I won't," she complained. "I'd rather eat buttered popcorn than a hotdog."

Jane detested buttered popcorn and refused to eat it. "I'm sure they have popcorn around here somewhere." He patted her thigh and started singing, "Take me out to the ballgame…"

"Be quiet," she said, interrupting his song. "This isn't baseball."

"No, but football is the great American pastime, Babe. Football, beer, and hotdogs. What's the worst that could happen if you eat a hotdog?"

She shot him a piercing glare.

"I'll find you something to eat." He gave her a kiss then turned to Jim and said, "Come with me."

"Where we goin'?" Jim asked.

"To find Jane something she'll eat. We'll grab a couple of beers too. Still have lots of time 'til kickoff."

Jane ended up with bean and kale curry and a Diet Pepsi. Randy and Jim both had a twenty ounce beer, a pulled pork sandwich, and a pile of garlic fries.

The size of their ales made Jane's jaw drop. "Oh my god, Randy. Do you think that's big enough?"

Randy tried to reason with her. "I'm not driving, and it's not every day I get to see my brother-in-law play football. I'm having fun." He picked up a garlic fry and held it in front of her face. "Want one?" he teased, knowing damn well she would never eat a French fry.

She repelled in disgust. "Gross."

"Suit yourself." He popped it in his mouth and savored every morsel.

After the game, Brian met the family at the house. In the middle of casual conversation, Brian turned to his father and said, "Hey, Dad, I want to show you something."

Brian led his father out to the driveway and handed him the keys to a shiny yellow 1969 Daytona Camaro Z-28. "It's yours."

Dale stared at his son, wide eyed. "What?"

"I know how much you love classic Camaros. When I found this one, I had to get it for you."

Randy's eyes popped open, ogling over this amazing vehicle. High performance, powerful, and one of the hottest-looking rides of the classic muscle car era. "Holy shit."

Dale's eyes teared up. "Brian."

"Go ahead," Brian said. "Check it out."

"Thank you." He gave his son a huge bear hug.

Under the hood, he and Randy inspected the recently rebuilt engine.

"That's a high-performance street machine you've got there, Dad," Randy said. "You don't often find classic cars in this kind of condition. Someone took care of this baby."

"You wanna go for a ride?" Dale asked. "I would love for you to join me."

Randy looked at Jane, uncertain what to think. Jane nodded, encouraging him to go. Randy rode shotgun while Dale took the Z-28 for a spin, fully enjoying the speed and grace of this classic muscle car.

Back at the Davine home, Jane sat on the porch with Brian, waiting for their father and Randy to return. "I can't believe you did that for Daddy."

"You know he's always wanted one. A buddy of mine restores cars, and when he told me he was selling it, I couldn't resist." Brian chuckled, "Did you see the look on your husband's face when he saw that car? I think he was a little jealous."

Chapter Twenty-Nine

The house appeared to be orderly when Jane and Randy returned home. Everything was in its place and to Randy's surprise, Robby had kept the house clean. The rambunctious parrot screamed at Randy, scolding him for leaving over the weekend, but it appeared Robby had tended to him well. His feathers were neatly preened and he was his normal, vibrant self.

"Hey, Birdbrain," Randy said to his squawking parrot.

"Hello, Doctor."

Randy unlatched the birdcage and let the bird fly around the house freely. "It looks like Robby took care of the house. I guess I worried over nothing."

Jane set her purse on the coffee table. "I'm glad he took responsibility for something."

"So am I."

Robby galloped down the stairs to greet them. "Hey."

Randy turned to face him. "Fingers looks good. Thanks for taking care of him."

"No problem." Robby pulled a Kleenex out his pocket and wiped his nose. "How was the game?"

"The game was good." When Robby wiped his nose again, Randy remarked, "You've had that sniffle for a while now. I know a good allergist I can refer you to."

Robby shrugged it off. "Nah. I'm fine." He bounced around the living room like a kangaroo on crack, shifting from the sofa, to the stairs, to the living room window, where he peered out as if on reconnaissance.

Randy hadn't seen him that pumped up in a long time. "Wow! You have a shit ton of energy. Did you eat a bunch of sugar before we got here?"

"No." He peeked out the window again. "Just waiting for a buddy of mine to drop something off."

While Randy unpacked, Jane shuffled through her jewelry box. Frantic, she dumped the contents onto the bed. "Oh my god."

Randy tossed his dirty clothes in the hamper. "What's wrong?"

"My ring is missing." She dug through the pile, searching for the misplaced item. "My ring. My mother's ring. It's gone." She began to breathe heavier.

Randy helped her look for it. "Are you sure you had it in here?"

"Yes."

Not only was the ring gone, several diamond earrings, a gold and sapphire bracelet, and a twenty-four karat gold and ruby necklace were also missing. Randy opened a dresser drawer to discover his Rolex watch had disappeared as well. "What the hell?"

Jane buried her face in her hands and sobbed. "That ring belonged to my mother. It was one of the only things I had that was hers. I can never replace that, ever." Her tears escalated. The sentimental importance attached to that ring was far more valuable than the monetary worth.

Randy wrapped her in his arms. The pain his wife felt broke his heart.

There was no indication of a break in. In fact, a burglary was pretty unlikely considering Randy lived in a secure gated community and had an active alarm system installed on his house. The only way this could have happened was if someone with full access to the house allowed it to happen. Only two people, besides him and Jane, had that kind of access—his father and Robby. Randy suspected his brother was to blame.

He softly kissed Jane's head. "I'll take care of it." He stepped out of the room and down the hall. Without a second thought, he barged into the guest room. "I need to talk to you."

Robby leaned over the bedside table and inhaled a line of white powder with a straw.

"What are you doing?" Randy flung the tray, along with a razor blade, a re-sealable bag of powder, and other paraphernalia, into the air. "Are you sniffing cocaine in my house?"

With his hand clenched in a fist and fury in his eyes, Robby rose to his feet and swung at his brother.

Randy dodged his punch, grabbed him by the wrist, and held him in a chokehold. "My wife is in the other room bawling her eyes out because you stole something from her of extreme sentimental value, something that can never be replaced. Not only that, you have illegal drugs in my house, potentially putting her in danger. When you mess with Jane, you deal with me."

Robby whimpered in pain and tried to pry himself free. "Let go of me!"

Randy gripped his arm tighter. "You're lucky I don't beat your ass and have you arrested. Is this how you support your drug habit, you little shit? By stealing from me? What did you do with the jewelry, Robert?

Did you pawn it? Trade it for drugs? You better start talking."

Robby's body weakened. Randy released him before he passed out.

Gasping for air, Robby leaned on his knees.

"Are you alright?" Randy asked. Although he was angry, he never intended to hurt his brother.

Robby coughed.

"Are you hurt? Can you breathe?"

Robby slowly stood upright. He sniffed and wiped white residue off his nose.

Randy picked the bag of powder off the floor. "Where'd you get this stuff?"

"That's none of your damn business."

Robby tried to snatch the bag from his brother's hand, but Randy pulled it away from him. "How long have you been using this?"

"I don't have to tell you that."

Randy held his palm open. "Turn over your key. I want you out of my house."

"Give me my stash."

"Give me my key."

Reluctantly, Robby handed Randy his key. "Now give me my stash." He snagged the bag out of Randy's hand and shoved it in his pocket.

"Get out." Randy escorted Robby out of the house and made sure he exited the neighborhood.

When Robby was gone, Randy headed back upstairs. He combed his fingers through his hair and sat on the bed. "Robby's been sniffing cocaine right under our noses. When I caught him, he tried to take a swing at me."

Jane covered her mouth with her hand. "Are you ok?"

"I'm fine." He exhaled heavily. "I feel so betrayed. My brother stole from us to support his drug addiction. How could he do something like that?"

Still weepy-eyed, Jane hugged him.

"I'm sorry, Honey. I really thought I could trust him."

Randy boxed up Robby's belongings and searched the guest room for any signs of the missing items. He didn't find any of them, but he did find a pawn ticket with an address on it. His Rolex and several other pieces of jewelry were listed on the ticket as pawned items. Unfortunately, Jane's ring was not among them.

Randy brought Robby's belongings over to his parents' house, explaining what happened. "I found the pawn ticket. He can't deny he stole them."

"Did you call the police?" his father asked.

"No."

"The only way you'll be able to get them back is by filing a police report or have Robby go to the pawn shop and retrieve them."

"That's pretty unlikely, considering I threw him out this afternoon," Randy said. "But if I call the police, he could be charged with a felony. I don't want to get Robby in trouble, and quite frankly I don't care about the missing items. The only thing I care about is that ring. It holds sentimental value for Jane and she was very upset it was taken. Can't we get him some help? Put him in a drug rehabilitation program or something?"

Mark Hanson explained, "We've offered to put him in rehab, but he refuses to go. If Robby doesn't recognize he has a problem, he won't take the necessary steps to clean himself up. I know you want to help him, Randy, and as much as I hate to admit it, the only way to do that might be to file charges against him."

Randy considered his father's advice, but didn't know what to do. "I just want to get that ring back."

Chapter Thirty

Randy and Jane lay naked under the bedsheet embraced in each other's arms. Jane rested her head on his shoulder with her hand on his chest. He wrapped his arm around her, stroking her long, beautiful hair.

"Randy?" She kissed his chest.

"Hmm?"

"I want to have a baby."

Randy choked when he swallowed, but didn't say a word. He knew Jane would get the baby bug sooner or later, but he wasn't expecting it to pop up quite like this.

When he didn't express an opinion, she asked, "You have nothing to say?"

"What do you want me to say?" Randy wished this conversation would disappear. He didn't feel ready to take on parenting but could tell by the tenacious tone in Jane's voice that this topic wasn't going away.

"How do you feel about it?"

"I think you need to stop hanging out with my mother." He gently moved Jane off his chest and sat up.

Jane propped herself up on her elbow. "You said you wanted to have children with me."

"I do," he claimed. "But I thought we were going to wait until I completed my residency?"

"We were, but I don't want to wait anymore."

Randy ran his fingers through his hair, searching for a convincing argument. "Why do you want to rush into this?"

"We're not rushing into it. We've been married for three years."

"I know how long we've been married, Jane. I don't need you to tell me." He put his feet on the floor and slipped on a pair of athletic shorts.

Jane sat up, still covered in a sheet. "I guess you don't want to then. Is that what you're saying?"

"I'm in the middle of my residency."

She didn't see what that had to do with anything. "So?"

"So, you knew I wanted to wait until I finished before we started talking about starting a family."

She abruptly crawled out of bed and put on some clothes.

"Jane, come on, don't be like that. I do want to have children with you, but not right now."

"Then when? When it's convenient for you?"

"Honey, please. Between work and all this crap going on with Robby, I'm not comfortable with that kind of commitment right now."

She whirled around with her hands on her hips. "And what about what I want?"

Randy could tell by the fiery look in Jane's eyes that her temper was going to erupt at any moment. He had to tread carefully or an argument would ensue. "Do you realize how much stuff babies need and the amount of time involved in caring for an infant? Spontaneity will be in the toilet, sleep will be minimal, privacy will be nonexistent. Bottles, diapers, and baby clothes scattered everywhere, paying for babysitters, a crib, stroller, cradle, car seat and whatever the hell else babies need. Are you really ready for all of that? 'Cause I'm not sure that I am." Definitive in his argument, he thought he made a valid point.

But she disputed his logic. "Why is everything always about you?" She turned away from him and exited the bedroom.

Bothered because Jane was so upset over this, but also not liking the tone she developed with him, he followed her downstairs. "It's not always about me. Where did that come from?"

"It is about you. If it doesn't fit into your schedule then we can't do it."

That accusation irritated him. "That is a load of crap and you know it."

"Did you ever once stop to consider my feelings?"

"I think about your feelings all the time, which is why I always ask how you feel before we make decisions. Why do you think I was so pissed off when Robby stole your mother's ring? It certainly wasn't because I don't care." Jane seemed overly moody. Something must have happened that put her in this foul mood. "What the hell is wrong with you tonight?"

"Wrong with me?" she argued. "You're the one who always wants me to work around your schedule. I miss family events and dinner dates because you have to go to the hospital. Do you know how many nights I've spent alone because you were on-call?"

"You knew I was an obstetrician before you married me, and you know all too well what medical training involves. If you didn't like what you were getting into then you shouldn't have said I do. Excuse me if my schedule cramps your style. But my schedule is my job, and my job is our livelihood and gives you this house and your car and all the luxuries we have."

She retorted, "And I told you I didn't care about all this materialistic crap, Randy."

Randy didn't sympathize with her. In fact, her attitude frustrated him so much that he raised his voice at her, something he never did. "You really shouldn't be complaining. As far as wives go, you have it pretty damn good, Mrs. Hanson. So I don't think you have grounds to be bitching at me. If you're that miserable then why the hell are you still here?"

Jane started to cry.

Randy hated to see his wife cry. It broke his heart. Even more so, he hated it when they fought. They hadn't had a blowout in years. And what the hell were they fighting about? A baby? Jane wanted to carry his child, and he became argumentative over it. He felt like an asshole. "Baby, please don't cry."

"You're yelling at me," she sobbed.

"You were yelling at me too." He twirled the wedding ring on his finger. "I don't want to fight. Can we please talk about this?"

"Why don't you want to have a baby with me?" she sniffled.

"You are not listening to what I'm saying," he charged. "I do want to have a baby with you, but the timing is bad. I want to wait until I'm finished with my residency."

"But you'll be finished by the time the baby comes."

She had a good point there. With his finger, he lifted her chin and wiped her tears. "Why is this so important to you?"

"I want us to have a family."

"Honey, we have lots of time for that. A baby will change things. Babies need constant attention. We'll lose that spontaneity we both love so much."

"But there's more in life to experience than that," she argued.

"I know, but…"

Not letting him finish, she asked, "When have I ever asked you to do something like this for me?"

Randy couldn't think of a time when Jane ever asked him to do anything life changing like this. Quite the contrary. He's the one who had done that to her when he drug her away from her family and friends and basically everything she ever knew to marry him and move to Seattle. "Never."

"I don't demand things of you, Randy," she declared.

He agreed. "I know."

"I'm not a nagging wife."

"No, you're not. Not at all."

"I really want this. Doesn't that matter?"

He looked Jane in the eye and knew right away how important this was to her. When he exchanged vows with her, he promised he would be a supportive husband and look out for her needs and wants. He wanted nothing more than to make her happy. "Yes, it does matter."

"Then I'm asking you to do this for me."

Randy didn't feel ready for this, but knew Jane was. He wasn't sure what to say to appease her, but realized he needed to give in a little and not be so damn stubborn. In an attempt to compromise, he offered, "Tell you what. First of the year you can go off the pill. Your prescription expires then anyway."

"You promise?"

Reluctantly, he agreed to her power of persuasion. "I promise."

"January first?"

"Yes," he nodded. "That will give me a bit of time to get used to the idea."

She threw her arms around him. "Thank you."

Jane always held a soft spot in his heart that made him want to do crazy things for her. Even though he didn't feel ready to take on fatherhood, he knew this was something she wanted. And for her, he would make that sacrifice.

Randy had been trying to reach his wife all afternoon. She wasn't answering her phone, and every time he called, her cellphone immediately went to voicemail. Unable to get in touch with her, he left a text message instead. *I love you. Been trying to reach you. Call me please.*

After a long day of physician duties, Randy stepped outside the hospital and checked his phone messages hoping Jane had responded. She left a text that simply said, *Went to SF. Will explain later.* She didn't say I love you or even place little hearts on the end of the message like she usually did. Overthinking this entire situation, he began to fear the worst. What the hell was she doing in San Francisco? And why didn't she tell him about this? Was she still upset because they were fighting last night? Frantically he dialed Jane's cellphone number again. Nothing. Voicemail. "Dammit, Jane, what the hell are you doing in San Francisco?"

When Randy got home, Jane's car was not in the garage and she was nowhere to be found. Muddle-headed, he dashed over to his parents' house.

When his mother answered the door, Randy had a horrorstricken look on his face. "What's wrong?" Ellen asked him.

He plopped on the couch.

His mother sat down beside him. "Honey, what is it?"

"It's Janey. I've been trying to call her all day, but she won't answer her phone. Apparently she went to San Francisco, but never told me she was leaving. All she did was leave a text message." He handed his phone to his mother to show her what the message said.

"What is she doing in San Francisco?"

"I don't know. She didn't even tell me she was leaving." His thoughts swirled a hundred miles a minute and a million questions bounced around in his head.

"Calm down," his mother advised. "I'm sure there's an explanation."

He raised his hand to his forehead and swallowed his pride. "You don't understand, Mom. Jane and I got into an argument last night, but I thought we worked it out."

"Let me get you something to drink. It'll clear your head." She ambled into the kitchen, leaving him to ponder his thoughts.

Mark heard the unnerved tone in Randy's voice and saw the fearful look on his face which made him chuckle a little, not because he found humor in this situation, but because he knew his son was a worry wart and most likely overdramatized this situation. "What were you arguing about?"

Randy explained, "Having a baby, then it escalated into a bunch of accusatory shit and I made her cry. I'm such an ass. Why do I do that to her?"

Teasing his son, Mark said, "Wait a minute, you two were discussing having a baby?"

"Yes." Irritated that his father dwelled on that statement, Randy declared, "But why does that matter right now? That is totally irrelevant."

Mark was certain Randy's anxiety was unfounded. "Randal, I'm sure your wife has a perfectly good reason for being in San Francisco. You are being irrational. Have you tried calling her?"

"I've been trying to call her all afternoon. That's my point. She isn't answering her phone. She seemed happy with what we agreed on last night and we even made love afterwards, that's why I don't understand this."

"You are jumping to conclusions. Is it that she isn't answering, or is her phone turned off for some reason?"

Her phone had been going directly to voicemail all day, which made his father's statement make sense, now that he thought about it. "But why would she go to San Francisco at the spur of the moment and not tell me?"

Mark chuckled at his oldest son's incessant worrying. "Why don't you pick up the phone and call her."

"I have been."

"Try again," Mark insisted.

Randy took in a cleansing breath and pressed the speed dial button for Jane's phone, praying she would pick up this time. When he heard her voice on the other end, he said, "Where the hell have you been? I have been trying to reach you for hours."

"You didn't get my message?" she asked.

"Yes, but what are you doing in San Francisco?"

"Daddy called me," she explained. "Brian's in the hospital. He's been hurt pretty badly, so I took the first flight I could."

"You scared the shit out of me."

"Why?"

"Because after last night, I thought…"

She knew exactly what he was thinking. "Randy, that's silly."

"You could have called and told me what was going on. I've been worried sick."

"I told you I'd let you know later. You worry too much," she declared.

Where had he heard that before? Seemed like people told him that all the time. "Brian's in the hospital? Is he ok?"

"I just got here, but it looks like he's gonna be on the injured reserve list for a while."

"What happened?" Randy asked.

"He dislocated his shoulder and broke his collarbone."

"Jesus, what the hell hit him, a mac truck?"

"No, a lineman bigger than him."

"I was unaware there was such a thing." Randy felt much better now that he talked to Jane. They spoke for a while before he asked, "When are you coming home?"

"Tomorrow afternoon. I needed to make sure Brian was alright. I'm sorry if I scared you."

After concluding this conversation, Randy hung up his phone and snorted under his breath, feeling foolish for being as melodramatic as he was.

"She had an explanation, didn't she?" Mark asked, knowing all along there was nothing to worry about.

Randy confirmed, "Yes she did."

"You are far too young to let minor issues like that bother you so much. You make mountains out of molehills. I'm surprised your blood pressure isn't higher than it is," Mark joked with his son. "I want to hear more about you and your wife discussing having a baby."

"Don't let Mom hear you say that."

Mark lowered his voice. "When is this happening?"

"We agreed to start trying after Christmas."

"Really?" Mark teased. "Another grandbaby, huh?"

Randy sighed heavily, "That's what Jane wants."

"You don't seem too thrilled about this."

"I'm not sure how I feel about this," Randy admitted. "I don't think I'm ready to be a father."

"Is anyone ever ready for that?"

Good point.

"Just enjoy it, Son. Use this opportunity to get closer to your wife."

Randy thought about the prospect of getting his wife pregnant, which would involve having sex with her over, and over, and over again. Hmm, maybe this wasn't so bad after all. "Have you heard from Robby?" he asked his father.

"No."

"Neither have I." Randy felt a burst of intense guilt. He rubbed his hand across his chin, and said, "I feel bad for throwing him out."

"You did what you had to do."

"But how do I know he's not starving to death on the street somewhere? He could be dead for all I know."

"Robert has to learn to face the consequences of his actions, Son. You did the right thing."

Randy wasn't so sure. "Then why do I feel so guilty about it?"

"Because he's your brother."

Chapter Thirty-One

It is a well-known fact that drug abuse takes a serious toll on a family's overall mental health. Fights between the user and other family members often tear apart the strongest relationships. Robby's addiction definitely fit into that mold. Randy hadn't heard from his brother in weeks. He had no idea where he was, what he was doing, or what kind of physical condition he was in. Cocaine users not only habitually used cocaine but also increased their dosage over time in a futile attempt to repeat or exceed the initial high. Not being able to do so, engrossed users stepped up their intake, which often led to deadly effects. Randy worried that Robby would fall into this self-destructive death trap.

Over a cup of coffee, Greg noticed Randy's distressed state of mind. "Are you alright?"

Randy set his cup on the table. "I'm worried about my brother. About a month ago I walked in on him sniffing cocaine. We got into a huge fight that turned physical and I threw him out of my house. We parted on very bad terms and I haven't seen him since. In fact, no one has seen or heard from him in almost a month. I keep waiting for a phone call telling me they found him passed out on the street or lying dead in a ditch somewhere. It scares the crap out of me."

"Have you tried calling him?"

"Yes, but he refuses to answer me," Randy said. "I hope he's alright."

Down in the ER, the ambulance wheeled in a patient who was vomiting, seizing, and drifting in and out of consciousness. These symptoms, along with the rapid heart rate, increased blood pressure, hyperthermia, and sweating, lead the ER staff to believe the patient was suffering from a drug overdose. His breathing became weak.

"Get an IV started on this patient." The doctor hooked him up to a cardiac monitoring system and gave him a sedative to decrease the elevated heart rate and blood pressure.

The EMT handed the doctor a small vial full of white powder. "We found this on him."

The doctor examined the vial's contents. The white powdery substance appeared to be cocaine. "Thank you." He handed the vial to a tech and said, "Send this and a blood sample down to the lab, asap."

"Yes, Doctor."

They injected the patient with drugs to manage seizures and minimize the stimulant effects on the Central Nervous System. To lower the patient's core body temperature, the ER crew used convection cooling methods, which involved spraying the patient's exposed body with tepid water while fans circulated air.

"Is there any ID on this patient? Did he come in with anyone?"

A nurse brought a wallet and a cellphone over to the doctor. "This is all we found."

He flipped through the patient's wallet searching for any form of identification. "Alright, call toxicology. I'll notify the family."

In the middle of his coffee break, Randy received a page. "Great," he said, glaring at his phone. "What's going on now?"

"Who is it?" Greg asked.

"The ER. Guess I better head down there." He gulped down the last of his coffee and rose to his feet. "I'll talk to you later, Greg." He tossed his cup in the trash and rushed down to the Emergency Room.

When he arrived, the ER physician on duty said, "Thank you for your prompt response, Dr. Hanson."

"No problem, Dr. Gallagher. What's up?"

"Will you come with me for a minute, please?"

"Sure."

He led Randy to a private room where his parents sat waiting. Surprised to see them, Randy asked, "What are you guys doing here?"

"Sit down, Randy," his father insisted.

"Why? What's going on?"

Dr. Gallagher answered, "Robert Hanson was brought in via ambulance about forty-five minutes ago."

"Robby?" Randy decided he better sit down.

"He was extremely disoriented, sweating profusely and convulsing. We thought he was going to slip into an unconscious state for a while, but we were able to sedate him long enough to stabilize his vitals. Blood tests indicated toxic levels of cocaine in his system. Does he have a history of usage?"

Randy answered the question, "Unfortunately, yes, but I didn't find out until about a month ago. Apparently he's been using for a while and none of us knew."

Dr. Gallagher interjected, "He's calm and resting at the moment. We have him on generous amounts of fluids and a sedative to help him relax, but I want to keep him for a few hours to monitor his vitals. As he detoxifies, he may develop chest pains or a headache. I want to make sure his cardiac status and seizures are under control before we release him."

Both Mark and Randy concurred that was the best treatment route.

The doctor exited the room, leaving Randy alone with his parents. Randy rested his elbows on his knees and stared down at the floor. "I should have seen this coming. I should've drug his ass in the car and drove him to rehab."

"Randy, be reasonable," his father said. "You and I both know that detox doesn't work unless the person affected is willing to embrace the treatment. He would have fought you every minute, and you know that."

"I know, but we should have done something. Maybe we could have prevented this."

"Robby has to admit he needs help before he will accept any help we offer him."

At the end of his shift that evening, Randy reported to the ER to check on Robby. He wasn't sure what he was going to say to him and didn't know if his brother even wanted to see him.

Dr. Gallagher was still on shift, scanning a computer monitor and jotting down some notes in a file.

"Good evening, Dr. Gallagher," Randy said.

The doctor looked up and grinned. "Hey."

"How's Robby doing?"

"His blood pressure has returned to normal and his heartrate has stabilized. Tests indicate no nerve damage. He's alert and coherent, but still a little groggy."

"Can I see him?"

"Of course." Dr. Gallagher escorted Randy back to the exam rooms. He skimmed through Robert's chart then tapped on the door. "Hello, Robert."

In a faint voice, Robby answered, "Hi, Doctor."

"You have a visitor," the doctor said.

Randy peeked his head in the door. "Hey, Rob."

Robert's eyes glossed over.

Dr. Gallagher sensed the emotional tension in the room and decided to give them some space. "I'll leave you two alone."

When Dr. Gallagher left the room, Randy pulled a chair up to Robby's bed. "How you feeling?"

"I'm a little shaky, but I'm doing ok." Before Randy spoke another word, Robby swallowed the lump in his throat and said, "Randy, I am so sorry."

"It's alright."

"No, it's not alright. You've done nothing but look out for me and I…" Tears clouded his vision. "I've hurt my family, I've betrayed your trust, and I totally fucked up my life. I'm the worst person in the world."

"No you're not. You just got mixed up with the wrong crowd and made some bad choices. But it's not too late to fix it."

"I don't know how."

"Let us help you. That's what family is for." Randy squeezed his brother's hand. "You gave us quite a scare today."

"It scared me too." Robby wiped his eyes and sniffled.

"You know I'll always be here for you. If you were having problems, why didn't come talk to me?"

"I don't know." He hung his head.

"You can't go through life keeping things bottled up and letting difficulties tear you down like this. You have friends and family who love you and want to help you. Don't try to go through life alone. Let me get you some help," Randy offered.

"I'm scared."

"I know you are, but there are good programs out there that can help you kick this habit and get you back on your feet."

Realizing how close to death he came and how much he'd hurt his family, Robby agreed to seek rehab.

The drug treatment center they checked him into offered around-the-clock medical supervision and a range of detox medications and techniques that would help ease the transition between intoxication and sobriety, allowing Robby to skip the intense discomfort and pain of withdrawal. Through exercise, group therapy, and staying active, this rehabilitation center offered a safe and sober environment where Robby could recover from his drug addiction and focus on living a healthy, productive life.

Randy offered his full support. Every day he stopped by to visit, which included bringing a container of Jane's homemade cookies and delivering a stack of Robby's favorite car magazines. Although Robby was on medication, he still suffered some physiological changes caused by cocaine withdrawal—vivid and unpleasant dreams, insomnia, and fatigue. Despite this, he remained in good spirits.

Shortly after checking Robby into detox, Randy received a 3x5 inch bubble envelope in the mail. It was postmarked Kirkland, WA but had no return address on it. He poked at it for a while before he broke the seal. Inside, wrapped in white tissue paper, was Jane's missing ring. Randy held it in his hand and stared at it. "Damn you, Robby."

Randy brought the ring to Jane. "Honey, look."

The moment she saw it, her eyed welled with tears. "You got it back?"

"No. Robby did. He mailed it to me. He didn't include a note or anything, but I know it was him."

Jane slipped the ring on her finger. "You have no idea how much this means to me."

"Yes I do. But more importantly, Robby figured it out."

"How's he doing?"

"He's irritable and feels overwhelmed, but he's doing ok. Detox isn't pleasant." He set the empty envelope on the table. "He says thank you for the cookies, by the way."

"I made him another batch this afternoon."

"He'll appreciate that. Every bit of encouragement helps. He's vulnerable right now, and at high risk for relapse. We need to keep offering our support in any way we can."

Since full drug rehabilitation could take as long as ninety days, the family had to celebrate the holidays without Robby. To help pep up his spirits, they brought him piles of gifts, delivered leftovers from their holiday feast, and gave him a personal-sized Christmas tree for his room. The support his family offered helped Robby overcome the detoxification process. He was well on his way to a life of sobriety.

Chapter Thirty-Two

To commemorate New Year's Day, Randy pulled a medicine bottle out of his lab coat pocket. "Honey, come here for a sec. I want to give you something."

With a book in her hand, Jane inched over to him. He handed her the bottle.

Staring at it oddly, she asked, "What's this?"

"Pre-natal vitamins. One a day."

The prescription label on the bottle had her name printed on it, with Dr. Randal Hanson as the prescribing physician.

"No more alcohol for you, and make sure you are eating properly. Cut down on the Pepsis; you need to lower your caffeine intake. Keep your body in shape and exercise every day. Take your vitamins and stay away from secondhand smoke. I want a healthy baby, so listen to your doctor, please."

"My doctor? Who said I wanted you to be my doctor?"

Randy was drawn back this comment. "You don't want me to be?"

"I definitely want you." She leaned over and kissed him. "I love you, Dr. Hanson. Thank you."

"You're welcome. But I have one condition with this."

"What's that?"

"We stay spontaneous and let nature take its course. No ovulation calendars, no menstrual cycle charts. If it happens, it happens. If not, we keep trying."

She agreed.

His thoughts turned to steamy imaginings. Randy took Jane's hand and led her toward the stairs.

"Where are we going?"

"Upstairs to make a baby. Can't do it alone though. Could use a little help."

A few weeks passed. Randy had an hour and a half break between patients, so he set out for a bite to eat. Right as he stepped into the parking lot, Greg called him. "Hey, Randy. You have time to grab some lunch?"

"That's where I was headed."

"Sweet," Greg said. "Meet me at Cantinetta's in ten."

"Sounds great." Randy hopped in his car and joined Greg for Tuscan-style Italian fare.

"What you been up to?" Greg asked. "Haven't talked to you in a while."

"Trying to get Jane pregnant."

Greg found this amusing. "Really?"

"Yup."

"Gee, rough life, Hanson. You wake up with a pretty wife by your side, drive your Porsche to the hospital, work all day at a job you love, then go home to a big comfortable house, eat a nice home-cooked meal, and have sex all night."

"Yup, pretty much."

"Let me know if you need help with any of that."

Teasingly, Randy said, "Screw you."

"What are you doing this weekend?" Greg asked.

"Trying to get my wife pregnant, I told you that."

"Ok, what are you going to do when you're not partaking in mindless sex?"

"I don't know. Why?"

"Lakers are playing this weekend."

And Randy had every intention of watching the game. "Yes they are. You want to come over?"

Greg flashed two concert tickets in Randy's face. "Better idea. Lakers game Saturday afternoon and concert Sunday night. I have an extra ticket to the Shinedown concert. Wanna go?"

"Oh, hell yeah. I would love to go."

When Randy came home that evening, Jane had a discouraged look on her face. He draped his lab coat over a chair and asked, "What's wrong, Babe?"

Thwarted, she said, "I started my period today."

"Sometimes it takes a while. We'll keep trying." Offering encouragement, he gave her a kiss. "What would you like to do for Valentine's Day?"

"I don't know."

"Well, you're picking. When you decide, let me know and I'll make reservations."

On February fourteenth, Randy waltzed in the door with a dozen roses, a box of chocolate, and a teddy bear in his hands. "Hello, Beautiful," he announced. He gave his wife a kiss and held the flowers out to her. "Happy Valentine's Day."

She sniffed the flowers, taking in their sweet scent. "These are beautiful. Thank you, Sweetie."

He handed her the teddy bear and a box of dark chocolate raspberry squares. "Are you going be ready to go out in about an hour?"

"Yes." She pulled a chocolate from the box and ate it. Then she fed one to Randy.

"I'm gonna hop in the shower real quick. I smell like a hospital."

After dinner, Randy kissed all over Jane as they stumbled into the house. He closed the door with his foot and they continued up the stairs to the bedroom, slowly taking one step at a time. While attempting to maneuver to the bed, he set his cellphone and keys on the dresser. The keys fell onto the floor, but he didn't care. He left them there. He laid Jane on the bed, with him on top of her. Throughout the night, not thinking about anything except being together, they let passion get the best of them.

About a month later, Randy woke to the sun beating through the window, warming his body. He peered outside, surprised it wasn't raining. He stretched and reached his hand over to touch Jane. She was not in bed, but her covers were turned back and the spot where she had been lying was still warm. "Janey?" he called out to her.

She peeked her head out of the bathroom, looking pale with a sour expression on her face.

Her funny face made him laugh. "You ok?"

"I feel awful. I think I have a stomach bug." She sat on the bed holding her stomach.

He scooted over and wrapped his arms around her, kissing her neck. "I'm sorry you're not feeling well."

"This happened yesterday too, after you left for work."

Randy probed for more information. "Are you running a fever?"

"No," she answered.

"Achy muscles?"

"No. But I've been tired lately, and the last two days I woke up with a headache."

He had a diagnosis in his head, but wanted to know more about her symptoms first. "Are you breasts tender?"

Jane jerked her head around and glared at him. "What do my breasts have to do with anything?"

"I'm serious. Are they?" he asked again.

"A little, why?"

"You're not ill."

She wrinkled her forehead and cocked her head slightly. "Why else would I have headaches, feel tired all day, and puke for no apparent reason?"

He offered his diagnosis. "Because you're pregnant."

"And you are a crazy person." She pulled herself to her feet and headed to the shower.

"You have all the classic symptoms. Nausea, tender breasts, fatigue, headaches, and you haven't started your period yet, have you?"

"I'm a few days late."

"Because you're pregnant."

"How do you know?"

Was she serious? "Did you forget I'm an obstetrician? I see these symptoms every day, and I'm telling you, you're pregnant."

She smirked at him.

"You don't believe me, do you?"

"No, I don't."

Trying to justify his opinion, Randy said, "Fine. I'll run to the drugstore and pick up a pregnancy test right now." He got up and slipped on some clothes. "But when it comes back positive you owe me breakfast."

When he returned home, he opened the box and handed Jane a urine cup. "Fill 'er up," he teased.

She humored him and took the specimen cup into the bathroom.

"Here," she said, handing it back to him.

Randy laughed.

When Jane left the room to put a load of clothes in the washer, Randy administered the test. It turned pink. "Uh, Honey," he called down the stairs. "Will you come up here please."

She trampled back upstairs. "What?"

He showed her the pink dip stick. "It's pink. Pink means pregnant." He stared at her with a smug grin on his face. "I told you so."

She snagged the box off the counter and read the instructions. "How does this thing work?"

He explained it to her, "It detects the presence of the hCG hormone, which is secreted by the placenta shortly after fertilization. The only way to get a positive test result is if the hCG hormone is in your system."

Sure enough, the box said pink was positive. Randy was right. With tears in her eyes, she held the pink indicator in her hand. "We're pregnant?"

"Yes, Ma'am." Randy was far more excited about this than he thought he was going to be. He didn't think he was ready to be a father, but now that it was becoming a reality, he couldn't stop smiling. "We're going to have a baby."

A tear rolled down her cheek.

Randy wiped it away and gave her a kiss. "Come on, Mrs. Hanson. You owe me breakfast, and pancakes sound mighty tasty." He winked at her and headed downstairs.

Monday, Jane reported to Harborview clinic about twenty minutes before Randy was scheduled to get off. No patients were in the waiting room, and everyone seemed to be wrapping things up for the day. She stepped up to the front counter. "Excuse me."

The receptionist looked up. "May I help you?"

"Yes," Jane replied. "I'm here to see Dr. Hanson."

"Do you have an appointment?"

"I suppose you could say I do. He's my husband."

The receptionist smiled at her. "You must be Jane."

"Yes."

"He said you'd be coming in," the receptionist confirmed. "Come on back."

Jane followed the receptionist back to the examination rooms. Randy and another physician stood in an office discussing some charts. The moment Randy he saw his wife, he set the chart down on the desk. "Hey, Baby. You ready for your examination?"

"Yup."

"Good." Randy summoned the nurse and a medical student to help him. "Diane, can we get a file started on her, please?"

"Yes, Doctor."

He gave a directive to the medical student. "We need weight, BP, proteins, and we'll need blood drawn when I'm finished with her."

"Blood?" Jane asked jeering at her husband, not at all liking what he said.

"Yes, blood," Randy clarified. "We'll need to do blood typing on you, check for diseases, and run a bunch of tests to make sure everything's normal. Go with Diane and she'll get you started."

Jane filled out some forms, stood on the scale, then sat in a room where the nurse took her blood pressure. She had to give a urine sample before she was led into an examination room. The nurse handed her a pink hospital gown. "You'll need to completely strip. Slip this gown on with the opening to the front and sit on the examination table. The doctor will be with you in a minute."

"Thank you." Jane did as she was asked and sat on the examining table waiting...and waiting...and waiting, moving her feet back and forth restlessly.

After what seemed like an eternity, Randy walked in with a medical chart in his hand. He flashed a big shit-eating grin, trying to contain the humor he found in this situation. He set her chart down by the sink and wheeled the stool closer to her so he could sit down. He stared at her for a moment.

"Why are you sitting there staring at me like the wolf in Little Red Riding Hood?"

"I find this funny. You playing patient and me playing doctor. I'm afraid that gown isn't very flattering on you, Babe."

Unimpressed with his mockery, she said, "Shut up and do whatever it is you're going to do to me."

He picked up her chart again and quickly read over it. The urine test confirmed pregnancy, which he already knew. He checked her weight, protein count, temperature, and blood pressure results before he set her chart back down and washed his hands. "Prelims look good. Now lie back."

"What are you gonna do?"

Randy stood next to the examination table. "First I'm going to give you a breast exam, then I'm going to give you a pelvic exam and see if I can determine, by the enlargement of your uterus, how far along you are. And I'm going to give you a Pap."

She curled her lip. "Yuck. I hate those."

"I know. But I'm gentle, I promise." He popped his head out the door and called out, "Diane."

The nurse came in while Randy slipped on a pair of latex gloves.

"Why do you have to have another person in the room with you?" Jane asked.

"Liability reasons. Don't want a sexual assault accusation."

"But I'm you wife."

"I know. But it's standard procedure; I have to do it. Now lie down and hold still," he ordered.

He opened her gown and quickly moved his hands over her breasts checking for abnormalities. "Scoot down more." He put her legs in stirrups and performed a Pap on her then pressed his fingers down on her abdomen.

"Ow!" she said, wiggling and squirming around.

"You are a terrible patient. Hold still." He paused his examination briefly and developed an odd expression on his face. "Hmm, probably about four weeks." He removed his gloves and tossed them in the medical waste bin. The nurse took the Pap sample and left the room. Randy washed his hands, took a quick measurement of her abdominal girth, then wrote something on her chart. When he was done, he whipped out his iPad and typed in some data.

"What are you doing?" Jane asked.

"Calculating a due date." He read the information on the screen. "We're due around November sixth." He wrote that down on her chart. "You can get dressed now. Before we leave, I'll need to get a few blood samples, then we'll head over to ultrasound to confirm the due date. That will give us a chance to get accurate measurements on the embryo and check for a heartbeat." He closed her chart and set his pen down, giving her a serious stare down. "If you want me to be your doctor then you need to take my medical advice."

"You're going to love telling me what to do, aren't you?" she scoffed.

"I mean it. I'm going to give you some orders and you better listen."

More serious now, she said, "I'm listening."

Randy leaned against the counter and crossed his arms. "Your weight is good, but you should be gaining about two to three pounds a month. Keep taking your vitamins. I'll write you a prescription for a six month supply. Do not take any other medications whatsoever without asking me first. Not even Tylenol."

"Ok," she giggled at his seriousness.

He stood up and gave her a kiss. "As soon as you're dressed, see Ms. Lu. She's going to draw some blood."

Jane came out of the lab holding a cotton ball bandage on the crook of her elbow.

The displeased expression on her face made Randy chuckle. "Nice face. What's up with that?"

"All of this poking and prodding at me. Is this really necessary?"

"You're done with most of it, for a while anyway. Goes with being pregnant."

Randy took several pictures of the embryo and printed out a few sonograms. Seeing his child for the first time nearly brought tears to his eyes. He turned the ultrasound monitor around so Jane could see too. "Look, Honey. It's our baby."

The image was so tiny, it was hard to make out it was a baby at all. "Where?"

Randy pointed out the tiny seven millimeter embryo. "And there's a healthy heartbeat." When he was finished, he handed her a paper towel so she could wipe imaging gel off her tummy. "Clean up. Let's go home."

Randy kept two sonograms for himself and had the others placed in Jane's file.

The next morning, Randy's cellphone rang. It was Jim. "Yo, Hanson. How's it goin'?"

"Got some interesting news last night," Randy answered, stepping into the bedroom so he could talk to his friend while he got ready for work.

"Oh yeah? What's that?"

"Jane's pregnant."

Jim wasn't sure if Randy was joking around or if he was telling the truth. "Are you serious?"

"Yup, about four weeks. She's due November sixth."

"It's about damn time. Congratulations, Bro."

"Thank you."

Randy decided it was time to tell his parents the news. After dinner that night, he and Jane took a walk to his parents' house. Over casual conversation with his father, Randy pulled out a sonogram. He had covered Jane's name with medical tape so his dad wouldn't know it was hers. "Take a look at this and tell me what you think."

Mark put on his glasses to get a better look. He carefully examined the image. "About four to five weeks gestation. Placenta normal." He looked up at Randy and said, "There's nothing unusual about this sonogram, Son."

"I know."

"Then why did you give it to me?"

"Take the tape off the top."

Mark didn't see the point, but to humor his son, he peeled off the medical tape to unveil the name Hanson, Jane. Mark took off his glasses and questioned his son. "Is this accurate?"

"Yes, Sir."

"I'll be damned." Mark called to his wife, "Ellie, come here."

Ellen and Jane emerged from the kitchen.

Mark handed his wife the image of the embryo. "Look at this."

Ellen immediately noticed the name on the top. Her hand covered her mouth. "Jane is…"

"Pregnant," Randy confirmed.

Ellen tightly squeezed her daughter-in-law. "Congratulations, Honey."

"Thank you," Jane replied.

She squeezed her son so tightly he could barely breathe. "I'm so excited."

"Mom, you're choking me." Randy tried to pry her off. "Please."

She let go and joined them in the living room.

Randy explained to his father, "I'm having her chart, ultrasound scans, and all the lab work I did on her today transferred up to your office. She wants me be her doctor, but I need a home to do it until I'm finished with my residency."

Happy to comply with his son's request, Mark replied, "No problem at all, Son."

"She's scheduled to come in, in four weeks, for her second appointment. Figured I'd do it in the evening, that way I won't interfere with you and your patients. Is that ok?"

"Sounds like a good plan," Mark stated.

Wallowing in bed with Jane's head on his chest, Randy thought about the prospect of becoming a father—the time commitment involved, all the furnishings and items the baby needed. He started to make a mental shopping list. Realizing the herculean task put before them, he said, "We have a lot of stuff to get."

"We do."

"We said that spare room would be a nursery someday. Guess we should get rolling on that."

"What do you think of teddy bears?" Jane asked him, hoping he would approve. "Pale yellow trim with teddy bears."

"Why am I not surprised you said that?" Randy moved his hand down to her tummy. "What do you think of Archibald?"

"Archibald?" she asked.

"Yeah. We'll name the baby Archibald Hanson." Of course he wasn't serious. He just wanted to see her reaction.

"That is a terrible name."

"What about Beelzebub?"

"Randy, be serious."

"I've got it. Zeus. That's a good strong name." His voice deepened as he flexed his muscles and puffed out his chest. "Zeus the thunder god."

"Randy."

He chuckled and kissed her head. "We'll think of something. We have thirty-six weeks to decide. We'll narrow it down once we determine gender. Right now we need to get the nursery done and buy a bunch of baby crap."

"I need to call Daddy tomorrow and tell him," Jane said.

"I already told Jim. I gave Bruce and Steph a call last night and let them know. I'll send a bulk e-mail out to everyone else later today." He rubbed her belly. "Seems strange, doesn't it?"

"What does?"

"We're gonna be parents."

Even though he was still uncertain about all of this, he did feel a sense of pride knowing he had fathered a child. More importantly, Jane was happy, and to him that's what mattered most.

Chapter Thirty-Three

To celebrate Robby's success at being six months drug free, the entire Hanson family gathered at Randy's parents' house. Randy, Bruce, Stephanie, and Jane sat on the deck in lawn chairs taking in the glorious view and carrying on pleasant conversation. Jane developed a sour expression and ran into the house. Randy set his beer down and followed her, tapping lightly on the bathroom door. "Honey, are you ok?"

He heard the toilet flush.

Jane opened the door with a repulsed scowl on her face. "What happened to morning sickness? I feel sick all day long."

"Try eating some crackers." He found a package of Saltines in the pantry and handed them to Jane. "Here. See if this helps."

Despite feeling queasy, Jane ate well at dinner. Randy snuck up behind her and placed his hand on her tummy. "Feeling any better?"

She placed her hand over his. "A little. I think I needed food."

"You always need food," he teased. "Pregnant or not. You and food are magnetized to each other."

She parted her lips and grunted at him. "That's not true."

"You are always hungry. And now that you're pregnant, I won't be able to keep the fridge stocked." He laughed and softly kissed her.

Later that night, Randy sat on the bed removing his shoes and socks. His wandering eyes followed Jane.

Jane pulled her shirt off exposing her tummy, which wasn't showing the slightest signs of carrying a baby. Her breasts, however, were more voluptuous than ever.

Making eyes at her, he said, "Come here." He patted the mattress, inviting her to sit down.

She plopped down next to him and scooted closer.

He grabbed his stethoscope off the bedside table and slipped it on his ears, moving the bell down to her tummy.

"What are you doing?"

"Ssh, Zeus is talking to me." He listened intently.

"Randy."

"Quiet. I can't hear." Seconds later, he removed the stethoscope and sat up. "Zeus says he wants Oreos."

"The baby did not say that," she denied. "And quit calling him Zeus."

"Zeus Hanson has a nice ring to it, don't you think?" he joked.

"No." She stood up and slipped a red negligee over her head.

Randy chanted, "O-re-os. O-re-os."

"Oreos will fry the baby's brain."

"They will not. You eat yogurt and I don't see any toxic effects."

"That's not funny." He leered at him and snuck into the bathroom.

Jane wasn't playing along with his silly antics like she usually did. In fact, she seemed irritated with him tonight. "You alright, Honey?"

"I'm fine."

He knew better. Concerned about her woefulness, he stood up and joined her. "What's wrong?"

Her eyes became weepy.

"Why are you crying?"

She sniveled and rested her head on his chest.

Fluctuating emotions were normal during pregnancy. Although deep down he found her hormonal changes amusing, he tried to be sympathetic towards her. "Baby, it's ok."

The waterworks began to flow. "I'm gonna get fat."

"You're not going to get fat. You're pregnant. There is a difference." He rubbed his hand across her cheek and wiped her tears away. "I think you're beautiful, and the fact the you're carrying my baby makes you even more beautiful." He kissed her softly on the lips. "I love you. I'll always love you." He held her a bit tighter and let her release her emotions.

Bruce had three days off before he had to return to his neurosurgery duties in L.A. Since Randy had patients on his schedule, Bruce took it upon himself to purchase paint, rollers, and paint brushes. He pulled up to Randy and Jane's house ready for a painting party.

"I'm here to decorate the nursery," he told Jane. He shuffled inside and set one of the paint cans on the kitchen island. "I picked up the paint you wanted. Which room do you want transformed?"

Jane was not expecting this. "Thank you. Randy will be so surprised."

Bruce lugged all the painting equipment up to the spare bedroom then moved furniture to the middle of the room and draped plastic over it. He spread drop cloths on the floor and opened the windows to provide ventilation. He worked for five hours, painting the walls pale yellow, putting up teddy bear decals, and hanging up curtains that Stephanie sewed from cute teddy bear fabric. By the time he was finished, the room was bright and cuddly-looking. Bruce moved the bookshelf back against the wall and Jane placed a few teddy bears on the top shelf.

"I hope he likes it," Jane said.

"He will," Bruce replied. "I saved him a butt load of work."

When they heard a car pull up, Jane peered out the window to see Randy standing by the bed of Mark's truck. She and Bruce both headed outside to investigate.

When Randy saw her, he greeted her with a kiss. "I picked up something for the baby today." He opened the tailgate to reveal a large cardboard box. "Hey, Buckman. Help me unload this thing."

The men lugged the box upstairs. As soon as Randy walked in the baby's room, a huge smile filled his face. "Wow! It looks great in here. Who did this?"

"I did," Bruce said.

"Thanks. I love it."

Bruce fixated on the box, imagining what mysteries would unleash from it. "What's in the box?"

"A crib," Randy said. He pulled out a pocket knife and cut though the cardboard. "Hopefully it won't be too much of a pain in the ass to put together."

When Bruce and Stephanie returned to Los Angeles, Bruce checked the bank account balance with his cellphone. Almost three-thousand dollars was missing. He studied the banking statement to discover several department store transactions, all of which occurred on the same day. At first he thought someone had gotten ahold of his credit card information and fraudulently used it as their own. Then he remembered seeing Stephanie in a new outfit this morning. He decided to question her before he notified the bank.

With his cellphone in his hand, he marched into the living room. "Steph, did you go shopping earlier this week?"

"I bought myself a few new outfits. Why?"

"A few?" He held his phone up to her face. "You spent three-thousand dollars."

She turned her eyes away.

"We have rent due, bills to pay, a daughter to feed, and I have student loan payments to make. You can't frivolously spend money like that."

"All I did was go shopping."

He tightened his jaw. "You spent money we don't have, and you did it without asking me."

"I have to have permission to go shopping?"

"When you carelessly exhaust our bank account like that, yes. If you want to go on shopping sprees then maybe you should get a job."

"How come you can spend money but I can't?" she snarled.

Her argumentative tone made him cringe. "I spend money on essentials. You blow away money on crap we don't need. You already have an entire closet full of outfits you never wear. How can you justify buying another three-thousand dollars' worth of clothes?"

"I think I should be able to buy whatever I want." She stomped out of the room.

Bruce didn't let her off that easily. He followed her into the bedroom and closed the door. "We need to talk about this."

"There's nothing to talk about."

"Yes there is," he argued. "I'm angry you chose to do this without consulting me, yet you act like it's no big deal. We're supposed to make decisions together."

"How can we make decisions together if you're never home?"

Ouch. That was a low blow. "What do you mean, I'm never home? I spend every minute I have off with you and Emily."

"Every time I try to call you, you refuse to answer your phone."

"I'm in the middle of a procedure, Steph. I can't just walk away from a man's exposed brain to check my phone messages. People's lives are at stake here."

"Obviously those people are more important to you than I am." Feeling neglected, she turned her back to him and stormed off.

Days later, Randy reached into the refrigerator to grab a carton of orange juice. Jane sat on a stool at the kitchen island and, for no apparent reason, started to cry.

"What's wrong?" Randy asked, setting the carton on the counter.

Tears flowed from her eyes. "Nothing."

Jane's moodiness flared up at inopportune times, like in the middle of meals, during sex, or pretty much any time she looked at her reflection in the mirror. Jane had expressed to him her concerns about putting on weight as her body expanded to accommodate pregnancy, and even though he complimented her daily and told her how beautiful she was, she felt self-conscious. The emotional rollercoaster she seemed to be plummeting down caused him as much stress as it did her. He sometimes felt like everything he said made her tear up.

With sympathetic eyes, he leaned against the counter. "Do you need something? Want something? Whatever you want, I'll give it to you, but you have to tell me. I can't read your mind, Babe."

"I don't know what I want."

Randy took a deep breath. Cautiously, he approached Jane and put his arms around her. "Honey, I don't know what you're going through right now, but I'm trying to understand. Talk to me. Tell me how you feel. Tell me what you want."

She melted into his arms, crying on his shoulder.

Pregnancy really seemed to be doing a number on her emotionally. Randy understood the complexity of increased hormonal levels and the elevated emotions pregnancy could cause, but never really comprehended its significance until he experienced it firsthand with Jane. Seeking advice, Randy met his father for lunch. "I'm worried about Jane."

"Why?" Mark asked.

"She has no idea what she wants. She laughs one second and cries the next. She's an emotional wreck."

"You know what increased hormonal levels can do."

"I know, but I had no idea it would affect Jane like this. I don't know how to help her because when I ask her what she wants, she says she doesn't know."

"She probably doesn't."

Randy fiddled with his wedding ring. "I hope this wears off soon. It's driving me nuts."

"It'll taper off," his father advised. "The best thing you can do for her right now is reassure her that you love her and be a supportive husband."

"I'm trying," he explained.

"This pregnancy experience you're going through with Jane will make you a better obstetrician, Randy.

You'll see and experience what Jane goes through, which will give you an alternative perspective. It will make you more empathic to your patients' needs and concerns. Use this as a learning experience."

"Did Mom get like this?"

"Not as badly as Jane seems to be affected by it, but every woman is different. How's she doing otherwise?"

"Nausea. She's tired all the time and her breasts are sore, so I have to be careful when I hug her," Randy said. "And she's been craving peanut butter sandwiches lately."

"How are you doing?"

Randy exhaled heavily. "I don't know if I'm ready for all this."

"I don't think anyone is ever ready for it, Son." He patted Randy on the shoulder. "You're going to be fine. Just support your wife right now, and enjoy watching her body change as your baby grows. Be actively involved."

"I am," Randy confirmed.

"Good. That's the best thing you can do."

Chapter Thirty-Four

Jim flew up to Seattle to spend the weekend with Randy. Together, the men took off in the Porsche, styling their sunglasses and leather jackets. Typically this time of year Seattle was damp and cool with overcast skies. But on this particular spring day, the weather was warm and sunny. By far it was the warmest day they'd had in May, reaching a high of seventy-eight degrees. The men took off their jackets and put the top down on the Porsche. Tunes cranked out as they cruised around the city in search of a suitable place to have lunch. They ended up at Pacific Inn Pub, relaxing on an outdoor deck munching on the city's best fish-and-chips and sipping on tasty brews.

"Bet you're lookin' forward to joinin' up with your dad next month, aren't ya?" Jim said.

"Very much so. Been working my whole life for this."

"Workin' your whole life so you can work your whole life."

Randy had to laugh. "Yes, but think about what we do, Jim. We're doctors. We make an impact on the world, saving lives and bringing new life into the world."

"For you, that's the literal truth right now. How's Jane doin'?"

Randy lifted a shoulder. "Morning sickness has hit her pretty hard. And the hormonal changes are getting the best of her. She's been really moody."

"That sounds about right." Jim took a sip of his beer. "You excited?"

"About what?"

"Bein' a dad."

Excited was not the word he would have chosen. Scared to death or nervous would have been more accurate. "Don't feel at all ready for this."

"Of course you don't. But that's not what I asked you."

"Let's put it this way," Randy said. "Sharing this experience with Jane has been bonding for both of us in a way we've never experienced."

"Good. Enjoy it while you can. Before you know it you'll be holdin' that baby in your arms, and that, my friend, will soften your heart more than you realize." Changing the subject, Jim stated, "I have some news I think you're going to like. Remember when I told you I wanted to get out of San Francisco and relocate after my residency?"

"Yeah."

"Swedish Medical Center was scopin' for Emergency Medical Personnel, an ER physician and RNs experienced in emergency care in particular. Jill and I inquired into this."

Swedish Medical Center was the hospital where Randy's father delivered all his private practice babies. Randy had done a few rotations there during his residency. "Swedish? Like Seattle's Swedish?"

"Yup, and they offered both me and Jill positions in the ER."

Jim was full of shit most of the time, so Randy didn't believe one iota of the crap that came out of his mouth. He was convinced this was another one of Jim's sick jokes. "That isn't funny."

"I'm serious, Dude. The director, Dr. Minosa, offered me the position last week. I start July fifteenth. Jill and I begin the moving process July first. While I'm up here, I was hopin' to check out a few houses we've been lookin' into."

The expression on Jim's face and the earnestness in his voice made Randy realize he was telling the truth. "You're moving to Seattle?"

"Yup. Just waitin' to get my Washington State License in the mail."

Randy's eyes widened. He didn't know what to say. "You didn't tell me you were looking into this."

"I wanted to surprise you, but didn't want to say anything until I knew Jill and I had positions secured here. Less than two months and I'm here, Bro. I'll be right down the street again. We can catch Lakers games, eat Oreos, and shoot hoops like we did before."

"Holy shit." Randy's entire face lit up. "This is awesome. Best news I've heard in a long time."

The article Randy wrote for his resident research project, Streets of the Lost, went out for publication in several medical journals and health magazines. The topic he focused on was youth and pregnancy. After dealing with so many pregnant young girls who had no prenatal care, Randy interviewed homeless adolescent girls to get their feelings and experiences about pregnancy. What he discovered over the course of the research was that ninety-two percent of the female youths on the streets of Seattle were sexually active, starting at very early ages. Average age of first consensual sex was thirteen years for these street girls. Several were underage prostitutes. Thirty-three percent of these girls reported becoming pregnant and none had prenatal care. Through these interviews, Randy discovered that for a lot of girls, getting pregnant was a big spur to leave the streets. The girls wanted to protect their child and therefore became more receptive to assistance. He was convinced that an intensive intervention, which led the girls toward community resources such as housing, health services, and educational or vocational training, would benefit greatly. There was no magic bullet or cure that would put these adolescents back together, but he knew that he and society couldn't afford to give up.

Because of his outstanding research endeavors with this project, the University of Washington awarded him the David Rothman Resident Research Award. After reading the publication himself, Greg said, "Congrats on the research award, Randy. That article was quite informative."

"Thank you."

"Only a few more weeks until you're official."

"I know. I'm excited."

"You ready for your Boards?"

Boards were specialized exams used to certify a physician in a particular specialty. The American Board of Obstetrics and Gynecology certified their doctors through a two-step process. The first was a day-long written examination consisting of objective, single-best answer, multiple-choice questions provided by board members where a doctor had to demonstrate that he or she had obtained the knowledge and skills required for the medical and surgical care of women. In the second step, the physician seeking certification took an oral exam. In order to become fully certified, a doctor had to pass both exams.

"Yup," Randy replied. "I spend a couple hours a night reviewing information from all my OB/GYN books and looking over my notes. My dad gave me some resources he used when he studied for his Boards. I've been checking those out too."

"Always best to be prepared. I take my oral next week," Greg said.

"Ooh, good luck with that."

"Thanks."

Randy took a sip of his coffee. "How's it going with Raquel?"

With a crooked smile, Greg replied, "Going well. Would like to move things forward a bit. I'm considering asking her to move in with me. Her lease is up the end of the month and she's looking for a new apartment. I thought I'd save her the search by offering mine."

"You think she's ready for that step?"

"We're getting pretty serious. I think she'll be open to it." Both men stood up and threw their coffee cups in the trash. "You want to play basketball this weekend?" Greg asked.

"Sunday would be best. Let's meet at the gym at nine."

"I'll be there."

The OB/GYN specialty only offered the Board exam once a year, on the last Monday in June. Randy's day was grueling, and by the time he came home, all he wanted to do was collapse on his couch. The first thing he did when he walked in the door was make a cup of coffee. "Jane!" he called to his wife from the kitchen.

She ran downstairs to greet him. "Hi, Sweetie. I didn't hear you come in."

He dumped sugar in his coffee cup and stirred. "How you feeling?"

"I haven't thrown up all day."

"I'd say that's better." He placed his hand on her tummy and met her with a kiss. "You ready to find out the gender of this baby?"

She nodded in anticipation.

"Good. Let me finish my coffee then we'll go."

Fetal gender determination was done by ultrasound at sixteen weeks or later with extremely high accuracy. Randy was well trained in ultrasonography and knew what to look for in a sonogram. As he examined the image of his baby on the monitor, the corners of his mouth raised.

His reaction made Jane ask, "What do you see?"

Randy turned the monitor and showed her. With the touch screen stylus, he drew a line around the outside of the fetus, pointing out the legs and buttocks. "And look here." He drew a circle around an appendage protruding between the legs. "It's a boy."

Jane squinted to get a better look. "I don't see it."

Randy again pointed out the identifying body part. "See? We're having a little boy."

Since the day they found out Jane was pregnant, Randy hoped for a boy. He was more worried about having a healthy baby, but now that he knew his child was a boy, he felt less apprehensive. In his eyes, raising a boy would be much easier than being the paranoid daddy of a little girl he was bound to overprotect.

He drew an arrow pointing to the baby's defining organs and wrote, It's a boy! He printed out the sonogram and handed it to Jane. He took a good shot of the baby's face and printed that out as well, keeping one copy for her file and one for himself. After he finished taking measurements, he wiped the imaging gel off her belly and pulled her shirt down. "You are done."

Jane sat up and stared at the ultrasound image. "Look at him."

"Yup. Baby Hanson," Randy said proudly. "And since he's a boy, the name Zeus still holds."

"We are not naming him Zeus."

He placed his hand on her thigh. "I know. I'm kidding."

Chapter Thirty-Five

Randy and Mark Hanson spent a good amount of time setting up a schedule that was workable for both of them. The University of Washington School of Medicine offered Randy a clinical supervisory opportunity, so they included that into the schedule as well. The endless hours Randy spent learning various gynecologic surgical procedures made him one of the more highly-trained OB/GYNs in the region. In addition to his office calls, hospital rounds, and delivery duties, they scheduled a day for Randy to be in the Physicians Ambulatory Surgery Center to perform any needed surgical procedures on their patients. In order to keep their clinic open five days a week and see patients daily, but still be able to spend quality time at home with family, Randy and his dad planned to alternate off days and on-call statuses. Randy was on-call for deliveries all day Saturday. His off days were Friday and Sunday.

His first day on the job, Randy bounced around the house all morning. When he stood up to put his cup in the sink, he came up behind Jane and placed his hand on her protruding tummy.

"I think I felt the baby move last night," Jane said.

"Did you?"

"I think so. It felt like a fish swimming around in there."

Confirming her observations, he replied, "That's good. An active baby is a healthy baby." He rubbed her belly once more. "I gotta go." He grabbed his stethoscope, cellphone, and car keys then kissed her goodbye. "I'll call you later. I love you, Honey."

"I love you, too. Drive safely and have a great day."

"I will." He winked at her then headed out the door.

The clinic was located in a suite of a medical complex right across the street from Swedish Medical Center. Several other medical offices, a radiology lab, Starbucks coffee shop, Spectrum Gym, and a soup and sandwich café were also located there. When Randy saw the painted glass on the clinic door, a huge smile filled his face.

Women's Healthcare Physicians

Obstetrics and Gynecology

Mark E. Hanson, M.D., FACOG

J. Randal Hanson, M.D.

This was the coolest thing he had ever seen. He dedicated twenty-two years of school and four years of advanced training for this moment.

A while back, Randy's father gave him a key and alarm codes to the clinic. Randy used his key to unlock the door. The waiting room was inviting with several comfortable chairs, a few potted plants, and interesting wall art. Tables displayed magazines for patients to read and a large screen TV hung on the wall for patients to view as they waited for appointments. A glass bowl full of candy cane striped mints was freely available along with free water bottles. The open receptionist's counter displayed information about breastfeeding, WIC, infant care, and other women's health issues. Next to the brochures was a set of appointment cards with the clinic's address and phone number, one set with Randy's name and another with his father's.

A door led from the waiting room to the examination rooms. Randy opened this door and headed to the back. To his surprise, the entire clinic staff, including his father, stood at the counter holding a huge banner. *Welcome Aboard, Dr. Hanson!*

"Welcome, Son. We've been looking forward to this day for a long time."

Randy couldn't believe the trouble the clinic personnel went through to make him feel welcome. "Wasn't expecting this kind of reception."

Nancy, one of the nurses, said, "We have coffee brewing in the back for you with creamer, sugar, and everything else you need. And we already gave your schedule to the hospital."

"This is too much. Thank you."

Aside from the four examination rooms and two bathrooms this clinic had, it also housed a small lab on site where blood was drawn and pregnancy tests were performed. It was complete with a sink, microscope, and a cabinet with extra medical supplies, as well as tons of other lab equipment. The nurses' area contained a scale, blood pressure cuff, and several temporal thermometers. The clinic also had a decent-sized office space with a comfortable couch, a desk and rolling chair, and bookshelves full of medical reference material. Mark had some family portraits hanging on the wall. Randy brought a picture of Jane to add to the collection. One wall displayed all of Mark's degrees and certificates, as well as his medical license. The wall space next to it was empty. Randy planned to fill it with all of his framed accomplishments.

Growing up, Randy had visited this clinic at least a hundred times, but today it had new meaning to it. It was his clinic now.

"Geez, Dad. You went all out here."

"Of course. This is a big day for us. We are getting an incredible asset to our team." Mark eyed the appointment book. "A lot of patients knew you were starting today and specifically requested you, so you have several appointments this morning. A few names I've never heard before have also been calling and setting up appointments with you."

"I've gained a few loyal patients through my residency."

"That's good," Mark said. "More patients are welcome."

"Jane needs to come in this week too. She's due for another monthly exam."

"We'll have Samantha set her up."

The receptionist knew exactly what he meant. "I'll put her on the schedule."

Randy scanned the schedule to see what appointments he had.

Veronica, the file clerk, handed Randy a stack of patient charts. "These are all of your appointments today. I sorted them by time for you."

"Thank you."

Mark gave Randy two prescription pads with his name and clinic address on them. "I had these made for you too."

"You didn't have to do that. I can get my own."

"Consider it my gift to you for finishing your residency."

"Thanks." Randy grabbed one and shoved it in his pocket. With his stethoscope draped around his neck, he intently studied the first medical chart in his hand. He flipped through pages and jotted down a few notes.

Nancy tittered at him.

Randy looked up from the chart. "What is so funny?"

"I remember the little boy who used to come in here with his dad all the time," she said. "And now look at you. Dr. Randal Hanson."

"Yup, and I'm anxious to get started."

Mark unlocked the clinic door and the staff prepared for a busy day of appointments.

Before his first scheduled appointment, Randy reorganized the supplies in his two examination rooms and placed his prescription pad on the shelf by the sink. He found the Doppler, speculums, and other necessary equipment and quickly adapted to his new environment.

After years of hearing about how good Randy was, Mark was finally able to witness his son in action. The rapport he established with patients was outstanding. He was easygoing, had a sense of humor, and the patients found him easy to talk to. The notes he made on charts were thorough and insightful. Randy was well-organized and stuck to the schedule. Every patient left his examination room with a smile. They rescheduled with him and grabbed his appointment card on the way out the door.

Randy had a few minutes between appointments so he stepped into the break room to grab a cup of coffee. Mark went with him. As Randy stirred his cup, his father commented, "You have proven to be very popular, my boy. The patients love you."

Randy set his spoon down and picked up his cup. "Just doing my job." He took a sip of his coffee and checked the time on his watch. "I have a few minutes before my next appointment. I'm gonna call Jane and see how she's doing."

Within his first two weeks, Randy performed many procedures—Pap tests, pelvic exams, labor inductions,

Caesarian sections, and countless vaginal deliveries. He provided pre-natal and post-partum care and ordered HPV vaccines. He referred women to radiology for ultrasound examinations and to screening centers for mammograms. He counseled patients on proper health and nutrition during pregnancy and discussed birth control options with young women. He calculated the gestational age of pregnancies and counseled older women about their menopausal symptoms. Regularly, he prescribed pre-natal vitamins, birth control pills, and hormone-modulating therapies as well as standard drug therapies such as antibiotics and diuretics. He helped treat cancer and pre-cancerous diseases of the reproductive organs, sometimes making referrals to gynecologic oncologists for further evaluation and testing. And occasionally, he dealt with pregnant women in the ER when his expertise in the field was required.

As a clinical supervisor for the University of Washington School of Medicine, Randy performed various surgical procedures and deliveries under the watchful eyes of eager medical students. He conducted seminars and Grand Rounds on gynecologic and obstetrical issues as they pertained to the procedures the students were learning and supervised medical students when they performed their OB/GYN clinical skills. Randy took on this role enthusiastically and tried to expose the medical students to as many procedures as possible while educating them about the aspects of gynecology and obstetrics.

Through his practice, Randy heard stories from patients that touched the core of what it meant to be human. And being in close proximity to his patients, he became a witness to that humanity. Whether the story was about a woman's desire to be pregnant or her desire not to be pregnant, her diagnosis of cancer or her yearly examination, the stories they shared with him sometimes captured the essence of his very soul. His eyes still watered at births, and that motion of placing a new baby on a woman's chest never ceased to move him. He felt honored when a woman, young or old, trusted him with the story of her miscarriage. In the same breath, he got excited when a young teenager came into his clinic and he was the first person to explain to her about how her reproductive system worked, how to protect herself from infection, and what to do if her birth control or partner failed her. Like every doctor, he was always in awe over the strength he witnessed when taking care of a woman near the end of her life. These were some of the most privileged conversations in medicine that made the entire journey to it worthwhile. These conversations often made Dr. J. Randal Hanson his patients' new best friend.

Images of newborns, which quickly festooned the clinic walls, were a testament of his commitment to the health and lives of women and their families. This was satisfying work. What he never realized was how much fun the job would be. But by far, the most important job he had right now was getting Jane through this pregnancy.

Jane lay on the bed in the hot and humid summer heat, wearing only a tee-shirt and her panties, sound asleep. Her tummy bulged.

Randy quietly crept into the room and set his stethoscope on the dresser. He changed into more comfortable clothes then sat on the loveseat with a book of baby names in his hand. He flipped through several pages, jotting down names he liked. After a forty-five minute nap, Jane started to stir. Randy looked up from the book. "Hey, Sleepyhead."

She sat up and stretched. "Hi."

"When you wake up all the way, come here and sit by me for a minute."

She hobbled to the restroom then took a seat next to him. "What are you reading?"

"A book of baby names." He showed her the piece of paper he wrote a few names on. "What do you think of Richard?"

"Everyone will call him Dick. I don't like that."

"How about Alberto?" he said, trilling the R.

"No."

He turned the page. "What about this one?"

Jane read the name he was pointing to. "I don't even know how to pronounce that."

"Vachel. It's a French name."

She glared at him.

"Ok. I guess that's a no." On the next page, he saw a name that made him laugh. "Here's a great name for a doctor's kid. Viral."

Jane laughed with him. "Whatever happened to names like Billy and Bob?"

"I don't know," he said. "But Zeus is sounding better and better." Randy flipped through some more pages while Jane looked on. When his phone rang, he handed the book to her.

Jim was on the line. "Yo, Randy. What you up to?"

"Picking out baby names."

"Find anything you like?"

"Only came up with Viral and Zeus so far," he replied. "Who the hell writes these baby name books? Where do they come up with these names?"

"I have no idea. Hey, Jill and I just finished loading the U-Haul. We're gonna crash in a hotel tonight and head out in the morning."

With Jim only days away, Randy's excitement level elevated. "Sweet."

"And since Bruce is up there quite a bit, we'll all be together again."

"Minus Mandy and Sarah," Randy reminded. "Not quite the same, but I'll take it."

"I gotta go. Need to feed the kids, but I'll call you en route tomorrow."

"Drive safely."

"I will. Talk to you later, Dude."

"Later." Randy hung up and returned to looking at baby names with Jane.

"What do you think of Nathan?" she asked him.

He pondered this for a moment. "Nathan Hanson sounds good. I like it. But we need a good middle name to go with it."

"What about Randal?" Jane suggested.

"Randal's my name."

"So?"

He shook his head in disapproval. "No. I want him to have his own name, not mine. Randal and Jonathan are out of the question." He rattled off a few alternatives before the perfect name came to him. "James. No one in my family has that name."

She tested it to see how it sounded. "Nathan James Hanson." A huge smile decorated her pretty face. "I like it."

"I like it too." Randy took the book out of her hand and set it on the table, leaning over to kiss Jane's belly as he did. "You hungry, Nathan?"

"He can't hear you."

"Sure he can. Fetuses can hear sounds. He hears your voice and your heartbeat. His vocal chords are forming, he can suck his thumb, blink, and swallow. He has fingernails and skin, and he's even starting to get hair on his head now. His lungs are developing, all of his major organs have formed, and his tiny heart pumps about six gallons of blood a day."

"Really?"

"Yup. All kinds of stuff going on in there," he said. "So, are you hungry?"

"Mmm hmm."

"Good. I'll fix dinner." He held out his hands and pulled her out of the loveseat.

Chapter Thirty-Six

The minute Jim hit the Seattle city limit sign on Interstate-5, he pulled out his phone and called Randy to let him know he was in town. Upon hearing this news, Randy drove over to Jim's new house, which was not far from the medical district. Leaning against his Porsche, Randy stood in the driveway anxiously waiting.

An orange and white U-Haul drove up the street and parked by the curb. A blonde man in a bright yellow tropical shirt, a pair of faded jeans, flip flops, and Oakley sunglasses stepped out of the truck.

The men greeted each other with a hug. "Damn it's good to see you." Randy quickly scanned the area. "Where's Jill?"

"She's comin'. She had to stop at the gas station to deal with an episode the kids had in the car." Jim took his sunglasses off and hung them on the front of his shirt. "Travelin' with kids is a pain in the ass. We had to stop more than I wanted to because they can't all seem to go to the bathroom at the same time. And they're hungry all the damn time."

"Great," Randy scoffed. "You're supposed to be telling me how wonderful fatherhood is."

"Oh, it is. I just don't like traveling long distances with the kids. Drives me fuckin' insane, which is why Jill took the kids in the car and I drove the truck."

"Good plan."

Jim breathed in a huge breath of air, clearing his lungs. "Fresh air. I haven't smelled that in a long time."

"We had some rain yesterday, but it's been clear all day today."

"Then help me unload this truck before it starts to rain again."

The men opened the truck's roll up door and began lugging furniture and boxes into the house.

About an hour later, Jill pulled up with a huge bucket of Kentucky Fried Chicken, mashed potatoes, coleslaw, and biscuits. She had a gallon of milk for the kids and a six pack of Corona for Jim and Randy.

"Oh sweet. Grindage," Jim said. He took the bucket of chicken from Jill and set it on the table. "Think Jane will want to join us?"

"Probably, but she won't eat this."

"That wife of yours doesn't eat anything."

"Yes she does. In fact she can eat quite a bit, especially lately." Randy pulled his cellphone out and dialed Jane's number. "I'll have her bring over some paper plates."

Randy and Jim were unloading the sofa from the moving van when Jane pulled up. They set it on the living room floor and collapsed in it.

With a cup carrier of coffee in one hand and a grocery bag in the other, Jane leaned over the sofa and gave Randy a kiss. "Hey, you."

"Hey."

"I see you're working hard."

"Yup. And I see you brought coffee. Thank you." He pulled one from the drink carrier, cupped both hands around it, and took a sip.

Jane's belly bulged, and she waddled when she walked. Jim got a kick out of seeing this. "You either swallowed a watermelon or you have a baby brewin'."

288

Jane turned her eyes to Jim. "Hi, Jim."

"You look fantastic," he remarked.

"Thanks."

"Won't be too much longer before we have a little Hanson runnin' around."

Jane pulled a box of popsicles and a deli sandwich out of the grocery bag. "I picked up some ice cream for the kids."

When Jim's children heard the word ice cream, they darted into the room. Sabrina stopped for a minute and stared at Jane. "You're having a baby."

Jane put her hand on her tummy. "Yes, we are. We're having a little boy."

"Boys are gross," she said with a sneer. She grabbed a red popsicle and exited the room almost as quickly as she entered it.

Randy and Jim looked at each other and laughed.

The physical brutality of moving heavy furniture and the knuckle-banging chore of putting beds and shelves together wore Randy and Jim out. The long trip exhausted the kids too, but the Ryan family was excited about their relocation prospects.

With Randy's help, Jim and Jill learned their way around the medical district of Seattle fairly quickly. They found a good babysitter for the kids and easily adjusted to life in the Pacific Northwest. Once established in their new home, Jim and Jill began their first shift at Swedish Medical Center.

Adding Jim and Jill to the Emergency Room staff was a definite asset to the hospital. And the coolest thing about it was that Randy had privileges at Swedish Medical Center. Working at the same hospital was an experience both Randy and Jim hoped for since they started this whole medical school journey. Their wish finally came true.

Randy and Mark tossed some lines into the lake searching for the perfect trout. The water was calm and a light layer of fog blanketed the lake. They had a half dozen donuts to munch on, a gallon of orange juice, and a couple cups of Starbucks coffee. Anticipating a big catch, Randy baited up his line.

"How's Jane doing?" Mark asked his son.

"She likes her job, and she's gained quite a few clients. Those kids she works with at the Y are making good progress. It's cute to watch them play basketball."

"No, I mean how's she doing with this pregnancy," Mark clarified. "She's your patient. I haven't looked at her chart."

"Oh," Randy chuckled. "She's coming along nicely. We heard the heartbeat last week and she's gained eight pounds." He cast his line out. "I see pregnant patients every day, but I've never witnessed pregnancy firsthand like this. I get to see the physical changes every day and experience the emotional aspects right along with my wife, and I have to say, I'm really enjoying this. I'm kind of jealous though."

"Why?" Mark asked his son.

"She can feel the baby squirming around. Can't wait 'til I can feel the baby move."

Mark reeled in his line and changed his bait. "I'm assuming you were planning on making this delivery."

"Yes I was," Randy confirmed.

"Delivering your own child is going to be difficult."

"I can handle it."

"I have no doubt you can handle it, Son. You've done many deliveries on your own. But I'm telling you that seeing your wife lying there going through labor is a lot different than having a patient on an examination table. You'll be present for every contraction, every pain she feels. It's going to be more challenging than you ever anticipated."

"I'm prepared for that."

"Delivering my own children was the scariest experience of my life. If you decide you need me…"

"I can handle it, Dad," Randy insisted. "I'll be fine."

Chapter Thirty-Seven

Randy and Jane were scheduled to go to a dinner party with Randy's parents that night. It was an important party that would allow Randy the opportunity to establish his reputation with local medical professionals, and he was looking forward to mingling with a few of them.

Randy was in the bathroom putting on his tie when he heard Jane crying. He stepped out to see what was wrong. She sat on the bed surrounded by dresses, frantically throwing them from one side of the bed to the other. "What's the matter?"

"I can't wear any of these. My tummy sticks out and it looks awful."

"You're pregnant. You can't expect to fit into your size six dresses."

Tears fell from her eyes. "Look at me. I'm fat."

"Stop it." He sat next to her and wiped her tears away. "You are the most beautiful woman in the world, and that baby you're carrying makes you even more beautiful."

"No it doesn't."

"Yes it does." He lifted her chin and grazed his thumb across her cheek. "Honey, you are beautiful, and I love you very much." He touched his lips onto hers. "I'll help you find something to wear. Calm down."

Three hours into the dinner party, Randy saw Jane mingling with a group of women. She was listening to what they were saying, but didn't appear to be participating in the conversation. One woman kept touching Jane's pregnant belly and, by the look on Jane's face, said something she didn't like.

Jane immediately left the conversation and plodded over to Randy. "Have I been sociable enough for you?" she complained.

"What?"

Her lips drew back in a snarl as if she was about to bite someone's head off. "Can we go please?"

It wasn't like Jane to rush away from social situations, so this sudden urge to leave surprised him. "You wanna leave now?"

"Yes."

"Why?"

"Because I do."

"Alright, but let me say goodbye to my parents first."

"Hurry up." Jane waited impatiently with her hands on her hips and a callous scowl on her face. She grew angrier by the second.

Randy said his goodbyes then ambled back over to Jane, who made it very clear she didn't want to be in that room another second. "What is wrong with you?"

"I want to go home." She darted out the door and headed toward the car.

After belting up, Randy started the engine and turned his eyes to Jane. She stared out the window, distant. Either something was bothering her or her hormones were in overdrive tonight.

Silence filled the car the entire drive home. Randy opted not to talk and risk aggravating his wife further.

He decided it was safer to let her mull it over for a bit rather than push the issue.

When they made it home, he leaned over to kiss her, but she turned away from him.

"I'm taking a shower." She stomped up the stairs without saying another word.

Randy drew back, wondering what he did that made her so mad. He traipsed upstairs and joined her in the bedroom. "Honey, what's wrong?"

"Nothing." Jane peeled off her dress and slipped on a robe.

"Something's bothering you. Don't tell me otherwise because I know better. Talk to me."

She ignored his question.

"If I've done something to piss you off, I really wish you'd tell me what it is."

She crinkled her forehead. "Are you that ignorant?"

He shoved his hands in his pockets, having no clue what she was talking about. "I guess I am."

She glared at him and retreated to the bathroom.

He barged in behind her.

"Do you mind?"

"Yes, I do, dammit. Don't shut me out. What is going on?"

She turned the water on and refused to answer him.

Begging for an explanation, he said, "Jane, please tell me what the hell I've done that has made you so angry tonight."

She turned off the faucet and stared at him. "You didn't do anything."

"Then what is it?"

She clenched her jaw and pursed her lips together. "That woman."

"What woman?"

"That woman in the sequined dress—all she did was talk about money and brag about how her husband bought her fur coats and big diamonds and how she travels around the world and only eats at the finest restaurants. She actually spent fifteen-thousand dollars to get her sofa reupholstered with Italian silk. She was bragging about the fact that she paid a guy thousands of dollars to redo her hardwood floors, but she didn't like the way it looked afterwards so she paid another guy to do it again. And if she touches my stomach one more time..."

Jane was about to lose her temper. Randy tried to calm her nerves before she snapped. "Honey, calm down. Some people are just fascinated by pregnant women."

"Well, I do not wish to be the object of her entertainment," Jane complained. "She's a rich, pampered snob. I do not want to be a spoiled doctor's wife like her."

He wasn't sure he liked that comment. "You married me knowing I was a doctor."

Her voice became hard. "That's not what I mean, and you know it. Are you even listening to me?"

"I am," he confirmed. "But I don't understand what you're talking about."

"I didn't marry you because you're a doctor," she proclaimed. "I married you because I love you. I don't care about wealth and all that materialistic crap. It drives me crazy when we get around people who live in a shell of money. Just because you're a doctor doesn't mean we have to live like pretentious brats."

"I wasn't aware that we were," he defended.

"It's not that simple, Randy."

"Then enlighten me."

"That uppity woman drives around in her Lexus wearing five-hundred dollar cashmere sweaters and Oscar de la Renta gowns. She only wears expensive Italian designer shoes and carries a twenty-five-hundred dollar Louis Vuitton handbag. She eats Caviar and drinks five-thousand dollar bottles of wine. Is that the way I'm supposed to act?"

What a ludicrous thing to say. Where in the world did she get that idea? "No. I want you to be who you are. I don't care what you wear. To me, you look good in shorts and a tee-shirt. And I can't stand Caviar. I use fish eggs as fishing bait, not as an hors d'oeuvre. I sure as hell don't want silk on my couch with a baby in the house. I'm happy with my sports car and would rather drink Corona or a good cup of coffee over an expensive glass of wine any day. Our life isn't like that, Jane. It never has been. I wasn't raised in snobbery and I will not raise our child that way."

In a raucous tone she said, "It drove me crazy when that woman talked like that."

"I know it did, but these dinner parties are necessary for me to establish myself in the medical community. I cannot fail to acknowledge my colleagues." Randy wrapped his arms around her, placing his hand on her tummy. "Are you going to get upset with me because I'm touching your tummy?"

"No. That's your baby."

He massaged her belly and gave several soft kisses to her neck and shoulders to try to get her to relax. "I'm sorry that woman bothered you so much."

"It's not your fault."

"No, but obviously you're upset about it." Then something she said earlier made him ask, "Who the hell pays five-thousand dollars for a bottle of wine? That's crazy." He tenderly kissed her neck, trying to get her mind off of it. The satin robe Jane had on conformed to her belly making it pooch out. Randy always thought pregnant women were beautiful, especially his wife. He gently lifted her robe and placed his hand on her tummy. "Has he been moving around a lot?"

"He's been really active today."

Randy grabbed his stethoscope off the bedside table and put it on his ears, placing the bell on her tummy.

"What are you doing?"

"We should be able to hear the heartbeat with a scope now." He listened intently to a faint but rapid heartbeat.

"Can you hear it?"

"Yup." He put a little pressure on the bell to hold it in place and had Jane take possession of the stethoscope so she could hear it too. "Listen closely. It's a fast rate, and it's kind of hard to hear."

When she heard it, a huge smile filled her face.

He let her listen for a minute before he removed the scope. He rested his hand on her tummy and a tiny bump pushed on his hand. The corner of his mouth lifted. "I felt that. The baby's kicking right here." Randy felt it again. Feeling his baby kick for the first time brought a few chuckles. Every time he pushed down with his hand, the baby pushed back. These movements fascinated him. He moved his hand all around her belly searching for more.

Jane had felt the baby move for a while and felt kind of alone in her experiences. But seeing the joy on her husband's face, now that he felt his baby move, was enough to bring tears to her eyes.

"He's an active little thing." He listened for a heartbeat with his scope again. He heard it for only a brief second before it faded. "Aw man. I lost it." He set the scope down and sat up against the headboard. Spreading his legs, he took Jane's hand and said, "Come here."

She scooted closer and sat between his legs.

He moved his hands down to her lower abdomen and began to practice Lamaze breathing with her. "Breathing will be a little different for us because I'm your coach and your doctor. When it comes time to push, I'm going to have to switch roles and play catch instead."

"I completely trust you, Dr. Hanson."

"You're gonna do great, Baby. You're a strong woman." He kissed her gently on the lips.

The next morning, Randy went outside to wash his Porsche and shine up his tires with Armor All. A red pickup he'd never seen before pulled up in front of his house. He couldn't tell who was behind the wheel, so he stood up to get a better look.

Greg stepped out of the vehicle.

"Hey, Man," Randy said, slapping Greg's palm with his. "Get a new rig?"

"Yes I did. You like it?"

"I do. Love the color too." Randy took a peek at the leather and fabric-trimmed interior and examined the fancy console of the extended cab Toyota Tundra. "Nice."

Greg closed the driver's side door and beeped the alarm.

"You want a beer?" Randy offered.

"Sure."

The men went inside the house to grab two beers. Seeing Greg in basketball attire, Randy changed his clothes. He pulled the Porsche into the garage to clear the driveway then grabbed a basketball and closed the garage door. He dribbled a few times before he fired a shot that bounced off the backboard and dropped into the hoop. "I felt the baby wiggling around last night. It was pretty awesome."

Greg retrieved the ball then converted a crossover and pivoted to evade Randy. He attempted a fade away; it went in, answering Randy's shot. "That's exciting."

Randy stood in the middle of the driveway holding the ball under his arm. "I'm excited about being a dad, but I'm worried about what having a child might mean for my marriage. Jane and I have always been pretty spontaneous. With a baby in the house, everything is going to be different. We won't have the freedom or the energy to go out whenever the urge hits. I'm not sure I'm ready to give that up."

"Having a baby will definitely change your life." Greg tried to ease some of Randy's worries. "My brother told me that he and his wife grew closer after having a child. I've even heard people say that having children enhances your life. With the kind of relationship you and Jane have, I don't think you need to worry."

When the men took a break to finish off their beers, Jim pulled up. "Sup, Bros?"

"Where the hell were you yesterday?" Randy asked.

Jim snatched the ball and spun it on his finger. "Why do you care?"

"Because I left you two messages and you never returned my call."

With a sigh, Jim said, "Jill got some bug up her butt to go downtown, so we ended up takin' the kids to the zoo. Then the hospital called me last night to cover a shift for a few hours. When I got home at two o'clock in the mornin' Jill decided she wanted a chocolate milkshake."

Greg interjected, "She's not pregnant is she?"

Jim's eyes enlarged and a terrified look overtook him. "Oh Jesus. I hope not."

Randy chuckled. "Jane's been craving weird things lately. Yesterday she wanted a BLT."

"That's not weird," Greg said.

"For Jane it is."

Jim chortled, "Apparently you've never seen the way that woman eats. Fatty foods or anything even remotely associated with grease…hell no. And bacon…Jane wouldn't be caught dead eatin' a piece of fried pig fat."

Randy couldn't have agreed more. "No she would not."

With three of them now, they couldn't play a balanced game. "We need a fourth man," Greg said.

"I can see if Jane wants to play," Randy suggested.

"She still plays?" Jim asked, dribbling the ball.

"Why wouldn't she?"

"Protruding belly, off balance, equilibrium all fucked up."

"She can still play, and she probably will until she can't see her feet. It's good exercise for her and it keeps her in shape. Besides, she loves basketball."

"Hell," Greg said. "I'll play with her."

Jim questioned this bold statement. "You've never played with her before, have you?"

"No, why?"

"Dude, she's gonna kick your ass. She's fuckin' mean on the basketball court."

Greg didn't seem to care. "I'm game. Go get her."

Randy went inside to fetch Jane. She joined the men in the driveway and their game resumed.

Chapter Thirty-Eight

The entire Hanson family gathered at Randy's house for a Fourth of July celebration. Stephanie and Bruce flew up to Seattle for this event, and the Ryans were also invited to attend. Randy stood on the deck preparing the grill when the family began to show up.

"Buckman." Excited to see each other, Randy slapped the palm of Bruce's hand. "It's good to see you."

"Good to see you too."

Randy handed him a beer. "How you been?"

Bruce popped the cap off his Corona and situated himself on a lawn chair on Randy's back deck. "I worked over eighty hours last week and performed sixteen surgeries within a seven-day span. It feels like I go from operating room to operating room all day. As soon as I make it out of one surgery, I get an emergency call for another."

"Isn't that what you wanted?"

"Yes, but damn. I barely have time to breathe."

The minute Bruce saw Jim step on the deck, he vaulted out of his seat. "Jim. How the hell are you?" The two men shook hands. "It has been too damn long, my friend."

"Yes it has," Jim replied.

"How's the ER treating you?"

Jim pulled up a lawn chair and sat down beside Bruce. "Mad busy. That place is trippin' with action. People do crazy shit to get themselves into the ER."

"And within the craziness of your day, you get the satisfaction of knowing you've set a few bone fractures, sutured someone's hand back together, and saved a few lives."

"You save lives too," Jim remarked.

"But it's different. Brains aren't like broken legs or skin. They're more like Jell-O. They can't exactly be sewn back together. The best I can do is alleviate swelling, remove blood clots, repair blood vessels, and control pressure inside the skull."

"True point," Jim said.

After the sun went down, Randy pulled out a box of sparklers for the kids. They lit a few fireworks, snacked on red, white, and blue Rice Krispie treats, and enjoyed family time together.

When Bruce and Stephanie returned to Randy's parents' house for the night, they laid Emily down and lounged on the pullout bed downstairs. Bruce kicked off his shoes and crossed his ankles.

"By the way, I wanted to tell you something," Stephanie said.

"What's that?"

"I think I might be pregnant."

His eyebrows seemed to frown, and his face slowly turned downward.

"In fact, I'm pretty sure I am."

Bruce sat up. "You and I discussed this, and we agreed to wait until I finished my residency before we decided to have another child."

"Well, I didn't want to wait."

"So you just took it upon yourself to get pregnant despite how I felt about it? You were supposed to be on the pill."

"I was...for a while."

He glared at Stephanie with blackness in his eyes. "You stopped taking them? Is that what you're telling me?"

"Yeah. What's the big deal?"

"What's the big deal?" he scorned. "Don't you think having another child was a decision I should have been involved in?"

"It's my body."

"And it's my child."

Stephanie shrugged it off as if she didn't care. "I didn't think you'd react this way."

"How did you think I was going to feel when you knew I didn't want another child right now?" Bruce's shoulders tensed. He held his hand across his chin, trying to remain calm. "You don't see anything wrong with this?"

"No."

He spelled it out for her. "You lied to me. You deceitfully tried to keep me in the dark and made a major life decision without consulting me. Are you capable of thinking about anyone but yourself?"

"Why are you so upset about this?"

He shot her an angry stare. "This is the second time you've lied to me about taking your pills. You seriously see nothing wrong with what you did?" He slipped on his shoes and prepared to leave the room. "If you would have been honest with me about it instead of sneaking around and being deceitful I wouldn't have cared so much."

"Well, if you'd learn to trust me maybe I wouldn't have to be."

"How can you expect me to trust you when every word that comes out of your mouth is a damn lie? Just once I'd like you to tell me the truth." He stood up and headed toward the stairs.

"Where are you going?"

He left before he said something he was going to regret.

Randy was about to head off to bed when Bruce showed up on his doorstep.

"Can I come in?" Bruce asked.

"Of course." Randy showed him inside, surprised he was here so late. "I thought you were putting Emily to bed?"

Bruce sat down on the sofa. "She's already asleep."

Randy closed the front door and joined his friend. "What's up?"

Bruce's face tensed. He was aggravated beyond belief. "She did it again."

"Who? And what did she do?"

"Your sister just told me she's pregnant."

The look on Bruce's face indicated he was not happy about this. "And I get the impression this is not good news for you."

"We decided we were going to wait. I made it very clear to her that I did not want to have another baby until my residency was complete. She was on the pill. One was missing from her pack every day, so I honestly thought that she was taking them. But she just admitted to me that she wasn't."

"If she wasn't taking them, where did they go?"

"The hell if I know. Knowing her, she probably flushed them thinking I wouldn't find out. Makes me wonder what else she's hiding from me."

Although Randy was shocked his sister would do something like this, he completely understood Bruce's reaction.

"I'm so sick of this shit. She hides things from me all the time, and when I question her about it, she lies through her teeth. And on top of everything else, she finds it necessary to go on thousand dollar shopping sprees without consulting me. I have to constantly monitor my bank account because I can't trust her with a credit card."

"Have you talked to her about this?"

"Yes, but she has the mentality that she can do whatever she wants, whenever she wants, and my feelings about it don't matter."

"Marriages don't work like that."

"I know, but evidently she doesn't care." Bruce hung his head, feeling defeated. "Do you mind if I hang out here for a while? I need to cool off before I go back over there."

"No problem. You want some coffee?"

"Coffee would be great."

Randy poured him a cup of coffee and the two of them stayed up late talking before Bruce reluctantly returned to his in-law's house to settle in for the night.

Mark and Ellen took the entire family out for brunch the next day. Tension between Bruce and Stephanie was painfully obvious. They stayed as far away from each other as possible and didn't speak all morning. Randy knew they were having problems, but so far no one else seemed to notice. Besides the unplanned pregnancy, and Bruce's claim that Stephanie always hid things from him and rarely told him the truth, Bruce openly shared with Randy other issues going on between him and Stephanie. Apparently, she expected him to drop everything on a whim, which his schedule didn't allow for, and when she didn't get her way, she'd throw a fit or stomp away in a tizzy. According to Bruce, they argued frequently, and he was to the point where he was afraid to say anything to her because she constantly picked fights with him over petty issues.

Randy didn't want to get involved in their squabble, but the tension in the air was too thick to ignore. He leaned toward Bruce and whispered, "Refusing to speak to each other isn't going to make things better."

"Can't make it any worse."

"Have you two sought the help of a marriage counselor? Maybe there's some underlying issue that's causing all of this."

"The issue is Stephanie demands attention 24/7, and she will do anything necessary to get it." Bruce excused himself to use the restroom. Sensing Bruce's frustration, Randy decided it was best to stay out of it and let them work it out themselves.

When the family returned from brunch, the women went shopping for infant clothes.

Stephanie held up a small outfit with puppy print pants and a matching tee-shirt. "Aww," she said. "Baby clothes are adorable."

Ellen brought over two packages of onesies and tossed them in the shopping cart. "You can never have too many of these," she said.

In the middle of shopping, Stephanie announced, "Since we're here buying baby stuff, this is a good time to announce that I'm pregnant."

Both Ellen and Jane's mouths hit the floor. "Oh my god, Stephanie," Jane said. "Congratulations!"

Ellen hugged her daughter. "Another grandbaby on the way. This is wonderful news."

While the women were shopping, the men engaged in a game of basketball. Randy offered a challenge to his dad. "Care to make a bet, Dr. Hanson?"

"Now, Son, every time you do that, you lose. Haven't you learned yet?"

But Randy insisted. "Name your stakes."

Humoring his son, Mark played along. "Alright. Twenty bucks."

Randy countered, "Twenty-five, and winning team takes all."

Getting away from Stephanie and engaging in a game of basketball made Bruce much more relaxed. He grabbed his wallet and pulled out a twenty and a five dollar bill. "I'm in."

Jim did the same. "Me too."

With an arrogant smirk, Randy directed his attention to his father again, waiting for his response. "Dad?"

Mark shook his head. "You never learn, do you, Son? You must enjoy a good beating."

"I live for it. You in or not?"

Mark pulled out twenty-five dollars.

Randy added his twenty-five and set the money on the front porch, held in place with a rock. "That's fifty bucks each to the winners." Randy pulled a quarter out of his pocket and flipped it in the air. "Buckman, you call it."

"Heads," Bruce replied.

It landed on heads. Mark patted his son-in-law's shoulder. "Good call, my boy." They met with a high five and the game proceeded. Bruce took the ball in his hand and headed out to the street, dribbling toward the basket. Jim guarded him.

Randy stood in front of his dad, arms up, trying to keep him from gaining access to the ball. "You can't win, you know," Randy claimed.

"Where's that cockiness come from?" Mark caught Bruce's pass and dribbled toward the basket. Bruce ran across the driveway and Mark tossed the ball back to him. Score. "Two nothing already? Looks like you're getting flaccid, my boy."

Defending himself against his father's statement, Randy replied, "I am anything but flaccid." He tossed the ball to Jim then ran to the end of the driveway. Jim dribbled around a bit before he passed the ball back to Randy, who in turn fired a shot into the basket. "Two, two. Eat your words, old man."

"Game's not over yet," Mark replied.

Randy and Jim ended up claiming victory, but only by a narrow margin. "See, you should have listened to me, Dad. You can't barter with the great one." He picked up the cash and gave half to Jim. "Call me flaccid will you."

"I'm sorry. Did I damage your ego?"

"His sexual ego maybe," Jim teased.

"I think I've proven myself sexually," Randy argued. "My wife is pregnant. Kind of hard to father a child if you're flaccid. So much for your theory, Ryan."

"All fathering a child proves is that your plumbing works. Doesn't prove you can produce sexual gratification."

"You saying I'm not good in bed?" Randy argued.

"How the hell would I know, and why would I care?"

"I'm very good in bed."

Jim laughed out loud. "If the millions of babes who flocked at our door every night beggin' to hop in the sack with you is any indication, then yes, you must be."

Mark raised an eyebrow at this comment. "Is that a fact?"

Red in the face about having this conversation in front of his father, Randy snarled at Jim, insistent that he drop this subject.

But Jim didn't drop it. Instead, he continued to torment him further. "Three or four every week."

"I see," Mark said. "Does your wife know about this?"

Bruce chimed in, "His wife was one of the flock."

"That is not true," Randy defended, wishing both of them would shut the hell up. "Jane was never one of my one night stands. And I really don't see how my private bedroom affairs are anyone else's business."

"I'm messin' with you, Dude," Jim remarked. "Quit buggin'."

Following the game, the men went inside to grab a beer and relax by the lake. Through his sunglasses, Jim looked over at his best friend, who sat in a lawn chair pouting. Knowing Randy was still upset, he eased over to tame the lion. "You seriously need to chillax, Dude. You know I was teasin'."

Randy snapped at him. "In front of my dad? That wasn't necessary and you know it."

"I'm sorry. I didn't mean to upset you." Randy's flustered facial expression told Jim that something else was bothering him. "You ok?"

Randy swallowed hard. "You know what my wife is doing right now? Shopping for baby clothes. I am four months away from becoming a father, and it scares the hell out of me."

Jim sat next to him, trying to offer counsel. "Being a dad is the most challenging and rewarding thing I've ever done, but I wouldn't trade it for anything."

Fear filled Randy's eyes. "I don't feel ready for this. What if I fuck it all up?"

"Parenting isn't perfect, Bro. You'll make mistakes and have times when you don't know what to do, but it all works out in the end. I didn't know what the hell I was doin' when I first had Chris. He didn't come with an instruction manual. But I figured it out and learned as I went along. So far everything has turned out fine."

"I want the best for my son. I want to raise him to be a good person."

"You will," Jim encouraged. "You're gonna be a good dad. Stop worrying. And I tell you what, holding your baby for the first time…nothin' compares to that. Your heart will melt." Jim placed his hand on Randy's shoulder. "C'mon. Let's set up the volleyball net. We'll play when the girls get back."

Randy got up to help him.

"We'll have a lot of grandbabies running around soon," Ellen said to her husband.

"Yes, I know."

"The other day I brought some baby stuff over to Jane. When Randy saw the package of diapers and pacifiers and receiving blankets, he stared at me with this look of pure terror on his face. I asked him what was wrong and he admitted to me that he was scared."

Mark scratched his head, surprised that his oldest son hadn't talked to him about this. "What's he so afraid of?"

"He's worried that he and Jane's relationship will change after the baby's born. He wants to share in the pregnancy experience with Jane but doesn't feel that he adequately is."

"He's been involved. Why would he think that?"

"I don't know. That's just what he told me," Ellen explained. "He rattled off a huge list, Mark. Mostly he's worried about Jane. He's hoping there are no complications during her delivery and is afraid that he might not be able to handle it if there are. He's uncertain as to whether he can keep Jane calm during contractions and still be able to perform his doctorly duties."

"I told him that delivering his own child was going to be intense. I offered to be there with him, but he seemed irritated that I even suggested that."

"He also mentioned that he's worried he's not going to be a good dad. He's afraid he's going to make mistakes and scar the child. You know how Randy is. Everything always has to be perfect."

Mark laughed, "If he thinks parenting is perfect, he is in for a big surprise."

"Talk to him, please," Ellen insisted.

"What would you like me to say to him, Ellie? Do you want me to tell him that parenting has times of failure and times when he'll try everything and nothing works and he really shouldn't worry about it? Do you really think he'll listen? Do you really think that will ease his mind?"

"No."

"The only thing that is going to take Randy's fears away is Randy. Right now his priorities are his wife and his life as a physician. He won't snap into dad mode until he holds that little boy for the first time. It doesn't really sink in with new dads until the baby is born, then it hits like a ton of bricks. Having a baby will open his eyes and make him consider things he otherwise would have never considered. Being a first time dad comes with a frenzy of epiphanies. They come fast and furious. His priorities will change and the rest will take care of itself. Nothing I say will make it easier for him or take the confusion and fears away. That will only happen with time."

When Jane returned from the beautician Saturday afternoon, Randy said to her, "Go up to the baby's room."

Jane arched her eyebrows, confused by this statement. "Why?"

"I want to show you what I did."

She waddled upstairs to take a peek. In the room, Randy set up a cradle with a sheet-covered cushion and had finished putting the furniture together, complete with a four drawer dresser, three drawer changing table, and rocking chair, all in cognac to match the crib. A teddy bear lamp with a blue lampshade sat on the dresser; a yellow ceramic teddy bear piggybank rested next to it. Draped over the crib was a cute little appliquéd soft chenille bear-patterned baby blanket that matched the curtains, crib sheet, diaper stacker, and bumper. A teddy bear mobile dangled over the crib. A sculpted bear rug was spread out in the middle of the floor and a junior rocking chair with a bear pattern sat alone in a corner of the room. On the wall hung an oversized furry bear wall hanging and a hand-painted shelf.

A tear came to Jane's eye. "Randy."

He opened the nursery closet and pulled out a portable crib. "I also got this so we'll be able to take Zeus with us to Mom and Dad's or lie him down in the living room. And…" Randy reached into a drawer and pulled out a small Lakers tee-shirt. "Look what I found." He held up the treasure he came across. "Baby and daddy can wear matching Lakers shirts on game day."

Inside the dresser drawers, tiny baby onesies, socks, outfits, receiving blankets, burp rags, and pajamas were neatly folded. The diaper stacker was full, and a basket on the changing table was carefully organized with diaper ointment, baby wash, baby shampoo, teething gel, baby lotion, and baby wipes. "I can't believe you did all this."

"Our baby needs a space of his own, and I know how much you wanted to finish the nursery, so I finished it." He put his arms around her, which was becoming more difficult to do. "Do you like it?"

"I love it. This is by far the sweetest and most thoughtful thing you have ever done." She kissed him softly on the lips, proud at how lovingly and willingly he took on his fatherly duties. "Thank you."

"You're welcome."

Chapter Thirty-Nine

Bruce came home from another busy day of neurosurgery later than he planned. He was exhausted and not in the mood to deal with attitude, which Stephanie seemed to fling at him constantly lately. As expected, the moment he walked in the door she started in on him.

"Why are you so late?" she snarled.

"Don't start, Steph."

"You could have called."

"I was in the middle of a procedure. I can't stop to call you when a patient's life is on the line." Bruce set his keys on the kitchen table and looked over at Stephanie, who had on another new outfit he hadn't seen before. "Did you go shopping again?"

"I bought some clothes for Emily."

"And for yourself," he corrected.

Stephanie sneered at him. "You have a problem with that?"

"What I have a problem with is you maxing out all the credit cards. If you want to spend money, why don't you buy stuff for the baby." Bruce was in a bad mood tonight, and her irresponsibility intensified his irritation.

"Why are you so pissy?" she huffed.

Bruce shot her an evil scowl. "I haven't been sleeping well because I am worried about what kind of bullshit you're going to pull when I'm not here to watch over you. You constantly bitch at me for doing my job, spend money without consulting me, and deliberately do things behind my back."

Stephanie was aghast by this accusation. "I do not."

He humorlessly tittered at her denial. "Yes you do. You flushed your damn birth control pills down the toilet."

"You're still dwelling on that?"

"This isn't the first time you've done it."

"When are you going to let that go?"

"I don't trust you, Stephanie. You lie to me constantly, and I'm fed up with it." All Bruce wanted to do was crash on his pillow and sleep. "I really don't want to argue with you tonight. It's been a long day and I'm tired. I'm going to bed." Bruce checked in on Emily then retreated to the bedroom for the night.

The rain Seattle received the night before had let up, but the ground was still wet. Randy opened the bedroom window to allow fresh air into the room. The smell of newly dampened concrete permeated the air. He stared out the window, deep in thought.

Jane stepped out of the shower wrapped in a towel, which barely covered her. She reached into a dresser drawer to get her undergarments. "Something interesting out there?"

Randy rubbed his chin. "No. Just thinking."

"About?"

"I'm worried about Bruce and Stephanie."

"Why?"

"Stephanie called me yesterday upset because she and Bruce can't communicate without arguing. I think their marriage is in serious jeopardy."

"Really?" Jane's face curled. "Stephanie hasn't said anything to me about it."

"She's trying to hide it from the family, but Bruce has opened up to me about it. She constantly nags him about work, she spends his paycheck as quickly as he makes it, and this pregnancy is dragging him down."

"What do you mean?" Jane began to get dressed, slowly sliding her clothes over her bulging belly.

"This was not a planned pregnancy, Jane. In fact, Bruce was pretty firm about not having another baby right now. Long story short, Stephanie led him to believe she was taking her pill every day when in reality she popped one from the pack and flushed it instead. She ended up pregnant because of it."

"She deceived him?"

"Exactly, and it's not the first time she's done this to him. She did a similar thing with Emily. Needless to say, he doesn't trust her. I can't say that I blame him," Randy admitted. "Apparently she lies to him all the time."

"Did you talk to Stephanie about this?"

"I'm trying not to get in the middle of it. Quite honestly, it doesn't surprise me. I told Bruce from the start that he and Stephanie weren't compatible. I even tried to talk him out of marrying her."

"Why would you do that?"

"Because Stephanie only married him for the money and status being a doctor's wife provided. He's a trophy husband, Jane. She doesn't love him."

Jane's mouth dropped. "That is a terrible thing to say."

"It's true," Randy declared in his defense. "She admitted it to me."

"If Bruce finds out…"

"He knows. Bruce married her because he didn't want to lose his daughter. Their marriage is not based on love, it's a marriage of convenience. That's why I tried to talk him out of it, but he was determined to go through with it. It's coming back to bite him in the butt now, and I fear they may be heading toward divorce."

Jane put her hand over her mouth. "That's awful."

"Unfortunately, it happens. I just wish it wasn't Bruce and my sister it was happening to." He turned around and put his hand on her tummy. The baby kicked. "Thirty-six weeks already. It went by quickly."

"Yes, it did."

Right now, holding Jane like this, Randy felt more confident about parenthood than he had throughout this entire process. "I'm ready to be a father."

Hearing those words from him made Jane smile. "Me too."

"You're ready to be a father?"

She giggled at him. "No, silly. A mom."

"Oh. Ok. Scared me there for a minute."

"I'm not sure who's going to be a bigger kid, you or this baby." She grazed her hand across his chest as she inched toward the door.

"I love you," he called to her.

"I love you too."

He winked at her and watched her pregnant body hobble out of the room.

Stephanie woke up Wednesday morning in a lousy mood. Every move Bruce made enticed her to pick a fight. "One request, Bruce. One. I didn't think that was asking too much," she bellowed.

"I told you already, I was busy yesterday. I was working and making money, which is more than I can say about you. I don't see you doing anything to contribute to the finances of this family. All you do is suck my pocketbook dry."

She snarled at him and stormed away.

Bruce exhaled heavily. Their entire marriage was one petty argument followed by another. "Dammit, Steph," he called out after her. "I love how quickly you bite my head off when you don't get what you want. If it was that damn important, maybe you should have taken care of it yourself. It's not like you don't have time. Speaking of which, what exactly were you doing yesterday?"

"What do you care?"

"Oh I care, because you're draining our bank account. You're the one who doesn't care. In fact, you don't care about much of anything, unless it benefits you."

Stephanie rolled her eyes at him, picked up her purse, and headed for the door.

He grabbed her arm. "Where are you going?"

"Let go of my arm," she demanded.

"No. Neither one of us is leaving until we work this out."

She yanked her arm out of his hand. "You are always occupied with your job."

"I'm a doctor. I have responsibilities to my patients. Unexpected things come up that I have no control over, emergency situations that can't wait. I try to save someone's life and you chew my ass for it."

"Your job is more important to you than we are."

"Don't even go there." Frustrated, he threw his hands in the air. "I have too much to deal with right now. I don't need this crap from you."

"Fine. Do whatever you want." She left the house, slamming the door on her way out.

Bruce put his hand up to his forehead, irritated not only by the fact that Stephanie stomped off, but also because she left without taking Emily to pre-school. Now he was going to have to drop her off on his way to work, which was probably going to make him late. "Shit." He finished getting Emily ready then prepared himself for another day of neurosurgery.

Feeling down and wishing he had a friend to talk to, Bruce called Mandy. Anytime he had something on his mind, Mandy was always there to listen. Since Bruce's apartment was close to UCLA and Mandy lived in Santa Monica, they decided to meet halfway.

Bruce sat and stared at his coffee cup while he poked at the muffin he had in front of him, not eating any of it.

"Bruce?" Mandy questioned. "You gonna talk to me or sit and poke at your food?"

Bruce looked up. "What?"

"You said you wanted to talk but haven't said two words since we got here."

He pushed his muffin aside. "Stephanie totally flipped out this morning over a damn box. She had a package she wanted me to mail, but I had that emergency brain hemorrhage last night. By the time I was done, the post office was closed. She bit my head off and told me I don't care about my family." He shook his head. "What a load of crap. If it was that big of a deal, she could have mailed it herself, but of course she was too busy shopping and frittering away all my money that heaven forbid she break away from her busy life to take care of necessary household tasks."

Sensing a bit of hostility in Bruce's tone, Mandy said, "Seems like a silly thing to argue about."

"We argue about stupid shit all the time."

It seemed like Stephanie caused Bruce unnecessary stress that he really didn't need.

"Did I tell you what else she did?" Bruce said.

"No."

"She's pregnant again."

This comment confused her. "Again? I thought you didn't want another baby?"

"I don't, but evidently she doesn't give a crap what I think. She deliberately flushed her pill every day, leading me to believe she was taking them," Bruce added. "She complains about every aspect of our lives and constantly gripes about my job. I can't fucking breathe. This isn't a marriage, Mandy. I live in a goddamn war zone. I'm to the point where I will gladly work a twenty-hour day so I don't have to go home and listen to her bitch at me."

The way Bruce talked about his wife led Mandy to believe there was more going on here than just an argument over a box. She'd suspected for a while that Bruce and Stephanie were having problems, but he never opened up about it until now. She gave him a sympathetic look and gently touched his hand to try to make him feel better. "I'm sorry."

Bruce pinched the bridge of his nose. "I am so tired of this."

"What are you going to do about it?"

"If it were only me, I would've been gone a long time ago, but Emily is involved."

"And you need to think about your daughter," Mandy said. "But you need to think about yourself too. You can't keep this up. I see what it's doing to you."

After coffee and muffins, Bruce reluctantly headed home, dreading what would happen when he got there.

"What have you been doing for the last hour?" Stephanie ranted.

"Not here," he begged, knowing Emily was sitting in the room and could hear them.

Emily ran over to him. "Daddy."

Bruce squatted down to her level and gave her a hug. "Hey, Princess. Did you have a good day?"

"We made cookies at school today," the child screeched.

"That's awesome. Did you save any for me?"

"Uh huh. I put them in the fridge for you."

Emily always wanted to do things for others, not at all like her mother. "Thank you, Sweetheart." He kissed her on the cheek. "I'll play with you in a minute."

"Ok." The little girl skipped off and returned to her dolls.

Stephanie snarled, "Are you going to answer me?"

Bruce disregarded Stephanie's question and went into the bedroom to change.

Stephanie trailed right behind him.

Bruce closed the door so Emily wouldn't hear them. "Why do you insist on picking fights in front of her?"

"I'm not picking a fight. I asked you a question."

"I was having coffee with a friend." He loosened his tie. "I didn't realize I had to ask you for permission."

"Which friend?"

"A colleague of mine. What difference does it make?" He removed his dress shirt and slipped a clean tee-shirt over his head.

"Do you know what I've been doing all afternoon?"

"Why do I have a feeling that I'm about to get my ass chewed about something? Go ahead. Get it out of your system. Then maybe I can grab some dinner, spend some time with my daughter, and relax for a while."

She snarled, "I had to pick Emily up from pre-school and take her to ballet class. Then I spent the last half hour on the phone trying to reschedule my doctor's appointment because the day I scheduled it is the same day as Emily's recital."

"Wow," he mocked with a smartass tone. "Was this before or after you went shopping? By the way, how much money did you spend today?"

She shot him an evil glare, appalled that he wasn't showing any sympathy towards her plight.

He kicked off his shoes and changed into jeans. "Would you like me to tell you what I had to do today?" Although he knew she didn't care in the slightest.

Stephanie simply exited the room.

"That's what I thought," he remarked.

Chapter Forty

Holding a garden rake in his hands, Randy stood in his front yard raking leaves into piles. He took a break for a moment to take in the vibrant scene around him. Shades of orange, yellow, and red painted the surroundings. Overhead, a flock of Canadian geese honked in formation, making their annual migration south. The distant snowcapped mountains hid behind a layer of clouds, which carried a misty drizzle with them. The sky was grey and gloomy, but the air was crisp, filled with the subtle scent of wet earth and chimney smoke. Overnight, the temperature had dropped by twenty degrees, sweeping a cool breeze through the city. Randy cupped his hands together and blew air into them to warm his fingertips, then he gripped the rake in his hands and continued to form leaf mounds.

He had already raked two piles and was working on a third when his cellphone rang. He reached into his back pocket and checked the incoming number. Robby. "Hey, Rob," he answered

His brother's trembling voice replied, "I'm dying for a fix, Man. My hands are shaking. You gotta talk me down."

"Where are you? Are you home right now?"

"Yeah."

"I'll be right there." Randy dropped the rake in the yard and dashed to his car. He was at his brother's apartment in under seven minutes.

Robby was curled up on the sofa hugging his knees. His hands trembled and sweat beads formed on his forehead. Randy sat next to him. "What's going on?"

Robby looked up at his brother. "I'm fiending bad."

It was normal for recovering drug addicts to experience intense cravings, especially in high stress situations. Cravings rarely lasted longer than half an hour, but battling against them was like trying to block a waterfall. It exerted a tremendous amount of energy. Sometimes the cravings were too strong to fight, and the recovering addict relapsed. Other times, the addict could resist urges, especially if there was no opportunity to use. In rehab, Robby was taught to fight these cravings with a strategy called urge surfing. This was a meditation strategy in which he waited the craving out until it peaked in intensity, then after a few minutes, gradually subsided into nothingness, just as a wave crests and falls. He could literally glide over and down a craving as naturally as surfing a wave on the ocean.

"Remember what your therapist said, just surf through it."

Robby shook his head. "I can't."

"Yes you can. You're stronger than this, Rob. Don't let that craving have power over you. You can do it. I'll stay here with you and we'll wait it out together."

Robby released the grip on his legs and put his feet flat on the floor. He took a few deep breaths to relax. "I feel a tightness in my legs and my stomach is jumpy."

"Surf through it," Randy said, offering encouragement.

"My arm is kind of itchy, like pins-and-needles. And I feel warm."

"Keep going. Ride it out."

After several minutes of talking himself down, Robby's craving waned.

"What triggered it?" Randy asked.

"I owed a guy some money. In an attempt to come clean with him and put that part of my life behind me, I stopped by his place to pay him off. The second I walked in the door, there was coke paraphernalia all over the place, and a chick was sniffing right in front of me. I started feeling that itch and got out of there as quick as I could."

"You did the right thing," Randy said. "You recognized your cravings, got yourself out of that situation, and called someone. You proved to yourself that you can do this."

Robby leaned back on the sofa and breathed deeply. "I guess I did."

"Keep in mind the reason why you changed your lifestyle in the first place."

"Oh, I remember. I hurt everyone I ever loved and an overdose almost killed me. I don't need to be reminded."

Although Robby sometimes experienced cravings, they no longer had power over him. He had the strength and mental capacity to overcome them. "You did great, Rob. I'm proud of you." Randy leaned over and hugged his brother.

"Thanks, Bro."

Once Randy was assured that Robby had full control, he headed back home.

When he stepped out of his car, he released a heavy sigh. The wind had blown all the leaves back into the yard. He slipped his car keys into his pocket and picked up his rake, returning to the chore of raking his lawn.

At thirty-eight weeks gestation, Jane was coming in for weekly checkups. Randy ran a Doppler on her; the heartbeat sounded strong. When he checked for dilation and effacement, what he discovered made him cock his head slightly. "Baby's turned, and you're dilated to almost three right now." He removed his latex gloves and threw them in the medical waste bin.

"Is that good?"

"The fact that you're dilated intrigues me. We're getting close." He washed his hands at the sink and tossed his paper towel in the trash. Then he picked up a pen and wrote some information on her chart. "Baby looks great. Only a couple more weeks to go." He lovingly patted her thigh. "Get dressed. I'll see you out front." He gave her a kiss before he left the room.

Randy handed Jane's file to the file clerk then moseyed over to his father, who was intently reading a medical chart in front of him. "Jane's dilated."

This announcement made Mark look up from his paperwork. "Is she?"

"Yup. And baby's turned," Randy said. "Everything's looking like a normal delivery."

"That's good. Your mother and I are going out tonight. I'll have my pager on if you need to buzz me for any reason."

It was Randy's on-call night, not his dad's. But his father had carried a pager around with him everywhere he went for years. He still did this out of habit even on days he wasn't on-call. Randy found it amusing how old school his father was. Their office had shelves stuffed full with paper and pencil patient files, and his father still carried an old-fashioned pager. The clinic desperately needed an upgrade as far as modern medical equipment and computer technology was concerned. "When are you going to get the pager app on your phone and get rid of that dinosaur attached to your belt? Time to upgrade to modern technology, Dad," Randy teased.

"You and your toys."

"I'm trying to make things easier for you. There's a lot of advanced modern equipment out there. I think you should check some of it out and get techy."

Mark snorted at his son's suggestion.

Jane waddled out of the exam room. "Do I need to make another appointment?"

"Yes, Ma'am," Randy said.

"I shouldn't have to make an appointment to see my own husband."

"My schedule fills up quickly. If you don't make an appointment you might not get in."

"What time will you be home tonight?"

"I don't know. Dad and I are both running about fifteen minutes behind right now. I'll get there as soon as I can."

"I'll have dinner ready," she said.

"Thanks."

"I love you," she said to him.

"I love you, too." While she scheduled another appointment, Randy went in to see his next patient.

Friday morning around 4:00 A.M., Jane woke up with cramps in her abdomen that kept her from sleeping. Thinking they were those nasty Braxton Hicks contractions she'd been having, she slipped out of bed and went downstairs on the couch to read a book. Usually when she switched positions or drank water, the cramps went away. This morning, however, the discomfort didn't subside no matter what she did.

Randy rolled over and reached for Jane only to discover she was not in bed. He opened his eyes and called her name. No answer. He noticed a light on downstairs, so he slipped on a pair of sweats and went down to look for her. He found her sitting on the couch reading. He came up behind her and gave her a kiss. "Hey, Baby. What are you doing up?"

"I can't sleep." She put her hand on her tummy.

"You ok?"

"I think I'm having contractions. I tried moving around and switching positions and I even drank some water, but they're not going away."

"Really?" Wanting to know if this was the real deal, Randy probed for more information. "Are they consistent? Have you been timing them?"

"Yes. They're running about ten minutes apart and last about thirty seconds or so."

"How long has this been going on?"

"A couple hours."

"Why didn't you wake me up?"

"I thought it was those fake contractions at first, but now I'm not so sure."

Sounded like she was going into labor. Most likely they were going to have a baby today. "Definitely a regular pattern. Could be the latent stage of labor. Tell me when you have another one. I want to feel what your abdomen is doing." He headed to the kitchen to put on a pot of coffee. "How you feeling otherwise?"

"I feel great." A painful grimace pierced her face.

Randy noticed it right away. "Contraction?"

She nodded.

He rushed over and put his hand on her tummy while he watched the hands tick on clock. Her tummy felt tight, and the look on her face told him she was uncomfortable. Thirty seconds passed; the discomfort decreased and the tightness in her abdomen abated. "No drumrolls or trumpets blaring yet, but enough activity for me to want to keep an eye on you."

Her hands started shaking and fear crossed her face. "I don't know if I can do this."

Randy held her hand. "You're going to be ok. I'll be right there with you. Probably won't see any action 'til later this afternoon or tonight though. Depends on how you progress. Every woman is different, and first pregnancies tend to take longer. Right now you need to relax. Try taking a shower."

Randy planned to play basketball with Jim, Greg, and Robby that morning, but with Jane having contractions like this, he wasn't sure he wanted to go. She wasn't in severe pain yet, but she was uncomfortable, and by 8:00 A.M. her contractions became more frequent. He wanted to be available for her, and since he was supposed to be on-call that day, he called his dad.

"Good morning, Randal."

"Morning. I need you to cover my on-call status today."

Mark knew something was going on. Randy wouldn't be asking him to do this if it wasn't important. "Why is that?"

"Jane's having contractions. Nothing big yet, but she's running about eight minutes apart and has been consistently for about an hour and a half now. I want to keep an eye on her today."

"Did you check her?" Mark asked.

"She's a hundred percent, three and a half centimeters."

Mark agreed keeping a watchful eye was a good idea. "Keep us posted on her progress."

"I will. Thanks, Dad." Randy hung up and returned to his wife.

"I thought you were playing basketball this morning," she said, rubbing her tummy.

"I was, but under the circumstances, I'm not going."

"I still want you to go."

Randy didn't like that idea. "No."

"You shouldn't have to sit here watching me all day."

Randy stared at her with a worried expression on his face.

"Go. I'll be fine. Just bring your phone in case I need you."

Jane was able to convince him to get out of the house. She was still several hours away from any action, and Randy needed to find something to do besides sit around the house watching her or he was going to drive her crazy.

"Keep an eye on your contractions. Call me if they get to be five minutes apart or if the intensity grows to the point that you are in pain. If your water breaks or if you start feeling a lot of pressure, call me immediately," Randy ordered.

"I will."

"Try to relax between contractions. I'll call and check on you later."

She snuffed at his incessant worrying. "Will you go, please."

"I'll be thinking about you." He gave her a kiss before he left. "Bye, Babe."

Randy didn't let his cellphone out of his sight. Before the game even started he announced, "Jane's in labor, so I might have to leave."

Jim gave a wide smile. "Looks like Randy Hanson is gonna be a daddy today."

"Most likely," he boasted proudly. "She's in the latent stage, but she is having contractions."

"How far apart are they?" Greg asked.

"Between seven and eight when I left. We're getting pretty close. I'm leaving my ringer on, and if she needs me, I'm leaving."

Almost exactly two hours later, Randy's cellphone rang. He rushed to the side of the court, missing his pass.

"Dude," Jim teased. "You're supposed to catch the ball."

"Fuck you, Ryan. My wife is on the phone." He picked up his phone and answered the call.

"Randy, I need you to come home." Her voice sounded tight. "These are running five minutes apart and they're starting to hurt." Feeling a contraction coming on, she groaned.

"Hang tight, Honey. I'm on my way." He hung up and grabbed his car keys. "Alright, guys. I'm out."

"How's she doin'?" Jim asked.

"She's in pain. I can tell by her voice."

"I'll be on shift tonight. You better call me."

"I will. But I gotta go."

Jim flashed the shaka sign. "Later, Dude."

And within seconds Randy was gone.

He sped home, not recklessly so, but he definitely drove faster than the speed limit.

When Randy walked through the door, Jane's hand was clenched to her abdomen and she had a horrible frown on her face. He leaned over and kissed her. "How you feeling?"

"I think we better go."

He gently rubbed her tummy. The contractions were pretty intense; she couldn't talk through them. There was no doubt she was in active labor. "Alright. Let me hop in the shower real quick. Give me five minutes."

She clenched her teeth and nodded as she felt a contraction coming on.

Randy took the fastest shower in history. Four minutes—a new record for him. He quickly dressed then threw Jane's bag, the diaper bag, and the car seat in Jane's car, all while talking to his dad on the phone. "Her contractions are increasing in intensity, and they're running about five minutes apart. I'm bringing her in."

"Alright," Mark said. "We will meet you over there."

"Thanks. See you in a bit."

Randy checked Jane in and wheeled her up to Labor & Delivery. He carried the bags up to room twelve, made sure she was situated comfortably, and let the nurses do their magic. They checked her blood pressure and temperature then placed a fetal monitor on her abdomen.

Mark and Ellen peeked into the room. "Hello."

Jane attempted a smile. "Hi."

Mark directed his attention to his son. "Randy, can I talk to you out in the hall for a minute?"

"Sure." He kissed Jane's forehead and stepped into the hall with his father. "Yes, Sir?"

"When I delivered you and your sister and brother, I had another OB in the room with me just in case. I didn't need him, but I was glad he was there. I'm not anticipating any problems, but if something happens, things could get tricky," Mark explained to his son. "Don't let your emotional state make judgment calls. Think clearly and keep Jane relaxed."

"I know."

"Jane is your number one priority right now. And if it comes down to it, you need to be a husband first. I think I should be in the room as a backup."

Randy didn't argue.

"Things are going to get intense. If it gets to be too much, you need to move aside and let me take over."

Even though he tried to hide the stress he felt, Randy was convinced his father saw right through him. He rubbed the back of his neck to relieve some tension.

"You ok?" Mark asked.

"Yeah." Randy closed his eyes and took a deep breath.

"I'll be right behind you if you need me."

Randy stared at his father with a million emotions circulating through his head.

Mark saw the gears turning. Self-doubt was kicking in. "You can do this. I have all the confidence in the world." Mark patted his son's shoulder. "Do you need anything?"

"How about some coffee?" Randy suggested with a chuckle.

"I'll get you some."

Before his father left, Randy called out, "Dad?"

Mark turned around. "Yes?"

"Thanks."

Mark headed to the coffee shop downstairs.

Randy reentered the room to find Jane in the middle of a contraction, trying hard to focus on breathing. When her contraction subsided, she looked at Randy and begged, "Don't leave me."

"I'm not going to. I'm right here." He checked the fetal monitor. Baby had a good, strong heartbeat, and he could see from the printout that her contractions were now about four minutes apart, lasting a solid sixty seconds each. "How you doing on pain?" he asked. "You want something?"

"I'm ok, for now."

"Let me know if you change your mind." He performed a standard pelvic exam to evaluate her cervix. She was five and a half centimeters and fully effaced. "Ok, Babe, I want to move things along here. I'm going to rupture your bag of waters. It will get your labor progressing more quickly."

She was about to have another contraction. Randy stood in a position where she could see him. He looked her in the eye and held her hand to get her attention. "Breathe, Baby." He demonstrated a slow, controlled breathing rate, loud enough so she could follow his lead, slowing her breathing to a quiet, rhythmic pace. "You are doing great. The baby looks good." When her contraction settled, he ruptured her water. "There. That should speed things up a bit."

Labor progressed normally for a few hours, with Randy massaging Jane's back and guiding her through breathing. She discovered she was more comfortable if she moved around, thus Randy walked the hall with her several times. Despite his valiant efforts to comfort her, Jane became extremely agitated. He held her hand, and she squeezed so hard it crushed his fingers. She attempted to breathe and tried to be strong, but the pain became unbearable. She buried her face in his chest and broke down in tears.

Randy suspected she had hit the transitional stage of labor, by far the worst on the pain threshold. Watching his wife endure this immense torture was more than he could bear. He held her close and said, "Please, let me get you something for the pain."

Another contraction came, a bad one, causing her to completely lose focus. Breathing was no longer working.

Randy was about to lose it. He nuzzled his forehead on hers and begged, "Let me help you."

With a nod, she agreed.

Randy immediately turned to the nurse. "Get anesthesia up here, STAT."

"Yes, Doctor."

They gave her fifty milligrams of Demerol by intramuscular route, which could be repeated at one to three hour intervals if needed. That seemed to take the edge off. She was able to focus more, which made Randy more able to focus. He checked her progress again. She was now dilated to seven and a half and her contractions came every two to three minutes. She had indeed hit transition.

Randy never experienced labor from this vantage point before. His job as an obstetrician was to pop in long enough to perform a D&E and check the fetal monitor only to return every half hour or so to repeat the process until dilation reached ten centimeters or he received a page to come back and make the delivery. The constant progression of contractions, the increasing pain threshold, and the tears was something he never really saw, let alone experienced firsthand. He found this aspect of labor and delivery unbearable.

Jane was fatigued, crying through contractions. She grew more and more restless, and the increased pelvic pressure made her irritable. "I can't do this," she said, speaking through tears.

"Yes you can." Trying to offer reassurance, he kissed the top of her head. "I know it hurts, but you are doing a wonderful job. Keep your breathing slow, relaxed, and even." Randy felt like crying. He couldn't stand to watch his wife endure this agony. Seeing labor progression from a doctor's point of view wasn't anywhere near as intense as this was. This was beyond intense. His father chose the wrong word for this hell.

Randy remained by Jane's side, massaging during contractions, holding her hand, and soothing her with his voice as they got closer and closer. Her transition from seven to ten occurred rapidly, much to Randy's relief. During her next contraction, she felt the sudden urge to push. Randy checked dilation one last time; she was at a full ten centimeters. Time for the show.

He looked her in the eye and said, "Honey, look at me."

With glossy eyes, she stared at him.

"I know you're feeling the urge, so next contraction I want you to push. Grab your knees if you have to, but push. Stop to breathe between pushes. The nurse will guide you by counting to ten. Don't stop pushing until she stops counting."

Her body tensed. "I can't."

Randy peeled his gloves off and stood beside his wife, holding her in his arms while the nurses called pediatrics and prepared for delivery. He knew she was frightened, but he did his best to calm her. "It's almost over." He lifted her chin and their eyes met. "Focus on my voice, my face. I'm right here with you. You can do this."

She nodded and began to breathe erratically as she felt pressure and intense pain.

"I love you, Honey. Now push." He put on a scrub shirt his dad fetched for him and slipped on a clean pair of latex gloves.

Jane pushed, with the nurse and Ellen Hanson guiding her.

Randy took position with Mark standing right behind him.

Jane screamed and began to panic. To make his presence felt, Randy used his calming voice to help her relax. "Listen to my voice, Honey." Her eyes were closed and drenched with tears. He gently touched her leg. "Open your eyes and look at me," he said. When her eyes popped open, he pointed to his. "Look right here. Focus on me, on my voice." Again, he demonstrated slow, deep breaths, trying to get her to breathe with him. She calmed down long enough to take a few breaths with him. "Good job, Babe. You're doing great."

Randy's heartrate skyrocketed, and he had more adrenaline careening through his body than he really cared to have right now. He had been a part of and witnessed many births in the past, but this one was far beyond comprehension. This was his wife, his child. He was only minutes away from seeing his son's face for the first time, and his wife was in severe pain. But he needed to stay calm. Feeling tightness in his hands, Randy flexed his fingers a few times to relieve the tension.

He found that if Jane could hear his voice, it helped her relax and control her pushes. So during the next contraction, he counted for her. Between pushes, he gazed into her eyes and helped her stay focused. This pattern continued for several minutes.

Five minutes into pushing, a huge smile decorated Randy's face. "I can see his head, Janey. He's right there, and he has lots of brown hair." Now that Randy could actually see his son's head, excitement grew. He looked up at his wife. "Let's finish this. We are so close. Come on, Baby, you can do it."

Jane was able to focus more on the delivery knowing she was near the end. While Randy counted, she pushed. Finally, at 3:35 P.M., the baby made his appearance.

Randy cradled the infant's head and suctioned his nose and mouth. He clamped the cord and cut. A loud cry echoed through the room. He held the infant and wrapped him up in a blanket. "He's beautiful, Honey. Absolutely beautiful." His voice was brittle, his face full of emotion. Even though Randy tried to hold them in, the tears came. His heart raced, and he couldn't remember a time in his life when he felt as much pride and joy as he did at this moment. This was the happiest day of his life. He was a father.

He performed the classic sweep, placing the baby on Jane's chest. Jane took the infant in her arms as a tear fell down her cheek.

The pediatrics team cleaned up the baby, took some vitals on him, and checked his overall appearance. They did it all right there in the room under a warming light so Randy and Jane were able to watch. He weighed seven pounds, six ounces and was twenty-one inches long. His vitals looked excellent. He was strong and alert, with vigorous motions.

"How is he?" Jane asked.

Randy took a peek at the baby. "He looks great."

When the pediatrician was finished, she handed the infant to Randy. "You have a strong, healthy son, Dr. Hanson. Congratulations."

"Thank you." Randy looked down at this tiny infant, who was wrapped up in a blue receiving blanket with a blue knitted hat on his head. He cradled the baby in his arms and sat on the bed beside Jane.

Jane slowly sat up, wincing.

The infant, not wanting to be restrained, pulled one arm out of the blanket. Randy reached down with his hand and touched the baby's fingers. In the softest, most loving voice he said, "Hey, Nathan. It's Daddy." He gently rubbed the baby's hand. "Can you open your eyes for me?"

The baby tightly gripped Randy's finger.

Mark and Ellen gathered around to ogle over the new addition to the family. "Good looking kid you got there," his father said.

Randy handed the baby to his dad. "This is Nathan James Hanson."

Mark nuzzled the baby. His eyes became hazy as he stared down at his grandson. "He looks like you did when you were a baby."

"He's perfect." Randy couldn't stop smiling. His son was the most beautiful baby he had ever seen. He was so proud to be a daddy.

While Jane and the infant were moved across the hall to postpartum, Randy stepped over to the nurses' station. He sat in a chair and leaned on his knees. The pressure, stress, and unstable emotional state he'd endured over the last few hours was more than he could handle. No longer could he contain his emotions. He held his head in his hands and cried.

Mark followed Randy into the hall. Recognizing his son's fragile emotional state, he put his hand on Randy's shoulder. "You alright, Son?"

Randy tried to lower his heart rate and relax his own breathing. As the adrenaline left his system, he suddenly felt weak. "That was the hardest thing I've ever had to do. And when she wouldn't take the pain medication…"

"I told you it was going to be intense."

"Intense?" Randy looked up at his father. "Intense is not the word I would have chosen. Holy shit."

"You were very professional, and a loving and supportive husband for Jane. You handled yourself well."

Randy took a deep breath to regain his composure. "I seriously need a cup of coffee."

"I need one too. I'll run downstairs and grab some."

"Thanks."

When the excitement settled down, Randy needed to de-stress. He did this by playing with the hospital's intercom system. "Dr. Ryan, report to L&D. Dr. Ryan to L&D please."

Jim recognized Randy's voice.

"You're being paged," Jill said to him.

"I know. Son-of-a-bitch said he'd call after the baby was born, but I wasn't expecting a grandiose announcement."

Holding a cup of coffee in his hand, Randy grabbed Jane's chart off the wall and entered her room.

She held the baby in her arms, smiling at him. "Hi, Daddy."

He opened her chart and flipped through it. "How you feeling?"

"I'm a little sore, and I'm hungry."

"I'll get you some Tylenol and send for some food." He wrote an order to keep her supplied in Tylenol then put his stethoscope on.

"What are you doing?"

"Checking your vitals."

"Randy, I'm fine."

He looked her dead in the eye. "Will you let me do my job please?"

He checked her heart rate, took her pulse and temperature, and checked her blood pressure and oxygen levels. All normal. He pulled up a rolling chair and wheeled over to the bedside. He placed the bell of his scope on the baby's chest. His heartbeat was strong and his lungs sounded great. Satisfied, Randy removed the scope from his ears and draped it around his neck. "You did a fabulous job today. I'm so proud of you." He leaned over and kissed her.

Right at that moment, the postpartum nurse walked into the room. "Dr. Hanson, I..." When she realized she was interrupting, she waited for them to finish.

Randy broke his kiss with his wife and acknowledged the RN. "Hey, Terri."

"I'm sorry to bother you, but the pediatrician wants to talk to you."

"Send her in."

The pediatrician went over information about infant care, gave them an immunization schedule, taught Jane how to clean the umbilical area, and they agreed to have the baby circumcised. They received a ton of supplies—infant thermometers, cleaning bulbs, pamphlets about breastfeeding and infant care, and lots of diapers. The pediatrician checked vitals on the baby before she left.

After meeting with the pediatrician, the nurse gave Jane some Tylenol and Randy called the cafeteria to have food brought up to her room.

Randy held his new son. He talked to him, touched him, and examined his tiny hands and feet. Finally the baby opened his eyes. They were a steel grey color. "Look, Janey. His eyes are open."

Jane watched her husband, who proudly nuzzled little Nathan in his arms.

"I love the color of his eyes," Randy said.

The baby began to fuss a bit. Randy used this opportunity to teach Jane how to breastfeed. It didn't take long for either one of them to figure it out.

While the baby was feeding, Jane gazed at Randy with pride in her eyes. "I can't even imagine how hard that must have been for you today."

"You did all the work, not me."

"But you stayed so calm. I know that wasn't easy."

He sat on the side of the bed. "You want the truth?"

She nodded.

"That was the most exhausting, difficult, and exhilarating experience of my life. But seeing our baby for the first time, being there when he took his first breath, hearing his first cry," he got all teary-eyed again. "No words can describe that feeling." He kissed her, being careful not to squash his son. "I love you, Honey."

"I love you too. You should eat something," she insisted, knowing that after that exhausting experience, he had to be hungry.

"I will. But I want you to get some rest."

"What about the baby?"

"I'll stick around. In fact, I'm going to grab some food while he's nursing. I'll be back in a bit."

Randy made a stop down in the ER before he went to the cafeteria. When Jill turned around and saw Randy standing there, she ran over and gave him a huge hug. "Congratulations."

"Thanks. Where's Jim?"

"He's with a patient. I'll tell him you're here. He won't be a minute."

Jim came out to the physician's work room and moved towards Randy, who was staring out the window. "Yo, Hanson."

He turned around. "Hey."

"Dr. Ryan to L&D? Like they would let me leave the ER to run up there." He shook Randy's hand. "Grats, Bro. How you feelin'?"

"I feel incredible. He is beautiful." Randy pulled out his phone and showed Jim a picture he took of the baby.

"Cute kid. How big is he?" Jim asked.

"Seven, six. Twenty-one inches."

"Good size. What name did you guys go with?"

"Nathan James Hanson."

Jim wanted to make sure he heard him correctly. "Nathan James?"

A self-satisfied smirk filled Randy's face. "Yup. James."

Jim's eyebrows rose. "Damn, Dude. I'm flattered. You gave your son my name."

"Yes we did," Randy declared. "He doesn't look a damn thing like you though."

"I sure as hell hope not."

Randy slipped his phone back in his pocket. "When do you get off?"

"Not 'til 2 A.M."

"If you slow down and get a break later, come up and see him."

"I will. I'll see if Jill can sneak away too."

"Cool. I'm going to grab some food. I'm starving."

"Well, yeah," Jim said with a chuckle. "You've had a busy day."

"Yes I have. I'll catch ya later." Randy started to walk away.

"Yo, Randy," Jim called out to him. "Get some coffee too, Bro. You look like shit."

Randy stuck his middle finger in the air and left the ER to get something to eat.

It wasn't long before the exhaustion of the day caught up with Jane. When she fell asleep, Randy sat with the baby, giving skin to skin contact, caressing his back, and talking to him. The baby stared at him with those big grey eyes. "Hey, Buddy." The newborn made little grunting noises and cute facial expressions. "Ssh, Momma's sleeping." The baby gripped Randy's finger. "You're a strong little guy, aren't you?" He kissed the baby's head. "I'm new to this whole daddy business, but I'll do my best to take care of you. You can depend on me. I'll always be here to talk to, I'll support you, and I'll love you unconditionally, Nathan Hanson." Randy cuddled the baby in his arms for a while, relishing this father/son moment.

The nurse came in to check Jane's vitals and heard Randy singing some sort of lullaby to the baby. "Sorry to interrupt, Dr. Hanson," she whispered.

"It's ok." He signaled for her to come inside.

"Vitals," the nurse said, following standard postpartum routines.

Jane was sound asleep. Randy didn't want to disturb her. "I just checked her. Let her sleep."

Maintaining a whisper, she asked, "May I?"

"Sure." Randy repositioned the infant a bit, allowing the nurse to see his face.

She peeked in and eyed the baby's features. "He looks like you."

"Everyone keeps saying that."

"Congratulations, Doctor."

"Thank you."

"You want a cup of coffee?" she offered.

"That would be great. Thanks."

"I'll have one brought up to you."

Randy managed to get the baby to go to sleep. He laid him in the bassinet the nursery provided and covered him up with a blanket. Hoping to relax for a while, he put his feet up on the recliner and lounged next to Jane. He reached his arm inside the bassinet and held his son's hand. It wasn't long before he, too, drifted off to sleep.

Jane awoke stiff and sore. She sat up slowly and turned her head to see both the baby and her husband sound asleep. Careful not to wake them, she rang for the nurse.

When the nurse stepped in the room, Jane held her finger up to her lips. "Ssh."

This particular nurse had worked with Randy many times. She adored the man on both a professional and a personal level. He was always respectful to everyone he worked with and was one of the nicest people she ever had the privilege to know. Seeing him asleep like this, holding his infant son's hand, was too precious to resist. "We need to get a camera."

Jane pointed to the counter where Randy had set all of their belongings. The nurse grabbed the digital camera and snapped the shot.

"Can I get some Tylenol, please?" Jane asked.

"Certainly," the nurse said, setting the camera back down. "I'll be right back."

"Thank you."

As the nurse left the room, Randy opened his eyes. He let go of Nathan's hand and sat up to stretch.

"Wake up, Sleepyhead," Jane said.

He ran his fingers through his hair a few times. "Guess I was more tired than I thought."

"Can we go home?"

Randy laughed at her insistence. "No, we cannot go home. I need to keep you here overnight to make sure you're clotting properly and not getting an infection. And peds have to monitor Nate and make sure he's ok."

Knock. Knock.

Randy looked over at the door. "Come in."

A blonde man wearing scrubs waltzed into the room bearing flowers and a huge blue Mylar balloon. He had a stethoscope draped around his neck and the name James Ryan, M.D. printed on his name badge. "Hey, hey. Sup Hanson family?" Jim peered into the bassinet at the sleeping baby. "You created that?"

"I know. Can you believe it?"

"He looks like you. Poor kid."

"Shut up," Randy said, knowing Jim was teasing him.

Jim didn't stay long because he was still on shift, but promised he and Jill would stop by the following day, once Randy and Jane arrived home with the baby.

Many visitors stopped by the hospital to meet the new addition to the Hanson family. Physicians and nurses Randy worked with, several of their friends, including Greg and Raquel, and unexpectedly, Robby made an appearance.

Randy picked up the baby and tried to hand him to his brother.

Robby was hesitant to take him. "Dude, I can't."

"This is your nephew, Robby."

"I don't want to hurt him."

"You won't." Randy placed the baby in his brother's arms.

Robby carefully sat down in the recliner, supporting the infant's head and staring at him. "He's tiny."

"Newborns are." Randy pulled up a chair and sat across from his brother. "I didn't get a chance to tell you this earlier, but you look healthier than I've seen you in months. You've put on some weight and don't seem as stressed."

"With this new job, I've been able to save enough money to pay off a lot of debts I owed."

"Good. I'm glad to see you getting your life back together."

Robby adjusted the baby onto his shoulder and supported him by placing his hand on his bottom. "I'm glad you were there for me the other day. You kept me from having a relapse."

"You know you can call me anytime you need to."

"I appreciate your support. Some days are tough, but as time passes, it gets easier."

"And it's good that you recognize that," Randy said. "You've accomplished a lot. It's been almost a year now, Rob. That's an important milestone. I'm proud of you and the progress you've made."

"Thanks."

"Nathan is going to look up to you and ask you for advice along the way. I'm counting on you to guide him in the right direction."

"You know I will." Robby nuzzled his nephew and kissed his head. "I love this little guy."

Randy's youngest sibling had been through hell and back over the last year, but as Robby held Nathan,

Randy caught him smiling. Robby finally found his inspiration, and it came in the smallest package.

Chapter Forty-One

Mark was scheduled to do rounds in the morning, but since Jane was the only patient they had in the hospital, Randy took over. Her vitals were normal, no infection indicated, and her appetite had returned. Since 6:00 A.M., she'd been complaining about being hungry. To satisfy her wishes, Randy ran down to the cafeteria to order some breakfast and fetch a cup of coffee.

Shortly after he returned, Bruce and Stephanie arrived. Seeing Bruce standing in the hall of the Maternity Ward with a bouquet of flowers in his hand brought a warm smile to Randy's face. "Hey, Buckman."

Bruce greeted him with a hug. "Congratulations."

"Thank you." Randy took the flowers from him, gave his sister a hug, then invited them into the room.

"Another Hanson in the clan." Bruce peeked over at the baby. "How you feeling, being a dad?"

Randy grinned proudly. "I love it. I wouldn't trade this for the world. The birth of my son was the most intense, yet joyful thing I've ever experienced. The adrenaline flow was insane. And when I held him for the first time, nothing compares to that. Nothing ever will."

"I know the feeling."

Randy took a sip from his steaming cup. "When did you guys get here?"

"Flew in about an hour ago. We wanted to stop by before we headed over to your parents' house. Steph's gonna stick around for a week or so. I'll be in town tomorrow, but I have to be back in L.A. Monday morning."

"I understand."

"I talked to Mandy on the way over here. She and Sarah checked into a hotel together. They wanted me to tell you they'd stop by later."

"Cool. It'll be good to see them again."

At 3:30 P.M., Randy checked Jane's vitals one last time before he signed off on her chart and gave her clearance to go home. He fetched Nathan's birth certificate and signed off on that as well, not only as the attending physician but also as the child's biological father. When the pediatrician cleared Nathan, Randy packed up all of their belongings, which somehow accumulated since they checked in, and lugged them down to the car. Jane dressed Nathan in a tiny pair of sweats and the Lakers tee-shirt Randy bought for him. She covered his feet with yellow socks, put his knitted hat on his head, and swaddled him in a blanket to keep him warm.

"I'll pull the car up to the hospital entrance. See you and Nathan out front." Randy gave Jane a kiss and grabbed his phone, the camera, and his keys. He threw the diaper bag over his shoulder and headed down the elevator to the parking lot.

The nurse wheeled Jane and Nathan downstairs to the automatic doors. Together, the RN and Randy helped escorted her to the passenger side of the car. Once Jane was secured, Randy took Nathan from her and buckled him into the car seat. With Nathan safely strapped in, he sat behind the wheel, closed the door, and they all drove home together as a family.

Blue crepe paper streamers were attached to their house and a bundle of blue balloons hung off the mailbox. An oversized *It's A Boy!* sign adorned the front yard. "Oh Jesus," Randy said. "How much you wanna bet my family is responsible for this?"

Although over the top, Jane found this amusing. "Probably."

Nathan was asleep. Randy left him strapped in the car seat and carried him inside. He set him on the sofa then fed the bird a cracker and released him from his cage to get him to stop squawking. Jane slowly moved to the couch and sat down.

"Get some rest," Randy insisted. "I'll pamper you for a while."

The new family received several visitors that day. Randy's neighbors brought the baby a squeaky toy, some teething rings, and a new outfit. Another neighbor gave them a package of diapers and a CD of lullabies. Sarah and Mandy visited for several hours, taking turns holding the baby. Mandy bought them a diaper bag filled with everything from teething gel and baby wipes to pacifiers and infant Tylenol. Sarah gave them a babybook to keep track of important events and milestones in Nathan's life, and an 11x14 frame to display baby's photograph and footprints. Jim and Jill brought the kids over to see the baby, bearing a huge bag full of baby clothes, some rattles and squeaky toys, and a wooden jigsaw puzzle that spelled NATHAN.

Jim bought Randy a gift too. "And this is for you," he said, handing him a gift bag.

Randy eyed him curiously. "Do I dare ask?"

"Just open it."

Inside was a coffee cup imprinted with *It's A Boy*. He also gave him a grey tee-shirt that said, *Assistance May Be Required, New Dad in Training*. Randy thought this was the funniest thing he had ever seen.

"If babies came with training manuals, I would have gotten that for you, but since they don't, a tee-shirt will have to do."

Randy took off the tee-shirt he was wearing and put this one on instead. "Thank you. I love it."

Dale and Brian surprised everyone by flying up from San Francisco. Brian brought a 49ers baby onesie and a fleece football blanket for Nathan. Dale brought his grandson a blue teddy bear. This baby had piles of stuff—toys, clothes, blankets, teething rings, several packages of diapers, pacifiers, bibs, and plush stuffed animals that squeaked, crinkled, and rattled. Their house was full of flowers and balloons welcoming the new addition to the family. Randy welcomed it all with open arms.

Randy's family came over that evening with a pan of lasagna and a basket of garlic bread. Ellen set the lasagna on the table and pulled some plates out of the cupboard. "We know you have your hands full, so we made dinner."

While the baby slept, they all sat around the table and enjoyed a relaxing family dinner together.

"I'd like to know who's responsible for papering and ballooning my house," Randy said.

Everyone pointed to Bruce. He grinned sheepishly and shrugged his shoulders. "Hey, my best friend and his wife had a baby. I couldn't let it slide."

"I think you went a little overboard, Buckman, but it looks great."

As the stars came out and the moon made its appearance, Stephanie and Emily got situated in the guestroom of Randy and Jane's house. Stephanie planned to help Jane out with the baby when Randy went back to work. This worked out well for everyone because Randy had patients to tend to but didn't want to leave Jane alone with a newborn. And since Stephanie had no job commitments in L.A., she could easily spend a week in Seattle.

Bruce kissed his daughter goodnight, said goodbye to the family, then Randy drove him to the airport.

"Looks like you and Stephanie are getting along better," Randy remarked.

"She's restraining herself around the family. The minute she gets back to L.A. she'll be all over my ass again."

"What's going on with you two?" Randy asked.

"There's no reasoning with her. She has to have her way all the time, and if she doesn't, she throws a fit. She picks fights on purpose and does whatever she can to get me riled up. And she doesn't see herself as being part of the problem. She blames everything on me."

"Have you guys considered talking to a marriage counselor?"

Bruce let out a heavy sigh. "I've mentioned it to her, but she wants nothing to do with it."

"Don't you think it's worth a try rather than just giving up on your marriage?"

"Honestly, Randy, I don't know how much good it would do. I feel like I'm the only one who's making an effort here."

Randy felt Bruce's pain. "What about Emily? The new baby?"

"That's the shitty part," Bruce declared. "The kids are going to be caught in the middle of this crap."

"There's really no way to work this out?"

"I'm trying, but I can't fix it by myself."

After Bruce checked in, he and Randy headed toward the security line.

"Let me know if there's anything you need or if you want to vent," Randy said.

"I will." Bruce gave him a hug. "Congrats. You have a beautiful baby."

"Thanks."

When Randy returned from the airport, he set up the cradle on Jane's side of the bed and laid baby Nathan in it. He looked over at Jane, who was preparing for bed. "Are you ok with me going into the clinic tomorrow? 'Cause I can cancel my appointments and stay home if you need me to."

"Stephanie's here. I'll be fine."

He removed his tee-shirt. "Make sure you rest. Sleep when Nathan sleeps and give your body time to recover."

She was a little sore but felt great. She didn't see why he was making such a fuss over her. "Randy, I'm fine."

"You just gave birth. Your body needs time to recover from the stress it's been through. You're going to exhaust yourself if you don't get rest. I know you, and you tend to try to do everything by yourself. But you need to take it easy and not overdue it. Let Stephanie help you."

"I will," she said, reassuring him with a kiss. She slowly sat on the bed and poked at her belly. "I still look pregnant."

"It'll go away. Nursing will help. Already you're ten pounds lighter from losing seven and half pounds of baby, and other two to three pounds of placenta, blood, and amniotic fluid. The weight will keep coming off. By week four, the uterus should be back to its normal pre-pregnancy weight and you'll notice a difference."

"Four weeks?" she replied, not liking what he said.

"Generally, yes. Anywhere from three to six weeks is pretty standard." Randy kicked off his shoes. "I'm going to get a drink. You want anything?"

"No thanks."

He left the room and headed downstairs. Stephanie was sprawled out on the couch watching TV. He walked past her and said, "Make sure Jane gets some rest. Don't let her do too much."

"I won't. You need to quit worrying."

"She's my wife, Steph," he reminded her as he stepped into the kitchen. "And she's my patient."

"Speaking of which." She sat on her knees, looking over the back of the couch. "I need you to do me a favor."

He pulled a glass out of the cupboard. "What's that?"

"Will you do an ultrasound on me?"

"Why?"

"I want to know if I'm having a boy or a girl."

"Have your OB do it."

"I want you to do it. You're my brother." She gave him puppy dog eyes. "Please."

"Don't you think Bruce might want to be present for that?"

She shrugged unenthusiastically. "Come on, Randy. Do this for me."

He rolled his eyes in disapproval. "Fine, but you're supposed to be staying with Jane and helping her out."

"Jane and Nathan can come with me. And I'm sure Mom would love to spend some time with Emily."

"I'm sure she will." Randy turned on the faucet and filled his glass with water. "I'm booked all day tomorrow, but I'll be at the hospital with med students on Tuesday. I'll schedule you in then."

"Thank you."

He gripped the glass in his hand and trotted toward the stairs. "Night, Sis."

At six o'clock in the morning, Randy was awakened by a screeching cry. Bleary-eyed, he sat up. He rubbed his eyes, groaned wearily, and flopped back onto his pillow, completely exhausted.

Jane picked Nathan up and cradled him in her arms while she nursed him.

The doorbell rang. Randy looked over at Jane. "You expecting anyone this early?"

"No."

Randy rolled out of bed, slipped on a pair of sweats, and stumbled downstairs to answer his front door. When he saw Jim standing on his doorstep, an unimpressed glare filled his face. "What are you doing here?"

"Nice greeting. You're not even gonna let me in?"

Randy opened the door.

Jim waltzed inside and made himself at home. "I know it's early, but I figured with a new baby in the house you weren't sleepin' anyway."

Randy yawned and combed his fingers through his hair, attempting to scrape up some energy. "What do you want?"

"Have you eaten?"

"No. I just woke up. Why?"

"Thought we'd snag some breakfast and a cup of coffee this mornin' before work," Jim suggested.

"Alright. But I need to shower first."

"No problem. Take your time."

While they waited for their meal, the two ordered coffee. "You know what Jane asked me last night?" Randy stated.

"What?"

"How soon we could have sex. I couldn't believe that she asked me that."

To Jim, this was a hoot. "Yeah, Dude. How you gonna handle six weeks with no sex?"

Randy hadn't really thought about this before. He offered medical advice from a doctor's point of view, not thinking about the implications for him as a husband. Waiting four to six weeks to be intimate with his wife was going to require a lot of self-control on his part. More than he thought he could muster.

"By the way, Jill is gonna be getting in touch with you this week."

"What for?"

"She's lookin' for a gynecologist, and we heard you were the best in the city. She brought all of her medical records with her if you wanna see them."

Randy took a sip of his coffee. "Have her call the office and schedule an appointment. She can bring her file with her when she comes in. I'll look at it then."

"A'ight. I shall tell her."

After breakfast, Randy reported to his clinic. Normally on a Monday, his dad did morning rounds at the hospital before he came to the office, and the clinic personnel didn't usually show until 8:00, yet the parking lot was full of cars. Randy checked his watch to make sure he wasn't running late. It was only 7:30. From the passenger seat, he grabbed an envelope crammed full of baby pictures, picked up his stethoscope, and stepped out of the car. He beeped the alarm on his car on the way to the door. When he entered the clinic, the security system had already been disarmed. Convinced that his sleep-deprived state was making him delirious, he opened the door that led back to the examination rooms. Blue helium-filled balloons floated in a bundle, and, to his surprise, his dad and the entire staff gathered at the counter holding a huge banner. *Congratulations, Dr. Hanson. It's a boy!*

"What is all this?" Randy asked.

"There's a new addition to our family," Mark said. "And I'm a proud grandpa."

"Is this really necessary?"

"Yes, it is."

Everyone who came into the clinic that day commented on the balloons and banner. They all sent congratulatory wishes Randy's way and patients asked to see pictures of the baby. Randy happily fulfilled their wishes. Nathan James Hanson seemed to be the object of discussion from both the staff and the patients who came in and out of the clinic throughout the day. Randy was a proud daddy and didn't realize how much he loved that little boy until he spent the day away from him. He missed his coos and cries. He posted pictures of Nathan in his office wall and on the bulletin board where the other baby photos were, since technically Nathan Hanson was a child he delivered.

When Randy came home that night, Nathan was asleep. Stephanie was in the kitchen fixing dinner, and Emily sat on the living room floor playing with her dolls.

"Hello, Emily," Randy said to her.

Emily turned her head. "Hi, Uncle Randy."

He set his stethoscope on the table and joined his sister in the kitchen. "Where's Jane?"

"Upstairs sleeping. She has been for two hours now."

"Good. She needs rest." He sat at the kitchen island and peeked over at the portable crib where Nathan lay peacefully. "How long has he been asleep?"

"About an hour. He took a nap around ten this morning, but was awake most of the day."

"Maybe he'll sleep more tonight."

"He's a good baby, Randy. He eats well and sleeps pretty soundly. And when he gets fussy, talking calms him down. He loves to hear voices."

The baby squirmed a bit. Randy peered into the crib and Nathan opened his eyes, looking right up at him. "Hey, Buddy." Randy held him close to his chest, supporting his head and bottom. The baby cooed and grasped Randy's shirt collar. Randy kissed his head and gently patted him on the back.

"Bruce called earlier to check on Emily," Stephanie remarked.

Trying to get Stephanie's side of the story, Randy stepped into the kitchen so he and his sister could have a more private conversation. "How are you and Bruce doing?"

She ignored the question.

"Steph, I know things aren't peachy between you two like you're trying to lead everyone to believe they are."

"What makes you say that?"

"The tension between you two. It's obvious there's friction there. What's going on?"

Emily was sitting in the adjacent room. Trying to weasel her way out of this conversation, Stephanie said, "I don't want to discuss this with Emily in the room."

"Do you really think she doesn't sense the strain between her parents? She's a smart girl, Steph. You're not going to be able to hide it from her." It was pretty apparent that he wasn't going to get far with Stephanie, so he dropped the conversation. With Nathan in his arms, he sat on the sofa near Emily. "Whatcha doing, Sweetheart?"

She held her doll the same way Randy held Nathan. "Feeding my baby." She handed Randy a toy baby bottle. "You want to feed her?"

He chuckled at her. "My hands are a little full at the moment. But if you sit up here with me, I'll let you hold Nathan."

Emily set her doll on the floor and crawled onto the couch with her uncle.

When Stephanie came in to get an ultrasound, Randy was surrounded by a group of people in lab coats, all of whom had notebooks in their hands. "What's going on?" she asked, wondering why she had an audience.

"I have a few medical students who would like to observe this procedure. Do you mind if they watch?"

"No. Not at all."

"Thank you." Three medical students stepped into the room with him and positioned themselves in a corner out of the way. Randy explained the procedure step by step, pointing out specifics on each image. When he got a good look at the defining gender parts, he grinned.

"What is it?" Stephanie insisted on knowing.

"You're having another girl." He showed her the image and printed out a few.

Stephanie was perfectly happy with this news, but Randy knew Bruce wanted a boy this time. Not going to happen. Instead, more girly, frilly pink stuff would be present in Dr. Buckman's life.

Chapter Forty-Two

During the first month of Nathan's life, Jane and Randy had to adjust their lifestyle to accommodate having a new baby in the family. Nathan was active and alert during the day and usually took a nap once in the morning and twice in the afternoon. He slept through most nights, only waking every three to four hours to nurse. Randy and Jane learned to recognize his distinctive cries and discovered ways to soothe him. Even though they were sleep deprived, they enjoyed their new baby and became quite proficient at being new parents.

Aside from adjusting to parenthood, Jane went back to work part time, taking on several sports psychology consultation cases while Randy squeezed in appointments, performed countless surgeries, conducted seminars, and delivered babies at all hours of the day. To add to the craziness, Randy was busy completing a large case list where he logged every surgery, hospital admission, and baby he delivered over the last six months. He had to turn this computerized database into the medical board prior to taking his oral board exam. Collecting relevant case files was a long and tedious process, and since Randy was in a partnership practice, he could only list patients he had been personally responsible for. Even though he'd already passed his written exam, he had to be in practice at least two years before he could take the oral exam and earn full certification. Despite his busy schedule, he took time every day to bond with his son.

It wasn't unusual to find Randy face to face with Nathan, making noises at him. They bought Nathan a play gym full of compelling toys to look at. One of Randy's favorite activities was to lie on the floor with Nathan while he swiped at the dangling toys, practicing his arm, hand, and finger coordination skills.

After tucking Nathan in for the night, Jane crawled onto the bed with Randy and kissed him quite fervently.

"Don't do that," Randy said between breaths.

"Why not?"

"Because you're getting me excited."

Jane didn't listen. Her sensuous kisses only escalated his craving.

"Baby, please," he begged. "We can't."

"Why can't we?"

"You're still healing. We really should wait. Six weeks is the standard recovery period for…"

She moved her mouth to his to get him to stop talking.

Randy wrapped her up tightly in his arms and closed his eyes, taking the kiss deeper. He always gave explicit orders to his patients to wait a full six weeks after birth before engaging in intercourse, but now that he was on the other end of this, he didn't want to wait. His desire grew, and kissing her like this made it next to impossible for him to exhibit restraint.

Jane took her shirt off and tossed it on the floor.

"I'm an obstetrician and I know…"

"I don't care if you're an obstetrician. I'm not listening to you." She unlatched her bra, exposing her voluptuous breasts, which were at least a cup size larger due to nursing. Taking initiative, she crawled on top of

L.M. NELSON

him and straddled his lap. She could feel he was erect. She grabbed the bottom of his shirt and pulled it over his head.

"What are you doing?" he asked.

"What we're doing." She began to unbutton his pants.

Wide eyed, his chest rose and fell with rapid breaths. He watched every move she made, but made no attempt to stop her. In fact, he helped her by sliding his pants over his hips and kicking them onto the floor. As soon as he was naked, Jane stripped her panties off. He stared at her in erotic delight. "You are so damn sexy."

Jane reached into the bedside table drawer and pulled out a condom. She tore the package open and unrolled the latex onto him. Without saying a word, she leaned over and kissed him.

He groped and fondled, wanting her in the worst way. When he slid inside, he let out a groan. He closed his eyes and took in every stimulating sensation she offered him.

In the morning, Nathan woke calmly with a few gurgles and coos. Randy peeked his head in the nursery door. The baby's grey eyes stared at him. "Good morning, little one." He took Nathan out of his crib and crept downstairs to prepare a bottle.

While Nathan gulped down milk, Randy's finger became an object of fascination. The baby stared at it intently and squeezed it with his hand.

"Whatcha looking at?"

Nathan spit out his bottle and gurgled.

"Not hungry?" Randy stared at the contents of the bottle and turned his nose up at it. "You need to get some teeth so you can eat real food, like Oreos. You'll like those. Stay away from Mommy's yogurt though. She'll poison you with that stuff."

When Jane heard her boys jabbering back and forth, she came downstairs to see what they were doing. Randy sat on the floor with Nathan, speaking in a soothing voice. Nathan answered with coos and gurgles. She snuck up behind the biggest boy and kissed him softly. "Good morning."

"Morning, Baby. Nathan and I are having a father/son talk here. He told me he wants Oreos."

"I'm sure that's exactly what he said." She stepped into the kitchen to prepare breakfast.

"He also said he wants to go fishing."

"He's too little," Jane replied.

"You're never too little to go fishing. You do need to be able to hold your own fishing pole however. A few more months and he'll be ready."

Jim came over that afternoon to find Randy traipsing around on his roof. He stepped out of his car and onto Randy's lawn. "Ho, ho, ho."

Randy peeked over the roof's edge. "Hey, Ryan."

"What are you doin' up there?"

"Hanging up Christmas lights. Why don't you get your lazy ass up here and help me."

Jim quickly negated that suggestion. "I don't do ladders, Dude."

"Why not?"

"I work in the ER. I've seen too many injuries that resulted from ladder mishaps."

Randy laughed and climbed down. "What brings you over here?"

"I brought you something." Jim handed him an envelope.

Randy opened the flap and pulled out two Lakers tickets. "Nice. How did you get ahold of these?"

"A colleague of mine bought them but won't be able to make the game. He sold them to me for a hotdog price. Will you be able to break free for a few days to join me?"

"Absolutely." Randy stuffed the tickets back in the envelope. "You want a cup of coffee?"

"Sure."

The two men went inside. Randy's house was all decked out in festive garlands and Christmas candles. The tree was decorated with shiny ornaments and lights, and several wrapped gifts nestled neatly underneath. Three red stockings, trimmed in white fuzz with the names Randy, Jane, and Nathan sewn on the front, hung on the fireplace mantle. Christmas-patterned placemats and hand towels adorned the kitchen area, and a large stuffed Santa sat on a barstool at the kitchen island. A tray of Christmas cookies cooled on the counter and Christmas music rang out from the sound system. The whole house looked, sounded, and smelled like Santa's workshop.

"Are you married to Mrs. Claus?" Jim teased.

"Jane and I like Christmas. And we have a baby this year celebrating his first one."

"You do know, don't you, that he won't remember any of this."

"So? What's your point?"

"Isn't this a bit extreme?"

Randy's lips formed a crooked grin. "Wait 'til you see the outside."

"Oh Jesus. You're not the National Lampoon guy are you?"

"Maybe." Randy took his sweatshirt off and poured some coffee into his Lakers mug.

Randy was a diehard Lakers fan. The Lakers history was one of the richest of all NBA teams. It included some of the brightest stars and personalities in basketball. In Randy's eyes, the Los Angeles Lakers were the top basketball team in the world. The Lakers banner on his office wall, the coffee cup he was drinking from, the mini Lakers basketball hoop that hung over the wastebasket in his clinic, and the Lakers logo on his keychain and watch were evidence of this.

"You gonna stay and watch the game with me tonight?" Randy asked. "Greg and Robby are coming over."

"When's game time?" Jim asked.

"Seven."

"Aren't you on-call tonight?"

"Yes, and dammit, I better not miss the game."

Greg, Jim, Robby, and Randy cheered when the Lakers made a three-point shot to take the lead. "Holy shit, that was an amazing shot."

Jane came out to the living room and glared at her husband. "Could you keep it down please. I just got Nathan to sleep."

"Sorry," Randy said with more of a whisper this time.

The buzzer sounded and the game finished with a 108-105 Lakers victory. Randy leaned back on the couch and took a sip of his Corona. "Oh man, that game was intense."

"Dude," Jim interjected. "That three pointer was off the charts, and that pick and roll in the last quarter, fuckin' righteous."

Usually Greg was outgoing and pretty talkative, but tonight he seemed kind of distant and withdrawn.

Concerned about his mood, Randy asked, "Hey, Greg. You alright?"

Greg took in a huge breath. "I have a lot on my mind."

Randy put his feet up on the coffee table, hoping Jane didn't see him. It pissed her off when he did that. "Like what?" He lifted a Corona bottle to his lips.

"I'm going to propose to Raquel."

Randy almost choked on his beer. "What?"

"I got her a ring and was thinking about giving it to her for Christmas. Maybe invite her over for dinner, share a bottle of wine while we watch Miracle on 34th Street." Seeking advice, he turned to Randy. "You don't think that's a corny way to ask her, do you?"

"It's certainly not something she'll expect. Sounds like a great idea to me."

Jim snickered under his breath.

"What is it with you and marriage proposals?" Randy asked. "Any time someone brings up the topic, you start laughing your ass off."

"Sorry, Dude," Jim said. "I find it funny how you, and now Greg, go out of your way to impress a babe hoping she'll be more inclined to marry you. If she loves you, she doesn't need a show. Tryin' to swoon her by gettin' down on one knee or takin' her out to some fancy ass restaurant isn't gonna change a damn thing."

"I know that, but how many times does a guy propose to his girlfriend?" Randy asked.

"Once."

"Exactly. Which is why I, personally, wanted to make it a memorable experience for her."

"That's all fine and dandy," Jim posed. "But some guys go through the motions all the time until they finally find some sucker who's willing to take the bait.

Before she even realizes what's happened, he reels her in with her mouth caught on the hook and her tail flappin' in the wind. Then there's those smooth talkin' dudes who are really slick. They get engaged to rich chicks, maybe even go as far as marrying the babe, then divorce her ass to get half the schwag. And they do it multiple times simply to get access to dinero."

Randy sneered at that absurd assumption. "Only a douchebag would do that."

"There are guys out there who do."

Greg added, "There are women out there who put on a show to suck guys in too. It goes both ways, Ryan. My ex was like that."

"Oh, I know they're out there," Jim said. "My point is if she loves you, you don't need to impress her with an expensive ring and all that romantic crap. She knows before you even ask her if she's gonna marry you or not. Some fancy show isn't gonna change her mind if you aren't the guy she wants to spend her life with, so why go through all that trouble?"

Jim desperately needed an intervention here. Randy took it upon himself to educate him. "You really need to hone in on your feminine side, Jim."

"Why? So I can be a fuckin' wuss?"

"No, so you can see things from a female point of view. Women love romance, and a woman needs to know you would go out of your way to make her happy. It makes her feel important. It makes her feel loved. You're damn lucky you found a woman who doesn't care that you're an insensitive ass."

"She loves my insensitive ass. In fact, she goes to bed with my insensitive ass every night."

Greg tried to get them back on track. "What the hell does that have to do with any of this? All I said was I bought her a ring and was thinking about giving it to her for Christmas. I never said I was gonna get on one knee and beg or show off with billboards and banners. I'm simply going to wrap a ring in a box and present it to her over dinner and a movie," Greg said. "When she opens the box, she'll know what it means."

Randy continued the debate. "You at least need to say the words. There was no feeling more powerful than looking into Jane's eyes and saying, will you marry me. It was the scariest and most exhilarating rush ever."

"All I did was tell Jill we should get married," Jim stated. "She agreed with me. Randy here made a damn show out of it. Fuckin' flowers and fancy dinner at the restaurant where they had their first date, and a three-thousand dollar ring or some shit."

Robby found that figure appalling. "You spent three grand on an engagement ring?"

"Two grand," Randy corrected.

Jim reemphasized his point. "She would have married you regardless of the damn show you put on."

"But buying her roses and taking her out to dinner was more fun," Randy defended. "Jane loves that kind of stuff. It's all about pleasing the woman, Jim. Haven't you figured that out yet?"

"I don't hear Jill complainin'. Quite the contrary, in fact."

Randy offered Greg a piece of advice. "Just let it flow and do what feels right. Marriage proposal is something no one can really tell you how to approach. You know Raquel, and you know what she likes. Feed off of that and you'll be good as gold."

Randy had on a tee-shirt with a chemical formula written on the front. Underneath the formula was the word OFF. All day long Robby had been trying to figure out what it meant. "What's with your shirt?"

Randy explained, "It's the chemical formula for urine."

Jim started laughing, knowing exactly what Randy's shirt said.

But Robby didn't get it. "Why would anyone care about that?"

Teasing his brother, Randy replied, "You mean you don't know the chemical formula for urine?"

"Who gives a crap what it is?"

Helping Robby out a bit, Jim clarified, "Urine, Rob. In other words, piss."

Robby still didn't get it.

"Think about it, Bro." Jim hoped Robby would figure it out for himself so he could see how twisted his brother was.

Once Robby put the pieces together, he too began to laugh. "Your shirt says Piss Off."

"Yes it does," Randy verified. "I usually get blank stares when I wear this shirt. Not many people get the humor. Jane hates this shirt. She thinks it's rude and doesn't like me wearing it in public."

Greg stood up and pulled another beer out of the fridge. "The baby's getting big."

"Yes he is," Randy said. "He eats like a horse. Weighs ten and a half pounds now."

"Big boy."

"Yup. He'll be shooting hoops with us in no time."

Jim and Randy met for lunch Monday. In the middle of the conversation, Jim pulled a photograph out of his wallet and handed it to Randy. "Jill and I were cleaning out a box of old pictures the other day and I came across this."

It was a picture of him and Randy standing in front of the gym in basketball shorts and tee-shirts. Randy was pointing to the camera with a basketball in his hand, and Jim's hand was in a fist with his pinky and thumb sticking up. Jim had what appeared to be flowers on his head.

"What the hell is on your head?"

"The lei Molly Ferguson gave me," Jim said. "That was the week Trina was pissed and hadn't spoken to me in three days."

"When was she not pissed at you?"

"Good point. Anyway, Molly felt bad because I wasn't getting laid, so she gave me a lei."

"I remember that." He handed the picture back to Jim. "Does Trina know you moved to Seattle?"

"Why should I tell her?" Jim asked. "I don't even know where she is. Don't care to know."

"Trina hated me. Every time you and I found mischief to get into, she always accused me of being a bad influence on you."

"She only said that because she was jealous. She knew I liked hangin' out with you more than her."

"You never actually said that to her, did you?" Randy asked.

"Hell yeah. I asked her once if she knew why I hung out with you so much."

This was bound to be good. Randy couldn't wait to hear how this story ended. "And what did she say?"

"She said she didn't know why. So I told her I hung out with you because you didn't bitch at me or throw shit at me. And you would shut up once in a while and let me talk."

"Ouch," Randy cringed. "That's harsh."

"I did add that she had one thing over you."

"And what was that?"

"She could make me wave horny and had a nicer ass than you."

Randy almost fell out of his seat. "Bet she didn't take that very well."

"No, she didn't. She called me an asshole and slammed the door in my face."

"That was when you guys broke up for like two months, wasn't it?" Randy recalled.

"Yup. But I knew she'd be back. She couldn't resist me. I gave her a good fuck and she knew it."

"Arrogant ass," Randy joked. "You have a high opinion of yourself, don't you?"

"Hey, I gave her what she wanted. You did the same thing when we were in college. The only difference is I did it with one woman. You slept with hundreds."

Although it was always fun reminiscing with Jim, Randy wasn't proud of some of the things he did during his college years. "That's a part of my past I really don't want to relive. I was a jerk to a lot of women and wish now that I hadn't broken as many hearts as I did."

"That's cool, Dude." Jim completely understood. He dropped the subject and slid the photo back in his wallet. "Sabrina is driving me nuts."

"Why?"

"That girl has an attitude that won't quit. I asked her to unload the dishwasher yesterday and she informed me that she didn't understand why we forced her to do all the work around the house."

"Unloading a dishwasher isn't asking that much."

"No, it's not. But according to her, we are terrible parents. Jill and I bought her a cellphone because I am tired of tryin' to reach her and never knowin' where she is. You would think she'd be grateful that we got her the phone she wanted, but instead she blurted out some kind of bullshit about how we don't trust her and never let her do anything. And heaven forbid we make our 10-year-old come in the house before it gets dark. She and some of her friends had a birthday party last weekend and when she returned home, she asked us if she could get her belly button pierced."

"She's too young for that."

"I know, but this girl thinks she's a grownup. I dropped her off at her friend's house for a sleepover the other day. She came home in a pair of really short shorts with the word Bubbly printed on the ass in big bold letters. I told her there was no way in hell she was wearin' that. I'm not havin' some perverted wave horny teenager starin' at my daughter's ass," Jim boldly declared.

"Man, she's rebellious, isn't she?"

"That's a fuckin' understatement. Jesus. She scares me," Jim said. "She's already interested in boys and she tries to dress provocatively to attract them."

"But she's only ten."

"I know. Besides the navel piercing and the eye-drawing words she wants printed on her ass, she also seems to think we should let her cake a crap ton of makeup on her face. Jill and I won't let her wear makeup, and we've cleaned all the crap out of her closet that we deem as inappropriate for her to wear. I grounded her the other day when she tried to sneak out of the house in super tight skinny jeans and a really low cut, tight-fitting tank top."

"What kind of people does she hang out with?"

Jim replied, "I've met a few of her friends. They're all nice girls, but Jill told me there's this older boy that's been hangin' around them."

"Sounds like she's trying to impress this boy," Randy assumed.

"So it seems, and I don't like that. Why is he hangin' out with 10-year-old girls?"

Randy found this entire situation amusing. He was glad Jim was dealing with it and not him. "You're going to have your hands full when she's a teenager, Jim. You better put her on the pill the day she starts her period."

Jim couldn't believe Randy suggested that. "The pill? My daughter is not old enough to have sex, Randy. No way. No guy is dickin' my daughter."

"You really think you'll be able to stop her if she wants to?" Randy asked. "It's better to protect her."

"I'll just lock her in the damn house." Jim's head hurt now. "Holy shit. I am not ready for this. What the hell happened to the sweet little girl in pigtails who used to draw me cute pictures and play with dolls all the time?"

"Girls grow up and become young women."

"Then they drive their fathers crazy with worry. I hope your next child is a girl so you can deal with this crap."

"I'm happy with my boy, thank you." Randy chuckled and looked down at his watch. "I better get back. I have a 1:15 appointment."

"A'ight. I'll give you a call tonight." The two men knuckle bumped. "Take care of that baby, Bro. Enjoy him while he's little. It doesn't last long."

"Will do." Randy left a twenty dollar bill on the table before he got up to leave. "I'll see you later."

Jim flashed him the shaka sign. "Later, Dude."

Chapter Forty-Three

Spring was in the air, and with it came warmer weather. Daffodils popped out of the ground and the trees around the Seattle area began to bud. Nathan was growing too. He could grab toys, support himself in a sitting position, and roll all over the room. He was able to get up on his hands and knees and looked like he was going to take off crawling at any moment. He was often seen playing with his toes, which he recently discovered. His personality blossomed. He was a lovable baby who liked being cuddled and held. Randy and Jane started him on solid foods and slowly began to wean him to only the bottle.

Randy came home from an early morning delivery emotionally and physically drained. The minute he walked in the door, he held Nathan in his arms.

Jane stepped into the room. The dejected look on Randy's face told her something was wrong. "You ok?"

"Had a rough morning. The tiny premature baby I delivered this morning came into the world barely alive. He has all kinds of health problems and had to be put on a ventilator." He kissed Nathan's head and sat him back down in the portable crib, where he rolled around and kicked his feet. "I thank God for Nathan every day. Our son is so strong, so healthy. He is such a vibrant little boy. But some of these babies, by no fault of their own, are struggling to survive. Innocent children and their lives are hanging by a thread. I feel helpless because I can't do anything for them. It breaks my heart."

"That's because you are a caring, compassionate man." Jane leaned in and kissed him rather fervently on the lips.

Nathan cooed and screeched, causing Randy to break away from Jane. He glanced into the crib to find the baby staring at them. "He's watching us."

Jane turned her head to look. "He is not. He's just making baby noises."

"No. He's watching us, and he's laughing. Look at that grin."

"Just like his daddy." She grazed her hand across his chest and sat on the sofa with a book in her hand.

Randy opened the kitchen window to allow the springtime breeze to circulate through the house. It was a beautiful morning. Fresh air, bright sun, and the birds happily twittered away in the tree outside. He washed his hands and put on a pot of coffee. While the coffee brewed, he chopped spinach, mushrooms, and red peppers and threw them in an omelet. He sprinkled it with the slightest bit of grated mozzarella cheese then added a fresh parsley sprig on top to spruce it up. When his omelet was done, he popped two slices of wheat bread in the toaster and sliced a grapefruit in half, sectioning it. He set all of this on the table then proceeded to prepare a bowl of baby cereal. Once it was mixed, he pulled a baby spoon from the drawer and brought it and the bowl over to the table.

He picked Nathan up and strapped him in the highchair. While Randy ate his breakfast, he attempted to feed the baby.

Jane sat and watched. Every time Randy took a bite of his omelet, he fed Nathan a spoonful of baby cereal. This became a comedy act because Nathan kept spitting the cereal out and Randy had to scoop it back in. "Are you getting any of that in his mouth?"

"He's eating. He keeps trying to grab my eggs though." He gave the baby another spoonful. "The thought of eating baby food grosses me out. This can't taste good."

"He doesn't know any different. That's all he's ever eaten. You're just spoiled because you get eggs."

Nathan had baby food all over his face and hands. Randy cleaned them with a baby wipe.

They decided to take Nathan to the park for a while to get some sunshine and outdoor air. They spread a blanket out on the grass and sat Nathan on it. They gave him a few toys to play with and watched him squirm around.

"Any word from Stephanie or Bruce?" Jane asked, wondering if Stephanie had her baby yet.

"Nope. Still waiting. If she doesn't have the baby this weekend, they're probably going to induce her. I would. I don't like letting patients go over forty-two weeks."

"Hopefully it won't be too much longer."

"Hopefully not." Randy rolled onto his tummy facing Nathan. He handed him a toddler-sized basketball. The baby grasped it with his tiny hand. A pretty yellow dandelion soon attracted his attention; he reached over to grab it. Dandelion petals immediately went to his mouth. Randy pulled his son's hand down and dusted the petals off. "No, Nathan. Yucky." The baby gripped Randy's finger and shoved it in his mouth, biting down. "You know, Honey, I think he might be teething. He's sure been chewing on things."

"Probably. Speaking of which, you can't leave your socks on the living room floor. Nathan scooted on his tummy to grab one the other day, and when I turned my back for a minute, he was chewing on it."

The thought of this made Randy cringe. "I'll make sure I put those in the hamper." Nathan had lost interest in Randy's finger and was now fascinated by a piece of grass. Once again he tried to put it in his mouth. Randy took it away from him.

Nathan scrunched his face up and shouted, "Da!"

Randy was a bit shocked by this. "Did you hear that? He said Dad."

Jane giggled. "I think he was yelling at you for taking that away from him."

"He can't eat grass, Baby."

"I know that. But he doesn't seem to agree with you."

Nathan picked up another handful of grass and tried to stick it in his mouth. "No, Nathan." Randy once again took it away from him, but this time the child started to cry.

"See, now you made him cry," Jane teased.

"I'm not going to let my son put grass in his mouth."

With sad eyes, Nathan pouted and whined. "Da."

"Aww," Jane said. "How can you resist that?"

"Man, he is strong-willed," Randy remarked, leering at Jane. "Wonder where he gets that from?"

For dinner that night, Randy and Jane decided to attempt going out to eat. Randy strapped Nathan into a highchair and scooted him closer to the table. The noises and people at the restaurant drew Nathan's attention. He looked all around and tried to grab things off the table. To appease his curiosity, Randy handed him a spoon. It immediately went in his mouth. Randy let him chew on it for a while, but as soon as Nathan started banging it on the highchair, Randy took it away.

Nathan frowned. "Da!"

"You cannot have that anymore." He gave him a quieter toy. "Here. Play with this."

Jane couldn't stop laughing.

"What is so funny?"

"He doesn't like it when you take things away from him."

"He was banging it on the highchair. We can't let him do that in a restaurant. People are trying to eat."

"You sound like a daddy."

Randy sat up a bit taller. "I am a daddy."

Nathan was fussy the next morning, and he kept tugging at his ear. Randy took his temperature and discovered he had a fever. He used his otoscope to look in his throat and ears. He had redness of the eardrum and one of his ears was clogged with fluid. "Owie."

"What is it?" Jane asked.

"He has an ear infection," Randy clarified.

"Aww. Poor baby."

"We can give him ibuprofen. Baby Motrin will do the trick. Putting him on Amoxicillin for a few days should help clear it up. Just to be safe, I'll call Mandy and see what she recommends." Randy cuddled his son and tried to soothe his crying. He kissed his warm forehead. "I'm sorry, Buddy." He pulled his cellphone out of his pocket and dialed Mandy's number.

Chapter Forty-Four

"Any contractions yet?" Bruce asked, wishing Stephanie would go into labor.

Stephanie shook her head. "Nothing. I see my doctor on Monday. I hope he induces me."

"So do I."

"How late are you going to be Monday?"

Bruce shrugged. "I don't know. But I'll have my phone on me. If you end up getting admitted into the hospital, please let me know."

"What difference will it make? You'll be too busy to show up anyway." She shot him a piercing glare and tore off into the other room.

Bruce got up and followed her. "Every time I have to work late or get called in for an emergency, you cock attitude with me. It's really getting old."

"Maybe you should think about your family once in a while and less about your damn reputation," she argued.

"What?" he bit back.

"You are so worried about what other doctors think that you bend over backwards and do more than you are required to do."

"Moving up the residency ladder means more responsibility, Steph. It has nothing to do with bending over backwards. Neurosurgery requires a lot of practice to be good at it."

"Eighty damn hours a week?"

"If necessary, yes." Stephanie never supported his medical training. Whenever he had to focus on research or take care of a sick patient, an argument almost always ensued. His medical career seemed to be a constant issue between them. "Is it really asking that much for you to support me? I have no control over my schedule. Neurosurgeons are in high demand, which often requires me to stay late and come in unexpectedly. It's the nature of the specialty."

"So you neglect your family because of it?" she reproached.

"Dammit, Stephanie, we've talked about this a hundred times. I am not neglecting my family."

"You never answer your phone when I call you. I always get voicemail."

"I can't drop everything and come home every time you call with a minor personal issue or a broken nail. People's lives are at stake."

"Oh, but you are sure quick to respond when the hospital calls, aren't you?" Her tone became increasingly more rash.

"I can't predict when a neurological emergency is going come up, and I can't ignore them when they do. Things like that are out of my control. Give me a break."

Emily walked into the room. "Daddy?"

Bruce looked down at his daughter. "Hi, Princess."

She hugged his legs. "Why are you and Mommy yelling?"

Bruce glowered at his wife, frustrated with her attitude. "Mommy and I are having a little discussion."

"It's loud."

"I'm sorry." He squatted down to her eye level. "You want a cookie?"

"Uh huh."

"Ok. Meet me in the kitchen and I'll get you one."

"Yay!" She skipped away joyfully.

Bruce stood up and turned his attention back to Stephanie. "Can you please control yourself in front of Emily? It upsets her."

"You're blaming this on me?"

"You're the one who brought this up. You always bring it up. Then it escalates because you refuse to let it go. Schedule and all, my job is what supports this family. I'm sorry if it cramps your style." He headed to the kitchen to get Emily a cookie.

As hoped, Stephanie was induced Monday afternoon. She gave birth to an eight pound girl. They named her Alyssa Christine Buckman. Bruce was able to get a week off to help Stephanie with the new baby, but shortly after he returned to his neurosurgery duties, he received a late night call from the hospital. It woke him from a dead sleep.

"Dr. Buckman," he answered groggily. He listened intently for a moment before he replied, "Yes, Sir. I'm on my way."

Stephanie sat out in the dimly lit living room nursing the baby. She watched Bruce gather his truck keys and shove his cellphone in his pocket, obviously in a hurry to get somewhere. "Where are you going?"

"Hospital called. There's an emergency situation that's come up," he explained.

"You're leaving?"

"Yes. I'm on-call tonight. They need me at the hospital."

She shot him a nasty glare. "What if I need you here?"

"Stephanie, not now. I'll come back after I see what's up."

"You always say you'll come right back, but you don't. They'll make you stay and operate or put you to work doing CAT scans and MRI's. You'll end up staying at the hospital for hours. You might as well not come back at all."

Bruce tightened his jaw, trying to dodge her harsh words. "I have to go."

Stephanie snarled and refused to look at him as he walked out of the apartment.

Because of the intricate and time consuming nature of neurological surgery, Bruce worked long hours and was often required to be on-call. When life-threatening situations arose, his services couldn't wait; he had to be available immediately. This posed several problems, most of which began with Stephanie. She constantly demanded Bruce's attention and expected him to take her out every night. When he didn't comply, she appeased herself by impulse shopping, yet she never told Bruce she had spent money. He usually found out by scanning through credit card transactions and checking the bank account balance. More often than not, an argument ensued, at which time she posted blame on him and accused him of neglecting the family because of his job. Bickering between them occurred almost daily, and the stress of it all was taking its toll on Bruce. He wasn't sleeping well and was to the point where he avoided coming home to evade a fight.

Needing a friend to talk to, Bruce met Mandy at a nearby coffee shop. "Thank you for meeting me here," he said to her.

"Of course. That's what friends are for. What's on your mind?"

With a frown, he said, "I live with constant negativity and yelling. It's extremely stressful and it's beginning to affect my work."

"That's not good."

"No, it's not." He huddled over his cup of coffee. "I need to get away, take some time to regroup."

"What did you have in mind?"

Bruce looked up at her. "Separation. Distance myself from her for a while. But I'm worried about my girls. Stephanie is vindictive, and I know she'll find a way to use Emily and Alyssa as leverage. To her it's all about winning and losing, and she never plays by the rules. She'll do anything she can to win." He set his cup down and stared at it.

"I hate seeing you like this, Buckman. You haven't smiled in months."

"I know. Which is why I need to get out of that apartment."

"You know my door is always open to you. You're more than welcome to stay with me," she offered.

He smiled at her. "I was hoping you'd say that."

Bruce walked into his apartment around 7:00 P.M. that night, just in time to give Emily a bath, read her a book, and tuck her into bed. He changed Alyssa, fed her a bottle, and burped her before kissing her goodnight. After the kids were settled, Bruce sat on the sofa across from Stephanie. He rested his elbows on his knees and tried to gather his thoughts. "We need to talk."

She pretended not to hear him. "Were you talking to me?"

"You know damn well I was talking to you." He twirled his wedding ring around his finger. "Our marriage has been on the rocks for a while now. We don't talk to each other. We can't stand being in the same room together. We haven't shared a bed in almost a year. There is so much tension and stress in this apartment all the time; I have to go to work to relax and unwind. I'm tired of arguing." Bruce waited for some kind of outburst from her. Instead he got silence. "Stephanie, look at me."

Their eyes met for the first time in a long time.

"You can't honestly tell me that you're happy living like this."

She shook her head.

"We're exposing our daughters to constant bitterness and bickering. That's not a healthy environment for them to be in, and you know that. Is that really how we want to raise our daughters?"

She admitted he was right. "No."

"Neither do I." He hung his head and stared at the floor. "I have a friend who's offered me housing until I can get my own place."

"What friend?" she insisted on knowing.

"That's irrelevant," he answered. "We both need time to rethink our commitment and figure out what we want. I think we should separate for a while."

"You're going to abandon your daughters?"

Even though she tried to pick another fight, he remained calm. "I'm not abandoning my girls. I have every intention of spending time with them, and I'll call Emily every day. But for now, I think separation is best for all of us." He took a cleansing breath and rose to his feet. "I'll stop by after work tomorrow to check on the girls. If you need anything until then, you know how to reach me."

After work the next day, Bruce stopped by the apartment to pick up some of his belongings. Every room was dark. "Emily?" He turned on a lamp in the living room. "Stephanie, are you here?" Panicking, he searched the entire apartment, moving from room to room. Emily's doll and blanket were gone and all the baby's diapers and clothes were missing. He looked for a note or some other clue telling him of their whereabouts. On the refrigerator, he found a folded piece of paper with his name on it. He pulled it off the magnet and read it.

Bruce,

Since separation is what you want, I've gone to my parents' house. The girls are with me, so don't worry about them. I'll have Emily call you later. Stephanie.

Bruce lurched over, both hands on his knees. With his head ducked low, he slid down the refrigerator and fell to the floor. His breathing escalated. He crinkled up the note and clenched it in his fist until his knuckles turned white.

Randy heard about this episode via a phone call from his father. Although he knew this was coming, it didn't dull the shock. "Does Bruce know she's up here?"

"I don't know," Mark replied.

"Has he called?"

"Not yet."

Randy tapped his finger on the desk, concerned about the circumstances behind this situation. "Let me talk to Stephanie."

"She's in no emotional condition to talk to anyone right now," Mark replied. "Give her some time to pull herself together."

By the time Bruce called, his initial state of panic turned to rage. Randy had to talk some sense into him. "Buddy, calm down."

"I'm so sick of her lying, sneaky deceitfulness. I can't believe she pulled this shit. She took my daughters away from me, my Emily, and she's denying me my chance to bond with Alyssa. She can't do this to me."

"I know, but you need to calm down."

Bruce took a moment to pull himself together. "Have you seen the girls? Are they ok?"

"The girls are fine. They're with my parents." Randy was able to talk Bruce down long enough to hear his side of the story.

Later that night, when Randy knew the girls would be asleep, he went over to his parents' house to talk to his sister.

The moment Stephanie saw him, she teared up.

Trying to be an understanding and supportive big brother, he held her for a minute and let her cry. "What happened?"

She wiped her tears and sniffled. "Bruce said he wanted to separate. He stayed at some friend's house last night but refused to tell me who it was. I'm married to a man who puts everything else before his family."

Randy found this hard to believe. Bruce loved his girls and spent every free minute he had with them. "You know he cares about those girls, Steph. He's a good father."

"His job is more important to him than we are, and I'm tired of being put on the back burner." She buried her face in her hands and sobbed.

Randy took a cleansing breath. He understood why Stephanie was upset. However, this story didn't mesh with the one he got from Bruce. "Have you two talked about this?"

"Bruce and I can't talk. Every time we try, we end up arguing. He says I'm uptight about his schedule and thinks I don't support his career. I've tried to support him. I have."

The fact that their stories didn't coincide made Randy wonder what was really going on. Bruce claimed Stephanie was constantly nagging at him because he couldn't be home every waking minute and had to go in at night for emergency calls. Stephanie contradicted this by saying Bruce neglected the family and was rarely home. Bruce accused Stephanie of spending frivolously and lying to him constantly. He maintained that he was left with no choice but to monitor her spending because she charged their credit card through the roof and was running the bank account into the ground. Yet Stephanie made it sound like Bruce was a dominating jerk who tried to control her. According to him, she was always picking fights and complaining about nitpicky things, but she denied this fact, saying she tried to support him. They each had a different story and Randy wasn't sure what to believe. Bruce and his sister had some serious problems they needed to work through, if that was even possible. Randy knew their marriage was rocky, but didn't realize how bad it was until the walls finally crumbled down.

Randy lifted her chin. "Steph. Look at me."

She wiped her tears and looked at her brother in desperation.

"What about your girls? You know how close Emily and Bruce are. And you have a newborn. He's their father, Steph. You can't keep Bruce from his children."

"I don't know what to do." She wept on Randy's shoulder.

Chapter Forty-Five

Despite efforts to try to rectify their differences, the next three months were stressful for both Bruce and Stephanie. They remained separated, and every time they tried to talk to each other, the conversation turned into a yelling match.

Randy offered to help out his sister by taking Emily to the park with them. Emily played on the slide and swung on the swings. Every now and then she'd stop to play with Nathan. After about an hour, she sat in the grass next to her Uncle Randy. "When can I go home and see Daddy?" she asked him.

Randy didn't know what to tell her. "I don't know, Sweetheart."

Tears welled in her eyes. "I want my daddy."

Randy put his arm around his niece, wishing he could take her pain away. "I know." Seeing tears fall from his niece's eye was more than Randy could handle. He hugged her and tried to offer comfort.

Later, when he dropped her off, he approached Stephanie with his concerns. "Steph, you have to let Bruce see his kids. I know you're upset, but they need their dad. Emily wouldn't stop crying for him today. He wants to come up and see them. He told me that he's asked you about it several times, but you refuse to work with him."

She glared at her brother.

"Come on. Be reasonable here. These are his kids. You can't deny them their father. He can stay with me so you don't have to talk to him or even see him if that's the issue, but you can't keep him from his girls, Steph. You know that isn't right."

After much convincing, Stephanie gave in.

Bruce took a week of vacation and flew up to Seattle. He housed himself in Randy's guestroom. "Thanks for letting me stay here."

"Not a problem," Randy said.

"This sucks. I can't tuck my girls in at night. Alyssa doesn't even know me." Bruce's eyes became misty. "I knew it was only a matter of time before she'd pull this kind of crap. She's not going to get away with this."

"She knows she can't keep the girls from you forever, Bruce. She's not that ignorant."

Bruce scoffed, "I hope not, because she has some serious explaining to do. I've already spoken to an attorney."

Randy questioned this decision, "An attorney?"

"Yes. I'm having divorce papers drawn up."

This wasn't something Randy expected Bruce to say, although he wasn't really surprised. "You're filing for divorce?"

"I can't live like this. Every day I dreaded coming home from work because I knew she was going to bitch at me about something the second I walked in the door. Everything I did was wrong, every word I said was misinterpreted, and I couldn't do my job without her griping about it constantly. I've spent the last three months trying to drag myself out of the financial hole she's buried me in. I'm tired of being lied to, tired of arguing, and tired of being used as her personal piggy bank. The last three months without her have been the calmest and happiest I've been in years. I desperately miss my daughters, and I fear what divorce may mean for them, but in the long run being away from Stephanie is a hell of a lot better than exposing my girls to constant hostility. This isn't a marriage, and it's not how I want to spend the rest of my life."

Randy could see where Bruce was coming from, he just hated to see his sister on the receiving end of it. "I didn't realize things were that bad."

"I'm sorry your family has to be involved. It was not my intention to hurt any of you. I hope there's no hard feelings over this."

Randy offered reassurance. "You and I are friends, Bruce, and nothing is going to change that."

"I hate to put my girls through this hell. I really want to avoid a court battle and see if we can come to some kind of settlement. I hope Stephanie doesn't try to drag the girls into this."

Randy helped Bruce get situated in the guestroom. They laid an air mattress and sleeping bag on the floor for Emily and set up the cradle for Alyssa. After everything was ready, Randy turned to Bruce and said, "Let's get your girls."

Bruce's demeanor turned tense. "I don't know how I'm going to react when I see Stephanie."

"I can go in and get the girls if you want," Randy offered. "That way you won't have to see her at all. Will that be easier?"

Bruce nodded. "It might."

And that's what he did. Randy came out of his parents' house with Emily holding his hand and Alyssa in his arms. He carried a diaper bag over one shoulder and another bag over the other.

Bruce started breathing heavier and almost lost it when he saw his girls.

Emily ran over to him and smothered him with hugs. "Daddy!"

Bruce threw his arms around her, lifting her off the ground. "Emmy."

Emily clung tightly to his neck. "I missed you."

"I missed you too, Princess." He kissed her cheek. "Daddy missed you too."

Witnessing this reunion brought tears to Randy's eyes. Emily and Bruce needed one another. Being separated like this had to be killing them.

Bruce held Emily's hand and carried Alyssa while Randy loaded the girls' bags in the trunk.

"Where are we going?" Emily asked her father.

"We're going to stay at Uncle Randy's house for a few days."

She jumped up and down excitedly. "Yay!"

Over the next six days, Bruce spent every waking moment with his girls, showering them with affection. He became reacquainted with Alyssa, stuffed Emily with ice cream, played with dolls, read bedtime books, and took the girls on more park excursions than any two children should have been allowed to participate in.

On his last day with his kids, Bruce fed Alyssa and laid her down for a nap. Once she was asleep, he sat on the sofa with Emily and they watched cartoons together.

"Daddy?" Emily asked him.

"Yes?"

"When can me and Allie go home with you and Mommy?"

Bruce fought to hold back tears. "Mommy and I are having a hard time getting along right now, Angel."

"Just tell her you're sorry."

He wished it was that simple. Emily had no way of understanding the complexity of this situation, and Bruce didn't want to shatter her with it. "Sometimes saying I'm sorry isn't enough."

"Can I go home with you?"

Bruce squeezed her and kissed her head. "I wish you could. But your little sister needs you to show her how things work. You have to teach her stuff. That's a big responsibility."

"Allie cries a lot," Emily complained.

"Babies do. But as she grows she'll need a big sister like you to help her."

"What about you? You're all alone. Don't you miss us?"

It took every ounce of effort he had to keep from crying. "Yes, Baby. I miss you very much."

Randy watched this interaction from the kitchen. He couldn't even begin to comprehend the emotional rollercoaster his friend was riding. Knowing this was the last day Bruce would spend with his girls until his next vacation was heartbreaking.

Randy stepped out to the deck and sat next to his wife, watching Nathan play. "Poor Bruce," he said. "The hell he must be going through."

Jane rested her head on Randy's shoulder. "Emily really misses him."

"I know she does. This is going to be hard on her." He handed Nathan a small basketball. "I don't see how Steph can consciously keep the kids away from Bruce. She says he's never home, but I just don't see it. He and Emily are so close. That kind of bond doesn't form between a father and daughter if the father's never around."

Nathan threw the ball at his dad. "Bah."

"Yes, that's a ball. Basketball." Randy handed the ball back to his son then held out his hands.

Nathan threw it. "Da, da! Bah!" he shouted. When the ball rolled away, Nathan crawled after it.

Jane asked, "How come his first word was Dad? Why couldn't Mom have been his first word?"

"Because he knows I'm going to take him fishing and let him eat Oreos. Smart kid."   He looked across the yard to see Nathan pulling himself up with a lawn chair. "He's gonna be walking soon, then we're in trouble."

Realizing her baby was becoming a toddler, Jane said, "He's growing so fast. He won't nap for me in the morning anymore."

"That's because he wants to play." Randy sat on his knees and held his hands out to his son. "Nathan. Come here."

Nathan fell on his bottom and rolled to his knees. Holding the basketball in his hand, he crawled over to Randy.

Randy picked him up and sat him on his lap. "You want a cookie, Buddy?"

Nathan cooed and baby babbled.

"Cool." He turned to his wife. "I'm gonna take him to the store and get some cookies. You wanna come?"

"Yes."

That night, Mark and Ellen Hanson agreed to babysit Nathan so Randy and Jane could have a date night, which left Bruce alone in the house with his girls. After he tucked them in for the night, he went downstairs and sat on the sofa. He twirled his wedding ring around his finger a few times before he took it off and placed it on the coffee table. One of Emily's dolls was on the sofa. He picked it up and stared at it, which instantly triggered tears. He decided to try to get his mind off everything by turning on the TV. As he flipped through channels, someone knocked on the door. He got off the couch to see who it was. His expression quickly turned sour when he saw Stephanie standing on Randy's porch. Even though he had a million things he wanted to say to her, he resisted the urge to say them. "What are you doing here?"

"This is my brother's house, remember?"

"You can't take the girls yet. I still get tonight."

"I'm not here for the girls. They should be sleeping anyway." She stepped inside and sat down. "Emily misses you."

"I miss her too."

"I've been thinking about you."

He knew damn well she was lying. "Don't do this." He closed the door and took a seat across from her. Trying to gather his thoughts, he leaned his elbows on his knees and stared at the floor. "You know, I've been thinking about the last words we said to each other. For once we were able to sit down and have a civilized conversation, only because the decisions involved affected the wellbeing of our children." He lifted his head. "Up to that point, every time one of us opened our mouth, a bitter argument erupted. We often went days, weeks where we didn't talk to each other. A dark cloud constantly hung over us." He hesitated for a moment before he said, "I don't want to live like this anymore. I want a divorce."

Her face turned down, almost saddened by this. "Bruce."

"Come on, Steph, you can't tell me you didn't seen this coming. But I'm worried about the girls. I don't want to drag them into a court battle."

"Neither do I."

Happy that they finally agreed about something, he said, "Good. Then let's try to find a way to resolve our differences long enough to negotiate, outside of court. We'll start with Emily and Alyssa."

"What about them?"

"I sent you numerous messages and called you multiple times to make arrangements to see my daughters and you completely blew me off. You can't keep them from me, Stephanie. I'm their father."

"I know that."

He questioned the sincerity of this statement. "You sure didn't seem to care too much when you ran off with them. You know damn well how difficult it is for me to get time off to come up here. You totally screwed me on that, and you know it."

"You said you wanted to separate," she reminded him.

"I did, but I was willing to move out. Taking my daughters away from me wasn't fair." His whole body tensed. Obviously she didn't see her wrongdoing. "I worked my ass off to try to make a good life for us and you never appreciated anything I did. Yet despite the crap we were going through, every night I came home to you."

"Do you know how many times I tried to reach you and you weren't available because you were in surgery?"

"That's my job, which is something you never understood." Frustrated, he leaned back on the couch and folded his arms across his chest.

Stephanie noticed Bruce's wedding ring sitting on the coffee table instead of on his finger where it belonged. "You're not wearing your ring."

"No, I'm not." Her left hand still wore a diamond. "Why are you wearing yours?"

"We're still married."

"We haven't had a marriage for a long time." Being around Stephanie caused him tension. Bruce didn't want to be in her presence any longer. "I think you should go." He stood up and opened the front door, inviting her to leave. "I'll drop the girls off in the morning." Bruce said nothing more. He had nothing else to say.

Stephanie rose to her feet and showed herself out.

The next morning, Bruce met Stephanie on the front porch. "Alyssa just ate and has a fresh diaper. She should be good for a while." He handed the baby to Stephanie then bent down and hugged Emily, kissing her softly on the cheek. "Bye, Princess."

"Bye, Daddy." She clung tightly to his neck. "I love you."

"I love you too, Baby. Be a good girl. Daddy will call you tonight."

Emily released him and ran off to see her grandma.

Bruce stood up and stared at Stephanie. "Do not blow off my requests for visitation. You can't deny me my daughters."

"You're their father, Bruce."

He scoffed, "That didn't stop you before. I don't want to have to go into a custody dispute with you, but if you try to prevent me from being with my girls, I will fight you."

The reality of what was happening hit Bruce like a freight train. When Randy drove him to the airport, he didn't talk. In fact, he stared blankly out the window, showing no signs of life at all other than the fact that he was breathing.

"You alright?" Randy asked as they cruised down the freeway.

Bruce took a deep breath and exhaled with a heavy sigh. "I can't believe this is happening. How can she be this cold? It wasn't enough for my marriage to fall apart, but she had to take my girls away from me too."

"I'm sorry, Buddy."

Bruce halfheartedly smiled at Randy's sympathy, although he didn't feel worthy of it. "No, I'm the one who's sorry. I'm sorry you got dragged into this, and I'm sorry things turned out the way they did. You definitely don't deserve to be caught in the middle of this crap."

"Regardless of what happens, Bruce, you'll always be family to me. And you'll always be my friend. Nothing will ever change that," Randy reassured him.

Bruce nodded gratefully, glad there were no hard feelings between him and Randy.

After Bruce checked in at the counter, he sat with Randy for a bit. The emotions of the week finally caught up to him. Tears formed in his eyes. "I really miss my girls. I miss Emily's dolls all over the floor. I miss the fuzzy pink blanket she always has with her. I miss her hair ribbons and hearing her sweet voice calling out to me in the morning." Feeling desperate, he looked at Randy and begged, "Promise me you'll look after my girls until we figure this out. Randy, please. You have to make sure they're being taken care of, and let me know what they need."

Bruce's voice was filled with more pain than Randy ever heard the man engulfed in. "I will. You know I'll always be here for you. And you're more than welcome to stay with us any time you need to. Just say the word."

Bruce took a few breaths to compose himself. "You are a good friend, Randy. Thank you."

"I'll e-mail all the pictures I took of you and the girls."

Thinking about the precious time he spent with his daughters this week made Bruce smile. "Thanks."

Randy wished there was something he could do to fix this situation and mend Bruce's broken heart. The next few months were going to be rough, not only for Bruce and Stephanie, but for the girls as well. He offered a friendly, supportive hug. "I love you, Man. Hang in there. Let me know if you need anything and call if you need to vent."

Bruce grabbed his carryon bag and threw it over his shoulder. Shaking Randy's hand, he said, "Thank you."

"Anytime."

Bruce waded his way through the security line and headed toward his gate.

Six weeks later, Bruce was anxious to return to Seattle to see his girls again. Being around them always cheered him up. When he came to Stephanie's new apartment to pick them up, he handed her a manila envelope. "I need you to sign these."

"What are they?" she sneered.

"Divorce papers."

She removed the envelope's contents and quickly turned to the part about splitting assets. Bruce offered her a decent sized child support check for the girls, half of the current assets, and joint custody. Since the day Stephanie left Los Angeles, Bruce had cut her name from the bank account and shut off every credit card in her possession, but on good faith, he included a clause in their divorce decree that said he would cover all divorce related legal expenses and any debt incurred during the course of their marriage, but in return she could have no access to his pension or any future income. To him, this seemed more than fair, but to her, it wasn't enough. "This is it? This is all I get?"

As it stood now, Stephanie was getting over a hundred thousand dollar from him and she didn't have to cough up a penny for the divorce or be accountable for any bills they had accrued. What the hell else did she want? "It's fifty percent of the assets. Half is perfectly fair." It was a good thing they didn't own a home together or she would have wanted that too. "I really don't want to fight you on this, but if you want to push me, I can and will drag your ass to court. You've already taken my daughters and depleted my bank account. How much more do you want from me?"

"Speaking of which, I need to talk to you."

"About what? This is my time with my girls and you are taking it away from me. Whatever the hell you have to say, get it over with quickly."

"Alyssa has outgrown all of her baby clothes and I need to get her new ones."

Oh, this was perfect. Stephanie must have found great pleasure in sucking every ounce of money out of him, not to mention the life she drained from him, because she sure seemed to do it a lot. "I just sent you a check. What did you do with it?"

"Emily needed clothes too."

Her greedy, selfish attitude made his blood boil. He snorted cynically at her request. "The entire time we were married you criticized everything I did and never once showed any appreciation. You constantly lied to me and deceived me to the point where I didn't trust you. You maxed out every credit card we had, which I am still paying for. When you took my girls away from me, you tore out every inch of my heart. Yet every month, I send you a check to cover expenses for the girls, and I offered you fifty percent in assets through the divorce settlement. But you still have the unmitigated gall to ask me for more." In a harsh, accusatory tone, he said, "This was your intention from the start, wasn't it? To make me your goddamn meal ticket."

She scowled at him but offered no response.

"Sign the damn papers, Stephanie, and get my girls so I can get the hell out of here."

As soon as he had his daughters, he loaded their bags in the car and drove over to Randy's house.

That night, after the girls were in to bed, Bruce blurted out, "Do you know what your sister had the audacity to ask me today?"

This seemed like a rather abrupt comment. Obviously something was wrong. "Do I really want to know?" Randy replied.

Bruce plopped on the sofa and told Randy what the divorce papers said. "But of course, that isn't enough for her," Bruce complained. "She wants more. And then she had the nerve to ask me for money when I recently sent her a check for three-thousand dollars."

"She failed to mention that."

"This hole she's digging keeps getting deeper and deeper and I am about to drown in this shit." Bruce rubbed his thumb and forefinger across the bridge of his nose. "I really don't have time to deal with this right now, and poor Emily isn't sure what to make of all this. She's the one who's going to be affected the most. I don't know how much more of this I can take before I lose my fucking mind."

Much to Bruce's relief, Stephanie agreed to sign the divorce papers. She didn't want to drag the girls through a court battle any more than he did. They maintained joint custody. She stayed in Seattle and he returned to his residency duties at UCLA. He wrote his child support check every month and acquired a bigger two-bedroom apartment to accommodate having his girls with him six months out of the year. Not an ideal situation, but it would have to do.

Chapter Forty-Six

Receiving a letter from the American Board of Obstetrics and Gynecology saying he passed his board exam and had earned the proud distinction of Diplomate of the American Board of Obstetrics and Gynecology was one of the most rewarding experiences in Randy's career. He could now practice the medicine he loved with the added benefit of being board certified.

"Randal?" his father said, catching him between patients. "Come over here for a minute and take a look at this."

"Yes, Sir." Randy walked over to his father to see what he wanted.

Mark handed him several sonograms. "How many embryos do you count?"

First Randy examined each image separately, then he spread out the images and compared them to ensure his count was accurate. "Five," he decided.

"That was my count as well."

"Is this one of our patients?"

"Yes, it is."

He combed his fingers through his hair. "Damn."

"We need to work together closely on this one," Mark said, trying to figure out how they were going to approach this case. "You have any experience with this many?"

"No. Triplets is as high as I've seen," Randy replied. "This should be interesting."

Now a year old, Nathan was mobile and getting into everything. This new mobility forced Randy to install a safety gate on the staircase and childproof latches on all the cupboards. These barriers restricted Nathan's exploration, but didn't suppress his curiosity. To encourage Nathan's inquisitiveness, Jane designated one low cabinet just for toddler play. She filled it with plastic containers and lids, empty boxes, and wooden spoons. This held Nathan's interest for hours.

Because Nathan loved to assert himself and say "no" all the time, Randy learned to alter the way he spoke to his son. He used phrases like "I'd like you to play over here" to try to alleviate the defiant no's Nathan always used. They began teaching him manners. Emphasizing "please" and "thank you" in everyday tasks added these words to Nathan's vocabulary.

Randy taught him how to put away his own toys by turning cleanup into a game of basketball, where he had Nathan pick up a toy and 'dunk' it in the toy tub. To help Nathan gain his independence, they encouraged him to attempt simple tasks such as brushing his hair or teeth, although the latter involved more chewing than brushing. He was learning how to use a sippy cup and a spoon, and was quite proficient at eating finger foods. He ate a variety of solid foods, checking out the texture of eggs and cottage cheese and discovering what grapes, cooked macaroni, and Cheerios did when thrown. When Randy gave him his first Oreo, Nathan shoved it in his mouth, getting cookie all over his face and hands.

"What is all over his face?" Jane said when she saw Nathan sitting in a highchair covered in chocolate.

"An Oreo," Randy proudly proclaimed as he wiped off his son's cheeks. "I fully intend to expose my son to the finer things in life. Oreos is definitely on that list."

Jane lifted Nathan from his highchair and gave him a bath, since he had gotten more cookie on himself than in his tummy.

They spent the afternoon setting up the Christmas tree. It wasn't more than five minutes after the tree was decorated that Nathan discovered ornaments. "Da da. Bah." He held one up to show his dad.

"That's not a ball. It's an ornament."

Nathan pulled another one off the tree.

"Leave the tree alone." Randy took the ornaments away then picked Nathan up and moved him across the room.

Nathan looked at his father with a pouty lip.

Jane tried to rush over to comfort him, but Randy stopped her. "Don't do it, Jane. He has to learn to listen." Randy ventured into the kitchen to fill his coffee cup. He looked over his shoulder at Nathan, who had forgotten the incident entirely and was now interested in the pretty ribbons and bows. Randy rolled his eyes. "Great. There he goes again."

Nathan toddled back over to the tree and ripped a bow off one of the packages.

Randy set his coffee cup down and walked over to his son. "Give that to Daddy." He attempted to pry the bow from Nathan's death grip, but the child pulled his hand back so Randy couldn't get it.

"No, Da!" Nathan screamed.

Randy couldn't believe his son did that. "Did you hear that? He's not even two years old yet and already my son is cocking attitude with me."

Jane thought this was funny. "Hmm, sounds like a man I know."

Scoffing her, he said, "Ha, ha. Very funny." He picked up Nathan's basketball, hoping it would distract him. The minute Nathan saw the ball in Randy's hand, he dropped the bow and hobbled over to get it.

Playing basketball with Daddy was one of Nathan's favorite activities. Randy had a plastic toddler basketball hoop set up in the living room. Nathan padded over to the net and dunked the ball. Randy got down on his knees and they took turns making baskets. This game kept Nathan occupied and drew his attention away from the Christmas tree.

"Christmas will be fun with him this year," Jane said.

"Yes it will," Randy agreed. "We need to keep an eye on him, though. He likes to get into things."

Somehow throughout the evening, Nathan managed to get his hands on a candy cane. Gelled in place by stickiness, his hair stuck straight up and his fingers were plastered together. Red streaks from the red-colored dye tinted his face.

Randy tried to take the candy cane away from him, which made Nathan grip it tighter, stubbornly fighting his father for possession of it.

Nathan was becoming quite a handful now that he was mobile, which made parenting much more challenging. He was an independent child—strong-willed and ornery as all get-out—who wanted to do things himself. If something was within his reach, you could guarantee Nathan would find it and pick it up. Any round object lying around the house was quickly discovered and thrown. The toddler was particularly fascinated with Daddy's cellphone, which he often tried to pull out of Randy's hand. Randy attempted to sidetrack him by offering other toys, but the distraction was often short-lived.

The few words Nathan knew, he used frequently. And he was quick in his mobility, running more than walking. Nathan Hanson had to be the most curious kid Randy had ever known, and he had no fear, even though he was only thirteen months old.

In the morning, Randy and his father planned to take Nathan out in the boat for his first fishing trip. Randy dressed Nathan in a baseball hat and a *Daddy's New Fishing Partner* sweatshirt. Randy also had on fishing attire, a tee-shirt with a picture of a fishing pole and the words, *I've got a big rod!*

"Do you have to wear that shirt?" Jane asked.

"What's wrong with it?"

"I've got a big rod, Randy? Really? That's perverted."

The sexual innuendo associated with the phrase is why he bought the shirt in the first place. "It's a fishing rod, Babe. It's not my fault you have a dirty mind."

She lovingly pushed him toward the door. "Go fishing, and bring home a big one."

"Oh, I will. Fish fear me."

"Uh huh. I'm sure they do." She gave him a kiss and sent him and her son on their way for Nathan's first fishing trip with Daddy and Grandpa.

Randy bought Nathan a toddler-sized fishing pole that he could handle and hold on his own. Randy cast Nathan's line out then handed him the pole. "Hold it tight, Nate."

Nathan gripped it with both hands.

Once Nathan was situated, Randy cast out his own line. "Did I tell you what Nathan did last night?"

"No," Mark replied. "But I would love to hear about it."

"He got ahold of a candy cane. He wouldn't let go of the damn thing either and I had to pry it out of his hand. Made him all sticky. He had it in his hair, all over his clothes. Yuk."

Mark remembered another little boy about thirty years ago who did the exact same thing.

"And I had to tell him six times to quit taking the ornaments off the tree. He finally left them alone, but then started pulling all the bows off the packages."

Mark offered Randy some advice. "I would strongly suggest you keep the packages off the floor."

"We kinda figured that out. He's getting pretty good at putting that basketball in the hoop."

"I know. I saw him do that the other day. He's becoming quite the talker too, isn't he?" Mark said.

"Yup. And he gets into everything. He snagged my car keys last week and hid them in the couch cushions. Took me all afternoon to find them."

"Where did you leave them?" Mark asked.

"On the coffee table."

Mark chuckled at Randy's parenting mishap. "Well, that was your first mistake. If you don't want Nathan to get them, keep them out of his reach. Once babies get mobile you have to be careful what you leave lying around."

"I'm discovering that. I'm also discovering he can reach places I didn't think he could."

"When you were his age, you hid my stethoscope and I had to buy another one. It took us three days to figure out where you put it."

Randy laughed. "Sounds like something Nathan would do."

"Feed his curiosity, but control it so he doesn't hurt himself," Mark advised.

"We're trying." Randy shook his head in disbelief. "This whole parenting thing has been quite a ride."

"You haven't seen anything yet, my boy. He'll throw more challenges at you as he grows."

"I'm looking forward to it."

And Nathan always delivered. Every day Nathan blew Randy away with the new words he used and new discoveries he made.

"Mama. Coocoo," Nathan said, extending his fingers into the air.

Jane had never heard him say this word before. "What do you want, Sweetie?"

Nathan pouted his lip.

Randy stepped into the kitchen to pour himself a cup of coffee. The pathetic look on his son's face made him chuckle. "What's wrong with him?"

"I don't know," Jane said.

Randy focused his attention to Nathan. "Whatcha need, little man?"

"Coocoo." He reached his hand toward the cupboard.

"I know what he wants." Randy opened the Oreo bag and handed one to Nathan. "Here you go."

Nathan took the cookie from him and stuck it in his mouth.

"Oh god, Randy. You have him hooked on Oreos."

"Cookies and milk. Every kid needs to experience that." Randy poured some milk into a sippy cup, screwed the lid on, and handed it to Nathan. Nathan took a big drink.

The toddler experienced separation anxiety when Jane and Randy would leave him, and waving bye-bye was sometimes traumatic. To ease the impact of departures, Nathan relied on the comfort of his favorite stuffed animal and dearest blanket. These transitional objects gave him a sense of security, especially when Mommy and Daddy were not around, and seemed to help him with the separation anxiety he possessed. Although Nathan struggled to master new skills every day with varying degrees of success, the cuddly blanket was one thing he could consistently return to for comfort.

Jane went Christmas shopping and left Randy and Nathan alone for some daddy/son bonding time. Randy stepped out of Nathan's sight to another area of the house. Nathan started to panic and began to whimper.

"Nathan," Randy called to him from his office.

Nathan searched for his father's voice. "Da."

"I'm in here."

He crept toward Randy's office and peeked his head in.

"Hey, Buddy."

The toddler held out his arms. Randy picked him up and sat him on his lap. Nathan was quite proficient at using non-verbal cues to indicate what he wanted. When he wanted to be held, he lifted his hands up; when he wanted to get down, he pointed down. However, Randy and Jane made it a point to encourage him to use words like up or down to express his wants. They both labeled objects for him and his vocabulary grew every day.

Taking an afternoon stroll, Randy narrated as they walked. He pointed out particular objects, and they watched beautifully colored birds dart in and out of trees. "Look at the pretty bluebird, Nate."

The bird's swooping feathers didn't capture Nathan's attention, but its song certainly did. "Bur," he shrieked.

"Yes, that's a bird," Randy confirmed.

They walked down to the lake to look at the fish and boats. Nathan was fearless around the water, which frightened Randy a little. Every time they took him to the lake, he ran toward the water and bent right down to touch it. The kid loved the shimmering ripples and the splash of the waves. He was fascinated by boats and loved the sound of the motors on fishing vessels. He enjoyed watching fish swim, and the seagulls flying overhead made him giggle.

Nathan's newly found independence made him reluctant to be held or carried. Once he had a taste of freedom, it was hard to hold him back. He wanted to walk on his own every time they went out, but he wasn't always stable when he walked. To help Nathan with this, Randy developed a little comic routine in which he walked along where Nathan could see him and then—whoops!—he would trip in a theatrical fashion and almost fall. Nathan found it hilarious, and it built his confidence to see a big person stumble. As long as Nathan got a kick out of it, Randy kept doing it.

These comic episodes with Nathan and Randy always made Jane laugh. She loved to see her husband and son bond like that. Even though he had a busy schedule, Randy made time for Nathan every day. He cherished these moments with his son more than he ever imagined he would.

Randy came home from work one night with a toy doctor kit in his hand. It had a plastic stethoscope in it. He introduced it to Nathan by showing him a real stethoscope first. "This is called a stethoscope." He placed the bell on Nathan's chest and let him listen.

Hearing the lub-dub sound made the little boy giggle.

Randy removed the scope and draped it around his neck. Nathan tried to reach for it, but Randy wouldn't let him touch it. "That's Daddy's." He handed Nathan the plastic one from the doctor kit. "This one is yours."

Nathan seemed satisfied with that. He put it on his ears and pretended to listen to his dad's heart. The two of them played doctor until it was time for dinner.

Chapter Forty-Seven

The week of Christmas, Bruce flew up to Seattle to spend time with his girls. Being around Stephanie was awkward and he had a difficult time looking at her without getting angry, but he bit his tongue and suffered through it. He never wanted to go through a divorce, but because the constant arguing took its toll on everyone involved, he felt like he had no choice. He was operating on autopilot, and doing a pretty good job of it. No one really noticed anything different about him, other than the fact that he seemed more rested than usual. Apparently having his life turned upside down didn't have any physical symptoms.

Randy and Jim knew Bruce had a lot on his mind. Before he caught his flight to Los Angeles, they took him out to lunch at their favorite burger place. Just because Bruce and Stephanie didn't get along and couldn't live together didn't mean the rest of the family held any begrudging feelings toward him.

"It kills me to say goodbye to my girls," Bruce said. "I've tried working more hours to get my mind off of it, but that doesn't make it any easier."

Randy felt sorry for him. If he was in Bruce's situation, he would be going crazy. "You know, Stephanie hasn't gone out much. She's not dating, and still uses the name Buckman."

"I know. I'm the one who writes her a check every month." Because of the girls, Bruce was going to be

413

involved with the family whether Stephanie liked it or not. Stephanie understood that. She also understood that Randy and Bruce were friends and that bond could not be severed.

When Bruce landed in L.A., Mandy greeted him with a hug. "Welcome home. How was your trip?"

"It was good. I hated leaving my girls though. I feel like I'm missing so much of their lives."

"But you talk to them every week and spend time with them as often as you can," Mandy assured him. "You're a good dad. Your girls love you."

Bruce smiled at her, grateful for her support. "Thank you. I needed that reassurance today." Amanda Stevens was such an understanding and compassionate person, and when push came to shove, she was always there for him when he needed a friend. "What are you doing tonight?"

"No plans. Why?"

"Join me for dinner?" he suggested.

She gladly agreed.

They reminisced about medical school and shared stories from their youth while they ate. "No way," Bruce said, laughing at a comment Mandy made.

"He ran through the kitchen as fast as he could with an open can of ravioli and a fork in his hand. He slid across the floor, ran into the door, and set the alarm off. My dad came out and asked what they were doing and why the house alarm was going off at two o'clock in the morning."

Bruce replied, "Never a dull moment in that house."

"With seven girls running around, no there wasn't."

Bruce refilled Mandy's wineglass then poured a glass for himself. "I love listening to your stories. They always make me laugh."

Mandy was about to take a drink when she noticed the never-ending smile on Bruce's face, something she hadn't seen in a long time. "It's good to see you smile again, Dr. Buckman."

"That's because I'm with you. Being around you always brightens my day. We need to get together more often."

"I agree. Next time you have a day off you should come down to Santa Monica. We'll hang out at the beach. Nothing like sand and sun to take your troubles away," she invited.

"That sounds like fun. I will definitely take you up on that offer."

They tapped their wine glasses together and continued to enjoy their meal.

In the morning, on what he called a slow day, Bruce showed up at the hospital at 5:30 A.M. and began to prepare for his first surgery. Surgery prep was quite a complicated routine. He dressed in scrubs and slipped blue sterile booties over his shoes. Over his scrubs, he wore a dark green sterile gown. Once dressed, he washed and sterilized his hands then put on a pair of latex gloves.

Neurosurgery required specialized equipment— glasses with magnifying lenses set into them and a headset with fiber optic cables that released a dull blue glow. The cables conducted light from a box behind him then wrapped over his hair and plugged into a spotlight which shined out from his forehead.

The brain he was operating on belonged to an anesthetized 50-year-old woman whose head was clamped to the operating table. He acted as the conductor of a small orchestra of fellow doctors, nurses, and technicians. An anesthesiologist stood on the opposite side of the table from him, watching a rack of monitors that displayed the patient's vital signs. With almost reverent care, Bruce sliced the skin on the skull to make a semi-circular flap, which he pushed aside. He drilled holes along the top of the skull, down toward the ear, and back up along the temple. He cut between the holes with a special burr then pulled off a section of bone and set it aside. He pushed down a fissure in the brain, moving toward an aneurysm so he could put a metal clip on it.

When he was ready to work under the microscope, a nurse stripped off his head gear. He sat in the microscope chair that was wrapped in sterilized plastic then rolled up to the patient so that his knees were under the table. To steady his hands, he rested his elbows on the armrests. He stared straight ahead into the eyepiece of a microscope, watching his surgical instruments move in a valley of brain tissue below the lens. His feet operated pedals that controlled the microscope, the drill, and an electrocautery device, which used electrical current to cut tissue. He held the electrocautery probe in his right hand and a suction tube to draw away blood in his left. He clipped the aneurysm.

"Run me a scan," he told the radiologist.

The angiogram indicated that an important artery wasn't filling up with blood. If the blood flow was blocked, the patient would have a stroke on the dominant side of her brain. She wouldn't be able to speak and she'd lose the use of her legs. To prevent problems, Bruce peered into the microscope to search for trouble. All visible arteries seemed to be fat with blood, so he asked the radiologist for another angiogram. A second image indicated all arteries were functioning. Job complete. He now began the painstaking task of closing up the patient's skull.

Dr. Bruce Buckman would operate like this about 350 more times this year. Dressed in blue scrubs and sneakers, he reflected on being drawn into neurosurgery by his fascination with the brain's complex anatomy. The life of a neurosurgeon was demanding. Many operations were long and technically difficult. Surgical emergencies, such as bleeding within the brain or sudden compression of the spinal cord, occurred at any hour of the day or night and demanded immediate attention. Cases involving severe brain injury, paralysis from damage to the spinal cord, or a brain tumor in a child were emotionally draining. Yet despite these challenges and demands, neurosurgery also offered a great deal of personal satisfaction. It was rewarding when he could restore a patient to normal function by relieving incapacitating pain, improve motor function, control a seizure disorder, or eliminate a tremor. He loved his work.

Neurosurgeons didn't have active social lives. Fitting social activities and friends into their lives was difficult. They often had to sacrifice career for family or vice versa, and surgeons, in general, had a high divorce rate. Bruce certainly didn't let the statistics down in that regard.

The following weekend, Bruce met Mandy in Santa Monica. They spent the day at the pier, toured the aquarium, rode the Ferris wheel at Pacific Park, and enjoyed a stroll on the beach together. Santa Monica State Beach offered a picturesque, panoramic view of the Pacific Ocean. The beach was well kept, raked daily, and, being right next to a police substation, was safe at night.

"Do you remember when we were in med school and the five of us went to that brunch buffet with all the ice sculptures?" Mandy asked him.

"I remember that place. They had awesome omelets."

"I saw a guy the other day who was carving bears from ice using a chainsaw."

"A chainsaw?"

"Yeah. It was really neat. I bet he gets soaked doing that, with ice flying everywhere."

"You mean like this?" Bruce reached his hand into the water and splashed her.

Her jaw dropped. "You are so dead."

He ran from her, kicking up sand, and she took off after him.

They sat on the beach and talked until the sun came up. Dedicated morning joggers arose on the beach and dolphins, who often chose this stretch of shore for a playful morning swim, splashed around offshore.

Neither one had slept, but they didn't care. Bruce reclined in the sand and looked up at the puffy white clouds. "The beach is always so calming."

Mandy lay back with him, staring at the nothingness. "It is. I don't understand why you don't come down here more often. It's not like we live that far away from each other." UCLA Medical Center was only about ten miles from Mandy's house in Santa Monica. It was a hop, skip, and jump down Sepulveda Boulevard to the Santa Monica freeway. "It would certainly help you relax."

"That's true." His stomach growled. He realized they hadn't eaten since lunch the day before. "You wanna get some breakfast?"

"Definitely."

He sprung to a standing position and held his hands out to Mandy. "Come on."

She took his hands and stood up with him.

Over scrambled eggs and coffee, Bruce caught himself gazing at Mandy. A huge smile painted his face. Being with her had a way of doing that to him. "I wanted to thank you."

"For what?"

"For cheering me up. You've always been able to take crappy circumstances in my life and turn them into sunshine."

"It's my pleasure," she replied.

He took a sip from his steaming mug. "Isn't your surgeon boyfriend going to wonder where you've been all night?"

"I'm not seeing him anymore."

"I'm sorry to hear that."

She blew off his comment. "Don't be. I broke it off."

"Why?"

"I didn't love him."

After breakfast they roamed back out to the beach, trying to catch one last breath of fresh Pacific Ocean air before Bruce had to head back to UCLA. Mandy gave Bruce a very serious stare and said, "Can I ask you something?"

"Of course. What's up?"

Not wanting to upset him, but needing an explanation, she asked, "I know we've never talked about this, but you had women at Berkeley who would have gladly stood by your side and given you the love and support you deserve. So why Stephanie? I mean, you two really had nothing in common. You didn't get along, and you seemed like complete opposites. I don't understand what the attraction was."

This was an odd question, but Bruce could see Mandy's reasons for asking it. "I don't know. She was different, exciting, a stimulating change from my mundane life. She brought out the crazy bad boy in me, the rebel."

"She also brought out the worst in you," Mandy countered. "I can kinda see the attraction. She is pretty, prettier than most women, prettier than me."

Bruce immediately interjected, "You are a beautiful woman, Mandy."

"Oh really? You never noticed before."

He slanted his eyebrows, which naturally looked like they were pointing downward anyway. "Why do you say that?"

Courageously, she held nothing back. "The day I found out you and Stephanie were together, I was so angry at you. And when you told me she was pregnant, even though I tried to support you, I was dying inside. At your wedding, when I should have been happy for you, I went home that night and cried."

Bruce didn't understand why Mandy was so upset or why she openly confessed all of this to him. He staggered for a response. "What? Why would you…"

"Because, dammit, I wanted it to be me. I was so jealous of her because she won you with almost no effort at all when I spent years trying to gain your affection. And she treated you like crap. You deserve so much better than that, Buckman."

Bruce stood in complete shock, trying to take in what Amanda said to him. He wasn't sure what to say or how to react at first. He stared at her with a dumbfounded expression on his face. He thought back to all the times he, Randy, Jim, and Amanda hung out together at Berkeley, yet couldn't recall one moment when anybody had even remotely implied that Mandy was interested in him. She never hinted it. She never said a word, at least not that he could remember. "How come you never said anything?"

"I did," she insisted. "But you were too wrapped up in med school to notice."

He could tell by the look on her face that she was serious. Bruce had known Amanda for eleven years. The two of them were always close, but the idea that there could potentially be more than friendship between them never crossed his mind. The more he pondered this, the more it mystified him. She was always supportive, and he could easily talk to her and share his deepest thoughts and best kept secrets. She was fun to hang out with and he could act silly around her. She was a woman he always trusted, and his best friend.

His eyes met hers and a tingly feeling grew in the pit of his stomach. As he gazed at her under the moonlight, he saw a different glow about Amanda Stevens than he never noticed before. He found himself unable to pull his eyes away from her.

They stood and stared at each other for a minute. This was the most bonding experience the two of them had ever shared. He took her hand in his and glanced down at it for a moment before he returned his gaze to her pretty face. Their eyes met again. Then he did something Mandy didn't expect. He leaned forward and softly pressed his lips on hers.

Mandy reached her arms around him and kissed him back with increased intensity.

Experiencing this level of passion with her made his tummy flutter. His heart leapt out of his chest.

When they came up for air, Mandy said to him, "I have waited eleven years for you to do that."

"All this time, and I never…"

She put her finger over his lips. "Ssh."

"But I…"

Before he could say another word, she drew him closer and kissed him again.

Bruce desperately needed sleep. In the restaurant parking lot, he held Mandy's hand and escorted her to her car. "Thank you for sharing this weekend with me. I haven't had this much fun in a long time."

"You're very welcome. But do me a favor, Buckman. Do a better job of keeping in touch, ok?"

"I will." He leaned forward and whispered in her ear, "I'll call you later." Without hesitation, he kissed her on the lips. "Drive safely."

"You too." With a content smile on her face, Mandy finally said something to him she always wanted to say. "I love you, Bruce. I always have."

"I love you too, Mandy."

She got in her car, backed out of her parking space, and waved as she drove away. He stood and watched until she was out of sight.

After a long nap and running a few errands, Bruce pulled out his cellphone and dialed Mandy's number.

Mandy was sitting on the sofa watching her favorite TV show when she got the call. She picked up her phone and answered, "Hey, Buckman. I see you were able to dodge L.A. traffic and make it home."

"Wasn't easy, but I made it. Did you know there was a triathlon in town this weekend?"

"No, why?" she asked.

"Wilshire was blocked off and they had everyone from the Medical District detouring to Sunset Boulevard."

"That's crazy. Bet that made your commute interesting."

"Maybe I should trade in my truck for the Batmobile, then I can just fly over the abysmal traffic."

She laughed at him.

With a sentimental voice, Bruce asked, "What are you doing next weekend?"

"Hanging out with you, I hope."

"Good, because I'm off Sunday and Monday."

The two of them made plans to meet at Amanda's beach house in Santa Monica.

Sunday morning, Bruce showed up on Mandy's front porch with a single long-stemmed pink rose and a bottle of champagne. "Hello." He handed her the rose, accompanied by a sweet kiss.

"Why, thank you, Dr. Buckman." She showed him inside. When she caught sight of the champagne bottle in his hand, she asked, "What's that?"

"Thought maybe we could pop the cork later."

"That sounds great. I could go for a glass."

"Thought so."

They spent the morning strolling along a bike path and visiting a local art gallery. As the afternoon sun warmed the air, they perused some of the shops along the 3rd Street Promenade. In the evening, they returned to Mandy's house, where they shared a Chicken Tetrazzini meal together, which they both helped prepare. After dinner, they sat on the sofa watching a movie and munching on popcorn. Mandy snuggled in closer, leaning against Bruce's chest.

Bruce put his arm around her. "You want some of that champagne?"

"I'll grab the glasses." She set the popcorn bowl on the coffee table and headed toward the kitchen.

Bruce ambled in after her. She was standing in front of a cabinet reaching for two crystal long-stemmed glasses. He snuck up behind her and wrapped her up in his arms. "Got any strawberries?" he whispered.

"Why do you want strawberries?"

"So I can dip them in champagne and feed them to you." He gently pushed her hair away from her neck and kissed the skin right below her ear.

"There's a container in the fridge."

He reached into the refrigerator to fetch the bottle of champagne, grabbing the strawberries as he did.

When Bruce's glass was empty, he set it down and pulled Amanda into his arms. His lips met hers in a passionate embrace, which almost made her spill her champagne on the floor. "Let me set my glass down."

He smiled and said, "Be my guest."

She set her glass on the table and rejoined him. They kissed for a solid thirty minutes before Bruce finally said, "It's getting late."

"It is, but it's an awfully long drive back to UCLA. And on weekends, traffic on the Santa Monica Freeway can be killer. You're welcome to stay here tonight if you'd like."

He stared at her seductively. "That all depends."

"On what?"

"Last time I stayed with you I slept in the guestroom. Do I get to share a bed with you this time?"

With lips close but not touching, Mandy responded, "Yes."

"Then I'll stay. Your room or mine?"

"Mine." She bounded off the couch and took his hands in hers. "Come on, Buckman. Get up."

Teasing her in suggestive overtones, he said, "I already am."

Amanda caught onto his suggestiveness and chuckled at him. She helped him off the sofa and they headed upstairs.

Bruce peeked out the plate glass door of her bedroom balcony at the amazing view of the beach and ocean. "Wow. Nice view." His eyes shifted to her. "Nice view here too." He pulled her into his arms and kissed her, gradually working his way to the bed. "You've always been able to cheer me up, make me laugh, and turn even my darkest days sunny again, but you know what else I've discovered about you?"

"What's that?" she replied.

"You also have the uncanny ability to turn me on." Bruce stared at her, longing to touch her. "You're beautiful, Amanda."

She sat down on the bed and slowly leaned back. "I have wanted this for so long, and if you think for one second that I'm going to lie here and not have you, you have another thing coming, Dr. Buckman."

Amanda always spoke her mind. Bruce wasn't about to argue with her. "I'm all yours."

She scooted further up the bed, dragging him with her.

The alarm sounded at 6:00 A.M. Lying in bed, wrapped in Bruce's arms, Amanda stretched gracefully. "Good morning, Dr. Buckman." She kissed his chest, overjoyed to be lying here with him like this.

"Good morning." Bruce stroked Mandy's hair and kissed the top of her head as a token of his affection for her. "It's nice to wake up not inhaling smog."

"Yes it is."

He took in a long breath and exhaled with a heavy sigh.

Mandy recognized that sigh. "What's on your mind, Bruce?"

"You're my best friend, Mandy. The woman I've always been able to count on, and the one person who knows me better than anyone." He gently rubbed her arm. "I've ruined every relationship I've ever been in. My work schedule and the demands placed on me always seem to get in the way. I don't want to lose what we have."

Mandy sat up and looked at him. "Dr. Buckman, I know all about your schedule and the demands of medicine. We went through medical school together, remember? I lived it with you. I know what you go through every day, and I will be here to support you."

Gazing at her, he replied, "Where have you been all my life?"

"Right in front of you."

Playfully, he rolled them over. "I learned something about you last night."

"What's that?" she asked.

"Besides the fact that you are an amazing lover, you have an incredible body underneath that lab coat, Dr. Stevens."

"About time you noticed."

Later that morning, Randy was preparing a cup of coffee when his cellphone rang. It was Bruce. "Hey, Buckman. What's up?"

"Not much. Saw Mandy yesterday."

"How's she doing?" Randy asked.

"Doing well. Her practice is really taking off. She stays pretty busy."

"That's good. From what I hear, she seems to like it down there."

"She does." Bruce hesitated for a minute before he bluntly stated, "A few weeks ago she and I spent the day together down in Santa Monica. She admitted how she felt about me and I kissed her."

Randy almost choked on his coffee. "You what?"

"I kissed her. Yesterday we strolled around the park for a while and checked out a local art museum. And last night, instead of driving back to UCLA, I slept at her place."

"You and Mandy?"

"Yup."

Randy was elated to hear this news. "Holy shit. It's about damn time. Since our first day in med school, that woman practically threw herself at you. Everybody saw it. We couldn't figure out why you never caught on."

"I'm a little dense I guess."

"A little?" Randy teased him. "She sent you every signal. Think about it."

Bruce had thought about it. All those dinners they had together back in med school and the times she invited him to stay and talk over coffee after their study sessions. The phone calls and text messages she sent just to say hello, the freshly baked bread she always made for him. She even had him go with her when she pick out her new car. She had made it pretty obvious. He was dense alright. "Too wrapped up in myself to notice, I guess," Bruce confessed. "I'm such an idiot. Why didn't someone hit me over the head and wake me up?"

"Would you have listened?" Randy asked.

"Hell yeah, I would have listened, if someone would have said something."

"She tried, relentlessly. I can't believe you didn't see it."

"When Stephanie and I started going out, Mandy got distant with me. At the time I didn't understand why. It wasn't until after Steph and I separated that Mandy started texting and calling me again. We started hanging out more often and reestablished that closeness she and I always had; she even broke up with her surgeon boyfriend." He laughed at his own ignorance. "All these years the woman I was meant to be with was standing right in front of me and I never noticed."

"That woman is crazy in love with you, and everyone knew it except you," Randy quipped. "It appears as though you've got it figured out now."

"Yes I do, and I am without a doubt in love with her too."

Exhilaration was present in Bruce's voice, something Randy hadn't heard from him in quite some time. "Congratulations, Bud. I'm happy for you."

Randy traipsed upstairs to the bedroom. Jane, wearing only her silk robe, stood in front of the bathroom mirror brushing her hair. He watched her for a moment, fascinated by the movements she made, before he slipped his phone back into his pocket. "I just got off the phone with Bruce."

"How's he doing?"

"Very well, actually. Apparently he and Mandy are together now."

Turning her head toward him, she declared, "No way."

"Yup. And he is happy as a clam." Slowly, his hand reached around her tummy. The body spray she was wearing had an enticing draw to it. His mouth

428

moved up to her ear. "You smell incredible," he whispered.

"Flattery will get you nowhere, Sir."

"How would you feel about going back to Bermuda for our anniversary?"

"Hmm. That's quite the proposition."

"Are you interested?"

"Perhaps." She turned her head so their lips were almost touching.

"I'll take that as a yes." He drew his mouth closer to hers and kissed her. "Get dressed. I'll make breakfast." He winked at her and patted her on the bottom before he slipped out of the room.

Chapter Forty-Eight

Ellen and Mark graciously volunteered to look after Nathan for a week so Randy and Jane could go to Bermuda for their sixth wedding anniversary. In their hotel room, Randy collapsed on the bed, kicked off his shoes, and clasped his hands behind his head. "Man it feels good to get away from it all. The last few months have been nuts."

Jane sat on the bed with him.

Randy reached over and touched her thigh. Jane was a beautiful woman. Her hypnotic green eyes, long brown hair, and mesmerizing smile always turned him on. "Eight days, just you and me, Baby." He wanted to kiss her, so he sat up and interlocked his mouth with hers. The moment he felt her warm lips and took a whiff of her sweet body spray, he wanted more. He worked on unbuttoning her blouse, slowly releasing one button at a time until her body was exposed to the warm night air. In one swift motion, he pulled off his shirt. He unbuttoned his jeans and inched the zipper down, watching her face the whole time.

She licked her lips and gazed upon him with that look he had seen in her eyes many times before—eyes full of longing.

He shifted his hand to the small of her back and pulled her close to him. His fingers moved along the waistband of her shorts. His tongue traced her lips then dipped inside in a slow, compelling rhythm. Slowly, he slid his pants down, followed by stripping off hers. Jane rubbed her hands all over his chest, feeling the shape of his muscles. Heat radiated from her body onto his. He grazed his lips across her neck and collarbone while he drew long, searching caresses all over her body.

As he sank into her, rushing pleasure overtook him. He quickly bombarded himself with reminders to go slow, take it easy, enjoy. He always saw to her pleasure first. Always. No exceptions. And Jane was incredibly responsive. Judging from the sounds resonating from her lips and the way she entwined her arms and legs around him, they seemed to be on the same page.

The intense physical desire they always had for one another hadn't faded over the years. In fact, Randy felt more attracted to Jane now than he did when they were dating. The sex was better, her body more desirable, and when they kissed, the feelings were more intense. His love for her grew stronger every day. Maybe it was the trust and devotion involved in marriage that made him feel closer to her. Maybe it was because he felt comfortable around her and they read each other so well. He didn't know the reason why. But he did know he wanted to soak in this moment and get lost in her for a while.

Their interlude, powerful and intimate, lasted a long time. Randy couldn't bring himself to move afterwards. He stayed joined with her for several minutes, feeling her deep in his soul, before he released her from his grip and let her go.

Jane crawled off the bed and walked toward the bathroom. Randy watched every move she made, following her with his eyes. When he heard the shower water turn on, he got up and snuck in with her.

"Randy," she said, startled to see him there.

"Care if I join you?" With his forearm against the shower wall, he closed his eyes and tasted her sweet lips. "You're so beautiful," he said in his bedroom voice. "I love you."

"I love you."

The physical aspects of their relationship made the emotional bond stronger, and the emotional bond began with engaging conversation. Lying on the hammock together in dreamy contentment, Jane rested her hand on Randy's chest. With his arm around her, he stroked her soft hair. "You know what I was thinking?" he said, releasing a relaxed sigh.

"What?"

"When I was a kid, I used to hang a hammock up between two trees in the backyard and contemplate my future, wondering where life would lead me. I remember one summer, when I was lounging in the hammock, Dad pulled a lawn chair next to me. He and I talked for hours about medicine, plans for college, fishing. We had a great time. My dad was always so supportive. Back in high school, he came to every one of my games. Even if it was only for the last ten minutes because he was on-call, his face was always in the stands," Randy said. "He's a wonderful father. He encouraged me to pursue my dreams and steered me in the right direction." He moved one arm behind his head. "I want Nathan to meet his full potential, and I'll support him any way I can, but I don't want to push him down a path he doesn't want to travel. I want to be a good dad, like my father was."

Jane propped herself up on Randy's chest. "You are a very good daddy, Randy. Nathan adores you. When you're gone, he stares out the window looking for you. He recognizes your car and goes crazy when he sees you pull up."

"He does?" Randy asked.

"Yes. And he loves to play basketball with you. Last week, he saw a basketball game on TV and instantly stopped what he was doing. He stared at it for a minute then looked at me and asked when Daddy was coming home."

"He did not."

"Yes he did. When he got ahold of one of your Sports Illustrated magazines, I thought he was going to tear it, but instead he flipped through the pages and pointed to every basketball he saw."

"That kid is fascinated with basketball," Randy said.

"And fishing. He put his fishing hat on the other day and asked me if I wanted to go fishing."

Hearing this made Randy smile. "He's Daddy's boy."

"He really is. I think it's cute."

Randy sighed. "I miss him."

"So do I."

Nathan missed them too. Nathan and his grandpa sat on the couch watching Elmo. Suddenly the child asked, "Daddy bye-bye?"

"Daddy will be home in a few days, Nathan. He and Mommy are spending some time together."

Nathan reached for his basketball. "Papa play ball?"

"Sure. We can play ball."

Nathan handed the ball to his grandfather, who got on the floor and played with him. Nathan quickly lost interest when he saw a picture of Jane and Randy on the shelf. He held the photograph in his hands and kissed it.

Mark's heart melted. Nathan was such a lovable little boy, playful and full of energy, much like Randy was as his age. It was scary how similar Nathan's personality was to Randy's. They even looked alike, aside from Nathan's charcoal grey eyes. It was like he was staring at his young son all over again.

Randy called his parents that evening to check on Nathan. Hearing his voice on the line brought a smile to Randy's face.

"Love you," the little boy said.

"We love you too, Nathan. We'll be home soon."

Jane and Randy strolled through the Botanical Garden together, holding hands along avenues opulently decorated with banyan trees, aromatic oleander, frangipani, bougainvillea, and hibiscus. Brightly plumed birds chattered at them.

"Nathan would enjoy this," Randy declared as he took a picture of the deep blue hue of an Indigo Bunting bird sitting on a branch of a tree. A bright lemon-yellow bird called out to them with its loud kis-ka-dee call. This birdcall sounded very similar to the French phrase, Qu'est-ce que dit. Randy found this amusing. "That bird speaks French." He gracefully bowed to the bird. "Bonsoir, mon petit ami à plumes."

Jane stared at him as if he was crazy. "He doesn't speak French."

"Sure he does." Kis-ka-dee, kis-ka-dee, the bird called to him. "See, he's asking me what I'm saying."

"That's because he doesn't understand you."

Randy snapped a picture of this bird. "Nate's gonna love these pictures."

Around one o'clock in the morning, red and orange tropical print swimming trunks and a hot pink bikini bottom ended up on the edge of a lagoon. Lovemaking under a waterfall, serenaded by the natural, nocturnal concert of tree frogs, was pure heaven.

Beautiful, colorful vegetation and the ancient relics mixed among the most modern amenities always made Bermuda paradise. With its private hidden coves and blushing pink beaches, it was the perfect place for relaxation and romance. Spending a week together in Bermuda, where they could enjoy each other's company with no other responsibilities on their plates, was not only amazingly romantic, but also bonding. Randy and Jane's vacation couldn't have been more perfect. Even though they enjoyed their alone time together, they couldn't wait to get home and see Nathan.

Chapter Forty-Nine

Caring for a patient carrying five fetuses was certainly the most challenging experience of Randy's career, and since it was only the second set of quintuplets in King County, the pregnancy put the Hanson clinic in the public eye. This was good for business, and good for their reputations.

Randy arrived back in town just in time for the big show. His patient, Alyssa Krueger, gave birth by Caesarean section after thirty-three weeks of pregnancy. The five babies, three boys and two girls, had a combined weight of twenty-one pounds, ranging from three pounds, six ounces to five pounds, two ounces. They were born tiny, but healthy. And since the babies were born prematurely, they would spend at least the next month in Swedish's Level III Neonatal Intensive Care Unit.

The morning Seattle Times headline read, *Western Washington Welcomes Its Second Set of Quintuplets.* The article that followed became talk of the city for many months.

"Guess you think you're some kind of hotshot now, don't ya?" Jim said when he saw Randy that afternoon. "Got your name in the paper as some damn Kahuna doctor makin' a historical delivery. That's just what you need for your swelled head."

"Hey, that quintuplet pregnancy was challenging."

"I know. I read the article. The entire hospital's been talkin' about it all morning." Jim sipped from his coffee then set the cup on the table. "How was Bermuda?"

"It was great. Nothing like the feel of sand between my toes. Lounging on the beach with my wife, relaxing. I love Bermuda."

"Sweet. Sounds like you two had a good time." Jim cast a stink-eye toward a man in a white lab coat. "That medical student is a squid."

The fowl expression on Jim's face made Randy ask, "Why?"

"We had a call come in the other night for a man with blood and fluid in his lungs. He was havin' difficulty breathing so I asked Spanky over there to help me with a chest tube, but he had no damn clue what I was talkin' about."

"That's a standard ER procedure that we all learned in med school."

"I know, but that arrogant son-of-a-bitch doesn't know shit. The dude is devoid of some serious brain cells. He makes excuses for everything and seems to think he can undermine my authority. Assmunch pisses me off, and if he tells me one more time that he's not familiar with a procedure, I'm gonna go postal on his ass."

Randy laughed at Jim's sardonic description.

"You wanna grab some lunch later?"

"Not today." Randy put his hand on his stomach. "Stomach isn't feeling too well."

"Coffee brick?"

"I think."

"Bummer. You need to eat somethin' when you drink coffee," Jim advised.

"Jane tells me that all the time."

"Listen to the wife, Bro. She knows what she's talkin' about." Jim checked the time on his watch. "Clock's tickin' and I gotta run. Hoops tonight?"

"Sure," Randy agreed.

"Sweet. Give me a call and we'll meet up at the gym." Jim made a fist with his thumb and pinky sticking up. "Peace out, Bro."

"Later."

In the ER, a patient was wheeled in with a weak pulse, hypotension, a swollen jugular vein, and an abnormal amount of fluid around the heart. He complained of dizziness and quickly developed breathlessness and a decreased level of consciousness.

"TTE," Jim ordered as he began the insertion of a needle through the skin, extracting fluid. "And get me a constant BP." The Emergency Room crew hooked the patient up to a heart monitor, took blood pressure readings, and provided oxygen. Jim looked at Jill. Right away she knew what to do. She treated the patient for shock by putting a pillow under his feet then checked and recorded breathing, pulse, and level of responsiveness, prepared to resuscitate if needed. Jim turned to the medical student he was working with, wondering why he wasn't doing anything to help. "Get cardiology on the phone."

The medical student didn't respond. He stood aloof with an odd expression on his face.

Jim repeated his orders. "Did you hear what I said? Get cardiology on the phone now, and get me a TTE on this patient. You do know what a TTE is, don't you?"

"I'm not familiar with that procedure."

"An echocardiogram. I need one on this patient. And call the cardiologist who's on-call. I hope you at least know how to use a telephone."

The medical student didn't move, so Jim grabbed the phone and called cardiology himself.

As soon as the patient was stabilized, Jim pulled this young medical student aside. "What is your problem?" he asked.

The man stared at Jim, blank-faced.

"I asked you to perform a simple procedure and make a phone call. It is extremely important for you to move quickly in an emergency situation."

"Yes, I know that."

"Are you sure? Because you didn't act like it. From now on you will do exactly what I say, when I say it," Jim demanded. "People's lives are at stake, and if you can't follow simple orders then you need to get out of here, because I will not be responsible for the death of a patient because of your ignorance. Do I make myself clear?"

"Yes, Doctor."

"Good." Jim stormed past Jill and the other ER nurses, resident doctors, and technicians into the locker room.

Jill followed right behind him. She carefully opened the door and peeked her head inside. "James?"

"What?" he snapped. Steam bellowed from his ears and his face was bright scarlet.

She sat next to him. "Talk to me."

With rage-filled eyes, he said, "That stupid cocksucker is going to kill someone. Why the hell is he in my ER?"

Trying to soothe his irritation, Jill put her hand on Jim's shoulder. "You need pull it together, Dr. Ryan."

"He doesn't belong here, Jill. How can any fourth year medical student not know how to pick up a phone and make a simple call?"

"This isn't his specialty," Jill tried to explain.

"I don't give a good goddamn what his specialty is. My patients' lives are on the line and that son-of-a-bitch doesn't seem to have the first damn clue what the fuck he's doin'. That man could have died tonight because of his lack of action. He is causin' me some serious aggro, and I do not have time to worry about an incompetent asshole who hasn't earned enough respect from me to even merit wearing scrubs in my ER."

Jim was exceptionally uptight and irritable. Jill tried to get him to relax. "James, calm down."

"No, Jill, I will not calm down. That fuckin' kook needs to get his act together or get the hell out of my hospital before he kills someone." Jim stood up and marched out of the room.

Jill let out a sigh. It was going to be a long day.

Jim met Randy at the gym that night. With a basketball in his hand, Randy said, "I have this patient who's been complaining of abdominal swelling. Pressure on the intestinal area, difficulty breathing and eating. At first I thought it was ovarian cancer, but when I did exploratory laparoscopy this afternoon, I found something unusual."

"What was it?"

"A mucinous tumor on the appendix. I've never seen anything like it. Any idea what it is?"

"Could be PMP," Jim thought.

"PMP? What's that?"

"Psuedomyxoma peritonei. It's pretty rare. I've only seen one case of it. If not treated, eventually the tumor ruptures and potential malignant cells spread. Generally it doesn't spread beyond the abdomen though."

Not what Randy wanted to hear. "Great. Might need an oncologist for this one."

Jim agreed. "Sounds like it."

Randy passed the ball to Jim.

"Guess what Spanky did today?" Jim said as he dribbled the ball across the court.

"Do I dare ask?"

"I had a patient with cardiac tamponade symptoms and he actually had no idea what a TTE was and didn't seem to realize that a cardiologist needed to be involved."

"Cardiac tamponade can be fatal if not treated properly," Randy stated.

"I know that and you know that, but the all-knowing mighty Dr. Assmunch didn't seem to think it was that big of a deal. He stood there staring at me like he was numb or some shit and actually told me he wasn't familiar with a TTE. And apparently the dumbass doesn't know how to use a damn phone."

"What year is he?" Randy wondered.

"Just finishing up his fourth year. He's about to graduate."

Randy didn't understand why this medical student was acting that way. "He should be more familiar with standard procedures than that."

"My point exactly. What the hell did they do, pull him off the street and throw a pair of scrubs on him? Doesn't merit M.D. behind his name, in my opinion, and I certainly won't recommend him. Must be one of those munchers who barely squeaked by in med school."

"Is he a UW student?" Randy asked, knowing that if the School of Medicine knew about this man's behavior, he would have consequences.

"Yeah."

"What's his name?"

"Olsen. Jeremy Olsen."

Being a clinical professor for University of Washington's School of Medicine, Randy had authority to say something to the powers that be about this person. Incompetence and lack of knowledge was not going to be tolerated in the clinical field. "Let me talk to some people and see what we can do."

"You can do that?"

"Yes I can," Randy said. "I'm a clinical professor for UW, remember? I do have some clout with the University."

Jim grinned. "Oh yeah, you're a muck-e-muck around here. That's kickass."

"I'll look into it tomorrow."

"Thank you," Jim said gratefully.

After an hour of game time, Jim and Randy sat courtside to rehydrate. "Dude, my daughter is drivin' me nuts," Jim said. "She's started to hang out with the skateboarding crew."

"Sidewalk surfers, Jim. I'd think you'd approve of that."

"She's eleven," Jim reminded him.

"She doesn't look eleven."

"I know. That's what scares me. She is so hung up on the way she looks. She wants to wear makeup and have all this jewelry and nail polish. She's pushin' me to have her navel pierced, and I know she's doin' it to try to attract boys. But a boyfriend is totally out of the question. She's too damn young. There is no fuckin' way I'm gonna have some wave-horny teenager all over my 11-year-old daughter."

"You know, don't you, that one out of every three American ninth graders has had sex. And there have been cases of 12-year-olds getting pregnant."

"And you're tellin' me that why?"

"Keep an eye on her, Jim. Once she hits puberty…"

"Dude," Jim said. "My daughter is not gonna be a statistic. Jill's talked to her about all that and we encourage abstinence. She knows it's not ok, and she knows damn well we won't let her leave the house in any kind of revealing clothing. No makeup, nothin' super short or tight-fitting, nothin' that exposes her chest, no questionable words. She has to tell us exactly where she's goin' and who she's with at all times, and we do call to confirm that's where she is. She's a child, regardless of what she thinks, and we'd like to keep her that way as long as possible."

"Has she started her period?" Randy asked.

"No. But it's only a matter of time before she does."

"When she does, bring her in to see me," Randy suggested. "I'll talk to her about all that. Maybe she needs to hear it from someone other than her parents."

Jim chugged down his Gatorade. "Can you believe my youngest daughter is starting Kindergarten in September?"

"Damn. Already?"

"Yup. And Chris is really gettin' into soccer. He loves that game. He's a smart young man—got all A's on his report card."

"Nice job," Randy commended.

"He likes math, and he's really good at it. Sabrina's more into reading and health class. It'll be interesting to see what Jalene likes."

"Watching Nathan's personality develop has been fun. He's really asserting his independence. He's gotten to the point where he wants to do everything for himself, so we gave him chores around the house."

"Good. That helps him learn responsibility," Jim advised. "I saw you guys got a bigger rig. You thinkin' about expanding?"

"Not yet," Randy said. "Wanna wait until Nate's potty trained before we think about another baby."

Right as Randy was about to head home from the weekend, Jim called him with an emergency OB situation. "I know you're getting ready to leave, but I need your help."

"What's up?"

"Had a woman from an automobile accident wheeled in a few minutes ago. She's thirty-seven weeks pregnant with vaginal hemorrhaging, severe back pain, and contractions. Her HCT is low and baby's heartrate is dropping. Fetal distress indicated."

These symptoms gravely concerned Randy. "Have you contacted her doctor?"

Jim hesitated for a second. "She's one of your patients."

Randy's heart plummeted to the floor. "Oh crap."

"We've got her on an IV."

"Run an ultrasound on her and keep the baby monitored. I'll be right there." He hung up, quickly grabbed his stethoscope, and dashed out the door. He reported to Swedish Medical Center's Emergency Room and immediately spotted Jim. "Where is she?"

Jim handed him the file. "Exam room two."

Randy examined the patient and studied all the test results, not liking anything he saw. "Get her prepped for surgery," he told Jim. "I need to do an emergency C-section." He didn't stay to chat. He raced to the operating room and scrubbed up.

Without hesitation, he made a transverse incision through the skin and into the abdomen, followed by a four-inch incision in the wall of the uterus. He removed the baby through this incision. The infant's skin was purple and his body was limp. He wasn't breathing. Randy immediately handed him off to the pediatrician.

The time from incision to delivery took about two minutes, with an additional forty-five minutes to remove the placenta, control the hemorrhaging, and suture the incisions. After completing the procedure and checking vitals on his patient, Randy washed his hands and headed back to the ER.

"How is she?" Jim asked.

"She's fine. She's in recovery and I'm having her checked into postpartum. Baby's Apgar wasn't as high as I'd hoped. Ox was low. They put him on oxygen for a while, and he seems to be doing fine now. Prognosis is good."

Jim breathed a sigh of relief. "That's good news."

"I'm glad you called. This could have turned out badly. Your quick action paid off."

"Lives were on the line, Dude. You know I don't fuck around with that."

"I know, and because of that, two lives were saved." Randy shook Jim's hand. "Nice job, Dr. Ryan. We make a good team."

"We always have," Jim concurred.

The two men smiled at each other with utmost respect. Randy removed the stethoscope from his neck and left the hospital, hoping no action would occur until tomorrow morning's rounds.

Greg and Raquel stopped by Randy and Jane's house that evening. "What's in the bag?" Randy asked when he saw Greg carrying a huge paper bag in his hand.

Raquel answered, "We're getting new products at Starbucks. I cleaned out the older syrups and coffee beans from the store. Instead of throwing them away, I thought you might like them."

"Thanks!"

Greg handed the bag to Randy. "You own a coffee grinder, right?"

"Yes I do." Randy entered the kitchen and reached into the fridge for a couple of Coronas. He handed one to Greg. "What you been up to?"

They stepped out on the deck to finish their conversation. "The clinic I'm in has me working crappy hours. Seems like I'm the only one who's ever on-call."

"That sucks." Randy took a drink of his beer and sat down in a lawn chair.

"I've often wondered if our patients have any clue what it's like being an OB. Ridiculous 4:00 A.M. phone calls, not only from my own patients but from people I don't even know. I guess their physician's answering system says, 'The doctor isn't here. We hope you have a friend who's an obstetrician.' And then for some reason they call me. Some days I want to throw my damn phone in the lake."

Randy couldn't have agreed more. "I hear ya. The cellphone is the leash attached to my collar, a modern ball and chain. For an obstetrician there is no respite. I wonder how pre-cellphone OB's functioned without them?"

"Sometimes I think they were better off. I know there are emergency situations, but…"

Randy finished the thought, "Don't call and interrupt my evening with non-urgent questions that can wait until an office visit."

"Exactly."

"I think patients forget that doctors are human. We have lives, families. And we do sleep. We don't go sauntering around at 4:00 A.M. waiting for medical emergencies." Randy deepened his voice. "Why yes, I was waiting for your call. I have been sitting at my desk for the last five hours going over my old manuals and I believe I have a solution to your problem."

Greg got a chuckle from Randy's commentary. "You know what I hate even more? People who think that because we're doctors our lives are perfect all the time. Just because I own everything I could possibly want doesn't mean my life is all beer and pretzels."

"No kidding."

Greg popped the top off his beer bottle and took a drink. "I wish Raquel would have taken my last name when we got married. It bothers me that she didn't."

"Did she ever tell you why she opted not to?"

"She says she doesn't want to lose her identity, whatever that means. I'm trying to convince her to change it though."

While the men chatted outside, inside Jane asked, "Are you and Greg planning to have children?"

"I don't know about the whole pregnancy and giving birth thing," Raquel replied. "Especially after hearing the stories Greg tells me. Sometimes he confuses me with the things he says. Most professions have their own lingo that excludes outsiders, but none is more intimidating to me than the medical profession."

Jane agreed. "Sometimes Randy rattles off things I don't understand, but I humor him and pretend to know what he's talking about."

"I love Greg's job," Raquel said, "but when your husband saves someone's life how do you, with any sense of self-worth, respond when he asks you how your day was? It makes my job seem so unimportant. All I do is serve people coffee."

"And Randy loves you for that."

"Does it ever bother you, using the name Jane Hanson and knowing your husband is a physician, that people see you only as a doctor's wife?"

Jane shrugged. "I've never had that problem. I took Randy's name, not his title. He spent five years in medical school and four in residency to earn that title. His professional standing has never been an issue in our marriage."

"Hmm," Raquel pondered.

"I am guilty, however, of abusing his professional standing," Jane admitted. "Whenever a friend of mine or someone I know becomes pregnant, I tend to offer his services. I give them Randy's card and tell them they are more than welcome to call if they have any questions. He cringes when I say that. He doesn't like giving advice to patients he's never met. He has gained a few new patients that way, and some people actually do call when their doctor is unavailable."

"How can a doctor be unavailable? Greg always has his phone on him." Raquel complained. "I despise my husband's cellphone. Don't get me wrong. I'm thrilled he's a doctor, but when he's on-call, there's a sense of anxiety in our house, waiting for the dreaded call to take him away to the hospital for the night. I try to avoid using the microwave on those days. It makes him jumpy."

"Randy gets like that too."

"I have no desire to see what Greg does all day. I have a feeling I would gag at the mere thought of it."

"I'd like to see Randy perform surgery," Jane said. "But he won't let me, partially out of respect for his patients. I picture him wielding a knife like Hawkeye Pierce."

Raquel thought that was funny. "I can see that."

"What I have seen is the preparation before the operation—the work he does the night before. That's when Randy brings his manuals and textbooks to bed, especially if there's an unusual procedure he needs to perform. Some of the things he looks at in his manuals are really gross. You haven't lived until you've seen page 567 in Surgical Procedures for Gynecology."

After a late night delivery call, Randy slept in. He rolled over and reached for Jane, but didn't feel her warm body. Only the sheet and pillow. He stretched and sat up. Combing his fingers through his hair, he looked at the alarm clock. 9:00 A.M. That's when he smelled it—coffee—that heavenly aroma that motivated him to get out of bed. The smell was a permanent fragrance in the Hanson house. Randy always had a pot brewing, and when he didn't, Jane brewed one for him.

He slipped on a pair of shorts and scurried barefoot down the stairs.

The parrot squawked at him. "Hello, Doctor."

"Hey, bird."

When Nathan saw Randy, he ran to him, throwing his arms around his leg. "Daddy."

"Good morning, little man." Randy picked the child up and hugged him.

"Me go Papa house."

Randy grinned. "Yup. We're going to see Grandma and Grandpa today."

"Fishie?"

"No. We're not going fishing. We're going to have a barbecue and take the boat out for some waterskiing."

Nathan squealed in excitement. "Boat go bye-bye?"

"Yes. We'll go bye-bye on the boat."

"Love you, Daddy."

"I love you too, Buddy." He kissed his son on the cheek and set him back down. He entered the kitchen and gave Jane a kiss. "Good morning, Gorgeous."

Jane scanned her husband from head to toe. His eyelids were saggy and he lacked his usual energy. "Late night last night?"

"I got a call at 2:00 A.M. and was at the hospital for three hours. Some complications arose and I ended up doing a C-section."

Jane touched his weary face. "You are a wonderful doctor. You care so much about your patients."

"I try." He pulled a coffee mug from the cupboard.

"There's some fruit salad in the fridge if you want some, Sweetie."

"Need to get the blood pumping first." He proceeded to pour himself a cup of coffee.

While Jane was in the shower, Nathan sat on the floor playing with his cars. Randy relaxed on the sofa, intently reading one of his medical journals, when a toy car came flying through the air and hit him on the head. "Ow!"

Nathan giggled.

Randy, however, didn't think this was funny. "We do not throw toys. That hurts," he firmly stated.

But Nathan didn't listen. He picked up another car and chucked it across the room.

Immediately Randy took the cars away from him.

Nathan screamed, "Mine!"

"If you throw the cars then you cannot have them. That is not nice."

The toddler flung himself on the floor, screaming and kicking his feet.

Randy had never seen him throw a tantrum like this before. "Wow. That's a good one." He ignored the fit and left the room.

As soon as Randy was out of sight, Nathan stopped screaming. "Daddy?" he called to his father. When Randy didn't answer, Nathan searched for him. He found him in the kitchen. With a pouty lip, Nathan looked up at his father and whined. "Car?"

Randy firmly stated, "You can't have the car. You threw it at me. We don't do that."

Nathan's lip quivered and he looked like he was about to cry.

Instilling discipline on his son, Randy said, "Throwing a fit and screaming will not get you what you want. That is not ok."

Nathan did it anyway.

Randy picked the child up off the floor, carried him into the living room, and sat him on the couch. "Fine. You want to act like that, then you can sit here with no toys. We do not throw toys and we do not scream and throw a fit."

Nathan sat there crying, but only for a few minutes. When he stopped, his lower lip stuck out and he looked pathetic.

Jane came out and saw Nathan sitting alone on the couch with a pout on his face. Her husband, on the other hand, looked annoyed. "What's wrong?"

"Our son felt it necessary to throw his car at me then proceeded to throw a fit when I took it away from him. So he is sitting there until he calms down."

"You're kidding?" Jane found this hard to believe. "I've never seen him do that before."

"Neither have I, but I will not put up with it."

Nathan calmed down and eventually became interested in playing with something else. Randy stepped into the kitchen to refill his coffee cup. "I am not ready for this two-year-old stuff. Those fits are gonna get old quick."

Jane and Randy needed to go grocery shopping. Nathan decided his Scooby Doo slippers were the latest trend in errand-running footwear, but rather than fighting the child on this and risk another tantrum, Randy played along. He put on his slippers then picked up the car keys and his wallet. "Ok, we can go now."

Nathan dissolved into laughter at the mere thought of Randy getting in the car in his slippers. "Shoe, Daddy." Nathan handed Randy his sneakers.

"Oh, you want me to put my shoes on?"

"Shoes go bye-bye," the child claimed.

"Yes, but Daddy can't wear his shoes if you don't have your shoes."

That was all it took for Nathan to fetch his shoes. He tried to put one on by himself but struggled with this task. Randy tried to help him. "Me do it," Nathan declared. He pulled the shoe away from his father and tried again.

Randy sat back and let him try. Nathan quickly got frustrated when he couldn't do it. He held his shoe up as if he was going to throw it, but Randy intervened before he did. "You want me to help you?" he asked. "I'll help you if you need help, but we do not throw things. Ask nicely."

Instead of throwing the shoe, Nathan handed it to his father. "Daddy, shoe?"

"Please?" Randy encouraged.

"Peas."

"That's better." He sat on the floor with Nathan and put his shoes on for him. "There."

"Me go bye-bye." The child sprang to his feet and toddled toward the door. Randy put on his own shoes and trod right behind him.

They reported to his parents' house around 1:00 that afternoon. Since this family get-together was a potluck barbecue, Randy and Jane brought potato salad and a huge watermelon. For Nathan, they packed a plastic shovel and pail, a blow up beach ball, floaties for the water, and a diaper bag full of necessary items he would need. Jane also brought a parasol to provide shade for Nathan.

Since the Ryans had become a permanent part of the Hanson family gatherings, Jim and his family were invited too. They brought fresh salad fixings and two bags of chips. Aside from Jim's normal surfing attire of flip flops, baggy swimming trunks, brightly colored Hawaiian print shirts, and a shark tooth necklace, he also had on a white tee-shirt with bold black letters: *You want to get my attention? Try bleeding.*

Randy chuckled when he saw it. "Nice shirt."

Jim removed his sunglasses. "I'm tired of people comin' into the ER for non-emergencies. It's called an Emergency Department for a reason."

"I hear ya."

"People's stupidity keeps me in a job. The shit they do to get themselves into the ER is ridiculous. We really need special triage tags for stupid people. Some dumbass came in last night with his hand nail-gunned to a two-by-four because he wasn't payin' attention to what he was doin', and he expected me to bend over backwards to accommodate him when I had someone in the next room goin' into cardiac arrest. I swear, every ER should be supplied with a valium lick for the uptight assholes who walk in there. My job is to save their ass, not kiss it." Jim reached into the ice chest and pulled out a Corona. "And just an FYI, a broken nail is not a medical emergency."

Randy loved hearing Jim's ER stories, and he was always so dramatic when he told them.

"I work eighteen-hour shifts in non-stop chaos. I don't get many breaks and it takes me ninety minutes to eat my lunch because I am constantly bein' interrupted. One minute of peace and quiet is a welcome sight. You know unspeakable evil will befall if someone dares to utter the words, 'Wow, it's quiet in here.' Then all hell breaks loose." Jim popped the top and took a quenching drink.

"And you love every minute of it."

"Hell yeah, I love it. Best damn job in the world," Jim said. "Jill made me laugh last night. We were on shift together and some dude was givin' her a hard time. I walked by the exam room and heard her say to him, 'Sir, if you don't keep the thermometer in your mouth I'll have to try a different approach.' Funniest damn thing I've ever heard."

Randy thought it was funny too. "That's great."

"And the best part is, she would have done it."

Randy watched his wife, who was on the beach with Nathan. She had on a pair of denim shorts and a black bikini top. Her long brown hair, up in a ponytail, swayed down the middle of her back. Her well-defined legs were tanned, and her bare toes were polished red. When she bent over to hand Nathan his pail and shovel, Randy stared at her backside.

"Quit starin' at your wife's ass," Jim said.

"I can't help it. She gets me hot."

"You have got to be the most wave-horny son-of-a-bitch I have ever known."

Randy continued to stare at Jane. "Look at her, Jim. She is the sexiest woman ever."

Jane spread a towel out in the sand then headed his direction. "Hey, Handsome."

He drew her closer to him and kissed her. As the kiss became more succulent, he slipped his fingers into her shorts and squeezed her butt.

She opened her eyes and cocked her head at him. "Randal Hanson, behave yourself."

He lovingly smacked her on the ass.

Before dinner, they got a few waterskiing runs in, shore starting to allow everyone on the beach the opportunity to ski. Randy drank a cup of coffee while he took control of the throttle. Jim sat by his side. Mark sat behind him holding 20-month-old Nathan, who was wearing a life jacket, and Jane sat opposite them serving as spotter for the skiers.

After all the skiers had their turn, Mark took over as driver so Randy could have a run. Randy was an excellent water skier—stable on one ski, jumping wakes, carving big rooster tails, and plowing through the water aggressively using advanced waterskiing techniques. He was very much at home in the water, but this was no surprise considering he grew up around water. Whether skiing, fishing, boating, using a Waverunner, or swimming, water was his second home.

Jim had never seen Randy waterski before. "Damn, Dude. You are a powerhouse on the water."

Randy stepped into the boat and grabbed a towel to dry off. "Been skiing since I was seven." He slipped his tee-shirt on and took control of the throttle again. They dropped Mark off at the beach then Randy turned the boat around and drove out to deeper water. He stopped the engine in the middle of the lake and stared at Jim. "Ok, Dr. Ryan. Your turn."

"Me?"

"Yes, you. Your wife tried it and your daughter gave it a whirl. Now it's your turn."

"Dude, I don't know how to waterski."

"Then it's time you learned." Randy threw a ski vest at him. "Get in the water."

Jim hesitated.

"Put on the vest, get in the damn water, and let's go."

Jim put on the ski vest and jumped in the water. Randy leaned over the side and handed him a ski. He talked him through how to put it on then handed him the other one. Jim struggled against the water current, waves, and the ski as he tried to put on the second one. Once he managed to get both skis on, he floated in the water with the tips sticking up.

"Ok. Important things to remember," Randy said. "Keep your knees bent and your skis together. The tips of your skis should be about one to one and half feet out of the water. Too much or too little will cause you to turn over sideways. Don't fight the water. Let the boat pull you. Allow for arm adjustment with the rope. Never pull your arms all the way to your chest, and never extend your arms out all the way. This gives you leeway to adjust for unpredictable difficulties that the water conditions may present you with. Your arms will get too tired otherwise."

"Alrighty."

"Now," Randy advised. "I'm gonna toss you the rope in a minute. Make sure it's between your skis and you have the handle tightly gripped in your hands. Once I push the throttle, you'll feel the boat pull you up. Keep your knees bent, feet together. When the boat pulls you on top of the water, don't try to move right away. Just get a feel for being pulled and try to balance. And final tip, always fall backwards. If you fall forward, your skis will come off and you'll get some serious water up your nose."

Jim cringed just thinking about that predicament. "Eww. Neptune cocktail."

"Not very fun. You ready?"

Jim took a deep breath, not feeling ready at all. "I guess."

Randy tossed him the rope. "I'm gonna take the slack out of the rope before I pull you up. Jane will be watching you and she'll communicate with me. When you're ready, give her a thumbs up."

Jim looked up at Jane. "Don't laugh at me."

"I won't," she assured him. "All of us had to go through this when we learned too. If you fall, let go of the rope or you'll get dragged."

"Leash lagged, huh?" He gave a mirthless laugh. "Fun fun." Then he turned to Randy and asked, "How fast does this thing go when you pull a skier?"

"Between twenty-five and thirty miles per hour."

"Great," Jim scoffed. "So when I fall and kill myself, I can be a patient in my own ER. I'll be triaged with the stupid people."

"You'll be fine." Randy took position behind the throttle and the boat began to slowly take up the extra slack in the rope. He looked at Jane and said, "Keep an eye on him. Don't let him get hurt."

"I won't."

"Maybe this will motivate him to move from skis to a surfboard."

Jim gave the thumbs up, and Randy accelerated the throttle. Jim popped right out of the water. Randy pulled him around for a while, but Jim got a little too ambitious and approached the wake, losing his balance and falling backwards.

Jane raised the orange flag and had Randy turn around. Randy circled around Jim and let him grab the rope for another shot at it. "Nice job," Randy said. "Got up your first time. Watch that wake, Buddy. It'll knock you on your ass."

"Now you tell me."

After dinner and a game of volleyball, people spread out on lawn chairs, kicking back and relaxing in the sand. Randy was cleaning up ski equipment when Jane ran over to him and threw herself in his arms. He lost his balance and they both fell backwards into the water. When they surfaced, Randy picked her up over his shoulder and carried her to deeper water.

Screaming and kicking her legs she said, "Randy, put me down."

"Ok." He dropped her in the water and headed back toward shore.

Nathan stared at Randy with an ornery scowl. "No, no, Daddy. Mommy wet."

Randy simply laughed.

As nightfall came, everyone went their separate ways. The minute Randy and Jane put Nathan to bed, Randy drug her into the bedroom. He fondled her buttocks and cupped her breasts with his hands. "My god, I want you." He removed her clothes, then stripped off his own shorts and tee-shirt as quickly as he could. Normally Randy didn't skip foreplay, but tonight he was about to explode. They maneuvered to the bed and he quickly accessed her, not wasting time with bedroom games. The intenseness that followed led them both to climax within minutes.

Panting, Randy asked, "You know what I was thinking?" He slowly meandered his index finger between her breasts, lovingly kissing the side of one. "Let's have another baby."

This was not what she expected him to say. "What?"

He looked her in the eye. "Nathan is getting more independent, starting to use the potty, and if you get pregnant now, he'll be two and a half by the time the baby is born."

She couldn't believe Randy suggested this. "You're serious?"

"I'm very serious. I wanna get you pregnant. How do you feel about that?"

The corners of her mouth arched upward. "I think that's a great idea."

"Alright. Then let's get started." He gripped her tightly and kissed her on the lips.

Chapter Fifty

Randy propped up on his elbow, watching Jane as she tied a silk robe around her waist. He always kept pretty good tabs on her menstrual cycle, especially since they were trying to conceive again. She stayed regular for the most part, and generally had mild to moderate PMS symptoms. However this month, she experienced no symptoms at all. "You're late this month."

Jane knew what was going through his head. "It's nothing."

"Are you sure about that?"

"I'm just a few days late. You're jumping to conclusions."

"I'll bring home a pregnancy test anyway."

She thought he was making a big deal over nothing. "Is that really necessary?"

"Yes, it's necessary." He pulled her onto the bed with him. "Are you arguing with your doctor?"

"No."

"Good." He pinned her on the bed and tickled her.

Before Randy left the office that day, he snagged a pregnancy test off the storage shelf and casually tossed it in the air, whistling as he caught it.

"What are you doing with that?" Mark asked him.

"It's for Jane."

Mark raised an eyebrow, assuming he knew what that meant. "She's pregnant?"

"Most likely."

"Let me know how that turns out."

"I will."

After dinner, Randy played with his son for a while then tucked him in for the night. He entered the bedroom and came over to Jane, who was at the bathroom vanity brushing her hair. He put his arms around her and kissed her neck. "I brought that pregnancy test home."

Jane looked at his reflection in the mirror.

"Let's check it out." He pulled the box off his bedside table and handed her a collection cup. "Here."

Thinking he was crazy, she took it from him. "Ok, fine." She stepped into the bathroom and closed the door. When she was finished, she handed the cup back to him.

Scoffing at her indifferent attitude, Randy stared at the specimen cup in his hand. "That's it? You're just gonna hand me a cup full of urine and walk away? You're not even a little curious?"

"Randy, I have no symptoms. I feel fine. I'm just a few days late."

"But every pregnancy is different," Randy explained. "You might not get the same symptoms you had last time."

"Humor yourself then." She changed into her blue silk nightie then propped herself up against the headboard and grabbed a book.

Randy administered the test and waited. Three minutes later, he called to her, "Uh, Honey, could you come here for a minute please."

Annoyed at his persistence with this, she got up and went to see what he wanted. "Yes, Doctor," she teased.

He held up the test strip. It was pink. "Told you."

She eyeballed him for a minute. "We're pregnant?"

"That's what the test says." With a smug grin on his face, he handed her the positive pregnancy test. "Stop by the clinic tomorrow afternoon. I want to do a pelvic on you and see if we can get in for an ultrasound. I have a seminar at 1:30 but should be finished by 3:00." Randy sat on the edge of the bed and reached over to the bedside table for his iPad. He turned it on and looked up her potential due date. "Looks like around April seventh."

"What about Nathan?"

Randy lifted his head. "What about him?"

"We have to prepare him for this."

"We will. There are tons of books out there about being a big brother, and we'll talk to him about babies and what they need. It's about time for him to move into a big boy bed anyway. I'll help him pick out furniture and he can help me set up his room. That'll help him transition when the time comes. He'll be fine, Jane. We have plenty of time to prepare him."

Randy drove over to his clinic the following afternoon to wait for his wife. Mark was surprised to see him, since he was supposed to be working with medical students at the hospital. "Good afternoon, Son. What are you doing over here?"

"Meeting Jane."

"Does this meeting have anything to do with the results of your test last night?"

Randy replied, "Yes it does."

Mark beamed. "Do I get to be a grandpa again?"

"Yes, Sir. We are due April seventh."

"Well, this is exciting."

When Jane showed up with Nathan, Mark held his arms out to the child. "Nathan. Come see Grandpa."

Nathan ran over to his grandpa and gave him a big hug.

Randy stepped out of an exam room and spotted his family. "Hey, little man." He kissed his son on the cheek.

"Hi, Daddy. Me go potty," Nathan boasted, proud of his accomplishment.

"You did?"

Jane added, "He went by himself all day."

Randy praised him. "Good job, Buddy." Randy sat him at a table behind the front desk with some paper and crayons. Then he turned to his wife and said, "You ready?"

"We can't just leave Nathan here," Jane said.

"He'll be fine. Veronica agreed to watch him for a minute so we can do this."

The receptionist reassured Jane, "It's not a problem at all. He's adorable."

With Jane's file in his hand, Randy escorted her into an examination room. He set her chart on the counter and pulled a pink hospital gown from the drawer. "My nurses are busy right now and the lab is pretty packed. Looks like I'll have to draw blood."

"You're going to draw blood?" Jane asked, not too keen on the prospect of her husband poking her with a needle.

"Yes, I am." He handed her the gown. "Put this on. I need to grab some things from the lab. I'll be right back." He kissed her before he left.

Randy returned with a specimen cup, three test tubes, self-stick labels, a permanent marker, a syringe with a capped needle attached, and a latex tourniquet.

He set all of this down on the counter and washed his hands.

After slipping on a pair of latex gloves, he grabbed a cotton ball out of a jar, a bottle of rubbing alcohol, the syringe, and three test tubes. He gently took Jane's hand and extended her arm. "I'm apologizing ahead of time for poking you. I don't mean to hurt you, but we have to do this."

He tied her arm in latex to extend the blood vessels and rubbed alcohol on the crook of her elbow. As soon as all necessary exams and tests were complete, he brought the three test tubes of blood to the lab. He had her get dressed then took a blood pressure measurement and recorded her weight. "Ok, you know the routine. No alcohol, eat balanced meals, limit caffeine consumption."

"Maybe you should take your own advice," she teased.

They headed to the hospital to get her an ultrasound. On the exam table, Randy lifted her shirt slightly and slid her waistband down to expose her tummy. He applied imaging gel to her abdomen and placed a transducer on her belly. He moved the wand around a bit to get a clearer picture. Confused by the image, he squinted his eyes. "What the hell?"

Jane tried to get him to tell her what he saw. "Is everything alright?"

He refocused the monitor and moved the transducer to a different location, ensuring that what he saw was real. "I can't believe this."

She grew worried that something was wrong. "Randal Hanson. What is wrong?"

"Nothing, Baby," he assured her. "Everything's fine." Randy took a still shot and turned the screen so Jane could see. "Look at this." He drew a circle around an embryo. "One." Then he drew a circle around a second one. "Two." His eyes met hers, astonished over this image. "You're carrying twins."

Jane's jaw dropped. Now she understood why Randy reacted the way he did. With her hand over her mouth, she gasped, "Twins?"

"Look." He pointed them out to her again. "One, two. They're right there, clear as day."

She wasn't sure how to react to this. "How did this happen?"

He examined the ultrasound again. One placenta, two embryos. Definitely twins. "These two are sharing a placenta." Randy pointed it out to her on the ultrasound image. "Which means they are monozygotic, or identical twins. Unlike dizygotic twins, who have separate placentas, MZ twins occur when one egg is fertilized by one sperm. The zygote splits for some unknown reason, forming two embryos. It's a totally random event."

"In other words, you don't know how this happened," she concluded.

"Exactly. It just happens. It's a fluke of nature."

"They're identical?" Jane questioned.

"MZ twins are always the same sex and blood type. They'll have the same physical features, but their fingerprints and personalities will be different." He printed off this image and took several more shots from different angles. "Well, Babe," he said, wiping the gel off her tummy. "You have now been bumped up to my high-risk pregnancy list."

"Why?"

"Multiple births are always high-risk. This pregnancy will look a lot different, and I'm going to handle it differently than I did with Nathan. I'm going to be monitoring you closely and you'll get more frequent ultrasounds. You'll get bigger sooner and you're going to gain more weight, upwards of thirty-five to forty pounds. In fact, your jeans will probably start getting tight in the next week or so."

She stopped him before he said another word. "Thirty-five pounds?"

Randy knew that weight gain was an issue for her with her last pregnancy. But for this one, it would be particularly important. "You're supporting two fetuses. You're going to need more calories, an extra six-hundred a day. You'll need to eat smaller, more frequent meals."

"I won't need a C-section will I?" she asked.

"Hopefully not. I wanna try a vaginal delivery. It is possible to deliver multiples vaginally, but sometimes, especially if the babies aren't in a head-down position, a C-section is safer. It's common for the first baby to be born head first, whereas the subsequent infant may be breech. We'll see how you progress. Regardless, twin pregnancies usually don't go full term."

He gave her all the facts about multiple births and tried his best to answer all of her questions. And because this pregnancy was so much different than the last one, she had a lot of questions.

Sensing her insecurity about all of this, Randy offered reassurance. "You'll be fine. I'll take care of you." With the ultrasound images in his hand, he checked the time on his watch. "I'm gonna put these in your file and talk to my dad really quick. Jim gets off in twenty minutes and I told him I'd shoot hoops with him today."

"Any idea what time you'll be home?"

"Around 6:00 probably." He leaned closer and gave her a kiss. "Love you, Babe. I'll see you tonight."

Jane left with Nathan, and Randy returned to his clinic. He placed several sonograms in Jane's file, but kept one for himself.

His father stood in front of a closed examination room reading through a patient file.

"Dad?" Randy said, trying to get his attention.

"Yes, Son?" Mark replied without looking up.

Randy placed the ultrasound image on the file his dad was studying. "Check this out."

"What is this?"

"Jane's sonogram."

After examining the image carefully, Mark's facial expression switched from a smile to a gasp of surprise. "There are two embryos here."

Randy grinned. "I know."

Mark removed his glasses. "Twins?"

"Yes, Sir." Randy hard a hard time soaking this in. "How are we supposed to handle twins? Two cribs, two feedings, double the diapers, double everything."

Mark put his hand on his son's shoulder. "We'll help you. Right now your priority is to keep Jane healthy and make sure you monitor her carefully."

"I know. I will."

Mark handed the ultrasound image back to Randy. "Don't forget to tell your mother."

When Randy walked into the ER, Jim was hovering over a screaming trauma patient who had been wheeled in from an ambulance. He barked orders at a resident doctor, an orderly, and several other personnel. "Hold his feet down, keep him still. Jill!" he hollered, trying to get her to come help him.

"Yes, Doctor. I'm on it." She monitored vitals and immediately got oxygen flowing through this man.

The ER staff diligently worked to sustain him while Jim tried to stop the profuse bleeding. With quick action, they were able to get this man's vitals back on track. After the excitement was over, Jim removed his latex gloves and headed toward the sink to wash his hands.

"Dr. Ryan," Randy inspected Jim's blood-covered scrubs. "Looks like you've been busy."

"Swamped."

"Will you be able to break free during shift change?"

"Yeah," Jim said. "Let me clean up first. Give me five minutes."

"Alright."

Once Jim was ready, he grabbed his athletic bag, carried on some kind of conversation with Jill, then gave her a kiss before he left the ER. "How was the land of medical school today?" Jim said as he and Randy left the hospital together.

"It was good," Randy replied. "I gave a seminar on pre-operative procedures this morning."

"Oh joy. I'll jump right on that one."

Clearly Jim was unimpressed. "Not the most exciting topic, but I did show them cool pictures of infections that could develop if they don't do it right. Got a few reactions from that."

"That's always fun," Jim chuckled. "What's new with you?"

Randy handed him Jane's sonogram. "This."

"What am I supposed to do with this?"

"That, my friend, is a sonogram."

"I know that, Dumbass, but why did you give it to me?"

"Look at it."

Jim did. "There are two embryos."

468

"Bravo, Mr. Wizard. Are you sure you're not an obstetrician?" Randy teased. "Now look at the name on the top."

When the name was revealed, Jim redirected his stare to Randy. "Jane's pregnant?"

"Why the hell else would there be an ultrasound image with her name on it? Yes, she's pregnant."

Thinking this entire situation was hilarious, Jim said, "Holy shit, Dude. Twins? What the hell are you and Jane gonna do with two babies?"

"The same thing we would do with one baby."

"Oh man. I hope they are both girls."

After work the next day, Randy picked Nathan up from his parents' house then stopped by the YMCA. He sat on the bench watching his wife put basketballs back on a rack while Nathan sat on his lap.

"Mommy play ball?" he asked his father.

"Yup. Mommy plays basketball."

"Me play too?"

"You have a basketball hoop at home," Randy said. "You can't play with these."

"My ball," Nathan insisted.

"No," Randy corrected. "These are not yours. These are Mommy's basketballs."

Randy ringtone went off. "Dr. Hanson." He paused for a second then lifted Nathan off his lap and sat him on a bleacher. "Symptoms?"

He appeared to be giving some sort of medical consultation over the phone. He did this periodically for some of his colleagues, especially for Jim if an obstetrical case came into the ER. But Jane could tell by the tone of her husband's voice that he was not talking to Jim.

"What are you doing for her now?" He stood up and listened attentively, drawing his eyebrows closer, deep in thought. "She needs to be continuously monitored. Run a creatinine and platelet count on her. Give her Magnesium Sulfate, twenty percent solution over the next five minutes. Once her blood pressure stabilizes, induce labor."

Randy started to pace around, agitated by something the other person was saying.

"I don't care. Prolonging this pregnancy could result in serious danger to her and death of this infant. The condition will be relieved with the delivery of the baby. Get her hooked up to an EFM. If the baby shows signs of compromise, we'll need to do an immediate C-section."

Randy stopped pacing. His tightened facial expression and snarled lip told Jane that he was about to lose his patience.

"That's why you monitor her. You'll discontinue the infusion of Pitocin in the event of fetal distress. Did anyone call her doctor?" He held his hand up to his forehead. "Alright, get her admitted to L&D and I'll come by and check on her later. Have someone up there call me if her condition worsens or if the baby has any problems."

Randy hung up and slipped his phone in his pocket. "Shit."

"What's the matter?" she asked.

"A woman in her third trimester came into the ER with symptoms of preeclampsia. She doesn't have a doctor and hasn't had any pre-natal care at all. The ER resident called me because he didn't know what to do."

"Jim's not there tonight?"

"No. Jim's off tonight."

"So you have to go to the hospital," Jane assumed.

"I can't leave her there in that condition. She needs to deliver this baby or she's going to run into some serious problems."

"Sounds like she needs you." She put the last basketball on the cart and wheeled it up against the wall.

"After dinner I need to run in and check on her." He bounded onto the court with Nathan by his side. "Speaking of which, what should we do about dinner tonight?"

Young Nathan joyfully expressed his opinion, "Chickie nuggie."

Nathan's boldness made Randy laugh. "Guess he wants chicken nuggets."

Jane sneered. "Fried food?"

"Hey, talk to your son. It was his suggestion."

"I'm not eating that."

"Tell you what, I'll snag some chicken nuggets for Nate then we'll stop by Subway and pick up some sandwiches. How's that?" Randy suggested.

"That sounds good."

"We'll meet you back at the house." He leaned over and gave her a kiss.

Nathan took Randy's hand and waved bye-bye to Jane. "Love you, Mommy." Then he and his dad exited the gym to go get dinner.

Chapter Fifty-One

Randy took a week off in November so he and Jane could fly to San Francisco for Thanksgiving. Aside from allowing Jane time to visit with her father and brother, this trip also gave Nathan the opportunity to take his first airplane ride.

While they waited to board, little Nathan, who had recently turned two, stared out the window wide-eyed, watching the airplanes take off and land. "Look, Daddy. Big plane."

Randy looked out the window with him. "That's a 747 jet. We're going to ride on one of those."

"Me go on dat plane?"

"One like it," Randy explained. "We're going to San Francisco to see Grandpa."

Once in the air, Nathan rested his head on Jane's lap and fell asleep.

Randy cast a watchful eye over his sleeping son, wondering where the last two years went. "When we get back, I'll take him to get a big boy bed. We need to get him into that other room so we can set up the nursery for the twins." They had already heard two heartbeats via Doppler and, at four months pregnant, Jane's belly grew bigger every day. "I'm gonna give you another ultrasound when we get back too. Check and see how they're doing."

"Lots of twitches and tickles going on." She placed her hand on her protruding tummy. "There's definitely two babies in there, either that or I'm carrying an octopus."

Randy laughed at her analogy. "When the kicks can be felt on the outside, make sure Nathan gets a chance to feel. We need to keep him as involved as possible."

When Dale Davine saw Jane waddling down the exit ramp, his face lit up. He struggled to put his arms around her. "Hi, Sweetheart. You look great."

"Thank you."

Dale gave Nathan a big hug and kissed his cheek. "Hello, Nathan. Look how big you've gotten."

"Me go potty," he proudly told his grandfather.

"Yes, I heard. Good job."

From the airport, they took Nathan to San Francisco's Academy of Sciences aquarium. This aquarium housed an aquatic world of 165 individual tank exhibits, each reflecting the natural environments of the inhabitants, including the Amazon underbelly, the California kelp forest, and a Hawaiian coral reef. The 6,000 gallon coral reef displayed dazzling fishes swimming in a complex mini-ecosystem of green fuzzy mushroom anemones and various colored corals. Nathan was able to get up close and personal with thousands of his favorite swimming, splashing sea creatures, including wonderful seahorses and a vast variety of fish.

"Fishie, Daddy!" Nathan squealed in excitement.

"Yup. Lots of fishies." Randy pointed out a pretty orange and white striped fish. "Look, Nate, this one is called a clownfish."

"Nemo!"

"Yes," Randy chuckled. "Just like Nemo."

At the Touch Tide Pool, Nathan got his hands wet handling sea stars, anemones, hermit crabs, and urchins. The anemones were his favorite because they would sprawl out their tentacles, then when he touched them they would quickly pull them back in.

Besides having about 5,000 specimens of fish, the aquarium maintained a collection of more than 200 kinds of reptiles and amphibians, along with three species of marine mammals, several birds, and large invertebrates.

Nathan and his adult chaperones enjoyed watching the adorable Black-Footed Penguins don their tuxedos while they waddled, swam, and gulped down fish at the daily feeding.

Nathan had never seen a penguin before, therefore he was naturally curious about them. "Daddy, what dat?"

"Those are penguins. Penguins are birds."

Those didn't look like any bird he'd ever seen. "Bird?"

"Yup. They don't fly though. They swim like fish."

"Fishie bird," Nathan concluded.

Nathan's childish classification made Randy laugh.

Dale stood back and watched Randy and Nathan's interaction. Nathan followed his dad around everywhere, and Randy taught him all kinds of things about science. The two of them were buddies.

To feed Nathan's fascination with fish, Randy decided to purchase a tropical aquarium for the house. He and Nathan spent an afternoon at a pet store looking at various types of fish and different tank styles. They ended up with a fifty-five gallon tank and a stand to put it on. Randy set it up against the living room wall. He and Nathan decorated it with natural pea gravel, a slate rock cave, decorative rocks to break up the aquascape, mock coral, and several natural live plants. Randy opted for a community tank with mild tempered fish that ranged in color from lustrous yellow with black stripes to vibrant gold and purple hues. The large colorful tank added life to the living room and excitement to Nathan's day. Nathan stood at the tank and watched the fish for hours.

Jane was at the point in her pregnancy where the hormones were kicking in, and because she was carrying twins, her moodiness multiplied. Everything she did was frustrating to her because she ran out of energy quickly. She felt heifer-like, and even though Randy told her morning, noon, and night how beautiful she was and embraced her new curves with hugs, she didn't feel beautiful at all.

After dinner, Randy carried Nathan on his shoulders and they all went for a walk around the neighborhood. Exercise was a big mood booster for her. It also tended to brew up sexual energy and usually led to them leaping under the sheets. But tonight, she was not in the mood. She was overly tired and kept complaining of her back hurting. To ease this discomfort, Randy had her lie on her side so he could rub it for her.

"My belly is sticking out," she remarked, no longer able to see her feet.

"Yes, but it's a beautiful belly."

"I look like Humpy Dumpty."

He offered his medical advice. "It's important for you to gain weight early in your pregnancy. The higher the weight at birth, the better the babies will do. Weight gain with multiples is not a minor issue, Babe. It's something you have to focus on."

"I feel like a balloon."

Jane had a hard time being a high-risk pregnancy. The likelihood of premature labor, high blood pressure, and C-section delivery was higher with multiples, and the babies were at greater-than-average risk of complications. Randy knew the significance of this; he had dealt with multiple births many times. But Jane didn't seem to understand the serious nature of her pregnancy.

"I've been so tired lately," she remarked.

"You're carrying two babies this time. Your body is working twice as hard. You need to take it easy and try not to do too much. Your primary job right now is to be an incubator. Anything else you can fit into to your life is a bonus. Feed yourself, feed these babies, and sleep. You have to take care of yourself."

She tried, but this pregnancy was wearing her down. Her feet were swollen, she was constantly tired and irritable, and felt heavy and weak. And because her belly was so big so early, she had a difficult time sleeping comfortably at night.

When they went in for an ultrasound, two heartbeats thumped steady and strong. The fetuses were growing normally; they were active and healthy. As Randy scanned over the images on the screen, he developed a smirk on his face. "Oh man. Jim is going to have a heyday with this."

"What are you talking about?" Jane asked.

He turned the monitor to show her. "They're girls."

As soon as Jim heard this news, he burst into laughter. "This is the best news I've heard all week. Not one, but two girls. Now you can go through the pink hair ribbons and Barbie dolls and watchin' your daughter mature into a young woman who wears a bra and bikini, not once, but twice."

"Twice the fun. Twice the love."

"Twice the work. Damn, Dude. Two girls at the same time. Good luck with that."

Randy and Jim sat on the couch, each with an X-Box controller in their hand. They raced and crashed sports cars down a racetrack while they munched on Oreos and drank coffee.

"Jill was pissed at me last night," Jim confessed.

"What'd you do?"

"My dad called, and you know how he gets. Anyway, he said somethin' that annoyed me and I started yellin' at him over the phone. Apparently the kids heard me talkin' to their grandfather that way and it upset them. Jill proceeded to inform me that what I said was inappropriate, and I shouldn't have yelled at my father in front of the children."

"What did you say to him?" Randy asked.

"He was houndin' me about bringin' the kids down to San Francisco for Christmas. I told him that if he really wanted to see the kids he would have make a conscious effort to get off his ass and buy a plane ticket to Seattle. They've never been up here to see the kids, my house, or where I work. He always expects us to fly down there. I told him it was his turn, and in the midst of the conversation, my daughter called me a Scrooge and told me I'm mean to old people. She hasn't talked to me all day."

"Wow," Randy snickered, finding this somewhat amusing.

"Pre-teen girls—moodier than hell."

Randy understood completely. "Jane's been really moody too. She hasn't been feeling well and this pregnancy's been rough on her. Trying to keep up with

Nathan all day is exhausting, and by the time she gets home from work at 6:30, she's completely worn out and sleeps for two hours. Then, since she took such a late nap, she has a hard time falling asleep at night."

"She needs to nap when Nathan naps," Jim advised.

"I've told her that, but she's usually getting ready for work when Nathan is napping."

"Maybe workin' is too much for her right now."

Randy disagreed. "I don't think her job is the problem. I think she's trying to do too much around the house. Aside from keeping up with Nathan all day, she insists on doing all the cleaning, laundry, and grocery shopping while I'm at the clinic."

"Don't let her," Jim said.

"I can't stop her, Jim. I've tried. I told her to save it for me to do, but she already has it done by the time I get home."

"I thought you were her doctor?" Jim reminded him.

"I am."

"Then be her doctor and lay it on the line. Her health comes first, Bro. With multiples, she needs rest. If she trusts your professional judgment, she'll listen to you. Offer her love and support, but tell her that because you care about her and her health, you need her to do these things."

Jim had a good point. This didn't happen often, but once in a blue moon Jim's words of wisdom made sense. "You know, that's a good idea."

"I know Jane has you wrapped around her finger, but dammit, sometimes you gotta put your foot down."

That evening, Randy had a conversation with his wife about his concerns. "You need to leave the housework and laundry for me to do. And if you text

478

me a list of groceries we need, I can stop by the store on my way home. Don't exert yourself so much. You're wearing yourself out."

"I am perfectly capable of washing a load of clothes, Randy. I'm not an invalid."

"I know, but you need to focus on getting rest right now."

She darted past him into the bathroom, completely blowing him off.

"Dammit, Jane, would you stop and look at me, please."

She turned around, agitated by his badgering. "What?"

"Why are you being so stubborn? I am your doctor, and I'm going to lay down the law on this one. You are carrying twins, making you a high-risk pregnancy. You are overexerting yourself, and I am ordering you to get some rest."

"You're ordering me?"

"In this situation, yes I am."

"I don't appreciate you ordering me around, Randy."

He remained persistent. "And I don't appreciate you ignoring my medical advice. You are going to wear yourself down to exhaustion, and when it's time to deliver these babies you will be too damn tired to endure labor. I am trying to keep you pregnant as long as possible to avoid complications that can severely affect your health. If our babies come too early, they will be put at serious risk. I'm not meaning to sound like a dominating asshole here, but you are scaring the hell out of me because you won't listen to my advice." Randy never demanded anything from her before, but right now he was downright serious. "Honey, I know it's hard for you to take orders from me, but you have got to get some rest. From now on, you are going to leave the housework and shopping for me. And if you need help with Nathan, call my mom. She'll be more than happy to come over for an hour or two and watch him so you can get some rest. Don't try to be Supermom."

"But I feel so useless right now," she complained.

"You are doing a huge job. You're raising our son and growing two babies."

"But there are things around the house that need to get done."

"Let me deal with that right now."

"I can't expect you to come home after a long day at the clinic and…"

He put his finger over her lips. "I am not going to argue about this anymore. You are going to take it easy and I will deal with the housework. You need to rest." He took her in his arms and held her tight.

She nodded her head in compliance. "Ok."

"Thank you."

Randy got Nathan involved in housework by making it into a game. He loved to help Daddy clean up toys, feed the bird, and fold clothes. Randy even had him fix Mommy a cold drink every night to help her relax.

The reality of becoming a big brother hadn't really hit Nathan yet. Randy tried to explain it to him and even had Nathan go with him when he picked up a second crib, cradle, highchair, and car seat. Despite this, Randy wasn't sure the child understood what was happening.

On one of their daddy/son outings, Randy took Nathan to Pottery Barn to pick out his own big boy bedroom furniture. They found a bedroom set with a white bedframe, dresser, and a nightstand that matched. Nathan wanted a basketball room. To accommodate this interest, Randy bought room décor centered around a basketball theme—bedding, a wallpaper border, a few accessories, and a lamp with a textured basketball base and blue lampshade.

With Nathan's help, Randy painted the walls light beige. Nathan was covered in paint by the time they were finished, but the two of them had a good time together. They took a break to let the paint dry, after which Randy stuck a wallpaper border around the wall's perimeter. Together, they hung blue sports ball print curtains on a curtain rod and Randy screwed it into the wall above the window. He attached a blue valance over it.

The classic sports bedding they bought came complete with twin bedsheets, a twin-sized comforter, and two throw pillows, one of which was a plush basketball Nathan could snuggle with. Randy placed a basketball-shaped rug on the floor beside Nathan's bed and hung a basketball clock on the wall above the dresser. He set a pair of blue bookends on the bookshelf and neatly displayed all of Nathan's books between them. The two of them transferred all of Nathan's toys, clothes, and shoes from his old room to this one then set up Nathan's basketball hoop in the corner. For a finishing touch, Randy bought Nathan a basketball-patterned beanbag chair to sit in.

"Wow, Nate. Look at this," Randy said to his son. "Pretty cool, Buddy."

"Dis my room."

"Yes it is."

The little boy padded down the hallway. To Randy's surprise, he stood in the doorway of the nursery, staring at what used to be his room. "Dis baby room now?" he asked.

"Yes. That's the babies' room."

Nathan returned to his new room and sat in his beanbag. "Nathan room."

"Yup. This is Nathan's room."

Nathan picked up his basketball and handed it to Randy. "Daddy play ball?"

"Sure. I'll play ball with you." Randy got down on his knees and together, he and Nathan took turns shooting the basketball into the hoop.

Monday after work, Randy changed into workout clothes and met Jim and Greg at the local athletic club. About forty-five minutes into their workout, they took a break to rehydrate.

Greg asked, "Do either of you know anyone in the city looking to hire an OB/GYN?"

"What's wrong with the clinic you're in?" Jim asked.

"Since I'm the new doctor on the team, they make me work all the shitty on-call hours, and I get last choice on vacation times. The females I work with seem to have a problem with me being a male gynecologist."

"Seattle Women's Clinic is looking for someone," Randy suggested. "You should check it out. That's a good clinic."

"I will definitely do that."

"Speaking of obstetrics," Jim cut in, "Jane's gettin' big."

"I know," Randy replied. "And she hates it. She says she feels like she's going to fall over, and the bad thing is she still has four months to go, but I doubt she'll make it that long."

"Two babies," Greg said, feeling overwhelmed just thinking about it. "You will never sleep."

"Jane and I were talking about that the other night. We both feel like we're being thrust into a situation for which we are ill-equipped and poorly prepared. It's definitely going to be one of the most challenging things we've ever done."

"No shit," Greg chuckled.

"Damn, Dude," Jim added. "That's gonna be a lot of fuckin' work. I don't envy you at all."

Randy took it all in stride. "We're looking at it as an opportunity to really work together as a team. It'll be a bonding experience. When we get through this and pull this off together, the rewards will be well worth it."

Jim set his Gatorade bottle on the floor. "You know Jill and I are committed to helpin' in any way we can."

Greg interjected, "Raquel and I are offering our assistance as well. You're gonna need all the help you can get."

Randy appreciated his friends' generous offers. "Thanks. I'm sure we'll take you up on it."

Chapter Fifty-Two

Down in L.A., Bruce was enjoying a rare day off. He did a few loads of laundry, washed the dishes in his sink, then lounged on the sofa channel surfing. A knock on his door forced him to get up. When he saw who it was, a huge smile filled his face. "Mandy." He greeted her with a kiss before he showed her inside. "What are you doing over here?"

"I was in the neighborhood running a few errands, so I thought I'd stop by."

"I'm glad you did."

They decided to grab a bite to eat at The Boiling Crab. Mandy struggled to crack open a crab leg. Every time she'd try, the crab cracker would slip out of her hands.

Bruce quipped, "Would you like some help with that, Dr. Stevens?"

"I can't believe I can't figure out how to crack open a stupid crab leg."

"You have to get it in the right position and squeeze." He placed his hands over hers and cracked it for her.

Bruce was having a hard time dealing with not being able to see his daughters over the holidays, and being the friend she was, Mandy tried to offer support. "How are the girls?"

"They're doing ok. It's been hard. I miss them."

"I know you do."

"It wouldn't bother me as much if I could be with them for Christmas. I feel like I'm letting them down."

"You shouldn't feel that way," Mandy said. "You talk to them regularly and spend time with them whenever you can. You're doing what you should." She reached across the table and held his hand. "I think you're doing a great job with your girls."

After lunch, they went for a stroll through the Japanese Garden, which was a lush, beautifully landscaped, 1.5-acre hillside garden featuring winding paths, a 20-foot waterfall, and a stone pagoda. A hand-carved gilt Buddha, along with stone lanterns and water basins, lined the paths. A central koi pond edged by a black pebble beach made its home among the dense plantings. Much of the vegetation surrounding the pond had Japanese origins, including pines, bamboo, magnolia, and camellia trees. Circular stepping stones and stone bridges allowed access across the water.

Holding hands, Bruce and Mandy meandered through this garden. They laughed about fun times and scoffed at difficulties that plagued them during medical school.

"I can't believe you said that right in front of Dr. Drenner," Mandy remarked. "She was not happy about it either."

"It didn't help that you and Jim stood in the corner laughing so loud the whole room could hear you. Randy just sat there staring at me with that shit-eating grin of his."

"He always has a shit-eating grin on his face."

Bruce chuckled. "I know he does."

When night fell, they drove back to Bruce's apartment.

"It's getting late," Mandy said. "I should probably head back."

Bruce took her hand and tried to entice her to stay. "Don't go. It's dark, and you never know what kind of crazy people might be out in the streets of L.A. at night. I'd feel safer if you stayed with me."

She agreed.

Without hesitation, he led her into his apartment, locking the door behind them.

Sifting through endless patient files and stacks of mindless paperwork was driving Randy crazy. He and his father needed a more efficient way to keep track of patients. To offer a solution, Randy did some research on the Electronic Medical Records (EMR) System. It was an easy, efficient way to transport patient data from office to home and back again. Patient files were stored in a central database and could easily be accessed, with a secure password, from any laptop, tablet, or mobile phone. Full EMR implementation allowed physicians to efficiently and cost-effectively manage their patients' full clinical experience, including appointment scheduling, office visits, labs, health maintenance, referrals, reporting of test results, and computerized orders for prescriptions.

Right now everything in their office was done paper and pencil, and prescriptions were handwritten. It was a paperwork nightmare, and it was out of date. This new technology would not only greatly reduce the horizontal migration of paper throughout their practice, it would also diminish the costs of maintaining a manual charting system. With the EMR System, they could focus more on patients and spend less time chasing paperwork. All Randy had to do was convince his father.

Randy discussed this idea with his dad and finally convinced him to switch over to the Electronic Medical

Records System. This was incredible progress, as Randy had been trying to entice his father to get 'techy' for quite some time. They purchased the necessary equipment and all the software then had their receptionist type a note to post in the clinic informing patients about the transition in progress.

Transferring all their medical files to the new system was going to be extremely time consuming. Randy thought it best to hire someone to start the data transfer process so the ladies up front could continue to focus on reception, scheduling, billing, and insurance verification. He brought this idea to his father. "I know the perfect person we can bring in to handle the data transfer."

"Who'd you have in mind?" Mark asked.

"What about Stephanie? She's good with computers and has experience in data entry work. She's looking for a new job anyway, and we can always use another person to help Sam and Veronica."

"True."

"With Steph focusing on the computer aspect, Veronica and Sam can focus more on patient relations. The clinic will be twice as efficient."

Mark agreed. "And she's family."

"Exactly."

"Alright. You want to talk to her or do you want me to?"

"I'll do it."

After work that evening, Randy stopped by Stephanie's apartment to present this idea to her. "Hey, Sis. How are you?"

"I'm ok, I guess."

Even though Stephanie and Bruce had been divorced for a while now, Stephanie was having a hard time adjusting. She carried a melancholy demeanor all the time and seemed overly stressed. Randy did his best to offer a listening ear. "What's wrong?"

"I hate my job. My hours are inconsistent and the pay sucks. I'm behind on my bills, and even with child support it's hard making ends meet. I told Bruce about it, but I'm not getting any sympathy from him." She stared at her brother with a frown on her face. "Did you know he has a girlfriend?"

"Yes, I did."

"Do you know who it is?"

"Why is that your business?"

"Because I have a right to know," she claimed.

Randy reminded her, "You're his ex-wife, Stephanie. He doesn't have to answer to you."

Stephanie glowered at him, not amused by his comment. "He doesn't seem to take any interest in my life at all and won't tell me what's going on in his. When I ask, he gets snarky with me. While he's gallivanting around Los Angeles living his life of luxury with whoever this woman is, I'm by myself struggling to raise these two girls."

Randy wanted to sympathize with his sister, but he couldn't bring himself to do it. "You brought this on yourself, you know."

"Me?"

"Yes, you. I warned you from the start that you and Bruce weren't right for each other, but you didn't listen to me."

"He cares too much about medicine," Stephanie tried to justify.

"And you care too much about sex and money and completely took advantage of him."

"I did not."

"Yes you did. You reeled him in with a pregnancy so you could get doctor's money to support your high-maintenance lifestyle. You knew neurosurgery was his life, but you put on a show and played out the lie."

"What lie?"

"You told me yourself you didn't love him. It was all about money and prestige. To you, it was all about the image. Don't stand here and tell me it wasn't."

She folded her arms across her chest and huffed at him.

"He's moved on, Steph. You didn't really expect him to crawl in a hole and mope around after you two split up, did you?"

"No, but he should tell me what's going on with his life. He owes me that much."

"He doesn't owe you anything, and he doesn't have to tell you anything. The only thing he has to do is take care of his daughters and send you a child support check every month. Other than that, he has no obligations, at least as far as you're concerned. There's no ring on his finger attaching him to you. He's entitled to carry on with his life and he has every right to be happy. If you have a problem with that, you should have considered all of this a long time ago."

"I didn't know it was going to be like this. I'm stressed out, I'm alone, and I'm struggling to make ends meet. And with Christmas around the corner, it's even harder. My life wouldn't be like this if it wasn't for him."

"You can't blame any of this on Bruce. He tried to make things work between you two, but you fought him every step of the way. You lied to him about birth control and let yourself get pregnant, not once, but twice. You constantly griped at him and complained about his career, even though he worked his ass off to provide for you and the kids. You took advantage of the money he made and spent every penny of it. You ran off and took his girls away from him. All of that, along with your bad attitude and negativity, led him to file for divorce. I'm sorry you're stressed, and I'm sorry life didn't turn out the way you wanted it to, but you have no one to blame but yourself. You need to face reality and deal with the consequences of your actions."

She snarled, "What happened to the sympathetic big brother who used to protect me?"

He retorted, "What happened to my little sister who used to consider consequences and think about other's feelings before she acted on impulse? Do you ever stop to think about how your actions affect other people?"

She stared at him with a black look.

He felt contrite now for upsetting her. "Look, Steph. I didn't come over here to lecture you."

"Then why did you?"

"I want to offer you a job with better hours and higher pay than you're currently making. It will help you get back on your feet."

"What kind of job?"

"Dad and I are switching our records over to the EMR System and we need someone to do data entry for us."

She was familiar with this system and had experience using it. "Computerized medical record keeping?"

"Precisely. You interested?" he offered.

"How much does it pay?"

"Twenty-five dollars an hour, and you'll get full medical coverage as well as free GYN services with us."

"And what will happen to me when all the data entry is finished?"

"You stay on to help Sam and Veronica up front."

This offer sounded too good to be true. "What's the catch?"

"No catch. You're family. You need a good paying job with regular hours, we need a computer tech with data entry and clerical experience. Everyone wins." Trying to convince her, he said, "We need you, Steph. You know the system and you have data entry experience. You'll be a great asset to our team."

Stephanie didn't need much convincing. She gladly accepted his offer.

Chapter Fifty-Three

Dinner with his family was interrupted when Randy's cellphone chimed. He looked at the incoming number before he answered, "Dr. Hanson." One of the nurses from the Maternity Ward updated him about one of his patients. "Is she dilated?" Anticipating a trip to the hospital, he checked the time on the clock. 6:47 P.M. "Ok. I'm on my way." He slid his phone in his pocket and quickly chugged down the rest of his milk.

"Delivery at the hospital?" Jane asked.

"Yeah. I have to go in for a few hours."

"Me go too," Nathan insisted.

Randy shook his head. "You can't come with me. Daddy has to work."

With begging eyes, the child said, "Please?"

Although Randy was proud of his son for asking nicely and using manners, he stood firm. "No. I have to go the hospital and you have to stay here and finish your beans." He grabbed his stethoscope and his car keys and kissed his wife goodbye. "I'll see you in a few hours."

"Drive safely."

"I will."

Nathan held a green bean out to his father. "Want a bean, Daddy?"

"No, thank you. You eat it. I already ate mine." Randy kissed him on the head. "Bye, Buddy. Be good for Mommy."

The entire first floor of the hospital was pure pandemonium. Nurses and doctors frantically ran in and out of patient rooms. Gurneys and wheelchairs crowded hallways. The hospital PA system announced one STAT call after another. Randy had to navigate through a maze of chaos to get to the elevator.

The Maternity Ward was hectic too. With wide eyes, Randy sighed deeply and headed to the nurses' station. "Good evening, ladies."

"Good evening, Doctor."

He skimmed over the names on the patient board. "Busy night?"

"In the last hour, we've had twelve patients check in." The nurse handed him a chart.

"How's she doing?"

"She's in pain, but she's hanging in there."

"Is her husband with her?"

"Yes."

"Good." He flipped through the chart to the second page and jotted down a few notes before he headed down the hall to her room.

His patient was making good progress—contractions regular, baby's heartrate strong. Randy asked about pain medication, but she denied. He honored her wishes and left her to progress on her own.

This woman's husband stopped Randy in the hallway. "Excuse me, Dr. Hanson."

Randy turned around. "Yes?"

"I know my wife said she didn't want any drugs, but can't you give her something?"

"I offered. She refused," Randy stated in a kind but affirmative voice.

"Isn't there a way around that?"

"I'm not going to give her pain medication against her wishes, Mr. Gromley. You should be having this discussion with your wife, not with me."

"But she's in pain."

"And she's denied medication. That is her call." This first-time dad had a horrified look on his face. To ease his worry, Randy offered some sound advice. "I know it's difficult to watch your wife go through labor. Believe me, I've been there. The best thing you can do right now is encourage her and help her relax. She's going to need you to guide her through this."

Mr. Gromley cracked his knuckles and rubbed his hand across his chin.

"If she changes her mind and decides she wants something for the pain, I'll call anesthesia." Randy placed his hand on Mr. Gromley's shoulder, offering reassurance. "Go on. She needs you now."

"Thank you, Doctor."

Randy was about to get a cup of coffee when his cellphone rang. It was Jim. "Hey, Jim."

Frantic, Jim replied, "Someone said they saw you at the hospital. Are you here?"

"Yes."

"Please tell me you're not busy right now."

"Not right this second. Why?"

"I need you in the ER."

Guess coffee would have to wait. "I'll be right there."

Randy rushed down to the first floor. Jim was tending to a screaming pregnant woman, who was being wheeled in on a blood-spotted ambulance gurney. Jim gave Randy the run down. "Profuse hemorrhaging, severe abdominal pain. She's crowning. Baby is breech and I can see a foot."

Well, this situation would certainly add some excitement to his night. "Tell her not to push." Randy hurried to the sink to wash his hands. "Prep her for surgery."

Jim gave the orders as directed.

In less than two minutes, Randy was scrubbed up, complete with latex gloves and surgical scrubs. He gathered his team and rushed into the OR. With a nurse's assistance, he made a small, horizontal incision in the skin above the pubic bone then cut through the underlying tissue working his way down to the uterus. Through the opening, he reached in and delivered the baby. He cleared the nose and mouth with a bulb syringe and cut the umbilical cord. At first, the baby didn't cry. In fact she didn't make any noise at all. Concerned about low oxygen levels or possible fluid in the lungs, Randy allowed the mother to hold her baby for a total of twenty seconds before he handed the infant off to a pediatrician. While the staff worked on the newborn, Randy began the process of closing up his patient.

After the surgery was complete and the patient was wheeled into a recovery room, Randy peeled off his gloves and removed his scrubs. He washed his hands then hurried back upstairs to check on his patient in the Maternity Ward. She was now dilated to nine centimeters. In preparation for the show, Randy called the pediatric staff and had the nurses on standby.

Around 9:30, Randy thought he would be able to go home. But as he was about to leave, one of the Maternity Ward nurses said to him, "Dr. Hanson?"

He turned around and looked at her. "Yes?"

"I'm sorry, Doctor, but we just got a call that another one of your patients has checked in."

"Where is she?" he asked.

"She's on her way up now."

"Alright. Get her situated in her room, get some vitals on her, and start a CTG. I'll pop in and check on her in a minute."

"Yes, Doctor."

A cup of coffee sounded awfully good right now, but no such luck, at least not yet. Once again coffee would have to wait.

The Maternity Ward was madness tonight. Babies everywhere, and why did they all seem to be his patients? He called Jane to tell her he was going to be later than he thought.

Over the course of the years, and after all the deliveries he'd made, Randy came to a conclusion he thought all men should take note of—women who gave birth were heroes. Amazingly, they survived the traumatic birth story, concluding it all with smiling faces. Even after enduring the excruciating pain from pushing a six-inch wide baby through a one-inch wide hole in their bodies, they came back for more with the next pregnancy. He was truly amazed.

Randy met Jim for lunch the next day. To dodge the torrential rainstorm, he ran from his car to the entrance of the restaurant. Safely under cover, he shook water off his jacket and searched for Jim. He spotted him sitting in a nearby booth. "Did you order already?"

"Just drinks. I got you a Pepsi."

"Thanks." Randy sat across from him then removed his jacket and draped it over the back of his chair.

"The ER was a madhouse last night," Jim remarked. "I worked from 7:00 A.M. 'til 10:00 P.M. without a break of any kind. My poor bladder and stomach. No wonder I have so many problems with them these days. One is overfilled and the other is never filled, and when it is, I can't cope with what's put in it."

Randy opened the menu and skimmed through the lunch choices. "L&D was nuts too. I didn't get out of there until after midnight. I was only expecting to come in long enough to do a quick delivery, but after that ER experience, I ended up bringing three other babies into the world last night. One was a delivery where the baby's shoulders got stuck, pinching the umbilical cord and cutting the oxygen supply from her not-quite-yet-born brain. For you or I to do the equivalent, we would have to press our shoulder up into our nose while a bulldozer on steroids pushed us through an amniotic fluid-filled mailbox. Don't try this at home, folks."

"No shit," Jim chuckled. "Hey, I was meanin' to tell you, awesome job last night, Bro. Give this man a team of nurses, a well-sharpened scalpel, and a pair of scissors and everything turns out great. Thanks for your quick thinkin'."

"That was a dangerous situation that could have turned out much worse."

"But it didn't, because of you. Baby is strong and mom is recovering nicely."

"I know. I checked on her this morning."

"Damn, I'm glad you were there last night. I hate those obstetrical emergencies. They scare the shit out of me."

The waiter brought their drinks and whipped out his notepad. "Are you ready to order?"

"Yes." The two of them placed their lunch orders then continued their conversation while they sipped on sodas.

Randy spent the next week sorting through all the baby items he and Jane had purchased. He put together the second crib and reorganized furniture to make more efficient use of the space in the nursery. They bought a side-by-side double stroller and stocked up on diapers, wipes, burp cloths, diaper rash cream, pacifiers, and baby wash. They purchased an ample supply of onesies and light sleepers, chose a few matching outfits for the girls, and sorted through Nathan's old infant attire, salvaging anything they could use. The amount of baby supplies they needed for these twins was ridiculous.

Ellen Hanson added to the accumulation when she came over with a bag full of matching outfits—double sets of everything. Pink dresses, pink socks, polka dot jumpers, Dr. Seuss Thing One and Thing Two tee-shirts, and little white pants with pink elephants on them. She also had two pink receiving blankets, two matching sets of pink crib sheets, and a large twin diaper bag.

Randy came home from his clinical supervisory duties earlier than usual that day. The house was quiet. He went upstairs to change his clothes, and as he passed by the nursery, he noticed it looked different. The original teddy bear accessories were still in place, but a few extra touches had been added, namely pink blankets, pink crib sheets, and two pink teddy bears. He peeked his head into Nathan's room to find him snoozing. Randy carefully closed the door and left him to take a nap.

When he moseyed into the bedroom, Jane was lying on her side with a body pillow between her legs. She looked over at him with heavy eyes. "You alright?"

"I can't walk, I can't sit, I can't lie down. No matter what I do I'm uncomfortable."

He unknotted his tie and loosened the buttons on his shirt.

"Your mom came over today to work in the babies' room."

"I saw. It looks nice."

"I tried to help her, but I couldn't bend over to put things away," she complained. "My back hurts and I feel so useless right now."

He pulled his shirt off and tossed it in the laundry basket. To help Jane relax and lift her spirits, he suggested, "Why don't I draw a bath for you."

"Sounds good."

He gave her a kiss then went into the bathroom to fill up the bathtub.

While she was soaking in the tub, Randy changed into a pair of jeans and a tee-shirt then went downstairs to make dinner.

The babies' movements could be felt externally now. To get Nathan involved in the pregnancy experience, Jane placed his hand on her belly hoping he would feel the babies kick. "Can you feel that?"

Nathan felt a little nudge. "What dat?"

"The babies are kicking."

"Do it hurt?"

"No, it doesn't hurt."

Randy came into the room with Nathan's stuffed bunny in his hand. "Alright, little man. Bedtime for you."

Nathan protested. "Me no want to."

"You have to. Big boys need their sleep. Give Mommy hugs night-night."

Nathan did as his father asked.

Randy read him a bedtime story and tucked him in. "Were you a good boy for Mommy today?"

"Yes. Me help."

"Good. I'm proud of you." He kissed his son on the cheek. "Now get some sleep. I love you, Buddy." Randy turned on Nathan's basketball nightlight and darkened the room.

"Love you, Daddy."

"Sweet dreams. Daddy will see you in the morning." As soon as Nathan was settled for the night, Randy returned downstairs and sat on the couch with Jane. He put one arm around her shoulders and placed the other on her tummy, hoping to feel a kick. "Lots of movement?"

She moved his hand to the other side of her belly. "They've been active today."

"That's good."

"Taking a soak was a good idea. Thank you for suggesting that."

He kissed the top of her head. "I want you to be comfortable. Try sleeping on your side with a pillow between your legs. That sometimes helps with the sore back. I'll give you a good back rub tonight too."

They sat on the sofa together feeling little kicks, talking about twin challenges they would face, discussing future plans, and openly sharing their fears about this upcoming undertaking. They both discovered that communication and understanding were key to enjoying this special time in their lives. And even though Jane was tired and moody, the quiet, private moments she and Randy shared together in the evenings strengthened their relationship and added to the joy of expecting twins.

In the morning, while Jane was brushing her hair, Randy snuck behind her and nibbled on her neck. "Did you sleep better last night?"

"A little."

"After breakfast I'm going to run over to my parents' house and grab the truck."

"What for?"

"I want to pick out our Christmas tree today." He placed his hand on her rounded tummy. "You are beautiful, and these baby girls of ours will be beautiful, just like their mother." He interlocked his mouth with hers, giving in to the erotic pleasure her lips offered him.

A little voice interrupted them. "Mommy."

They both turned around to see Nathan, still half asleep, in his jammies holding his stuffed bunny. "Good morning, Sweetie."

"Me hungry."

Randy squatted down to Nathan's level. "You wanna go get our Christmas tree today?"

"Me bring bunny?" Nathan asked.

"Yes, you can bring your bunny. But what do you say we make pancakes first?" Nathan loved pancakes, and Randy always spruced them up by decorating them with syrup and blueberry smiley faces.

Nathan's face lit up. "Pantakes!"

Randy shared his son's enthusiasm. "Alright. Let's make some pancakes."

"Me stir."

"You got it."

Randy and his family came home that afternoon with a huge Douglas Fir tied to the back of his dad's truck. While he worked to untie it, Nathan stood off to the side and watched, wide-eyed. "Dat a big tree, Daddy."

"Yes, it is a big tree," Randy replied. "We're going to decorate it and make it pretty for Santa."

"Santa come now?" Nathan asked.

"Not yet. Still have a couple weeks. Why don't you go inside and see if Mommy needs help with anything. Daddy's going to hang lights up outside."

"Me help," Nathan insisted.

"No, you can't help this time. I'm going to be on the roof. You can't go up there, it's too dangerous."

Nathan's eyes got huge. "No fall, Daddy. No get owies."

Randy got a chuckle out of his son's concern for his safety. "I'll be careful. You can help Mommy put twinkle lights and ornaments on the Christmas tree."

After setting up the tree, Randy began the chore of pulling all the Christmas lights out of the garage. Before he started hanging them, he called Robby to enlist his help.

Robby was about to hop in his car and go over to his brother's house when he saw a young woman attempting to start her car. All it did was make a clicking sound. He could tell she was frustrated, so he offered his assistance. "You need some help?" he asked.

She looked up at his unfamiliar face. "I don't know what's wrong with it. It was working fine yesterday."

"Pop the hood and I'll take a look."

Robby played around with some wires and quickly discovered what the problem was. "Your battery cable is loose." He peeked around the hood. "I have a toolbox in my car. Hold on a sec. I'll be right back."

His car was parked only three spaces down from hers. He opened his trunk and reached in to grab a wrench. Twirling the wrench in his hand, he strolled back over and tightened the cable, ensuring it was snug. "Try it now," he said.

It started right up. "Thank you so much."

"No problem." He closed the hood of her car and reached into his wallet for a business card. "I'm a certified mechanic. If you ever need anything, please call."

She read the name on the card. "Thank you, Robert Hanson. I will definitely do that."

"You know my name, but you didn't tell me yours."

"Evie Wilkinson." She held out an open palm to him.

He stared at her hand, but didn't touch it. "I would love to shake your hand, but I was just under the hood of your car. My hands are dirty."

"Rain check then." She checked the time on her phone. "I have to get to work. Thank you for your help."

"Anytime," he replied.

She backed her car out and drove away. Robby returned his wrench to its proper place then went inside to wash his hands before he headed over to Randy's house.

Robby stepped out of his car and into the middle of his brother's yard. Tons of large plastic tubs were spread out in every direction. "Every year you seem to have more lights than you had the year before," Robby claimed.

"Probably," Randy said, fetching the light-up Santa from the garage. "What took you so long to get here?"

"Some girl from my apartment complex couldn't get her car to start."

"Did you help her out?"

"Of course. I gave her my card and she introduced herself as Evie Wilkinson."

Randy stopped what he was doing and looked over at Robby. "Evie Wilkinson? I know her. She's a nurse in the Maternity Ward. She started a few weeks ago."

Randy's comment roused Robby's interest. "A nurse, huh?"

"An RN to be precise." Randy saw the gears turning in Robby's head. "I know what you're thinking, Rob. She's pretty, isn't she?"

"She is. She's also way out of my league."

"No she's not. She's a nice girl. And she likes water sports and snowboarding like you. Already you have something in common."

The entire time Randy and his brother hung up lights, Robby wouldn't stop talking about Evie. He made it pretty obvious he was attracted to her.

The following afternoon, the hospital called Randy in for a delivery. Evie happened to be on shift. After assisting him in the delivery room, she retreated to the nurse's station. Randy draped his stethoscope around his neck and followed her. "Heard you had some car trouble yesterday," he remarked.

She turned to face him. "How do you know that?"

"The mechanic who got it started for you, he's my brother. He was on his way to my house yesterday when he saw you. He told me all about it."

She covered her mouth with her hand. "Are you serious?"

"Yup," Randy teased her. "Your name came up quite a few times yesterday."

She bit her bottom lip, just like Jane did. Apparently she liked him too.

"He said he gave you his card yesterday," Randy remarked.

"Yes, he did."

"He's at work right now. We have a few minutes, you should pop into the break room and give him a call."

Robert was at his desk ordering parts when his office phone rang. "Burien Auto Repair."

"May I speak with Robert Hanson please."

"This is Robert Hanson. How may I help you?"

"This is Evie Wilkinson. You helped me with my car yesterday."

"Yes, I remember." Robert put his paperwork down and sat up confidently.

"I'm sorry to bother you at work, but I didn't have your cell number and I don't know what apartment you live in."

"It's not a problem. What can I do for you?"

"I was wondering if you wanted to have dinner tonight."

Robby wasn't sure how to take this. Other than his mother and sister-in-law, he'd never had a woman invite him to dinner before. "You called to ask me out?"

"Yes, but I don't get off 'til six, and I'll need to come home and change first. Is seven o'clock ok?" she suggested.

His heart raced in anticipation. "Seven is fine."

"Can I meet you at your apartment?"

"Sure. I'm in 208."

"Ok. I'll see you tonight."

"I'm looking forward to it."

Following their dinner date, Robby and Evie sat in the courtyard of the apartment building and continued their conversation. Throughout the evening, they discovered they had many things in common—water sports, skiing, and a shared love of horror movies. As the cold winter air kicked in, Evie said, "I should go. I have to be at the hospital early tomorrow morning."

"I'll walk you to your door." Standing on the front porch, Robby stared at her for a minute. "Thank you for dinner. I had a great time tonight."

"I did too."

He wanted to kiss her, but wasn't sure how she'd react if he tried. Before he had a chance to find out, to his surprise, she kissed him. She was passionate, shameless, and, evident by her kiss, liked to jump right in.

"I'll see you tomorrow," she said.

Spellbound, Robby watched her enter apartment 103 and close the door. With a self-satisfied smirk on his face, he traipsed upstairs to his apartment. He couldn't wait to see her again.

Before he reported to the hospital in the morning, Randy popped into his clinic to double check his surgical schedule. The entire place was decked out in garlands and Christmas lights, and a fully decorated Christmas tree was set up in the corner of the waiting room. Stephanie was already there, booting up computers and laptops. "Morning, Steph," he said to her.

"Hey, Brat."

"Who put all these decorations up?"

"I did. Dad asked me to spruce up the place and make it more festive."

"It looks nice."

"Thank you."

He scanned the appointment calendar. "Why are you here so early?"

"Getting everything ready for the day."

He raised his head. "You enjoy working here, don't you?"

"In all honesty, Randy, when I agreed to take this job, I thought it would be uncomfortable working with my father and brother, but you know, I like working here."

"Not what you were expecting?"

"Not at all what I was expecting. Seeing what you and Dad do all day has certainly given me a new perspective. It's been a wonderful experience."

"Guess that means you'll stick around for a while?"

"I'd like to."

Randy read a phone message that was left on the counter for him. "You have done an outstanding job getting us EMR ready. You've worked the bugs out of the system, and I know Sam and Veronica like having you around to help out when they get backed up. You've been an invaluable addition to our team."

Usually Randy picked on Stephanie or teased her about something. The fact that he complimented her like this almost brought tears to her eyes. "That is the nicest thing you've ever said to me."

"I'm being honest. You've done a great job, and it's incredible having another Hanson here. This clinic truly is a family endeavor. Thank you for your help." Even though they had their differences and didn't always see eye to eye, Randy and Stephanie still cared about one another. "I have to do rounds and get prepped for surgery."

She handed him his tablet. "Here, don't forget this."

"Thank you. And thanks for decorating. It looks great in here." He shoved the phone message in his pocket and headed out the door.

Later that week, while pumping gasoline in his car, Randy ran into Robby. He waved to get his attention. "Hey, Rob."

Robby bounded across the lot to his brother's side. "I'm glad I ran into you. I need to ask you something."

"What's up?"

"Do you think Mom and Dad will mind if I invite Evie for Christmas dinner? Her family lives in Wisconsin, and with her work schedule, she can't go home for the holidays. I know we haven't been dating long, but I don't want her to be alone on Christmas."

"I don't think they'll mind. They wouldn't want her to be alone either."

"Cool. Can't wait for them to meet her."

Randy put the nozzle back in place and screwed his gas cap on. "Bringing a girl home to meet the family. Sounds like things are going well."

Robby smiled widely. "Things are great between us. We enjoy being together and have a lot to talk about."

"I'm glad to hear that. I think she'll be good for you."

"I'm meeting her for dinner tonight."

"Where you guys going?"

"Sarducci's. Speaking of which, I have to go."

Randy laughed at his brother's giddiness. "Have fun."

"We will." Robby bounded away, leaping about like a gazelle.

Randy was thrilled to see his brother in such good spirits. Over the last few years, Robby had fought off temptation to keep himself clean, overcame a drinking problem, and worked hard to pay off his debts. Now living a life of sobriety, he lived in a nice apartment complex, received his mechanics certification, and had a good paying job he enjoyed. And to top it all off, he had a stable, supportive woman in his life. Robby really pulled himself together. Randy was proud of him.

Chapter Fifty-Four

Bruce had a long and emotionally draining day. He dragged himself through the door and kicked off his shoes. As he was about to hop in the shower, his cellphone rang. "Hello?"

"Dr. Bruce Buckman?" an unfamiliar voice said.

"Yes, this is Dr. Buckman."

"Dr. Buckman, this is UC Medical Center in San Diego."

Odd that they were calling. He didn't remember having any consultation work down there.

"We have your father here."

Bruce lowered his eyebrows. "My father?"

"He's complaining of chest pains and shortness of breath. His blood pressure is dangerously high and his heart is palpitating at an alarming rate. He needs treatment but refuses to cooperate with doctors."

Bruce's stomach plummeted to the floor. He couldn't speak, mainly because he was worried about his father, but also because the hospital called him to deal with it.

Trying to get Bruce to respond, the hospital representative asked, "Dr. Buckman, are you there?"

"Yes, I'm sorry. I'm here."

"His symptoms are life-threatening, and we're afraid that without treatment his condition might worsen."

Bruce gathered his thoughts and replied, "Sedate him if you have to. I'm on my way." He dashed out to his truck, dialing Mandy's number on the way.

She immediately recognized the sense of urgency in his voice. "San Diego?"

"My father is in the hospital with myocardial symptoms, but he's refusing treatment. If he continues to fight the medical staff, he'll most likely go into arrest. I have to get down there."

"Stop by and get me. I'm coming with you."

"I can't expect you to drop everything and do this."

"I'm coming with you, Buckman," she insisted.

Obviously she wasn't taking no for an answer. "Ok. I'll be right there."

When they arrived at the hospital, Bruce's father was hooked up to an intravenous line and connected to an electrocardiogram, which displayed a rapid, erratic rhythm. Apparently the sedation medication had worn off, because he was arguing with the hospital staff again. "Get these damn tubes off me now! I'm going home!"

The doctor and other clinical staff fought to get him to leave the connections alone and lie back down. "Sir, you are in no condition to go home right now."

"Get me out of here!"

Bruce stepped into the room. "Dad."

Mr. Buckman looked up, snarling at his son. "You!" He waved a finger at him. "What are you doing here?"

"Let these people help you."

He tugged at the EKG leads and tried to rip the IV out of his arm. "I don't have to listen to you or any of these damn doctors. I want out of here!"

"Dad, please." Bruce rushed over to his father's side and attempted to pull his hand away from the IV line so he wouldn't hurt himself.

"Get away from me! Don't touch me! I want…" He gasped, grabbed his chest, and lost consciousness. Within seconds, his blood pressure plummeted and the electrical impulses on the EKG went flatline.

Hospital staff immediately began CPR.

Bruce tried to jump in to help, but Mandy held him back. "Bruce, no. Stay back."

The doctor administered defibrillation. Nothing. He tried injecting him with antiarrhythmic drugs. Still nothing. A long, drawn-out, high-pitched beep echoed through the room. It was the worst sound Bruce had ever heard.

For several minutes the staff attempted lifesaving efforts, all to no avail. There was nothing more they could do. The attending physician looked over at Bruce. "I'm sorry."

Bruce was shaken. His hands trembled and his breathing thickened. He had dealt with death many times before—he dissected cadavers in medical school, lost his brother to a fatal motorcycle accident many years ago, and even worked with patients who died from brain related diseases or injuries—but losing his father right before his eyes was by far the worst thing he'd ever encountered. His knees buckled underneath him and he almost fell to the floor.

Mandy supported him and led him to a chair. "Bruce, look at me."

He was unresponsive, frozen, numb.

"Buckman." She touched his cheek with her hand. "Look at me."

Bruce's eyes found Mandy's. He fought to contain his tears.

"I am so sorry." She hugged him tightly.

He held her close, letting his emotions flow. "I never had a chance to tell him. He didn't know how I felt."

"He knew you loved him."

Bruce pulled himself away from her and shook his head. "No, Mandy, you don't understand. I haven't seen my father in almost five years. The last time we spoke, we said hurtful things to each other. I told him I hated him and slammed a door in his face."

No wonder Bruce was upset. What an awful thing to have on his conscience.

"I should have put forth more of an effort to patch things up. I should have been here when he needed me."

Mandy tried to get him to calm down. "There's nothing you could have done."

"I could have told him. I…" He couldn't continue. The pangs of guilt were too overwhelming. "I'm a heartless ass."

"No you're not. You are a wonderful man, Dr. Buckman. A very loving, caring person." Amanda held him, trying to help him get through the emotional turmoil and guilt he was feeling. "There's nothing you could have done."

Christmas was a bit rough for Bruce, not only because he didn't have his girls with him, but also because he recently dealt with funeral arrangements and other legal issues concerning his father. Around New Years, when he had a three days off, he embraced the opportunity and flew to Seattle to see his kids. Mandy took time off and went with him. Instead of imposing on Randy and Jane, they opted to rent a car and check into a nearby hotel. The room they reserved had a separate double-sized bed for the girls to sleep in.

"It feels good to get out of L.A. for a while." Bruce dropped their bags on the floor by the dresser. "There's only so much of that madness I can handle before I lose my mind."

"If you'd stay with me at the beach, you wouldn't be in the middle of it all."

"I would, if you weren't so far away from UCLA. It takes forever to get from your house to work in the morning. Have you ever been on Santa Monica Boulevard at 7:00 A.M.? Traffic is horrendous."

"Point taken." Mandy kicked off her shoes and plopped onto the bed.

He sat on the bed next to her and placed his hand on her thigh. "I'm not sure what Stephanie is going to do tomorrow or what she's going to say when she sees us."

"She knows you're here, right?" Mandy asked.

"She knows, but Steph seems to think I need to explain my life to her. She might have one of her episodes when she sees us together is all I'm saying."

Amanda sat up. "Did you tell her about us?"

"Obliquely."

Questioning this statement, Mandy arched an eyebrow. "What does that mean?"

"She knows I'm involved in a relationship but doesn't know it's with you."

"You didn't tell her?"

"It's none of her damn business who I choose to be with. I told you, I will not answer to her."

Mandy tightened her lips, realizing that this situation had the potential to turn sour quickly. "If it will ease the tension, I can stay here while you pick up your girls."

He immediately shot down that idea. "Absolutely not. You are a part of my life and she is going to have to deal with that. I frankly don't give a shit if she likes it or not."

"Don't let her cause a scene in front of the girls, Buckman."

"I can't control what Stephanie does. She's going to do and say whatever she wants."

But Mandy was genuinely concerned. "She better not freak out in front of the kids."

"Let me handle Stephanie."

When Bruce knocked on Stephanie's door, right away she noticed he was holding Mandy's hand. "Her?" she snarled. "That's the woman you're involved with?"

"I did not come here to discuss my personal life with you. What I do and who I'm with is no longer your concern. That's the magic of divorce, Stephanie."

"I can't believe you're sharing a bed with her." She sneered at Mandy, eyeballing her as if she were a fungus.

Bruce didn't like her vile tone or the way she glared at Amanda. "Are you finished?"

Stephanie rolled her eyes and huffed.

The minute Emily heard her father's voice, she ran out to him, squeezing him hard and almost knocking him over. "Daddy! I missed you."

"I missed you too, Princess." He kissed the top of the child's head. "You remember Mandy?"

Emily looked up at Amanda. "I remember her."

"She's going to be with us this weekend."

"Yay!" the girl cheered.

"Do you have a bag, Baby?" he asked his daughter.
"Uh huh."

"Hurry and get it."

Emily ran to get her things.

Once Bruce had the girls and all of their belonging, he had Mandy take them out to the rental car and get them strapped in while he stayed on the porch to talk to Stephanie. "I'll have the girls back Monday after dinner. We have a late flight to catch that night."

He was about to walk away when Stephanie stopped him. "Bruce?"

He pivoted his body and gawped at her. "What?"

With pain in her eyes, she asked, "Do you love her?"

Bruce didn't feel that was any of her business, but maybe if she knew the truth she'd stop bugging him about it. "I love her very much. I always have." He stepped off the porch, got in the car, and drove away.

Bruce stopped by Randy and Jane's house, which not only allotted a few hours for them to hang out with their dearest friends, but also gave Alyssa and Nathan time to play together.

They spent the afternoon at KidsQuest Children's Museum. Randy loved this place. It was an interactive hands-on children's museum that integrated art, science, and technology. This museum fostered ingenuity, creativity, and experimentation—great for children to delve into the discovery of science and enrich their curiosity. The kids examined the microscopic world of dirt, bugs, and other interesting things. The Wild Wonders of Nature area featured animals peeking from their homes. Giant birdhouses beckoned the young children inside a huge playroom where they investigated the natural world. They built

516

blanket forts, climbed and slid on oversized leaves, and plunged their hands into a garden tub of sensory delights.

A second room featured tons of hands-on activities that allowed the children to tinker with tools, explore the mechanics of basic machines, climb into a full-size truck, and create water paintings on oversized rocks. An indoor treehouse invited Nathan and the girls to climb platforms, find hidden animals, enjoy a cozy tea party, and use a telescope to zoom in on exciting exhibits. At Water World, they pumped, poured, and sprayed water then built bridges, dams, and waterfalls. They even made music with water chimes and water drums. Randy and Bruce got right into the action, racing boats down a rocky stream and exploring the physical properties of water with their children.

Jane was convinced the men were having more fun here than the kids were. "Look at them."

"Yup," Mandy replied. "Two great minds encouraging their children to be aspiring scientists, budding engineers, and great inventors. Leave it to Randy and Bruce to find toys to play with."

Wasn't that the truth. "Randy's love of science has gotten Nathan interested in it. He loves fish and birds and figuring out how things work."

"It's captivating to see how the kids are developing. I can't believe how big they're all getting."

The children had a stimulating time at the museum and were worn out by the time they left. Before heading to the hotel, Bruce and Mandy stopped to get dinner for the girls. He had them take a bath then read them a bedtime story. With their eyes now heavy, he tucked them in. It didn't take long before they both drifted off to sleep.

"They're out," he told Mandy, joining her on the sofa while she flipped through channels. "The girls had a good time today."

"I think you had fun too."

"I love spending time with my girls." He removed his shoes and peeled off his shirt. "I overheard you and Emily talking. Sounded like the two of you were bonding a little."

"She's a sweetheart."

He reached his hand around Mandy's shoulders and pulled her closer to him. "Thank you for coming up here with me."

"This is your family, Bruce, and I want to share it with you."

"I love you more than you know. I should have taken you into my arms and kissed you when we were in med school. It would have saved me from a lot of stress and made me a happier man."

"But if you did that, you wouldn't have your girls."

He begged to differ. "Yes I would. The only difference is you would be their mother."

She closed her eyes, inviting him to kiss her. He did, rather intensely, but she didn't resist in any way.

When it was time to take the girls back to Stephanie, Emily clung to her father and refused to let go. "I don't want to go. I want to stay with you."

Trying to soothe her tears, Bruce said, "You have to go back to school. You need to be a big girl and learn lots of stuff in Preschool so you can be ready for Kindergarten next year."

"But I wanna be with you," the child whimpered.

"I know, Princess. I want to be with you too."

Emily sniffled and sobbed, gripping Bruce's neck.

"Ssh," he said trying to console her. "It's ok. Daddy will call you every day, and I'll come back to see you as soon as I can."

"Why can't I stay with you?" she cried.

Bruce stared at Stephanie who stood on the porch watching this entire incident, paying no mind to the pain her daughter felt. "I wish you could, Baby. Allie needs you to take care of her. You have to be a big girl and be brave. Can you do that for me?"

She wiped her eyes with the back of her hand. "Ok."

"That's my girl." He kissed Emily's forehead. "Be good, and listen to your teacher."

"I will."

"I'll call you tomorrow."

She finally released the grip she had on him.

"Go on, now. I love you."

"I love you, Daddy." She sniffled and slowly inched into Stephanie's apartment.

Bruce stood up, throwing daggers from his eyes aimed directly at Stephanie. "You see what you did to her, don't you?"

"I did not do that."

"The hell you didn't. You tore that little girl's world apart. She was Daddy's girl and you took that away from her."

"Don't even start, Bruce," Stephanie said, developing an argumentative tone.

"You are the one who did this, dammit. You stole my girls away from me, and my daughter is miserable because of it."

"She's a little girl," Stephanie snarled. "She doesn't understand any of this."

"Oh yes she does. You heard what she said. She wants to be with me."

"She's too young to make that choice, isn't she?"

"Then maybe I'll make it for her," he threatened.

"Implying what?"

"Physical custody of Emily."

Stephanie fumed at Bruce's suggestion. "You wouldn't dare."

"Wouldn't I? Don't push me, Steph. According to the divorce decree we have joint custody. That doesn't mean you make the rules and you get to decide how visitation is divided. I'm supposed to get six months. I've been generous by allowing you to have the kids during the school year so Emily's Preschool schedule wouldn't be disrupted, but I don't have to do that. I could fight you on this."

"She's my daughter."

"She's my daughter too, and the words joint custody mean we share. Oh, but I forgot," he taunted. "You don't know what that word share means. You must have everything for yourself and things always have to go your way. Well I've got news for you. You damn well better start putting other people first or I swear, your selfishness will hurt you and I will fight you on this. You need to think about how you want to approach this, because if Emily says she wants to be with me and wants to talk to me and wants to see me and you prevent that from happening, you will be on the receiving end of hell. Do not try to keep my daughter from me." He turned his back and returned to the car.

When Bruce took his seat behind the wheel, his lips were pressed together tightly and he had a death grip on the steering wheel, squeezing the life out of it. "I swear, I hate that woman," he said to Mandy, who was sitting in the passenger's seat. "She has got to be the most selfish, egocentric, uncaring person I've ever known."

"What happened?"

He took a deep breath to try to calm himself. "Emily was crying inconsolably and wouldn't let go of my neck. Every time I talk to her she says the same thing. When does she get to come home, when will she get to see me, and she wants to know why we can't be together. Stephanie knows this and ignores it. Today she stood on the porch with a smirk on her face and watched as her daughter cried. Dammit, I've had enough. I will not sit here and let my little girl suffer and tear up day after day because her mother won't allow her be with me."

"She can't keep Emily from you," Amanda reminded him.

"According to the divorce decree, no she can't, but obviously she doesn't care about that. We have joint custody, which means lodging and care of the children is supposed to be shared equally. If Stephanie doesn't want to work with me then she'll leave me no choice but to get a court-ordered custody schedule or fight for physical custody."

"Did you tell her that?" Mandy asked.

"Yeah, I told her that."

"So what are you gonna do?"

"I want Emily," Bruce plainly stated. "And I told Stephanie to figure out how to make it happen or I would have a judge figure it out for her. I guarantee she doesn't want that."

Amanda fully supported Bruce's decision with this. "Do you think she'll comply?"

"If she cares about her daughter and doesn't want a court battle she will," Bruce warned. "I want to wait a week and see what she does. If I don't hear from her, I'll call her…then I'll call my lawyer."

Chapter Fifty-Five

After cleaning out his car, Jim came inside to find Sabrina sitting on the sofa wearing headphones and browsing the internet from her iPad. "Whatcha doin'?" he asked her.

She took off her headphones. "Did you say something, Daddy?"

"What are you doing?"

"Looking up information about the life cycle of a chicken. I need it for my science project."

He sat next to her. "Who was on the phone earlier?"

"Natalie. I was giving her advice about her boyfriend."

"Natalie has a boyfriend?" Jim asked, a bit worried that Sabrina's friends were getting involved in adult relationships at such a young age.

"She thinks she does."

Thinks she does? What did that mean? "So she really doesn't?"

"She's been hanging out with this boy named Kenneth a lot, but he hadn't kissed her. He's a friend of Nick's, that guy in my science class."

"The boy with the skateboard?"

"Yes."

"Is he your boyfriend?" Jim said, hoping he wasn't.

"I don't have a boyfriend."

"He hasn't kissed you?" Jim teased her.

Sabrina curled her lip, grossed out that her father even suggested such a thing. "Yuk! I don't want him to."

He peered over her shoulder at the information she was reading. "Chickens huh?"

"Uh huh."

"What are you doin' for your science project?"

"Hatching chicken eggs under various environmental conditions to see which ones hatch first," she told him. "By the way, I need to get some fertilized chicken eggs."

Jim nodded in approval. "I can get you some. When do you need them?"

"As soon as possible. I need to get them in the incubator. Oh, I need one of those too. Sorry, Daddy," she apologized, thinking she was asking too much from him.

"No problem. We can get one. Did you get your science test back?"

"Yup."

He probed for a more detailed response. "How'd ya do?"

"I got a ninety-seven on it."

"Good job. How's math comin' along? Do you need help with anything?"

"Nope. I'm good," she replied confidently.

It appeared his daughter didn't need him. He patted her on the thigh and stood up. "Ok then."

"Daddy?" she called to him.

"Yes?"

"I love you."

Jim gave a half grin. "Love you too, Angel."

Out in the backyard, Christopher was kicking a soccer ball up in the air and bouncing it off his knee. Jim slipped on a hoodie and opened the back door.

"Hey, Dad. Watch this." Christopher bounced the ball off his knee twice, kicked it with his foot, and bounced it off his head back to his knee again.

"That's really cool," Jim said. "Where'd you learn to do that?"

"I figured it out by myself."

"Pretty talented there, Son."

Chris handed the ball to his dad. "You try."

Jim chuckled. "You want me to try that?"

"Just bounce it off your knee. It's not hard."

"Alright." He could only get the ball to bounce a couple times before it fell to the ground.

When Jill came home from working an ER shift, Sabrina was on her tablet and Jalene was happily playing with dolls on the living room floor. Jim and Chris were in the backyard playing soccer. She set her purse on the kitchen table and peeked her head out the back door. "James?"

Jim replied, "Yes, Honeybun?"

"Can you come in here for a minute. I need to talk to you."

Jim handed the ball back to Christopher then went into the bedroom where his wife was changing out of her scrubs. He greeted her with a kiss. "How was your day?"

"Busy." She pulled a folded piece of paper out of her pocket and handed it to Jim. "Here."

"What's this?" he asked.

"That is Chris's progress report. His grades have gone down quite a bit. I got a call from his teacher this morning."

"What?" He unfolded the paper and could not believe what he saw. Christopher had a D in reading, a C in Math, and only one A, which was in P.E. "How the hell did this happen?"

"I don't know. Did you know he was having trouble in school?"

"No," he discerned. "His last report card had all A's. It didn't look anything like this."

"We have to go in and talk to his teacher tomorrow after school."

"What time?"

"4:00," she replied.

Jim considered his schedule. Jill was off tomorrow, but because one of the doctors was on vacation and they were shorthanded, the ER director asked Jim to work a double shift. He was going in at 2:00 in the morning and wouldn't get off until 6:00 P.M. tomorrow night. Trying to squeeze a parent/teacher conference into his schedule was going to be tight. He would have to find someone to cover the last few hours of his shift. "I'll have to meet you over there." Jim examined Chris's grades again. "Shit. Wonder what's goin' on?"

"Why don't you talk to him and see what he tells you before we meet with his teacher tomorrow," Jill suggested.

With grades in hand, Jim went back outside with his son. "Hey, Chris, come 'ere for a minute."

Christopher dribbled the ball toward his father.

"Is something goin' on in school, Bud?"

Chris shrugged, pretending he didn't know what his father was talking about. "No."

"That's not what this says." Jim handed his son the progress report. "Can you explain this?"

Christopher knew he was busted. He held the ball in his hands and shifted from one foot to the other.

"What's up with your grades?"

"I dunno."

Jim knew his son was lying. "Your mother and I are meeting with your teacher tomorrow. What's she gonna tell us?"

"Mrs. Granger called you?"

"Yes, she did. Before we meet with her, I'm givin' you an opportunity to explain this. And you better be honest with me, because if we find out otherwise, you'll be in trouble. Fess up, Son."

"Dad, I…" Christopher didn't finish. He simply stared at his father trying to figure out how to get out of this.

"Start talkin', and start talkin' now," Jim demanded.

Chris gave his explanation, which ended up coinciding with what his teacher said.

A few days later, Jim drove to Randy's house to watch a Lakers game. As he leaned back on the sofa and took a drink of Corona he said, "Found out my son's grades have dropped significantly. Damn kid has been slackin' off with his classwork and hasn't turned in a homework assignment in two weeks."

"Are you serious?" Randy asked.

"Yup. Apparently he had some major book report project due, but I knew nothing about it. The kid reads all the time too. What pisses me off is he's been tellin' me he finished his homework. Since we've never had problems with his grades before, I didn't question this."

"He lied to you?"

"Yes he did."

"Ouch."

Jim couldn't have agreed more. "Obviously we're gonna have to keep closer tabs on him 'cause he's shown us that we can't trust him. And since soccer seems to be takin' up such a huge chunk of his study time, I pulled him out until he brings his grades up."

"Damn, you're a hardass aren't you?"

"I'm not gonna let the kid take time to play soccer if he can't dedicate time to get his homework done. I'm hopin' this will motivate him to hit the books. He's not steppin' foot on a soccer field again until I see an improvement in his grades."

"He's only nine-years-old, Jim. Did you ever stop to think that maybe fourth grade is hard for him?"

"Negatory," Jim insisted. "Chris is a bright kid and has always been a good student. He schnarfed on this one. I don't know who he's tryin' to impress, but I'm not puttin' up with it."

Randy had to laugh.

"What's so funny?"

"You sound like my dad," Randy said. "While we're on the topic, guess what my lovely two-year-old decided to do yesterday?"

"Do I dare ask?" Jim replied, anxious to hear the tales of the two-year-old terror.

"He somehow got ahold of my cellphone."

"Not your new phone, I hope."

"Yup, my new one, which, as you know, is also my pager."

Jim cringed. "Ooh, Dude, that's not good."

"I must have left it in the pocket of my lab coat or something. Anyway, he was messing with the buttons on it, and when I tried to take it from him, he threw it across the room. It landed on the ceramic tile and shattered all to hell."

"Sounds like a two-year-old."

"Needless to say, I had to replace my phone. Took me three hours to reprogram the damn thing and re-download my apps and ringtones."

"Does Nathan have a toy phone to play with?" Jim asked.

"No."

"You should get him one. That way he won't be as tempted to mess with yours."

Randy snorted under his breath. "Why'd he have to ruin with my phone? Why couldn't he have messed with Jane's phone?"

Jim found Randy's discontentment amusing. "You're lucky he didn't do that while you were on-call."

"Oh I know, that would have been far worse," Randy concurred. "I finally got my dad hooked up with a paging app. With all the cellphones and pagers he had, he was starting to look like he was carrying a Batman utility belt. To lessen the load, I helped him combine everything into one device."

"You're becomin' a technology guru aren't you, Mr. Gates?"

"It makes things easier and more convenient."

"Speakin' of which, how's that EMR system workin' out for ya?"

"It's awesome," Randy replied. "Easy to use and simple to transport. All I have to do is load it up on my iPad and voila—patient files, appointment schedules, prescriptions, lab reports, referrals, everything I need is right there. It's great."

"How's your dad doin' with all this techno stuff?"

"It's taking him a while to get used to it, but he likes it. He says it's more efficient. I have to agree. It's really cut down on paper clutter. Steph's been working on uploading all the patient files for us and has been training our office staff how to use the system. She's good at that sort of thing."

"So it's workin' out havin' her there?" Jim asked.

"She's great at what she does. Best decision we ever made was hiring her."

That may have been true, but that didn't change the fact that Stephanie was having a custodial dispute with Bruce. To avoid taking things to court, Stephanie gave in to Bruce's request.

"Did I hear you correctly?" he asked. "You're willing to let Emily live with me during the school year?"

"Yes," Stephanie clarified. "She talks about you all time, cries for you at bedtime, constantly asks me when she'll get to see you again. That's what she wants."

"Let me talk to her."

Stephanie put Emily on the phone. "Daddy?" a sad little voice said.

"Hey, Baby. How are you?"

"I miss you."

"I know, Princess. I miss you too. But we'll be together soon and you'll be able to come down to Los Angeles and stay with me."

"Really?"

"Really, really. Mommy and I were just talking about that."

"Yay!" she cheered.

"I'm excited too, but I need to talk to Mommy so we can figure out when I'm going to come get you, ok?"

"Ok. I love you, Daddy."

"I love you too, Princess. Give Mommy the phone," Bruce instructed.

He and Stephanie worked out details and they decided to give Stephanie six weeks to get all of Emily's things packed up and get her medical and school records gathered and ready to go. This gave Bruce some time to put in for vacation days so he could make the flight up there to get his daughter.

Chapter Fifty-Six

Randy was about to go in to see a patient when his receptionist, Samantha, said, "Dr. Hanson, your wife is on line two."

Jane rarely called Randy at work. If she needed him, she usually left a voicemail on his cell or sent him a text. The fact that she chose to call him at the clinic indicated something was wrong. "I'll take it in my office." He stepped into his office, set his iPad on the desk, and picked up the receiver. "Hey, Baby."

"I'm having contractions."

She had been pregnant for thirty-six weeks and four days, which meant she was almost four weeks pre-term. Not unusual for a multiple birth. "How long?"

"About four solid hours now."

"Four hours?" He couldn't believe she hadn't said anything to him until now. "Why didn't you call me?"

"I didn't want to bother you unless they got bad."

"I take it they're getting bad."

"Yeah," she said.

"You been timing them?"

"Running about five to seven minutes apart."

She was ready to come in. "Do you have your bag and Nathan's stuff ready?"

"Yes."

"Alright. I'm going to call Mom and have her take you to the hospital," he declared. "I'll meet you over there."

"Tell her to hurry."

"I will." He hung up and immediately called his mother.

The minute he got off the phone, Randy approached his father, who stood outside an examination room looking over a file. "Dad, I have to leave."

"Why is that?"

"Jane's in labor," he explained. "Mom's picking her up and bringing her to the hospital. I'll meet with my last patient then I need to head over there."

Mark could tell his son's nerves were shaky. "You ok, Son?"

Randy took a deep breath. "I'm doing alright. It's just that the twins are coming today. That's kinda scary."

As soon as his mother called saying she and Jane had pulled into the hospital parking lot, Randy grabbed his belongings and darted out the door.

Stephanie questioned her brother's urgency. "Why is Randy in such a hurry to get out of here?"

Mark told her why. "Jane's in labor."

Stephanie clapped softly. "How exciting. We're going to have two more babies in the family."

When Randy arrived at Swedish Medical Center, Ellen was ushering Jane to the door, with Nathan right beside her. He ran up behind them, panting. "Thanks, Mom."

"You're welcome."

Randy took Jane's arms and escorted her inside the building.

Once checked in, the hospital staff wheeled Jane upstairs. Randy knelt down in front of Nathan and said, "You're going to stay with Grandma for a while."

Nathan hugged his stuffed bunny. "Is Mommy ok?"

"Yes, Mommy's fine. But the babies are coming today and Daddy needs to help."

"Me help too. Me big boy." Nathan stood up straight to show how big he was.

"Yes you are, but you can't help, Buddy. You'll get to see the babies after they're born." Randy gave his son a kiss on the cheek. "Go with Grandma, and be a good boy. Mommy and I will see you later."

"Ok." Nathan skipped over to his grandmother.

Randy stood up and hugged his mother. "Thanks again, Mom."

"Randy, get upstairs," she insisted.

He waved goodbye to Nathan and bolted up to the Maternity Ward.

By the time Randy got there, Jane was already in a hospital gown and hooked up to a fetal monitor. "Hey," he said in a loving voice. "How you doing?"

With a wince on her face, she placed her hand on her oversized tummy. "I'm doing ok."

"Let's take a look." He examined her contraction spikes and checked the babies' heartrates, distinctly listening to each one. "The babies look good, but I want to see how we're progressing." As he feared, the limited space prevented the two fetuses from moving into the head-down position. A vaginal delivery would not be feasible. He suspected this would happen if she went into pre-term labor.

The worried expression on Randy's face made Jane ask, "Is something wrong?"

He threw his latex gloves away and stood by her side, taking her hand in his. "Honey, the babies haven't turned."

"What does that mean? Is that bad?"

Jane's birthing plan was now shot to hell, and Randy knew she would be upset about that. "It means we're going to have to do a Cesarean."

Unprepared for this, she shook her head. "No."

"We have to. These babies are breech and it's not safe to do a vaginal delivery like that."

She covered her mouth with her hand and cried.

Randy turned to the nurse and said, "Can you give us a minute please?"

"Yes, Doctor." The nurse exited the room, leaving Randy and Jane alone.

Randy hugged his wife and lovingly kissed the top of her head. "It's ok."

Even though Randy had explained to her the high probability of having a Cesarean with multiples, she didn't feel prepared for this. "This isn't what I wanted."

"I know, but we don't have a choice." He held her close and let her cry for a minute. "It'll be ok. I'll be right there with you the whole time."

She wiped her eyes and looked at him. "What's going to happen?"

He explained everything to her and tried to get her to feel more comfortable about this situation. After explaining the procedure, he kissed her on the lips and sat on the bed beside her. "What we're going to do now is get you to pre-op. The nurses will get you prepped and an anesthesiologist will numb you from the waist down. You'll be alert and awake during the procedure, that way you can hear what's going on and see the babies. I can even get a mirror so you can watch if you want."

"I really don't think I want to watch you cut into me, Randy. It's eerie knowing my husband is going to be standing over me holding a knife in his hand."

Knowing she was scared, Randy nuzzled his forehead to hers. "You ok?"

She nodded her head.

"I can't do this procedure by myself. Other people will be in the room. The pediatric crew, the anesthesiologist, and I'll have some nurses and surgical assistants helping me. Dad is on his way too," Randy explained.

"Alright."

"We need to prep you for surgery. I won't be with you while they're doing that because I have to scrub up and get my support staff in order. But I'll be right behind you, ok?"

"Ok."

He kissed her reassuringly. "I'll see you in a few minutes."

Randy's dad was scrubbed up and ready to go by the time Randy stepped into the OR. The room had been prepped, his equipment was lined up neatly on the stainless steel surgical tray, and pediatrics was setting up.

Mark's eyes followed Randy as he took position at the operating station. "How you doing?"

"I'm doing ok. Jane's a little freaked out, and I feel kind of strange."

"Why?"

Randy picked up the scalpel and stared at it. "There's something not right about wielding a scalpel to operate on my wife."

"You want me to do it?"

"No." Randy set the scalpel back down. "I got it."

They wheeled Jane in and Randy stepped over to her side. "Hey, Honey. We'll have our babies in about four or five minutes." He kissed her softly. "Try to relax. I love you."

"I love you."

Randy took position. To reassure Jane and make his presence known, he asked, "Can you hear me, Babe?"

"Yes," she confirmed.

"Alright. Let's do this." He held out his hand. "Scalpel." The surgical assistant handed Randy the scalpel and the procedure began. As he made the first incision, he wanted to ensure Jane was numb and comfortable. "How you doin', Honey?"

"I'm fine."

"Good." He continued.

The room was quiet for a solid three minutes. "Hold that," Randy finally said. He reached in and pulled out baby number one. "Syringe."

The assistant handed him the bulb syringe and he cleaned out the baby's nose and mouth. He clamped the umbilical cord then took a pair of scissors and cut. The baby cried, quite loudly, which made everyone in the room chuckle. "There's the first one. She's beautiful...and loud." He handed the baby to the nurse, who in turn brought her over to Jane so she could to see the infant's face before handing her off to the pediatricians. Time for baby number two.

"A little pressure," Randy said as he pushed on Jane's abdomen to move the baby down. He reached in and pulled out the second one, once again cleaning out her nose and mouth before clamping and cutting the cord. The second one didn't have as strong of a cry as the first one did, but her lungs worked.

Pediatrics did a workup on the babies while Randy finished up with Jane.

"Are they both ok?" she asked.

"They look great," he replied, trying to make conversation to get her mind off the procedure. "They're small, but strong for their size. The first one is bigger than the second one is. She has a tiny birthmark on her foot," Randy stated. "They look identical so we'll use that to tell them apart for now." As he sutured her up he asked, "Are we sticking with the original names we picked out?"

"Yes."

"Which one is the first one?" he asked.

"Lauren."

"Alright, Lauren Marie is the one with the birthmark on her foot and Lacy Nicole is the other one."

After Randy finished the job, he took a cleansing breath and set his equipment back on the tray. "There. You are all done. You're going to have a scar at your bikini line."

"That's ok."

He removed his latex gloves and tossed them in the hazardous waste bin. "I'm going to clean up and have them move you to the recovery room. We need to keep an eye on you for a few hours until this anesthesia wears off." He leaned over and gave her a kiss. "I'll see you in a bit."

Once his hands were washed and he was out of his scrubs, Randy spoke to the pediatrician who did the workup on his daughters. "How do they look?" he asked.

"They look good. The little one had some problems getting oxygen at first, but she's doing well now."

"Weights?"

"Five pounds, six ounces and five pounds, one ounce."

Randy raised an eyebrow. "Damn, that's over ten pounds of baby she was carrying."

"Yes it was."

"When will they be ready to come into the room?" Randy was anxious to hold his daughters and begin the bonding process.

"As soon as your wife is in postpartum we'll bring them to you." The pediatrician shook Randy's hand. "Congratulations, Dr. Hanson."

"Thank you."

In the hallway, Mark put his hand on his son's shoulder. "Nice job. How do you feel being the daddy of two girls?"

"I feel great. Still unsure about this whole twin thing, but my daughters are beautiful."

He handed Randy a gift bag. "Your mother and I got this for you."

Inside the bag was a white tee-shirt with two sets of baby footprints printed on the front. Along the bottom were the words, *Proud Dad of Twins.* "I love this. Thanks."

"You did a good job today," Mark said to his son. "I'll call your mom and tell her Jane is in the recovery room."

"Hey, bring Nathan up to postpartum as soon as Jane's ready. I'll call you when we move her over there."

"Will do." Mark joined his wife while Randy headed to Jane's recovery room, stopped on the way by several congratulatory well-wishers.

Jane was lying in bed with several monitors hooked up to her. Randy pulled a chair up bedside her and sat down, taking her hand in his. "How you feeling?"

"I can't feel my legs."

"That will start wearing off soon, then you're going to be pretty sore." He looked up at her vitals to check her numbers. Everything was normal. "I had them put an Oxycodone drip in your IV. It's probably going to make you sleepy, but it'll minimize the pain."

Concerned about the effect this drug could have on her nursing babies, she asked, "Is that safe for the babies?"

"The dosage I'm giving you is. It won't eliminate pain completely, but it will take the edge off. In a few days we'll wean you over to Tylenol." He looked down at the IV needle that was poked into her arm. "I'm sorry we had to do it this way."

"You did what you had to do," she said to him, knowing he wouldn't have resorted to a C-section if he didn't deem it necessary. "Can I see the babies?" she asked.

"They're on their way. I don't want you picking them up though. Just lie on your side and I'll put them on the bed next to you. You shouldn't be lifting anything right now." He stood up and began unbuttoning his shirt.

"What are you doing?" she asked, wondering why he was undressing.

He took off the blue button up dress shirt he had on and put on the tee-shirt his dad gave him. "My parents bought me a tee-shirt."

Jane read the print on the front. "That's great." Already tired of being in this room, she asked, "How long do I have to stay in here?"

"We need to monitor you for a couple hours to make sure you're stabilized." He folded his dress shirt and sat back down. "As soon as you can wiggle your legs we'll move you to postpartum."

She really didn't want to be cooped up in a hospital. "When can I go home?"

He reached over and held her hand. "It depends on how you're doing. In three to four days I'll check your sutures to see if they're healing properly. If they are, then you'll get to go home. If not, you'll be here a few more days."

Disappointed by this news, she protested, "I have to stay here for four days?"

"Maybe longer. You just had major surgery. We need to keep an eye on you to make sure you're healing properly and not getting any infections."

She started to poke at all the tubes and wires coming out of her. "Can you at least unhook me from all this stuff?"

He chuckled at her lack of enthusiasm. "Wow, you are impatient."

"I don't want to stay in here."

"I know, but you need to recover. Some of your equipment will be traveling with you to postpartum. The IV will stay until your intestines begin working again—when I hear rumbling sounds in there."

She glanced down at her incision, which was hidden under layers of gauze. "How bad is my scar?"

"It's not bad," he assured her. "I tried to make it as small as possible. It's about five inches long and will be about one-sixteenth of an inch wide by the time it's done healing. It's a low-lying scar that will eventually be hidden by the waistband of your underwear or bikini bottom. No one will notice."

As they were getting settled into postpartum, a nurse knocked and peeked her head inside. "Excuse me, Dr. Hanson. Your daughters are here."

Randy moved things out of the way.

The nursery staff wheeled both babies into the room. They were lying in their plastic bassinets wrapped up in pink blankets with pink knitted hats on their heads. The nurses put some diapers on the table and brought in a small diaper bag full of essential supplies. "Let us know if you need anything."

"Thank you," Randy replied. One of the babies was asleep and the other was wide awake. He picked up the alert one and brought her over to Jane.

"Which one is this?"

Randy took off the infant's right sock to see if she had a birthmark on her foot. She didn't. "This one is Lacy." He put her sock back on and gently laid her on the bed next to Jane, allowing Mom and baby some time to bond.

While Jane nuzzled with her daughter, Randy made a couple of phone calls. First he called Jane's father and brother, followed by Robby and Stephanie. The next call he made was to the University of Washington School of Medicine. He was scheduled to work with medical students the next day but called to cancel the seminar he was supposed to give and arranged for someone else to supervise the medical students for him. He was not going to work tomorrow.

Then he dialed Jim's cell number.

After two rings Jim answered, "Hanson. What's up, Bro?"

"We have the twins."

Jim didn't even know Jane had gone into labor. "What? When did this happen?"

"I got the call a little over two hours ago. Mom drove her over here and I had to do a C-section on her, so I didn't really have time to call you."

"Oh wow," Jim exclaimed. "Did you perform the procedure?"

"Yup."

"Bet that was intense."

"It was different."

"Gratz, Bro. How you doin'?" Jim asked, concerned about his best friend's wellbeing after an intense experience like that.

"I'm doing great. They're beautiful, Jim," Randy declared. "I'm in love with them already."

"Are you at the hospital now?"

"Yes."

"Sweet. Jill and I are off today. We're on our way to scout for some grub with the kids, but we'll stop by afterwards. You want me to bring you anything?" Jim offered.

"No. I'm good. I'll eat later. Thanks though."

When Randy got off the phone with Jim, he sent out a bulk e-mail to all their friends and family announcing the birth of their daughters.

Randy's parents brought Nathan up to the Maternity Ward to meet his sisters. While Randy's parents snuggled and cuddled with Lacy, Randy carried Lauren over to Nathan. "Hey, Buddy," he said to his son. "This is your sister."

Nathan was reluctant to get close to the baby. "She little."

"Yes, she is very little, which is why she's going to need her big brother to look after her." Randy held the baby at an angle that allowed Nathan to see her face. "This is Lauren."

Nathan slowly approached the infant, examining her features. "Me kiss the baby?"

"Sure. You can give her a kiss."

He leaned over and kissed his sister on the cheek. This was the sweetest thing Randy had ever seen.

Several other visitors came by the hospital that night, including Stephanie, Jim and Jill, and Greg and Raquel. After the exhausting day they had, Randy wanted Jane to rest. At 10:00 P.M. he politely asked people to leave and sent Nathan with his parents for the night. Finally alone, Jane nursed both babies. It didn't take long before she and the twins were asleep.

Randy quietly crept out of the room and headed over to the nurses' station. The Maternity Ward had just changed shifts and Evie Wilkinson happened to be on the night staff.

"Hi, Doctor," she said. "I hear congratulations are in order."

"Yes, thank you."

"Robby sent me a picture earlier. Your daughters are beautiful."

"Like their mother." He smiled at her and said, "I'm gonna run downstairs and get a cup of coffee. I'll be back in a few minutes."

"Did you want me to check on your wife?" she asked.

"No, that's alright. She and the twins are asleep. They should be fine."

Randy stayed at the hospital that night, crashed out on a recliner in the room. Around one o'clock in the morning, one of the babies began to stir. Randy woke up, hoping to intercede before the baby's noises woke Jane. He picked up his daughter and quietly slipped out to the dimly lit hall of the Maternity Ward. Snuggling with her, he sang, "Hush little baby don't say a word. Daddy's gonna buy you a mockingbird…"

Evie heard Randy singing this lullaby to his daughter, and he appeared to be dancing with her.

"Connie," she said to the other nurse who was on shift. "Look at Dr. Hanson."

The two nurses watched him, in awe over the delicate way he handled his newborn daughter.

"That is adorable."

Evie walked over and whispered, "Dr. Hanson?"

Randy pivoted his body, facing her.

"Can I get you a bottle of water? A cup of coffee?"

"No, that's alright," he said. "She was just getting a bit fussy. Thought a walk might help."

"Let me know if you need anything."

"We will. Thanks."

The next day, Randy assisted Jane with infant care and showed her comfortable ways to nurse with a sore belly. They had a few more visitors too, including Brian Davine, who took a day off from his busy football schedule to fly up and see his new nieces. Robby stopped by after work, and Randy's parents came by with Nathan.

Randy took Nathan home with him that night. He tried to maintain a normal schedule by fixing Nathan's favorite dinner, playing basketball, and reading books together. Before bed, he gave Nathan a bath. Their lives were about to change. Caring for twins, with a very active two-year-old in the house, was going to be the most challenging experience of their lives. Randy always knew he and Jane could make it through anything, and being parents of twins was going to give them a chance to prove it.

Jane and Randy focused on caring for their new bundles of joy and let little household tasks slide. They both figured they'd have time to catch up on those other things a few months down the road when the twins had established a regular schedule. Many friends, neighbors, and family members volunteered to help. They delivered meals for the family and came for visits that allowed Jane, and ideally the babies, time to nap while the visitor would do a load of laundry, empty the dishwasher, or clean a bathroom. Gift cards for baby product providers, like Babies "R" Us, Target, or the grocery store, were offered as gifts, and diapers were often left at the door with a note of support.

The entertainment level in their household increased exponentially with the arrival of the twins. The babies didn't communicate about their schedules for the benefit of their parents. In fact, it sometimes felt as if they were conspiring to make things as difficult as possible. In an average week the babies went through 140 to 200 diapers, twelve to fifteen cotton snap onesies, twelve one-piece leg-snap pajamas, twelve receiving blankets, and four to six fitted crib sheets. They had eight to ten diaper changes and six to eight feedings a day. Bottles became a necessity. Jane pumped a bit of milk and stored it so Randy could take over a few feedings while she took a nap. Bouncy chairs and a battery driven mobile that played tunes were a must; they often kept one quiet while the other was feeding, and it helped them get back to sleep. They had a few different pacifiers. Lacy needed to suck on something but wasn't picky about what it was. Lauren, however, had definite preferences. Not any pacifier would do. She had to have a special one.

The babies usually derived comfort from being placed in close proximity to one another during the early weeks after birth. They often slept side by side in one crib during nap time.

Jane and Randy still took time every once in a while to focus on themselves and Nathan by taking a soak in the tub, going on a nature walk, or simply taking a nap, which they both discovered they desperately needed. Family outings were limited with the twins being so needy right now. Because of this, Randy often took care of any errands that needed to be run, bringing Nathan with him. Parenting became more of a chore, but one Randy took on with enthusiasm. He loved being a father.

Chapter Fifty-Seven

A few weeks after the twins were born, Bruce flew up to Seattle with Mandy, not only to see Randy's new daughters, but also to spend time with Alyssa and bring Emily back to Los Angeles with him. When Bruce saw Stephanie, he didn't say a word to her other than, "I'll have Emily call you when we get to L.A."

To Stephanie, this was unacceptable. "That's it? You have nothing else to say to me?"

He looked over at Amanda and said, "Meet me in the car. I'll be right there."

Mandy held Emily's hand and ushered her out to the car.

Since their divorce, Bruce had been plagued with pent-up emotions and resentment. He had a multitude of things he wanted to say to Stephanie but never had the heart to do it. Maybe now was the appropriate time. "Every time I see you, you pierce right through me. I wasted too many years of my life trying to make you happy. Over the last few months, I've thought about everything you ever said to me, and I've concluded that every word that ever came out of your mouth was a lie. Most of the time you acted like you couldn't stand to be around me. You were never there for me and you never heard a word I said. You spent all your time thinking about yourself and whining about how I never gave you anything you wanted, but you never once took the time to notice when I needed you."

"What about what I needed?" she asked.

Stephanie's tone became snarky, but he didn't care. He needed to get this off his chest. "I no longer care about what you need. I am going to spend my life caring about somebody I love, someone who cares about me and loves me in return, someone who will be there when I need her. I refuse to be your doormat." He turned his back and walked away.

When he got out to the car, he sat there for a minute staring out the window, but didn't make a sound.

"Everything alright?" Mandy asked him.

"Yes. Everything is fine." Bruce felt better now that he had that out of his system. He felt liberated, free from the boulder that held him down. He looked at Emily in the back seat. "You ready?"

The little girl nodded. "Uh huh."

"Then let's go home." He started the car and the three of them went back to the hotel. Tomorrow he, Mandy, and Emily would fly to L.A. together.

Bruce was only months away from finishing his last year of residency. Following a fourteen-hour day at the hospital, he picked Emily up from daycare then drove down to Mandy's beach house in Santa Monica. After lying Emily down for the night, Bruce kicked back on the couch and put his feet up. Amanda stood behind him and rubbed his shoulders.

"That feels incredible." He closed his eyes and absorbed her tension-lifting massage.

"Busy day?"

"Busy week," he said.

"Have you heard back from the Neurosurgical Group yet?" she asked him, knowing he applied for a position there as a neurosurgeon.

"Yes, actually, I did."

"What did they say?"

"They're interested. I have an interview scheduled next week."

"See, I told you."

"Yup," he agreed. "You were right. And if I get the job, I'll have hospital affiliations at Santa Monica Medical Center."

"You'll get it." She moved her lips to his ear. "And when you do, you'll be closer to me."

"Yes, I will." His lips met hers in a loving embrace.

She moved to the other side of the couch and sat next to him. "My parents are coming over for dinner this weekend. I'd like you and Emily to join us."

"Your parents?"

"Yes, you've met them before."

"Oh, I remember. Your dad's an Aerospace Engineer with a double Ph.D. from Purdue. Kinda hard to forget that," Bruce said. "Brain surgery and rocket science. Two things that are real conversation stoppers. I can see where that tea party talk will go. You know any nuclear physicists? We'll throw them into the pot too."

Mandy thought this was funny. "Bruce."

"I don't know about having a rocket scientist and a brain surgeon in the same room together, Amanda. I think that's asking for trouble." Bruce deepened his voice a bit. "Got any summer plans? Why yes, next Tuesday I'm performing brain surgery. It's not rocket science, but hey, it's my job."

"Will you come or not?"

"Yes, I'll be there." He put his arm around her. "Stephanie and I made an arrangement."

"What kind of arrangement?"

"We're going to schedule visitation so the girls can be together as often as possible. We've decided to alternate holidays and spread visitations out. I'll get my six months, but in spurts. I agreed to let Stephanie have the girls during the summer as long as I get Alyssa for April and May. I'll have to fly up to Seattle to get her though."

"At least she's working with you now," Mandy scoffed.

"She doesn't have a choice. If she wants to play hardball with me, I'll get my attorney involved. And believe me, she doesn't want to go there."

Chapter Fifty-Eight

Jane peered into the crib, intently watching her daughters snuggled close together, sleeping soundly. Randy came into the room and put his arm around Jane, guarding over his baby girls like a sentinel.

"They sleep so much better when they're nuzzled side by side," Jane remarked.

"Well, they were housed together for thirty-six weeks. They got used to the other one being there." Randy slowly moved Jane's hair off her neck and nibbled at her soft skin.

She closed her eyes and let him.

He moved his hand to her tummy and whispered, "All the kids are napping. We should take advantage of this moment."

"Implying what, Doctor?"

"Oh, I think you know what I'm implying." A lustful tone resonated in his voice as he slowly moved his hand down her waist to her hips. He closed his eyes and soaked in the sweet taste of her kiss. "What do you say we go into the bedroom." He took her hand in his and led her across the hall.

In one quick motion, he closed the door with his foot and pulled his shirt over his head. "Now, where were we?" He drew her closer to him and once again his lips found hers. His body heat rose as they made their way to the bed.

"Please tell me you bought a box of condoms," she said.

"Oh yeah." He fumbled inside the bedside table drawer to find one. "Been looking forward to this for a long time."

Between kisses, she said, "It's been so long."

Randy quickly removed the rest of his clothes then helped Jane strip off hers. "I want you so bad." Attempting to open the condom package with one hand proved to be more of a battle than he anticipated. To simplify things, he held it between his thumb and forefinger and tore it open with his teeth.

"Here," Jane said. She took it out of his hand, threw the wrapper on the floor, and helped him put it on.

It had been nearly six weeks since Randy and his wife had been physically intimate, and he was about to burst. Wasting no time, he rubbed his hands all over her silky skin and kissed her. As he slid inside, he watched her facial expression. Her lips parted and her breathing became more erratic. Sexual gratification was never an issue in their marriage. Jane showed him every time how much she enjoyed the physical bond they shared, and he reciprocated with his own satisfaction.

Now sweaty and slightly out of breath, Randy closed his eyes and buried his head in Jane's shoulder, touching cheek to cheek. He lay there for several minutes holding her, unable to move, while he tried to regain air.

"Randy, we need to talk about something."

"Uh oh. What did I do?" he said, hoping he hadn't done anything to upset her.

She rolled onto her side. With her elbow bent, she supported her head with her hand. "I don't want to be on the pill anymore."

Pressing his lips together firmly, he questioned this decision. "What do you want to do then? We have to have some kind of contraception, because abstinence is completely out of the question."

"We have three children now. I don't really want more than that. Do you?"

"I think three is more than enough," he chuckled, completely agreeing with her. "Are you thinking sterilization?"

With a nod, she replied, "Yes."

"You sure?" he asked. "We can't reverse that if we change our minds."

"I know."

They discussed all the options and decided on a non-surgical procedure in which micro-inserts were placed into the fallopian tubes by a catheter. Once in place, the device was designed to elicit scarring in and around the micro-insert, and over a period of three months, a blockage formed. The procedure was as effective as the pill, but with no hormones.

"Do you want me to do the procedure?" he asked.

"If you can."

"I can, but we'll have to use alternative methods of contraception for the first few months until I make sure it scarred like it's supposed to."

"That's fine."

He grinned at her and said, "Alright. I'll put you on the schedule."

Randy picked up a copy of Seattle Metropolitan Magazine simply because the cover story intrigued him —*Seattle's Best Doctors*. He sipped on a cup of coffee and thumbed through the pages, fascinated by the medical talent in the city. When he came to the OB/GYN section, he stopped drinking and set his cup down. Printed in big bold letters on the top of the page were the names *Mark E. Hanson, M.D.* and *J. Randal Hanson, M.D.* With a smug grin, he read the article. It presented him and his father as medical gurus in the OB/GYN field. Randy didn't feel that important. To him, he was an ordinary guy with a wife and children. He had a mortgage and car payments. He washed his car, mowed his grass, and took out his trash. And just like the millions of dads before and after him, he changed his share of diapers. Yet his name and photo were plastered in a magazine for the entire city to see. Seattle's Best Doctors. There had to have been thousands of doctors in the Emerald City. How did he merit such recognition?

"Hey, Jane, come here," he called to his wife. "Check this out."

Jane stepped into the dining room. "What is it?"

He pushed the article toward her.

Jane pulled the magazine closer and read it. "You're famous."

"I don't know about that, but it is pretty cool." The digital clock on the microwave read 7:30 A.M. Randy gulped down the rest of his coffee then grabbed his cellphone, car keys, and stethoscope. "I have to get going. I'm running late. Save that magazine. I want to hang it my office." He gave Jane a parting kiss. "Love you, Babe."

"I love you too. Have a great day."

"I will." He kissed the top of Nathan's head. "I'll see you later, Nate. Be good for Mommy. Help her out today by cleaning up your toys."

"Me help. Me big boy." Nathan waved bye-bye before Randy slipped out the door.

When Randy got home that night, his two daughters were asleep on a blanket in the middle of the living room floor. Nathan was crashed out right next to them with his arm over both his sisters. This was a picture perfect scene. Randy whipped out his cellphone and snapped a picture with his camera. Quietly, he set his stethoscope on the dining room table.

Jane was slicing carrots at the kitchen sink. Randy came up behind her and kissed her neck then picked up a carrot and crunched on it. "Did you see the kids sleeping in the living room?"

"Yes. Aren't they sweet?" She tossed the carrot slices into a salad bowl. "I put some coffee on for you."

"Thanks, Honey." He pulled a coffee cup out of the cupboard and filled it. While he stirred in sugar and creamer, he said, "Dr. Stephens sent me an e-mail today."

Jane wondered who he was talking about. "Mandy?"

Randy tried to jog her memory. "No. The other Dr. Stephens. I used to work for him back in med school."

"Pete Stephens?"

"Yup."

"What did he want?"

"He said something about coming to Seattle. He wants me to call him."

"Might want to do it now while the house is quiet, before the kids wake up."

Randy gave her a kiss and crept into his home office, clenching his steaming mug in his hand. He looked up Dr. Stephens number then dialed it on his cellphone.

"Hello?" a familiar voice on the other line answered.

"Dr. Stephens. This is Randy Hanson."

"Well, hello, Dr. Hanson. Thank you for calling. It's good to hear from you."

"You too, Sir."

Dr. Stephens corrected him. "You don't have to call me that. We are colleagues now."

"Sorry. Just a habit, I guess. What can I do for you?"

"I'm flying into Seattle tomorrow and was wondering if you might want to snag a cup of coffee with me while I'm in town."

Randy hadn't seen Dr. Stephens in years. He looked forward to visiting with him again. "I would love to. Where will you be staying?"

"Downtown Sheraton. I have a conference from 9:00 A.M. until 4:00, but I'm available in the evening."

"Perhaps you'd like to join us for dinner?" Randy suggested.

"If you'd like, yes."

"We would be honored to have you."

As soon as the conference was over, Dr. Stephens called Randy, who in turn picked him up from the hotel and chauffeured him back to his house.

"How's the medical practice going?" Pete asked.

"Going well. Staying busy."

"Saw your name listed in Seattle Metropolitan magazine as one of Seattle's best."

"Not sure I deserve that title."

Pete disagreed, "Oh, I think you do."

When they arrived at the house, Randy gave him a tour. Several family photos were displayed throughout the home and a plastic tub full of toys sat in the corner of the living room. Parenting magazines and a copy of Psychology Today were spread out neatly on the coffee table, intermixed among Randy's medical journals and several children's picture books. The home was comfortable and kid friendly. The young charmer Dr. Stephens once knew had become a devoted family man. "Looks like you're doing quite well up here."

"Can't complain."

Nathan ran into the room to greet his father. "Daddy!"

Randy bent down and picked him up. "Nathan, this is Daddy's friend, Dr. Stephens. Can you say hello?"

Nathan shied away. "You Daddy friend?"

Pete replied, "Yes. Your father and I worked together when he was in medical school." He held out his hand to the child. "It's nice to meet you, Nathan."

Nathan wasn't sure what to do. Randy showed him. "You shake a man's hand when he offers it to you."

Nathan shook his hand.

"Daddy's going to talk to his friend now."

"Me play with my truck?"

"Yes." Randy set Nathan back down on the floor. "You can play with your truck if you want to."

Nathan toddled up the stairs to get it.

"Cute kid," Pete remarked. "How old is he?"

"Two." Randy offered Pete a chair then picked up one of his daughters and fed her a bottle.

"I have a favor to ask you. A friend of mine has a daughter who was recently accepted to UW's School of Medicine," Pete said. "Her name is Christina Sang. She's a good student, dedicated, eager to learn. She was hoping to find some work up here in the medical field to help pay for school. Do you have connections or know anyone she can contact to get the ball rolling?"

"I can do better than that."

"What did you have in mind?" Pete asked.

"You took a chance on me as a first year student and gave me the opportunity to learn from you and experience the medical field firsthand. I would love to reciprocate that." Randy moved his daughter to a burping position and patted her on the back. With his free hand, he reached into his pocket and handed his business card to Pete. "Have her call me and I'll set something up."

"Thank you. I will do that."

Chapter Fifty-Nine

The cool night air, combined with the smog, made the lights from the city of Los Angeles emit a misty glow. Street lights reflected off city ponds and local traffic zipped through the streets with their swooshing tires and blaring horns. Skyscraper lights set the night sky aglow while traffic signals blinked in red, green, and yellow. The coastal sage scrub, California poppy, and diverse palm trees with their large, compound leaves added serene beauty to the rolling boil of noise in the city.

Before tucking Emily in, Bruce sat on the edge of her bed. "Emmy, I need to talk to you for a minute." He scooted a bit closer to her. "How do you feel about Mandy?"

Emily told him, "She let me eat chips with my hotdog yesterday."

"Chips with hotdogs is always yummy." He looked his daughter in the eye and openly asked, "Do you like Mandy?"

"She's nice."

"I'm glad to hear you say that, because Daddy loves her very much. I'm thinking about asking her to marry me. How would you feel about that?"

"What about Mommy?"

"You'd still have your mommy in Seattle, but Mandy would be your mommy down here. You'd have two mommies," he explained. "And if Mandy was your mommy, she'd live with us all the time. She'd feed you hotdogs and chips, make you macaroni and cheese, and play playdough and Barbies with you every day. Would you like that?"

"Yes."

Emily's beautiful smile gave Bruce the reassurance he needed. "Ok. I will talk to her. Wish me luck."

"Good luck, Daddy."

He kissed his daughter's cheek and tucked her in for the night.

Mandy came over to Bruce's apartment the next day to spend the afternoon with him and Emily. They rode their bikes around the park, went to see a movie, then had dinner at Chuck-E-Cheese's. At the day's end, Mandy helped Bruce tuck Emily in.

Once she was snug in bed, Mandy and Bruce had some time to be alone. He turned down the lights in the apartment, making a more romantic ambiance, then stood behind Amanda and wrapped his arms around her. "Thank you for hanging out with us today."

"I had fun. Emily is so sweet. She's really well behaved, and I just love her little giggles."

He loved her giggles too. "She adores you, you know."

"I adore her."

He moved his mouth to her ear and whispered, "Marry me."

Her lips parted slightly, hoping she heard him correctly. "What did you say?"

Bruce reached into his pocket and pulled out a diamond ring, holding it in front of her. "Will you marry me?" he asked again, swallowing the lump in his throat.

With tears in her eyes, she lifted her chin so they were face to face. "Of course I will."

He kissed her then carefully slid the ring on her finger. "I love you, Amanda."

"I love you."

In the middle of the night, Bruce rolled over and tucked his hand under the pillow. With his other hand, he reached out to Mandy and snuggled in behind her.

She let out a content sigh. "Bruce?"

"Hmm?" he said, still half asleep.

"Were you serious when you asked me to marry you?"

"Were you serious when you gave me your answer?"

"Yes."

"Good. Then go back to sleep." He yawned and nuzzled in closer.

"When do you want to get married?"

As much as he loved discussing this with her, two o'clock in the morning was not the most ideal time to do it. All he wanted to do was sleep. "We can pick a date tomorrow if you want."

But Mandy couldn't sleep. She was too excited. "We have a lot to do to plan our ceremony."

He rubbed his heavy eyes. "I know you're excited about this; am I too. But do we have to discuss this right now?"

"I'm sorry. I'm keeping you awake, aren't I?"

"Yes, and I have to work in the morning," he reminded her.

She didn't want to disturb him, so she crawled out of bed, put on her robe, and crept out of the room, lightly closing the door behind her.

In the morning, Bruce slipped on a pair of pajama bottoms and trudged into the kitchen. His overly cheerful girlfriend was sitting at the table sipping on a cup of tea and watching the morning news. "Morning," he grumbled. His eyelids sagged and his hair was disheveled.

"You look tired. Did you not sleep well?"

He pulled the coffee out of the cupboard and began to prepare a pot. "Someone decided she wanted to talk at two o'clock in the morning."

"I'm sorry."

"It's alright. A good cup of coffee and a shower will wake me up." While the coffee brewed, he sat at the table with her. He took a deep breath to get the oxygen moving then reached over and held her hand. "I did hear what you said last night, and the two of us will sit down and discuss a date today. I'll look at my schedule. But right now I need to get ready for work." He moved her hand up to his lips and kissed it then returned to the kitchen to pour himself a cup of coffee. "I'm meeting with a couple of patients, and I have a surgery scheduled this morning. You have appointments today?"

"All day. First one is at 9:00. I'm doing a circumcision this morning," she stated.

Bruce flinched at that thought. "That's glorious. Thank you so much for putting that image in my head. Keep your scalpel away from me."

She tittered at his reaction. "I should be done by four or so."

"Good." He reached into the fridge and pulled out the coffee creamer. "Will you do me a favor?"

"What do you need?"

"Can you pick Emily up from daycare and take her to ballet when you get off?"

"Sure."

"Thanks. Hopefully I won't be too late."

"What surgeries do you have today?" she asked.

"I have a patient with a low-grade brain glioma on the left parietal lobe. I need to take care of that resection this morning."

"Is that complicated?"

"It's a four or five hour procedure." Now with caffeine in his system, Bruce sat back down. "And this afternoon, I need to run an MRI on another patient whose been having chronic headaches and dizziness. As long as no emergencies come up, I shouldn't be too late."

But he spoke too soon. While he was studying the MRI images, a patient was wheeled into the ER with a ruptured aneurysm that needed immediate attention. Bruce was called downstairs, which meant he would be staying late.

By the time he got home, it was almost 9:00 P.M., and Mandy had already put Emily to bed. An intense feeling of guilt swept over him for leaving Mandy alone with his daughter all night. He set his stethoscope, keys, and cellphone on the table and tried to justify his tardiness. "Sorry I'm so late. We had an emergency that came up and I…"

She didn't let him finish. "Don't ever apologize for doing your job, Buckman."

He stared at her, surprised by her reaction. He expected her to be upset with him, but she wasn't. "You're not mad?"

"Why would I be mad?"

"Because it's almost nine o'clock and I'm just getting home. I asked you to get Emmy for me, not expecting to be gone this long. You got stuck here dealing with her."

Mandy knew why he said that. His ex-wife would have been angry. "I understand emergency situations.

I'm not going to get angry with you for trying to save someone's life."

"But she's my daughter. She's my responsibility, not yours."

Mandy rose to her feet. "If I'm going to be your wife then you need to let me be a mother to your children."

"And I want you to be," he stated. "But I shouldn't shove it in your face and force it on you like that."

"You didn't know you were going to be this late. It's not your fault." To offer reassurance, she tenderly kissed him. "Emily and I had fun tonight. We played with dolls and colored and got to know each other better. We had a good time." He had a discouraged look on his face and his mood tonight was far from cheerful. She could see that something was bothering him. "What is it?"

"It's just…" he sighed. "Are you sure you want to get involved with this?"

She hoped he wasn't having second thoughts about proposing to her. "What are you trying to say?"

"This is how it is, Mandy. This is my life. I'm a neurosurgeon. There aren't many of us around, which means I have to stay late or come in at inopportune moments. Some days my schedule gets pretty sticky. I don't want to lose you over things I can't control." The thought of losing Amanda made Bruce teary-eyed. His heart felt heavy and he had a difficult time controlling his emotions

"Sweetheart, look at me." She touched his face with her hands. "I understand that work schedules and life-threatening situations happen. There are times when I have emergencies come up and I have to stay late too. I'm in your shoes, I know how it is. You keep forgetting that. I dissected a cadaver with you. We both drank too much caffeine and were sleep deprived together when we pulled all-night study sessions. When you had to work double shifts in an ER rotation, I did it too. When resident doctors humiliated you with their needless pimping, I experienced that right alongside you. We took the same exams, sat through the same courses, went through the same crap. I know what you've been through. I know what it takes. Yes, Bruce, you are a neurosurgeon, and a damn good one. But you've worked hard for that distinction. This is what you've always dreamed of, and I will be by your side to dream it and live it with you."

Mandy had a valid point. There were times when her schedule was just as crazy as his. She truly understood what the life of a physician was like because she was one. Hearing these words from her eased his mind. "You know, you're right. You have always shared my accomplishments and my griefs…and the lovely smell of formaldehyde." He put his arms around her waist and looked her in the eye. "Thank you for always being here for me."

"I always will be."

"Daddy, lookie," Nathan said, holding up an orange Goldfish cracker. "Fishie!"

"Is that good?" Randy asked him.

"Uh huh." He stuck the cracker in his mouth.

Gripping a steaming cup of coffee in his hand, Randy waked to the table where his son was sitting. "You want to go fishing with me and Grandpa today, Buddy?"

Nathan bounced in his chair. "Yay! Me go on boat!"

"Finish up your crackers and drink your milk first. Daddy's gonna get some snacks ready for us."

"You bring cookies?" Nathan asked, hoping his dad would bring a few along.

"Yes, I can bring some Oreos."

Overhearing this conversation, Jane said, "You've made him into a cookie junkie."

"He loves those things. But don't worry, Honey, I'll make sure he eats a good lunch and drinks all of his juice."

"I know you will." She grazed her hand across his chest.

"Bruce called this morning and you'll never guess what he told me."

"What?" she asked curiously.

"He and Mandy are engaged."

Jane moved her hand up to her mouth and gasped. "Are you serious?"

"Yup, but don't tell Stephanie. He doesn't want her to know. If she finds out, she'll probably show up at the wedding uninvited."

"Why would she do that?"

"To make a scene," Randy boldly declared. "He has a lot of exciting things happening in June. He's finishing his residency, he and Mandy are getting married, and he's starting a new job. June is going to be a busy month for them."

"Are they going on a honeymoon?"

"They only have a week available, but he's thinking about taking her to Hawaii."

"When are you taking me to Hawaii?"

He put his arms around her and replied, "Maybe you'd like to go to Hawaii for our anniversary next year instead of Bermuda."

"Can we?"

"I can certainly arrange that, Mrs. Hanson. I would love to relax on the beach holding you in my arms under the warm Hawaiian sun. We'll eat pineapple and share tropical drinks together. I'll even give you a lei under the stars," he hinted as he bowed his eyebrows suggestively.

"You are so bad."

"And you love every minute of it." He closed his eyes and kissed her, pulling her closer to him as their embrace intensified.

Nathan stared them down with his face all scrunched up.

Randy broke away from Jane and saw the dirty look their son was giving them. "What's the matter with you?" he asked, wondering why his son was glaring at them like that.

"You kissie Mommy. That my Mommy."

Jane desperately tried not to laugh. "See, look what you did."

"I didn't do anything," Randy said, trying to defend himself. "I kissed my wife. That is not a crime."

"Nathan got a little jealous there I think. He doesn't like your hands all over me."

"Well, that's too bad. He better deal with it because I'm kissing my wife." He kissed her again.

"No, Daddy!" Nathan scolded.

Jane tried to maintain a straight face as she stepped into the other room to take care of one of the twins.

Randy explain to his young son, "I can kiss Mommy, Nathan. She's my wife."

Nathan didn't see how it was possible for his mommy to be anything except his mother. "Mommy you wife?"

"Yes. She's a wife, a mommy, a psychologist, a basketball coach, a sister, and a daughter. She has a lot of jobs."

Nathan understood jobs. "Daddy doctor."

"That's right, but Daddy has other jobs too. I'm a husband and a daddy and a son and a big brother. Daddy also teaches medical students."

"Me have job?" the child asked his father.

"Well, yeah. You're a son and a big brother like me, and you're Daddy's little helper."

"Me be doctor too," Nathan confidently declared.

Hearing Nathan say that made Randy smile. If Nathan wanted to pursue that dream, Randy would support him all the way. "You can be whatever you want to be. You about ready to go fishing, little man?"

"Me catch big fishie." Nathan spread his hands out wide to show his father how big his fish was going to be.

"I hope you do, Buddy. Finish up so we can go."

On April first, Mandy stepped out of the car with Bruce, questioning him about something that bothered her. "How come you always go out of your way to pick up the girls and bring them back to Seattle? Shouldn't Stephanie be making the trip to L.A. to make exchanges too?"

"Technically, yes."

"Then why doesn't she?"

"She says she doesn't have the money."

This didn't make any sense. "But you said Randy was paying her well now, and you give her a hefty check every month. What does she do with it?"

"I don't know," Bruce replied. "Pisses it away most likely."

Amanda didn't understand why Bruce didn't seem to care about this. "She's supposed to be using it for your girls, Bruce."

"Honestly, Mandy, I really don't give a shit what she uses it for. As long as my girls are getting what they need, I'm happy." He looked over at the car. "Confrontations with Stephanie can get ugly. I don't know if you want to witness this. You might want to wait in the car."

"I'm going to be by your side to support you, Buckman."

Reluctantly, Bruce agreed to let her stay.

When Stephanie answered the door, she looked around as if she had lost something. "Where's Emily?"

Bruce told her, "She's spending the weekend with Mandy's parents."

"Mandy's parents?" Stephanie snarled, appalled that Bruce had the nerve to leave their daughter with someone she didn't trust. "Mandy is not their mother, and her parents are not family. What right do they have to spend the weekend with Emily?"

Annoyed by her attitude, Bruce gritted his teeth. "You know, I really don't want to have this debate with you again. Please get Alyssa so we can go."

"Well excuse me, Doctor." She fetched Alyssa's belongings and handed the child over to Bruce.

"You're going to have to come down and get the girls in June," he said.

"Why?"

"Because I won't have time. I'm finishing up my residency and preparing for a new job. You are going to have to fly down to L.A. to pick them up."

She gave him an evil glare. "Oh, great. Now I have to drop everything to work around your schedule?"

Bruce retorted, "I have always picked up the girls and brought them back to you. I take my vacation time to do that. I am going to be busy in June and I will not be able to use my vacation time to bring the girls to you. You are going to have to take the initiative to get down to L.A. and get your daughters. You cannot rely on me to do that all the time. I have a life."

"Yeah, a life with your bimbo doctor girlfriend," Stephanie scowled at Mandy with a wicked sneer.

Mandy drew back, shocked that Stephanie held her in such contempt.

Bruce was not about to tolerate Stephanie's disrespectful disparagement. He shot her and angry fixed stare. "That was rude and very inconsiderate. I will not allow you to badmouth Amanda like that. When are you going to act like a grown up and be a responsible human being?"

She dropped her jaw. "Did you just tell me to grow up?"

"Yes. You are a spoiled brat. Why do you insist that the whole damn world revolve around you? Get your head out of the clouds and look reality in the face, Steph. Life doesn't come served on a silver platter." He slowly trailed away.

"Bruce," Stephanie called to him.

He ignored her.

"Bruce," she howled again. "Don't walk away from me."

But he didn't turn around. He buckled Alyssa into the car and drove away.

As they headed down the road, Mandy stared at Bruce, a bit concerned over what she witnessed. "That was…interesting."

"I told you not go up there with me. I knew it was gonna get ugly."

"Is she always like that?"

He simply replied, "Yes. All the damn time."

"What a snob."

"That's a nice word for her. Not my word of choice, however." He tried to hide his frustration with a smile. "Let's go home." Together they returned to L.A. to prepare for the last weeks of his residency, a new job, and their wedding.

Chapter Sixty

In preparation for another busy week with patients, Stephanie read over the appointment calendar. Both Randy and her father were booked solid all week. She double checked the surgery schedule and on-call statuses for both of them and noticed a discrepancy. "Randy?"

Randy reached over the counter for a pen, scribbling on a note pad to make sure it worked. It was out of ink. He put it back and tried another one. "How come none of the pens around here work? This is a medical facility. You would think we would have properly working writing utensils."

Stephanie ignored his remark and went straight to the point. "Why is Dad covering your on-call status Saturday?"

"Jane and I are going out of town this weekend."

"Where you going?"

"Down to Santa Monica for a wedding."

Sticking her nose where it didn't belong, Stephanie asked, "Who's getting married?"

Randy opted not to answer.

But he didn't have to. She was able to put the pieces together herself. "It's Bruce, isn't it?"

Randy turned his eyes to her. "Yes, it is."

"That's why he wanted me to go down to L.A. to pick up the girls. He was too pre-occupied with his wedding. How long have you known about this?"

"He proposed to her two months ago."

"Why didn't he bother to tell me?"

"Why does he have to tell you?" Randy's first appointment was scheduled in ten minutes. "I can't talk to you about this right now. I have patients to see." He took the working pen and returned to the back where the examination rooms were.

Friday morning, Randy and Jane dropped Nathan and the twins off at his parents' house where they would be spending the weekend. As soon as the kids were situated, they drove to the airport to catch their flight to Santa Monica.

Bruce was standing by the baggage claim waiting when the Hansons exited their flight. He greeted both of them with a hug. "Hey, Man. It's good to see you."

"You too," Randy said. "Bet you feel pretty good now that you've finally completed your residency."

Bruce flashed a huge grin. "I feel great. Start at my new clinic soon too. I'm excited about that."

"I bet you are." Randy wondered why Bruce came to the airport alone. "Where's Mandy?"

"She had a few appointments this morning," Bruce explained. "She'll be home around noon."

"Cool."

Jim and Jill were on their way down as well. Since school was out, the kids were going to spend the weekend in San Francisco with Jim's parents while he and Jill attended the wedding.

"Jim's flight is supposed to get here in an hour," Bruce said. "I figured we'd hang out here, grab a cup of coffee, and maybe eat something while we wait."

"That sounds good."

Amanda, Jill, and Jane spent the afternoon shopping and picking Sarah up from the airport while Bruce, Randy, and Jim headed to the tux shop. The tuxes Bruce picked out were simple—solid black slacks and sport coats with white shirts and black neckties.

Bruce stood with his arms spread out getting a final fitting. "Can't wait 'til eleven o'clock tomorrow."

"Third time on the altar, Man," Jim teased. "Aren't you nervous about that?"

"Jim," Randy rebuked. "Shut the fuck up. Why the hell would you say something like that?"

"It's ok, Randy," Bruce uttered. "And to answer your question, no, I'm not nervous. This is Mandy. She's the woman I was meant to be with."

"Took you long enough to figure it out," Jim said. "I've never seen a chick give a guy fuck me eyes the way she did with you. She was full-on hot for your ass, Dude. I don't know why you didn't hop on every opportunity she presented to you. Mandy's a hot blonde with some bodacious curves."

"She's also my best friend," Bruce explained. "She was a flirt from the day I met her. That's always been the nature of her personality so I didn't think anything of it."

"She only flirted with you. At least Mandy's a real blonde, unlike your ex. That woman is totally fake. Fake hair, fake nails, fake intentions."

"Hey now," Randy warned. "Watch the ex-wife bashing, Jim. She's still my sister, you know."

"I know she is, but she also ragdolled him. You told me yourself."

"I never denied that. I simply said be careful what you say because she is my sister."

A soon as they were done getting fitted for tuxes, they headed over to Amanda's beach house. The two story, four bedroom, three bath home had a large open floor plan with lots of skylights and windows to allow the sun in. Large potted plants and mini palm trees decorated the entire house. Pictures of ocean scenes covered the walls. A huge plated glass door led out to a large sundeck, and the terrace upstairs had a spectacular view of the Southern California Pacific Ocean. They could sit on the deck in lawn furniture and watch surfers, pelicans, and dolphins, feeling the energy of the ocean, the sun, and the surf. Steps led down to the sand of her own private beach, with additional miles of public beach for daily activities and exercise.

"Holy shit," Jim said as he scoped the interior of the house. "This place is fuckin' sweet."

Bruce agreed. "Welcome to Mandy's beach house. Actually it was her parents' vacation home when she was a kid, but her dad gave it to her because they don't use it anymore."

"Spoiled rotten brat," Jim said. "I wanna retire here."

Randy peeked out the sliding glass door at the amazing ocean view. The waves lapped on the shore and the palm tree by the deck swayed in the breeze. "Wow! This is nice."

"Yes it is," Bruce said. "I'm in the process of moving all my stuff over here and setting up the girl's rooms. That way, when Emily gets back, she'll have her own space. There's some guest beds up there right now, so take your pick, gentlemen."

"Dude," Jim said, still in awe over the view this place offered. "This is badass. Give me a hammock, some coconut oil, a surfboard, and an umbrella-shaped margarita and I'm chillaxin'. This is my modus operandi."

Even though Randy had been around Jim long enough to understand the majority of his surfer slang, this was one phrase he had never heard before. "Your what?"

"Surfer heaven, Bro."

Randy replied, "Since we're in surfer heaven, why don't you quit boasting about how you're rippin', get on a surfboard, and learn how to ride the damn thing."

Bruce laughed at Randy's facetious comeback. "You know, he has a point, Jim. People who take surf lesson here are standing their first time out."

This confirmed Randy's point.

Trying to entice Jim further, Bruce added, "The lessons are two hours, all equipment included. You could catch one tomorrow afternoon."

Both Bruce and Randy saw the gears spinning in Jim's head. He always wanted to learn how to surf. This was the perfect opportunity.

"Sweet," Jim said with a huge grin. "I may have to do that."

"You all brought your suits, right?" Bruce asked.

"Of course," Randy said. "Don't go to the beach without it."

"Bruce," Mandy's voice trailed from the other room. "I see your truck parked out front. Are you guys here?"

Sarah and Jane filed in behind Mandy. When Sarah saw the whole clan together, she screeched and ran over to Randy with open arms.

Randy squeezed her with a bear hug while they exchanged pleasantries. "How have you been?"

"Doing well." Sarah stood back. "You look great. How are those new babies?"

"Growing and gaining weight every day."

Sarah spread her arms out to Jim. "It's been way too long, Dr. Ryan. It's good to see you."

"It's good to see you too."

Thrilled to have all of his friends gathered in one location, Bruce chimed in, "Now that everyone's here, who wants to go out on the beach?"

"Count me in," Jim responded.

For sleeping arrangements, Sarah planned to crash on the sofa leaving the two guestrooms for the couples. Jim and Randy raced upstairs and debated over the two available rooms. One had a large window with a fabulous view of the ocean. The other had a bigger bed and a private bathroom, but the window was facing the street.

"I get the room with a view," Randy said.

"The hell you do."

To diplomatically solve this problem, Randy suggested, "Rock, paper, scissors for it."

"You're on," Jim agreed.

They both made a fist and counted, "One, two, three." Jim's paper smothered Randy's rock.

"Ha, Chump," Jim teased. "We get the ocean view."

"But Jane and I get the bigger bed," he said with a smirk. "More fun for me."

The couples claimed their spaces then everyone put on their swimsuits and shuffled out to the beach.

The Santa Monica beach, with its clear sky and light winds, was full of diversity. It was an international mecca for the surfing culture. Nestled on the vast and open Santa Monica Bay, this Southern California tourist area enjoyed an average of 325 days of sunshine a year. Temperatures in June reached the mid-eighties. Morning fog and haze, caused by ocean temperature variations and currents, were a common phenomenon. During the month of June, the overcast skies kept the beach cool, even when other parts of Los Angeles enjoyed warmer temperatures. Breezes blowing in from the ocean circulated the air, therefore smog was less of a problem for Santa Monica than elsewhere around Los Angeles.

Randy and Jane playfully frolicking around in the water, splashing each other. Jim and Jill sat on lawn chairs drinking Coronas with lime, and Sarah sunbathed on a nearby beach towel. Bruce and Mandy leaned back on a blanket watching everyone. "It's good to see the gang together again," Bruce remarked.

"It is. And the best thing is, no one is stressed from school."

Bruce gazed out at the water's edge right as Randy and Jane embraced in a kiss. "Married life has been good to him, and he really enjoys being a father."

Mandy touched Bruce's face to get him to look at her. "Sounds like another man I know."

Lounging on the beach in his shades, shark tooth necklace, and a pair of baggy tropical print swim shorts, Jim said, "You know what, Honeybun? I think I'm gonna try my hand at surfin' while we're down here."

Jill questioned this statement. "You can't be serious."

"Why not? We're not in a hurry to get back. I would love to grind some waves."

"You're actually going to take Randy's advice and learn how to surf?"

"Hell yeah," he replied. "I've always wanted to, you know that. I have the time and the opportunity, so I'm gonna give it a shot. The big mama is gonna be fully mackin' some gnarly grinders." He flashed the shaka symbol at her. "Total Karma, Baby."

She thought he had lost his mind. "I have no idea what you just said."

He kicked back in the lounge chair and sipped from his beer bottle. "Man, this is livin'. Laidback mode, enjoyin' the sand and the surf. Life doesn't get much better than this."

When the sun sat lower in the sky, everyone gathered around the deck. Bruce fired up the grill and they partook in barbecued chicken and fresh tossed salad. The seven friends talked for hours as the sun slowly sank behind the Santa Monica mountains.

With the ceremony being held on Mandy's sundeck, the house buzzed in the morning. The noise woke Randy up. Jane wasn't in bed and her towel hung over the rack in the bathroom. Apparently she had already showered and gotten dressed.

Since sleeping through all this racket was impossible, Randy decided to get up. He grabbed a clean towel and hopped in the shower.

When he got downstairs, everyone seemed occupied with some sort of 'set up' chore. Several people ran around setting up tables and chairs, arranging flowers, and preparing food for the guests. Bruce was at the kitchen counter fiddling with a camera. Randy walked over to him and said, "Good morning."

Bruce looked up. "Good morning."

"Busy place this morning. Who are all these people?"

"Mandy's family. One of her sisters owns a catering company so she and her staff are getting situated. Her other sister is a beautician and offered to do Mandy's hair for her. She's setting up in the other room ."

A pretty blonde woman Randy had never seen before came inside from the back deck. "Bruce?"

Bruce turned his head. "Yes?"

"I called the minister. He said he'd be here by 10:45."

"Great, thanks."

"Mom and some of your friends are outside setting up flowers," she confirmed. "The champagne is chilling in the refrigerator, Dad's picking up the cake, and as soon as I get all the food prepped, I'll start on the punch."

"Thanks, Tiffani."

She left the room and returned to her duties.

Randy looked at Bruce, curious about this woman. "Who was that?"

"Mandy's sister," he answered. "Well, one of her sisters. She has six."

"Have you seen Jane?"

Bruce pointed toward the deck. "She's outside."

"Thanks." Randy moseyed that direction. Rows of foldup chairs lined the beach. Pretty yellow and white flower arrangements sat on an elevated platform where the bride and groom would exchange vows. Jane was placing yellow rose bouquets on tables. "Good morning, Baby."

"Hey, Sleepyhead."

"Why didn't you wake me up when all these people started showing up?" he asked. "Everyone's helping out and I was still in bed."

"We have everything under control. Besides, aren't you Bruce's Best Man?"

"Yes."

"Then you should be with him, not setting up flowers." She kissed him and returned to her flower duties.

Randy hollered down to the beach at Jim, who was wading in the water. "Yo, Ryan! Come up here!"

Jim ran up to see what Randy wanted. "Sup?"

"Let's take Bruce and get some coffee. Get him out of here for a while."

"Sounds like a plan. Let me slip on some shoes and snag my wallet."

The three men had a fun conversation over coffee. Bruce was in extremely high spirits. He didn't seem nervous at all.

"You know," Randy said. "For a man who's getting married in less than an hour, you are amazingly solid."

Bruce took a sip of his coffee. As he swallowed, he made a repulsed face. "Solid like this coffee sludge." He set the cup down and chose not to drink it. "Actually, I feel great," he admitted. "I'm marrying my best friend today."

"You shoulda married her from the start and avoided all the bullshit you endured," Jim remarked.

"I should have. Just took me a while to figure it out."

"Too damn long, if you ask me."

Randy interjected his two cents worth, "I'm glad you wised up and are marrying the right woman for the right reasons."

"Mandy is amazing," Bruce said. "And her family is incredible. They've adopted my girls and have supported both of us tremendously. I've never been so happy."

Randy could tell. Bruce couldn't stop smiling. "That's great."

Amanda looked stunning in her strapless white gown that tied behind her neck. Her hair was up in a simple twist, held in place by a yellow flowered hair comb. Her makeup was simple, a touch of eyeshadow and light pink lipstick that highlighted her pretty features. The small yellow roses and delicate white baby's breath bouquet she held in her hand was fragrant and feminine, just like Mandy always was.

Bruce was freshly shaven with his mustache neatly trimmed. He had a small yellow rose boutonnière pinned to the lapel of his tux. He stood proud at the altar, alongside his best friends, as he and Amanda exchanged wedding vows. It was obvious they were in love. The way they looked into each other's eyes and the smiles they wore on their faces brought tears to the eyes of many guests. This was a long-awaited, well overdue event.

When Dr. Bruce Michael Buckman and Dr. Amanda Renee Stevens were pronounced husband and wife, Randy was truly touched. He even felt a tear or two come to his eye. As they joined together to seal their union, he witnessed the most heartfelt kiss he had ever seen. They were the perfect pair, and the ceremony, although simple, was one of the most beautiful weddings Randy had ever attended. It was truly a joyous occasion.

Friends and family members mingled for a lunch of finger sandwiches, fresh fruits and vegetables, various cheeses, and a huge bowl of pink punch. It was festive and rather refreshing in the warm summer heat. Champagne bottles quickly cracked open celebrating the happy couple, who had been glued to each other's side since they said 'I do'.

The intense expression on Randy's face drew Jane over to him. "Deep thoughts there, Doctor?"

"It's good to see Bruce smiling. He's living it up in a beach bungalow in sunny California with a loving, supportive woman. He's happy, and he deserves to be. He's a great guy."

"They've been inseparable all day."

Randy reached his arm across Jane's shoulders. "They've always been inseparable. They're going to be very happy together." Randy stood and watched the newlyweds. Bruce held Amanda in his arms and mouthed the words, I love you, in his new wife's ear before he released her for the first time all day. "I'm gonna go talk to him for a minute," Randy declared. "Be right back." He parted from his wife and sauntered over to Bruce. Holding a glass of champagne in his hand, he said, "Life is looking pretty damn good for you, my friend."

Bruce admired the gold band on his finger. "Never been so proud in my life to wear a ring as I am to wear this one."

Randy put his hand on Bruce's shoulder. "Congratulations."

"Thank you."

With the rising of the sun, the bride and groom took off for a week in Hawaii. Jane and Randy turned in all the tuxes then spent the remainder of the afternoon at the Santa Monica Pier. They took a ride on the giant Ferris wheel and got a bird's-eye view of the surrounding beaches, ocean, and coastal mountains. After exploring the culture the pier had to offer, they ate dinner at a seafood restaurant before they checked into a hotel to get a good night's sleep.

When they returned to Seattle to pick up their kids, Randy's mom looked like she hadn't slept in days. Her hair was disheveled and her blouse was on crooked. "I don't know how you and Jane have the stamina to keep up with an active two-year-old and two infants, Randy. I've only had them for three days and I'm exhausted."

Randy found this situation amusing. "Some days are like that. Nathan does have a lot of energy."

"He is one busy little boy."

When Nathan heard Randy's voice, he ran to his father as fast as he could. "Daddy!"

"Hey, little man." Randy picked up the child and hugged him. "Did you have a good time at Grandma and Grandpa's house?"

"Me go in boat. Gampie buyed doughnuts," the child said with wide eyes.

"Grandpa bought doughnuts?"

The child nodded. "Uh huh. Me eated some."

"Yum." Randy asked mother, "How was he?"

"He was well-behaved and such a good helper. He helped Grandpa with yardwork outside."

"Good. That's what I like to hear," Randy said, proud of the way his son behaved. "You ready to go home, Buddy?"

"Uh huh."

They buckled all the kids up in their car seats and drove home.

The following week, Jim spotted Randy down at the hospital cafeteria. "Yo, Hanson," Jim called to his best friend.

Randy joined him at the table. "You guys get back last night?"

"Yup."

"You finally get on a damn surfboard?"

"Yup. Dude, we had a blast in Santa Monica. Nothin' like chillin' on the beach with my baggies, a board, and my babe. It was totally rippin'. I'm gonna buy a board and find a place around here to surf. I'm hooked."

Randy took a sip of his coffee. "Are you the king of the waves now?"

"Master of the waves. And as much as I love the action in the ER, I'll take sand over sutures any day of the week."

Randy noticed a new accessory to Jim's attire—a woven blend of tiny black, tan, and white beads on cord-wrapped leather. "Nice wares. Souvenir from Santa Monica?"

"Actually a guy I was surfin' with gave it to me. Total guru. He could ride the sickest pit I've ever seen." Jim stuck his straw in his drink and took a sip. "He totally got cactus juiced though. Came down from a six-foot floater and landed with his leg in a twisted position. Tore the meniscus in his right knee."

Randy cringed thinking about that. "Ouch. Damn."

"He couldn't stand up, was in hellacious pain, and his knee was totally swellin' up, but he tried to get back on his board."

"That's crazy," Randy proclaimed.

"Yeah, it is. Needless to say I couldn't watch him do that. I informed him I was a doctor and explained to him the seriousness of his injury. I was finally able to get him to plant back down in the sand and get his weight off his knee. I had someone run and get some ice while Jill snagged my first aid kit and called an ambulance. She and I worked to immobilize his leg 'til EMS came and took him to the hospital. Made a few friends out on the beach that day and the dude gave me his necklace. For the rest of the afternoon, his crew called me Doc Cooleo."

Randy laughed. "Doc Cooleo. That's funny. He's going to have some serious knee problems."

"Well, he certainly won't be shreddin' the waves like he used to after that gnarly wipeout."

"No kidding." Randy set his cup on the table. "ER slow today?"

"Been busy as hell actually, but we had a slight slowdown and I needed to get somethin' in my stomach. The resident docs and PAs can handle what's in there right now. No action at the moment." Jim managed to eat some of his food before he heard, "Dr. Ryan report to the ER, STAT. Dr. Ryan to the ER, please." He smirked, clearly unimpressed. "Dammit. Never fails. As soon as I sit down to eat, I get a damn STAT call."

"Sorry, Bud," Randy said, offering sympathy.

Jim grabbed his food and quickly tossed it in a 'to go' bag to munch on when he had time. "I'll call you later, Dude."

"Later."

Jim darted off, and Randy finished his cup of coffee before reporting for his next scheduled surgery.

Chapter Sixty-One

August first, Bruce and Amanda flew up to Seattle to bring Emily home. Bruce sent her out to the rental car with Mandy so he could talk to Stephanie alone. He reached into his pocket and handed her a check. "Here's your check for the month."

She stared at the wedding ring on his finger. "You know, I love how you took the time to tell me that you were getting married. You didn't even send me an invitation."

"Because I did not want you there."

Stephanie jeered at Mandy with a callous frown.

Bruce found her negativity and evil demeanor offensive. "Stop it."

"Stop what?"

"Don't sneer at her like that. What did Mandy ever do to you?"

"She has no right barging in on my family, trying to raise my kids."

"They're my kids too," Bruce reminded her. "And Amanda is very good with them. She gets down on the floor and plays with them and looks out for their best interests. She attends all of Emily's ballet recitals and even works with the girls on manners and helps them learn responsibility. She's a great mom."

"She is not their mother."

He explained, "She has taken on the role of being a parent when she didn't have to, and she does it with open arms."

"Well, goody for Ms. Perfect." Stephanie turned her nose up.

"You know nothing about her. I, however, have known Amanda for twelve years. She's honest, compassionate, and goes out of her way to help others. You, on the other hand, are a liar and a deceiver and don't give a shit about anyone except yourself. Just because you have a problem with Mandy doesn't mean the girls do. She is very much a mother to them, and I have every intention of making sure she is treated as such, respected as such, and that the girls refer to her as such. You damn well better not put negative thoughts into their heads either."

"Now why would I do that?"

Her condescending attitude and threatening words were more than Bruce was willing to tolerate. "You better back the hell off my wife."

"Or what?"

His hand tightened into a fist and his mouth set in a hard line. He hurried away to the car, leaving Stephanie to wallow in her own self-pity.

He sat behind the wheel for a minute, fuming. Veins popped out of his neck and his jaw tightened. He gripped the steering wheel so hard, Mandy thought he was going to break it off.

"Everything ok?"

He clenched his teeth and took a few cleansing breaths to calm down. "Everything's fine." He turned on the ignition, put the car in drive, and pulled into the street.

Mandy knew he was lying. "No it's not, Buckman. What happened?"

"I'll tell you later. I don't want to discuss it in front of Emily."

Mandy understood. Bruce was always good about not discussing grownup issues in front of the girls. She left him to stew a bit, hoping the drive back to the hotel and being with Emily would brighten his mood.

The Hansons had a family barbecue at Mark and Ellen's house that weekend. Randy and Jane showed up with their three kids. Stephanie came with Alyssa. Robby stopped by with Evie. The entire Ryan family made their appearance as well.

While the kids played in the sand, swam in the lake, and entertained themselves with toys, the adults all sat on the deck sipping on Coronas. In the middle of a conversation, Stephanie unexpectedly blurted out, "Bruce's wife is a bitch."

Jim's head swung to the right, outraged by that blatant disrespect. "Excuse me?"

Randy interjected, "Keep your mouth shut, Steph."

"Why?" she insisted on knowing.

"Because. Not only is Mandy Bruce's wife, she also happens to be a friend of mine. Back off."

Stephanie didn't heed his advice. "What right does she have to invade my turf?"

"Your turf?" Randy questioned. "What the hell are you talking about?"

"She's caring for my children, spending my money, has stolen my name, and is sharing a bed with my ex-husband. She's a thief."

"For Christ sake, Stephanie. Get a grip," Randy said. "Mandy didn't do anything to you."

"She doesn't deserve to have the name Buckman."

Stephanie's harsh tone infuriated Jim. He could no longer contain his opinion. "You never should have had the name Buckman in the first place. All you did was wear the name as a fuckin' status symbol. You stole Bruce's money, took his kids away from him, and lied to his face. Mandy would never do any of those things. She's a hellatiously cool chick who doesn't have an ounce of selfishness in her blood. You have no right to talk about her like that. Looks to me like you're the one who's bein' the bitch."

How dare Jim say such a thing to her. She glared at him and shouted, "Go to hell!"

"Hey," Randy interceded. "Don't talk to Jim like that."

Mark overheard this bickering going on between his children and immediately put a stop to it. "Stephanie Lynn, keep your personal opinions to yourself. That was not necessary. We are all family here and you will not denote any negative connotations toward anyone in this family, do you hear me?"

"Bruce doesn't belong in this family anymore, does he?" Stephanie argued. "And that woman never will."

Insulted that Stephanie had the gall to say things like that about his friends, Randy blew up a her. "You have a serious attitude problem. Don't badmouth my friends. They're good people, honest and caring individuals who are hardworking and dedicated doctors. They deserve your respect. I don't see your life all punch and cookies, so what gives you the right to be dissin' anyone else? The world does not revolve around you, Miss Snooty Pants, so get your stuck-up nose out of your ass and get over it already."

"Randal," Mark said. "That's enough."

"She started it."

"And you're going to end it," Mark insisted. "Now."

Randy didn't want to be around Stephanie anymore. He picked up his bottle of Corona, stood up, and moved down to the beach to get away from her. Jim was right behind him.

Mark shook his head at his daughter, outraged by her actions. "Stephanie, what is wrong with you?"

"What?" she asked, acting as if she didn't know.

"Never again are you to make derogatory comments about the people who are close to this family. That was extremely rude." He glared at her with fire in his eyes. "You owe Jim and Randy an apology."

While Mark was talking to his daughter, Jim and Randy had a conversation of their own. "Damn, Dude. Your sister is a cold, heartless bitch," Jim said.

"She can be sometimes. I hate it when she acts like that."

"What the fuck was that all about?"

"Bruce and Mandy came up here earlier this week to pick up Emily. Stephanie made some spiteful comments about Mandy and Bruce almost lost it."

"I don't blame him," Jim concurred. "I'd be pissed too if someone spouted off mean shit about my wife."

"I think Stephanie is beginning to regret all the bad decisions she made as far as Bruce is concerned." Randy leaned back in the sand and took a sip of his beer. "She sees how happy he is, and the girls love being with him. She's jealous as hell. But instead of dealing with it and admitting she screwed up, like a mature adult would do, she rags on Mandy instead."

"Dude, Mandy is awesome. I'm so glad Bruce married her."

"As am I." From the corner of his eye, Randy saw his sister making her way toward them. "Great, what does she want now?" he scorned.

Stephanie sat in the sand opposite them. "I'm sorry, guys."

Randy stared at her for a minute before he said, "That wasn't nice."

"I know. I'm sorry. I shouldn't have said that."

Randy teased her a little, "Guess being married to a neurosurgeon isn't sounding so bad now, is it? You could have had all that, you know, if you would have been honest and treated Bruce with respect."

She looked down at the sand, sulking. "I know."

"And you do know it's not Amanda's fault that you don't, right?" he asked, expecting her to admit it.

"Yes."

"Ok. Then leave her alone." Trying to ease the tension, he suggested, "What do you say we go for another round of skiing?"

"I think that's a great idea."

Randy turned to Jim, wanting his input. "Dr. Ryan? You up for another run?"

"Absolutely, Bro."

Randy hopped up, dusted the sand off himself, and the three of them went out to the boat to get ready for another round of water skiing.

Chapter Sixty-Two

The Emergency Room at Swedish Medical Center was the most efficient ER Jim ever had the privilege to work in. They treated more than 94,000 patients annually. Ninety-five percent of those patients were taken directly to a treatment room and never had to sit in the waiting room. Twenty-four hours a day, emergency physicians were available to address patients' questions.

Jim and Jill were both on duty when an ambulance pulled up. The woman lying on the gurney held her stomach, complaining of feeling faint and having severe, sharp, and sudden pain in the lower abdominal area.

"Get an EKG on this patient, Ox, BP, saline IV initiated, STAT!" Jim ordered.

The crew promptly responded.

"Jill!" he hollered.

She and Jim worked together so well that she knew exactly what he wanted. "I got it." She immediately started blood work on this patient.

Jim found out from this patient's husband that she had recently tested positive on a home pregnancy test. Two lives were at stake here, which gravely complicated things. He decided to call in a specialist. "Get Randy Hanson on the phone."

This patient's skin turned clammy and pale and her breathing became shallow. He checked her vitals.

Blood pressure dropping. Pulse rapid and weak. Body temperature below normal. This situation grew more and more serious. Every second was crucial. "She's going into shock, people. Get her stabilized, now." His medical team seemed to be operating in slow motion today. The fact that things were moving at snail's pace made Jim quickly lose his patience. "Time is something we don't have here." Jim hooked her up to an IV while his team raised her legs, gave her oxygen, and worked to keep the woman warm. Fluids were given intravenously and they monitored her heartrate and blood pressure on an EKG.

Finally stabilized, Jim proceeded to examine the patient, checking pupil dilation, feeling her abdomen for signs of internal bleeding, and looking for injuries. "Where's my OB consultant?" he asked. "I needed Hanson ten minutes ago."

"Ringing now, Doctor."

Randy was at his clinic typing up some information on a patient file when he received the call. "Dr. Hanson."

Jim's voice rang out, "Randy, get over here!"

"What's going on?"

"A 26-year-old female with extreme abdominal pain. She's feeling faint, dizziness, pelvic area tender, probably some internal bleeding there. Husband says she tested positive for pregnancy. She's showing symptoms of shock, but we have her stabilized."

This sounded like something he'd handled before. "Ok, get a full CBC on her and run an ultrasound. I'm on my way." Randy slipped his phone back in his pocket and darted across the street to the hospital.

When he got there, he scanned the ultrasound image they took and saw no enlargement in the uterus, but he did see a growth and abnormality on the fallopian tube. "Where's my CBC?" he asked.

Jill handed Randy the results of the blood workup. Elevated hCG hormone indicated a pregnancy, however her levels were lower than expected. Blood tests indicated signs of a hemorrhage. Randy performed a pelvic exam and ran a few tests. He conclusively diagnosed her condition as an ectopic pregnancy rupture. Rupture could lead to shock, dizziness, severe abdominal pain, and tenderness in the abdomen, all symptoms she had. This condition was life-threatening. She needed surgery and she needed it now. "Get her prepped for surgery," Randy ordered.

"What is it?" Jim asked.

"Ruptured ectopic it looks like. I'll see when I get in there."

"Damn. That's not good."

"No it's not. Could lead to infertility. Ten to fifteen percent of women who have ectopic pregnancies become infertile."

This was disappointing news. "She's so young."

The surgery was successful. Randy stopped the bleeding and was able to repair the damaged fallopian tube without having to remove it. As soon as he was finished, Jim pointed out the woman's husband, who anxiously sat in the waiting area with a worried expression on his face. Randy tread carefully into the room. "Mr. Riessler?"

When this woman's husband saw Randy enter the room dressed in scrubs, he stood up respectfully. "Yes?"

"I'm Dr. Hanson, the obstetrician who was called in for your wife."

The man shook his hand. "How is she?"

"She's still recovering from the anesthesia, but she's going to be ok."

He breathed a sigh of relief.

"Please, have a seat." Randy directed this man to a chair, taking a seat alongside him. "We confirmed her pregnancy, but it turned out to be what we call an ectopic pregnancy. Are you familiar with that?"

"No."

Randy explained it to him. "What happened was the egg implanted on the fallopian tube wall and started to grow. The problem with that is there's not enough room inside the tube for an embryo to grow. The pregnancy ruptured her tube, which caused the abdominal pain she was having. She had a lot of blood loss, but I got in there and removed the pregnancy and was able to repair the rupture."

"By remove the pregnancy you mean terminate?"

"Yes, Sir. Tubal pregnancies cannot continue. Even if it hadn't ruptured, your obstetrician would have terminated it. It's potentially life-threatening for the mother and an ectopic pregnancy never develops into a live birth," Randy explained.

"But she's alright?"

Randy reassured him. "She's fine."

"Will we be able to have children after this?" the man asked, concerned about what this all meant.

"It's pretty likely that you can still have children naturally, but if she does get pregnant again there is a chance it might be a repeated ectopic."

"And if we can't get pregnant?"

"There are options," Randy assured him. "If it comes to that, I can help you."

"Hanson is your name?" he asked.

"Yes, Randy Hanson." Randy reached into his pocket and handed this man his card. "If you have any questions or need help with anything, call me. I'm a board certified obstetrician."

Mr. Riessler took the card from him. "Thank you, Dr. Hanson. Can I see her?"

"Absolutely," Randy said. "She might be a little groggy or drift in and out of sleep for a while, but it will wear off. She's right this way, if you'll follow me." Randy led the man to his wife then stepped into the physician's locker room to remove his scrubs.

Jim caught up with him. "Nice job, Bro."

"Thanks. I've dealt with ectopics before. If caught early, an injection of methotrexate eliminates the potential problem of rupture. But if the woman doesn't suspect she's pregnant or doesn't test positive for pregnancy, it can be harder to detect. Sometimes by the time it's noticed, it's pretty large, then you can run into some serious problems."

"Bogus," Jim declared.

"Yup. Nasty shit."

On his way home from the hospital, Randy stopped at a gas station to fill up his car. He leaned against his Porsche with a gas pump in his hand and saw a familiar face walk out of the convenience store. "Dad!"

Holding a water bottle in one hand and his car keys in the other, Mark approached Randy's car. "What was up in the ER?"

"Ectopic pregnancy rupture. I was able to repair it. She's fine."

"That's good news. What are you doing Sunday afternoon?"

"Spending time with my family, washing my car, and Robby's giving me an oil change. Why?"

"Can you break away long enough to have lunch with me? I need to talk to you."

Randy screwed his gas cap back on and closed the opening. He wondered what was so important that his father felt it necessary to discuss it with him over lunch instead of just telling him now. "Sure."

"Great. Meet me at my house at 1:00 and we'll go to lunch from there. Have a good night, Son."

"You too, Dad."

Sunday morning, Randy took his family to Lake Sammamish State Park in Issaquah, Washington. The lake was active with swimmers, boats, and watercraft sports. Young people and families played volleyball and barbecued, enjoying the clear, sunny weather this Sunday offered. Aside from the many recreational activities, this picturesque 512-acre waterfront park provided deciduous forest and wetland vegetation. Jane and Randy enjoyed exploring nature along the 1.5 mile hiking trail. Nathan rode on Daddy's shoulders while the twins were lulled by the motion of Jane pushing them along in the double stroller. They witnessed all kinds of wildlife—mallard ducks swimming in the lake, a great blue heron rookery, and pretty yellow daffodils. Several squirrels gathered wares for winter and a red-headed woodpecker drilled on the trunk of a tree.

Nathan couldn't figure out what the woodpecker was doing. Being the curious little boy he was, he asked, "Why that birdie bang him head on that tree?"

"He's not banging his head on the tree," Randy explained. "He's using his beak to make a hole."

"Why?"

"He eats the bugs that live in there. That's his lunch."

Nathan curled his lip. "Yucky. Me no want to eat bugs."

"Don't worry, Buddy. You don't have to eat bugs."

They fed the kids a picnic snack and allowed Nathan some time to play on the playground before heading home.

While Nathan and the twins took their afternoon nap, Randy scooted away for a couple hours to have lunch with his father. They discussed cases, talked about fishing, and Randy shared stories about kid antics. Randy had the feeling his dad was creating small talk to avoid whatever issue he had brought him here to discuss. He stirred sugar and creamer into his coffee and eyed his father from across the table. "You said you had something you wanted to talk to me about?"

Mark filled his lungs with air and exhaled heavily, knowing what he was about to tell his son was probably going to upset him. "As you know, I turned sixty-five this year. Your mother and I would like to do some traveling and enjoy our golden years together. Over the last few months we've been discussing our future plans, and in the midst of the conversation your name and our medical practice came up quite often. You have done more for the practice than I ever imagined you would. You have gained a good reputation and made a name for yourself in the medical field. You are an outstanding doctor and more than capable of keeping the clinic going on your own."

Unsure what his father meant, Randy asked for clarification. "What are you saying? That you don't want to be in practice with me anymore?"

Mark tried to explain, "No, Randy, that is not what I'm saying. I thoroughly enjoy working with you. You are an amazing physician, and I have learned many things from you. What I'm saying is I've been practicing medicine for thirty-five years. Obstetrics is a busy profession to be in. You know that all too well. Since the day you told me you wanted to be a doctor, I have worked hard to get that clinic going so you could join me and eventually take over. I have given you the resources you needed to pursue your dreams, and you've done it quite well. I am very proud of you for that. But your mother and I want to spend some time together without having to worry about schedules or waking up in the middle of the night for an emergency call. She and I have discussed this in depth and the decision has been made. This will be my final year practicing medicine. Next summer, I'm retiring, handing the practice over to you, and I'm going to spend the remaining years of my life with my wife."

Randy shook his head, devastated that his father would abandon him like this. "I can't believe I'm hearing this from you."

"Did you honestly think I would stay in the practice forever?"

"Well no, but…" He tried to find a way to reason with his father. "I need you, Dad. Without your support I never would have made it this far. I can't do this without you."

"Yes you can. It was you who established a working, much more efficient electronic medical filing system. You're the one who opened up the practice to medical students. You've brought in many patients and maintained the ones I already had. You have won the hearts of the staff, and the patients like you. You will be just fine on your own. There's no doubt in my mind about that."

Randy refused to accept his father's words. "You can't do this to me."

"I've done my time, Randy. Now it's your time to shine."

Randy's eyes became glossy. "Dad, please."

"Find yourself another partner if you choose or practice alone. That will be your decision. But after thirty-five years, I'm ready to retire and spend time with your mother."

"What am I supposed to do?"

"Be the good doctor you've always been, bring healthy babies into the world, share your skills with others. You have more heart for this than anyone, Son. Medicine is in your blood, in your soul, it's what drives you."

Randy closed his eyes trying to hide the pain he felt. "But it's always been you and me. This is what we planned, this is what I worked so hard for."

"Yes, I know that, and believe me, this is not a spur of the moment decision. This is something your mother and I have mulled over for months now." Mark put his hand on his son's shoulder, trying to ease his uncertainty. "We have time. June 30th will be my last day."

Knowing there was nothing he could do or say to change his father's mind, Randy replied, "Yes, Sir."

The expression on Randy's face made Mark laugh. He looked like he lost a beloved pet. "Don't be so glum. Look at you. You're acting like I'm asking you to give up your life. I'm letting you live it, Son."

"I know, but it won't be same without you."

Over a romantic candlelight dinner, Randy discussed this issue with his wife. "I had a conversation with my dad today."

"About what?" she asked as she lifted her glass to her lips.

"He told me he's retiring next summer."

Jane knew he was bothered by this. The entire time Randy was in medical school, all he talked about was joining his father's medical practice. The day it finally happened, he could hardly contain his excitement. Losing this was going to be hard on him. "How do you feel about that?"

"How do you think I feel? I think it sucks. This is what Dad and I planned, what I worked so hard to achieve, and now he abandons me as if it means nothing."

"Isn't he sixty-five now?"

"So what? People work past sixty-five all the time." He gulped down his wine and took his dinner dishes to the sink. He rinsed his plate then leaned against the counter with his hands supporting his body weight. With a frown on his face, he stared down at the sink.

Jane stood up and joined him. "Sweetie," she gently placed her hand on his back. "I know you're upset, but being angry isn't going to change anything. Obviously your father has made up his mind."

"I know, but it doesn't mean I have to like it."

"No, but you do have to accept it. Try to think about this from your father's point of view."

Randy breathed a heavy sigh. "What am I supposed to do?"

To her it seemed pretty obvious. "Be the wonderful doctor you are."

After dinner clean up, Randy turned all the lights off in the house, leaving only the flickering glow of the fireplace. He took Jane's hand and led her over to the couch with him. They lounged in front of the fire enjoying the romantic ambiance.

"Randy," Jane said, noticing he was still feeling down. "Don't let this get to you so much."

"I'm trying not to. But it bugs me that he can throw all of this away and give up his career and our medical partnership so haphazardly."

"It wasn't haphazardly. I'm sure he's been contemplating it for a while."

"He said something to me that I don't understand. He said he did all of this for me. That he got the clinic going so I would have a place to practice medicine. Why would he go through all that trouble?"

She told him why. "You're his son."

"So?" he shrugged.

"You would do the same thing for Nathan and you know it."

And she was right. He would do whatever was necessary to help his son be successful.

"You're a good father, Randy, as is your dad."

Mark Hanson was a wonderful father—supportive and understanding, and a disciplinarian when he needed to be. He encouraged his children and allowed them to grow and develop into the individuals they were. When Randy was growing up, Mark Hanson spent quality time with his children, helped them with their homework, and showed up to take pictures and cheer them on at life events. He even knocked them off their pedestal occasionally, when they needed it. Randy loved the man. "I'm gonna miss him."

"He lives right down the street."

"I know, but it's not the same as looking over a patient file with him or working together on an obscure case or having him by my side when our children were born. Once he leaves the practice, I'll never be able to share those moments with him again."

"But you've shared other things with him that were just as memorable and have nothing to do with the fact that you two are medical partners."

"Like what?" he asked cynically.

"Like all the times the two of you went fishing together or the look on his face when you addressed your entire graduating class at your medical school banquet. When he stood up on that stage with you when you became a doctor, you should have seen him, Randy. He was so proud. He watched when we became husband and wife, and your dad would have been by your side when our children were born whether you were practicing medicine together or not. He's your father, and that's what fathers do for their sons."

She was right. All of those things, which meant more to him than any patient file, had nothing to do with them being working partners. It had to do with the fact that they were father and son.

"Those things won't change when he leaves," Jane reassured him. "He'll still be your father and he'll still be there for you."

He managed to crack a smile. "You never cease to amaze me. You always know exactly what to say to uplift my spirits. I've always loved that about you."

"I just want you to be happy," she replied.

"I am happy." He moved his mouth to hers and kissed her. "You know, I've been thinking. I'd like to get a car with a little more oomph. My Porsche is a nice car, but I miss sitting behind the wheel of a muscle machine."

Randy always had a boyish obsession with sports cars. The fact that he said this, didn't surprise her at all. "What did you have in mind?"

Randy's face lit up, glad she asked. "I've been looking at Dodge Vipers. Those things are race bred. They have a six-hundred horsepower V10 engine, zero to sixty in less than four seconds. America's fastest production sports car."

"Ten cylinders?" she questioned, thinking that was a bit extreme.

"And six-hundred horsepower," he said, lusting over this vehicle.

"Is that a lot?"

"Oh yeah. That's some high-speed stability. It averages over two-hundred miles per hour even with the top down."

"Why do you need a car that goes that fast?"

"Because it can go that fast. There is nothing in the world like sitting behind the wheel of a powerful vehicle and knowing you have control over a badass piece of equipment like that. That V10 engine will hum like a beast."

"Sounds like a gas guzzler," she complained.

"Thirteen city, twenty-two highway. Not as good as the Porsche, but for the speed and sheer look of a Viper, it's worth it. I'd like to get one, but I wanted to talk to you first."

"Why?"

"Because," he explained. "I'm not going to make a major purchase like that without consulting my wife. We make decisions together, remember?"

"Randy, if you want to trade in the Porsche to get another car, go ahead. You're the one who has to drive it."

Jane was the perfect wife. She was always understanding and generally played along with his crazy whims. "Thank you, Babe." He moved his mouth to hers and touched the back of her head, where he felt her long, soft hair between his fingertips. He leaned back onto the pillow and drew her in with him, taking the kiss deeper. This continued for several minutes before clothes made their way to the floor. Their bodies conformed into one, and the romantic glow from the fire made the feeling that much more intense.

Chapter Sixty-Three

"I found this totally kickass place to surf," Jim said over burgers, fries, and Dr. Pepper.

"Where's that?" Randy asked, popping a French fry in his mouth.

"Westport. I'm off Friday. You wanna come with me?"

Randy had nothing better to do on Friday. "What the hell, why not."

At the crack of dawn Friday morning, Randy was rudely awakened by someone pounding on his front door. He wearily rolled out of bed and slogged down the stairs. Jim stood on his doorstep dressed in red and yellow patterned board shorts, a navy blue Swami's tee-shirt, and black flip flops. He had Quicksilver sunglasses propped up on his head. "What the fuck, Jim? It's 7:00 A.M."

"I know, Dude, but I'm amped. We gotta get there early so I can hit the gnarlatious waves. Come on, Bro. We need to jet. Get your ass dressed."

"Alright, alright. Chill." Randy combed his fingers through his hair. "You owe me a cup of coffee for waking me up this early on my day off."

"I can do better than that. I'll buy you breakfast."

Randy grinned. "Even better. Let me hop in the shower first."

Before they made the two and a half hour drive to Westport, Jim stopped at the Cheka Looka Surf Shop in Seattle to pick up a can of Mr. Zogs Sex Wax.

Randy got a chuckle out of the label on the can. "I'm not even going to ask what you do with something called sex wax, Jim."

"Perv. It's for my board. I gotta wax my stick."

"Wax your stick?" He raised an eyebrow. "And you call me a perv."

The small fishing town of Westport was considered the surf capital of Washington. The main beach, Westhaven State Park, drew thousands of people every year, but unlike Hawaii or Southern California, surfing here was uniquely Northwest. The average water temperature ranged from forty to almost sixty degrees, making a full wetsuit essential year-round. Despite the chill and ruggedness, surfing had found a toehold and grown here considerably over the years. Because of the volatile conditions, Westport surfers tended to be hardy and dedicated to their sport. Many local surfers were in their twenties and thirties, snowboarded in the winter, and hit the beaches when ski season was over. Surfing here was wilderness surfing, where the surf changed dramatically with the seasons.

Jim pulled his backpack full of supplies out of the Jeep and carried his bagged up surfboard to the beach. Randy trailed behind with a small cooler of Coronas in one hand and two fold-up lawn chairs in the other. Jim unzipped his board and stuffed it upright in the sand. Randy set the two lawn chairs up and sat back to relax.

As Jim put on his shiny black neoprene wetsuit, he looked at Randy and said, "Surfin' is juice. Pure, raw juice."

"Juice?" Randy asked, wondering what the hell Jim was talking about.

"Totally. When I'm out there in the water ridin' along the crest of the waves, my senses are bombarded by the beauty of the ocean. It's addicting. When the surf's up, I just wanna get in the water and forget everything. My board glides toward shore and I breathe in the salt mist, and for a second or two, pure loping cadence. It's kickass!" Jim grabbed his board and ran out to paddle the waves.

Randy chilled on the beach jamming some tunes on his iPhone while he sipped on a Corona and watched the surfers and other beachgoers. Through his observation, he discovered that surfers were a unique breed. They carved water, skimmed whitecaps, and commanded their own vocabulary. They talked about riding a tube and catching a wave as if a wave were some elusive, mind-blowing virus everyone had to have. It was sixty degrees outside with a thirty mile an hour wind and these guys would paddle out in the chilly water without hesitation to check out the waves. And Jim Ryan—a bronzed, blonde-haired, blue-eyed, 34-year-old ER physician—had become one of them, sharing sessions and rubbing shoulders with the surfing gurus.

After a few hours in the water, Jim emerged carrying his surfboard under his arm. "Dude, I'm noodle armed," he said to Randy. "Totally cashed after that three-hour session." Jim stuffed his board in the sand and the two men went up to The Surf Shop.

The sign outside this local surf shop caught Randy's attention. It announced *Cowabunga!* and *Tap the Source*. A mural painted on the side displayed a large wave with a surfer silhouette in the foreground. Several surfboards and other coastal décor accented the exterior.

Jim introduced Randy to the surf shop owner. "Yo, this is my best bro, Randy Hanson."

"Howzit?" The shop owner flashed him the Shaka sign.

Being friends with Jim, Randy learned a few relevant surfer phrases over the years. "Just layin' low," he replied.

"You a doc too?"

"Yup."

"Sweet."

As they talked, a teenage boy, who reeked of alcohol, staggered into the shop. He mumbled some obscenities under his breath, stuck his middle finger up at them, and continued on his way.

The shop owner sneered, giving the boy a stink eye. "That dude just flipped me the bird."

"He's drunk off his ass," Randy added.

The men turned their heads to see the young man vomit by a trashcan, throwing up everything he'd eaten in the last three days. The shop owner cringed in disgust. "He hurled on my walkway. Nasty."

The young man hobbled his poorly coordinated body over to a truck, where some other teenagers made fun of him.

Chortling at this scene, Jim turned to Randy and said, "Yo, Dude. I'm starvin'. I need some grub."

Randy agreed. "I could eat."

"Sweet. Let's grind." Jim loaded up his gear then removed his wetsuit and hung it on a hanger in the back of the Jeep. He pulled his tee-shirt over his head and put his flip flops back on before he hopped in the Jeep and cruised the freeway back to Seattle.

"You've gotten pretty good on that surfboard," Randy remarked, fiddling with the dial on the radio.

"I try to get out at least once a week. It helps me relax. Sabrina wants to learn to surf now."

"Take her with you," Randy suggested. "She'll catch on pretty quickly, I bet."

"We want to hit the slopes this winter and try out our new snowboards."

"I'll go on the mountain with you. My whole family skis."

"Cool. We'll make a day trip out of it." Jim changed lanes and put the car on cruise control.

That evening in Santa Monica, after tucking Emily into bed, Bruce reclined on the terrace of his bedroom, gazing out at the ocean and listening to the lapping waves. The moonlight glistened off the water and the stars twinkled in the night sky.

Mandy tied her robe around her waist and sat in the cushioned wicker chair next to him. "Do you know what my mother asked me today?"

"No."

"She wanted to know when we were planning to have a baby."

Bruce eyed the odd expression on Mandy's face, not sure what to make of it. "What did you tell her?"

"I didn't know what to tell her."

"Why not?"

"Because we have never discussed this."

"Then let's discuss it now," he said.

"You have your girls, Bruce. I don't want to complicate things."

He reached over and held her hand. "My girls have nothing to do with this. What do you want? Do you want to have a baby?"

612

She looked at him and said, "Is that what you want?"

"There is nothing in the world I would love more than to have a baby with you, Amanda," he replied seductively. "But if we're going to make a baby, we might as well not waste any time. The sooner we start, the better." He pulled her onto his lap. "We have nowhere to go and nothing else to do. I say we start tonight." He kissed her tenderly on the lips.

She hopped off his lap, took both of his hands in hers, and led him over to the bed.

After the act, Mandy slipped her robe on and went downstairs. She came back with a half-gallon ice cream container in one hand and a spoon in the other. Cross-legged, she sat on the bed and took the lid off the ice cream container.

Bruce chuckled under his breath. "Hungry much?"

"You want some?"

"No, thanks."

"Suit yourself." She dipped her spoon in and took a bite, eating ice cream right from the tub while she flipped through channels on the television.

Bruce watched her intently. He loved the random, spontaneous things Mandy did. "You're cute," he remarked.

With a spoonful of ice cream in her mouth, she asked, "What did you say?"

He stared at her in loving adoration. "You are absolutely adorable. I love when your blondeness comes out." He clasped his hands behind his head and crossed his feet at his ankles.

"Are you picking on me?"

"No. Not at all. Your randomness is one of the things I love about you. Back in med school people referred to you as the airheaded blonde chick, but I always defended you."

Mandy left her spoon standing in the ice cream. "They really said that about me?"

"You are a gifted woman, Amanda, but you have arbitrary tendencies that make you unpredictable. People who don't know you think you're eccentric." Bruce rolled over onto his side.

"What do they know? They were all a bunch of freakshows anyway." She took another bite of ice cream. "Medical school was the most awkward, embarrassing, and humiliating experience of my life."

"I'm with you on that."

"And that surgery rotation was the worst."

"Surgery is easy."

"For you maybe. For me it was a pain in the ass," she stated. "The first time I was given a chance to suture a patient all by myself was during a Vascular Surgery case. The attending surgeon was performing a carotid endarterectomy and he used part of the saphenous vein for the procedure. While he was finishing up in the neck, he looked over at me and said, 'Ms. Stevens, why don't you close up the leg incision?' Of course I agreed. So the nurse handed me the proper gear and I got started. At the far end of the incision I threw in a stitch, tied a knot, then worked my way up, one stitch at a time. I was extremely careful, did everything by the book like we were taught, and made sure both sides lined up."

"How'd it turn out?" he asked.

"The end result looked pretty good. One end was a little dog-eared, but the surgeon didn't seem to mind. He told me to throw a steri-strip on it. However, when I tied the final knot, I looked up and realized that the main surgery was long over and the entire surgical team had spent the last hour watching me sew up what amounted to a four-inch incision."

Bruce laughed at her. "An hour? Wow, Mandy, that's pretty bad."

"Hush." She smacked him with a pillow. "I was mortified. The members of the surgical team were all good sports about it, but I was sure I flunked my rotation. The surgeon gave me another chance to suture the next day, so I probably wasn't as bad as I remember—or maybe I was, and he thought I needed all the practice I could get. Either way, he gave me a good grade at the end. I'd like to think I finished the rotation with at least some decent suturing skills."

"I'm sure you did just fine," he assured her. "You know, despite the tension we all felt, medical school wasn't so bad. If there was even the slightest opportunity for a professor or one of our classmates to seize a moment to lessen the stress, you could guarantee something outrageously funny would happen when we least expected it."

"But that's what made it less painful."

"Yes, it most certainly did," he concurred. "Medical school was the hardest thing I've ever done, but it was also the best time of my life. Every experience we had, good and bad, I wouldn't trade them for anything."

"Neither would I."

Chapter Sixty-Four

Temperatures in the Emerald City seemed to drop overnight. Eerie dark grey clouds disseminated, and with the clouds came rain, heaps of it.

On any normal Tuesday, Randy conducted Grand Rounds in the morning, performed a few surgical procedures before lunch, and supervised medical students at the hospital during the day, all while being available on-call for his private practice patients. But today was not a normal day. Automatic doors in the Maternity Ward kept sticking, phones randomly disconnected, and lights flickered on and off. A psychotic pregnant woman came into the ER with deep, self-inflicted scratches all over her stomach, and a man in a trench coat had to be escorted off the premises for flashing people when they walked through the entrance.

Before heading home that night, Randy popped into the ER hoping to track down Jim.

Jill was at the nurses' station reading over a chart when Randy arrived. "Hello, Mrs. Ryan."

She looked up. "Hey, Randy."

"Is your husband around here somewhere?"

"He's with a patient. I'll tell him you're here."

While he waited, Randy scribbled on a Post-It note and fiddled with various objects on the counter.

"Yo, Hanson," Jim said when he stepped into the room. "What brings you down here?"

Randy dropped the pen he was playing with and turned around. "I wanted to show you something. When do you get off?"

Jim peered over at the clock. "We have a shift change in about fifteen minutes."

"Will you be able to leave then?" Randy asked.

"Yeah. We haven't been that busy today. Let me finish up some paperwork and I'll be right out"

"I'll wait for you." Randy took a seat and waited.

A few minutes later, a guard paced around the hallway with a walkie-talkie in his hand while swarms of security began to mobilize.

"Secure the area," the guard said into his radio.

Within seconds, the hospital PA system openly announced, "Attention all staff. Code silver. Repeat, code silver."

Code silver was the signal for a total hospital lockdown, which meant all perimeter doors were going into lock mode. No one would be allowed to enter or exit the facility. Guards immediately secured the area, blocking all elevators and doors leading to and from the Emergency Department. Randy was trained in hospital lockdown protocols but had never rehearsed them. Acting strictly on impulse, he took charge of the situation. Careful not to cause a panic, he quickly ushered people to a secure location then did a sweep of the hallway and restrooms of the surrounding area, pulling everyone into safety. As soon as they were in a lockable room, he secured the door, drew the blinds, and dimmed the lights.

"Get down. Stay hidden," he instructed. "And if anyone has a cellphone, please silence it now."

He and the others crouched behind furniture and cabinets, hiding themselves from potential danger.

Outside, shots fired, followed by the sound of shattered glass and a car alarm. Randy's heart jumped out of his chest and his whole body tensed up. Fear swept over him. Blind to what was happening, images of Jane, Nathan, and his baby girls flashed before his eyes. And where was Jim? Randy had no idea where he was or if he was safe. He'd never been so terrified.

A young woman locked in the room with him shook in fear; tears flowed down her cheeks. As the physician responsible for this room full of frightened people, Randy had to maintain his composure and do his best to keep everyone calm. He swallowed the knot in his throat and crawled across the floor to the woman's side. Offering reassurance, he squeezed her hand. "We're safe here," he whispered. "Just be still."

Moments later, sirens blared, which hopefully meant police were on the scene. A male voice hollered obscenities outside their window, followed by another gun shot. Feet stomped past them in the hallway and two-way radios called out codes to the officers on the other side. Randy checked the time on his watch. 6:37 P.M. They'd only been locked in this room for seventeen minutes, the longest seventeen minutes of his life.

The hospital remained in lockdown for another hour and a half before the threat was finally lifted. As soon as the all clear was given, the first thing Randy did was track down Jim. The moment they spotted each other, they embraced in a hug.

"Are you ok?" Randy asked.

"Yeah. You?"

Randy rubbed the back of his neck, trying to release some tension. "That was the most frightening thing I've ever experienced. I think the gunman was standing right outside my window. Scared the shit out of me." Randy surveyed the scene. Several police officers—some wielding automatic weapons—stood around the main entrance of the Emergency Room. An influx of television cameras were on the scene and local media ran around trying to collect interviews from people. "Do you know what happened?"

"I don't know all the details, but apparently a witness reported hearing a man yellin' and runnin' around the parking lot with a rifle butt extending out from under his coat. She immediately reported it to security, who called the police and notified the hospital director."

Randy's knees felt weak and his stomach was queasy. He needed to sit down. "Was anyone hurt?"

"No, I don't think so. A few shots were fired at cars in the parking lot and some windows were shattered, but as far as I know no one was injured," Jim said. "According to police, the guy was lookin' for his wife. She's a nurse in the ICU. She recently left him, so he was scopin' the place tryin' to find her with the intention of gunning her down. When the police apprehended him, they found two guns in his possession."

Trying to decelerate his heartrate, Randy combed his fingers through his hair. "No doubt this is all over the news."

"Most likely."

"I need to call Jane. She's probably worried sick." Randy pulled his cellphone out of his pocket and dialed Jane's number.

She immediately answered. "Oh my god, Randy. I heard about the lockdown. Are you ok?"

"I'm fine. They have the suspect in custody."

"What happened?"

Randy explained the situation, reassuring her that no one was hurt, then returned to his duties of calming patients, reuniting people with their families, and assuring everyone was accounted for.

When things settled down, Jim grabbed his jacket and put it on over his scrubs. He met Randy by the main hospital entrance, relieved to finally be leaving the building. "You said you wanted to show me something?" Jim reminded him.

"Yes." Randy reached into his wallet and pulled out a game day ticket with the Lakers logo printed on the front. "The Lakers have their first pre-season game in L.A. on October seventh. I got four tickets. Think your wife will let you get away for a couple days?"

"I don't see why not. In fact, she'll probably be glad to have me out of her hair for a while."

"Cool. I wanted to tell you early so you could switch your schedule around and get days off. I'm going to invite Greg and see if Bruce wants to go too."

Jim nodded in approval. "A weekend with the guys. That's gonna be kickass."

"Yes it will," Randy declared, excited about spending a weekend with his closest friends. And after the crazy day he had, he desperately needed the downtime.

Randy braved the weather and drove home. Windshield wipers slapped rain off his windshield. Puddles covered the roads, splashing and spraying water everywhere. The wind howled, and with the torrential rainstorm and black, moonless sky, visibility was low. Only a few cars were out this time of night, but with the slippery road conditions, Randy drove cautiously.

He walked in the door, grateful to be in the safety of his home. The house was dark. Nothing stirred and no sound was heard other than the soft tick of a clock. Even the parrot was asleep. Careful not to wake his family, Randy locked the door then crept upstairs to check on his kids. He peeked his head into the nursery first. The teddy bear nightlight glowed, creating an angelic aura around his sleeping girls. He closed the door and left them to rest. Next he checked on Nathan. Sound asleep with his bunny in his arms. Satisfied that all was well, Randy headed down the hall to his bedroom.

He carefully entered the room, expecting to see his wife peacefully slumbering, but to his surprise, Jane was curled up on the loveseat with a bowl of popcorn on her lap. The room was pitch black, other than the light that emitted from the TV. Her eyes were glued to the screen in eerie anticipation. She had one piece of popcorn between her thumb and forefinger, slowly moving it to her mouth. The show she was watching obviously frightened her because when Randy closed the bedroom door, she flinched and screamed, spilling popcorn all over the floor. "Don't sneak up on me like that."

"All I did was walk in the room." He set his stethoscope, cellphone, and car keys on the dresser then kicked off his shoes. "Maybe you shouldn't stay up late watching horror movies alone in a dark house." He looked over at the screen. "What is this anyway?"

Jane set the popcorn bowl on the table. "Pet Sematary. This movie scares the bejesus out of me."

Randy looked down at the mess she made on the floor. "I can see that."

Jane popped up and embraced Randy with a hug, thankful he was home.

"Today was the craziest day of my life," Randy remarked.

"Because of the lockdown?"

"It wasn't just that. All kinds of strange things happened."

"Like what?" Jane clicked on the bedside table lamp and turned off the TV.

While she cleaned up popcorn, Randy undressed. "All day the door that leads from the Maternity Ward to the main hallway kept malfunctioning. The phones weren't working properly, and the lights in the hallway kept flickering on and off. And this afternoon, a woman came into the ER in labor. Normally, labor pains make women moan, or scream, or cry, or even start swearing at people, but this woman didn't do any of that. She just sat there blank-faced and scratched at her belly. She made herself bleed from the gouges she made all over her skin, and some of them were pretty deep. The look on her face reminded me of that evil stare Hannibal Lector had in Silence of the Lambs, like she was possessed or something."

"That's a bit disturbing."

"We had to call in a psychiatrist for that one, but even he was a little off."

"What was wrong with the psychiatrist?" Jane asked.

"Well, for one thing he walked into the ER humming the tune to the Addams Family. He wearing sweats and a grey zip-up hoodie, his hair was all messed up, and the laces of his sneakers were untied. He looked like he just rolled out of bed. I wouldn't have even known he was a doctor if he hadn't flashed his name badge in my face. Anyway, he tried to get the patient to relax, but let me emphasize his method for doing that—he used t'ai chi or some shit and kept talking to her about getting in touch with her inner spirit. He did manage to get her to calm down a bit, but as soon as he stepped out of the examination room, he reached into the pocket of his sweatshirt and pulled out a banana. He started eating it right there in the hall. But the strange thing was that as he pulled this banana out, a condom came out with it and landed on the floor. He bent down and picked it up then tore it open and blew it up like a balloon, tying the end off. He set in on the nurses' station, shoved the wrapper back in his pocket, and left the building."

"How odd."

"That's what I thought." Randy sat on the bed and leaned back, clasping his hands behind his head. "I've seen some unusual things over the years, but that was definitely up there on the weird shit-o-meter. With everything that happened today, I can almost guarantee there's a full moon out tonight underneath all those clouds."

The leaves on the deciduous trees changed from green to shades of red, yellow, orange, and brown. Fall was Randy's favorite time of year, not only because of the cooler weather and natural color scheme, but also because fall meant basketball season. Time for his favorite team, the Los Angeles Lakers, to take the court.

Since Jim, Randy, and Greg were staying in Los Angeles for two nights, they decided to go in style. The Ayres Hotel in Anaheim greeted them with European stone, climbing ivy, and gas lantern lighting. The hotel lobby, beautifully adorned in a warm yellow and green French-style motif, created an inviting, elegant setting with its central fireplace, marble flooring, imported rugs, and regal oil paintings.

The room they were in had two queen-sized beds and a couch that folded out to a sleeper. It had all the charm and style of a French country inn with all the comforts of home, including satellite TV, in-room refrigerator and microwave, and Wi-Fi.

Worn from a long day of traveling, Jim collapsed on the couch. "I'm starvin'. Where's a good place to eat around here?"

"Don't know," Randy said. "But let's call Bruce and ask him to join us."

Bruce met them at JT Schmidt's Restaurant & Brewery. This casual sports bar-style restaurant featured handcrafted microbrews, juicy Angus steaks, salads, burgers, and wood-fired pizzas. ESPN played on plasma televisions throughout the dining area, and through the full-length glass wall, they were able to watch the talented chefs and brewmaster.

Greg, the newest member of this group, directed his attention to Bruce. "Randy tells me you attended medical school with him and Jim."

"Yup," Bruce replied. "At Berkeley, along with my wife. After graduation, we all went our separate ways for residency."

Randy added, "Mandy went into pediatrics and Bruce here is a neurosurgeon."

"That's a complicated specialty," Greg remarked.

"Tedious at times," Bruce explained. "But I love it." He reached across the table to grab another slice of pizza.

"How long have you and your wife been married?"

"About four months. We've known each other for twelve years though."

Randy realized he hadn't told Greg all the facts about Bruce. "Remember when I told you Stephanie was married to a friend of mine from med school?"

Greg considered what Randy was implying, which made him chuckle. He turned to Bruce and said, "Your Stephanie's ex?"

"Yes," Bruce replied. "Emily and Alyssa's dad."

"How is Mandy anyway?" Jim asked.

Bruce's thoughts drifted to Amanda. "She's doing well. We're trying to get pregnant."

Randy eyes brightened at this news. "You are?"

"Yes we are."

Jim thought this was funny. "I'm gonna laugh my ass off if you have another girl."

Curious about Greg's plans as far as this topic was concerned, Randy pulled him into the conversation. "You and Raquel planning to have kids?"

Greg gave a half shrug. "I don't know. Raquel's not too keen on the whole pregnancy/childbirth thing."

"There's always adoption," Bruce suggested. "There are a lot of kids out there who need loving homes. It's definitely something to consider."

"Perhaps," Greg said.

In the morning, after a complimentary breakfast buffet of scrambled eggs, French toast, fresh fruit, and coffee, Randy, Jim, and Greg all dressed in Lakers shirts and met Bruce at Flightdeck Air Combat Center. They had a blast pretending to be fighter pilots in actual cockpit simulators. They were transported from their world of coffee shops, cellphones, and freeways to a parallel universe, flying the cyber skies in an F-18 Hornet. Going 450 miles per hour a hundred feet off the deck made the Viper in Randy's garage a pitiful ride indeed.

"That was awesome!" Randy declared, recalling the rush he felt when he shot Jim's plane out of the sky. "I blew your ass all over the place."

"Bring it on!" Jim challenged.

"I've always wanted to fly an airplane, and that was intense. We have got to do that again."

"I'm down, Dude."

With giant smiles on their faces, they went to grab some chili dogs before heading over to Staples Center for the Lakers game.

Jim, Greg, and Randy returned to Seattle boasting about how much fun they had in L.A. The trip was amazingly bonding. It helped them all unwind and gave them a chance to get to know Greg better. It was the best weekend they had in years, and one they talked about for months.

Chapter Sixty-Five

Dressed in jeans, tee-shirts, long sleeved zip-up hoodies, and sneakers, both Nathan and Randy were out in the front yard raking leaves. The air was chilly and the sky was overcast and grey. It looked like it was going to rain. Randy bagged up six bags of leaves, with Nathan's help, and set them by the trash bin. He leaned his rake against the side of the house and stretched. He grabbed his insulated portable cup off the front porch, sat on the stairs, and let the steamy coffee warm his body.

Nathan, who had recently turned three, sat on the stairs next to his father. The new independence Nathan gained allowed him more freedom to do more difficult tasks. He liked to dress himself, and was getting pretty good at it. He had problems with buttons, snaps, zippers, and ties, and sometimes put his shoes on backwards, but he insisted on doing it himself. Randy always let him try. Getting on and off his tricycle was a piece of cake for him now. He could peddle up and down the sidewalk or in the backyard with ease. Playing basketball was one of his favorite things to do, and since Nathan's eye-hand coordination had improved considerably, Randy taught him how to dribble. He had recently discovered building with blocks and liked to use his toy medical kit on his stuffed bunny and on Daddy. Nathan enjoyed watching the fish swim in the aquarium and discovered that fish, plants, and birds needed different things to survive.

He was a smart little boy. He knew several letters, could count to twenty, and easily named colors and basic shapes. He recognized his name in print and could write the first three letters by himself. It was messy, kind of like Daddy's handwriting, but he could do it. He loved being read to and enjoyed exploring things. Most of all, he loved hanging out with his dad.

"I helped," Nathan said to his father.

"Yes you did, and you were a good helper. The yard looks much better." Randy gave his son a high five.

Nathan eyeballed the six bags full of leaves. "That lots of leaves, Daddy."

"Yes it is, and more will fall. We'll have to rake those up later."

Nathan looked up at the branches of the nearby tree and developed a puzzled expression on his face. "Why the leaves fall down?"

Nathan was a curious child and was constantly asking questions about the world around him. Randy heard about young children asking where babies came from, and he was prepared to answer that. But Nathan didn't ask questions like that. He asked about things that had multifaceted explanations and scientific complexities. Randy responded in a way he thought Nathan would understand. "The leaves fall down because the tree doesn't need them anymore."

"Why?"

He tried to explain, "Leaves soak up sun for the tree to help it make food so it can grow. But in the winter the tree goes dormant, which means it goes to sleep. Since trees don't grow when they're sleeping, they don't need their leaves, therefore the leaves fall off."

"Do trees get cold in the snow?"

"No. Trees don't have nerve receptors like we do. We feel cold and heat and pain because we have nerves and a brain that tells us when something is cold or if it hurts. Trees don't have those things."

"Why?"

"Because trees are built differently than we are."

"No blankie for the tree?" the child asked.

Randy chuckled at his son's naivety. "No, Son. Trees don't need blankets."

Nathan moved over to his father's lap. "My tummy hungry. Where's Mommy?"

"Mommy went to the store with Lauren and Lacy. She'll be home soon." He kissed his son on the head. "It's chilly out here. You want some cocoa?"

"Uh huh." Nathan got off his father's lap and the two of them walked into the house together.

Randy removed his sweatshirt while Nathan struggled to unzip his. Every time he tried, the zipper kept getting stuck. "You want me to help you?" Randy offered.

"No. I do it."

"Pull down on the zipper, not out."

With a little perseverance, Nathan was able to unzip it. "Thank you, Daddy."

"You're welcome." Randy stepped into the kitchen and grabbed two mugs from the cupboard. He filled one with hot tap water so Nathan wouldn't burn his mouth, and the other with water he heated up in the microwave. He stirred a packet of cocoa into each one, put a dab of whipped cream on the top, then brought both mugs over to the table. "Nate, come drink your cocoa."

Nathan ran over to the table and took his seat.

Jane came home about twenty minutes later. She had one nine-month-old baby on each hip. Randy took Lacy from her, and Jane set Lauren down on the floor to crawl around. "You want to help me with the groceries?" she asked.

"I help," Nathan said as he leapt off his chair.

"Thank you, Sweetie."

Randy gave Jane a kiss then set Lacy down to explore with her sister. "I'll get them."

Randy and his son unloaded groceries from the car. Nathan could only carry one bag at a time, and they had to be lightweight ones, but he liked to help with household chores. It made him feel like a big boy.

After they brought in the last bag, Jane said, "I bought lunch for you and Nathan. It's on the passenger's seat."

"Yay!" Nathan cheered.

"Wash your hands before you eat," Randy instructed his son.

Nathan trotted into the bathroom to wash his hands. Jane tried to help him.

"Honey," Randy said, washing his hands at the kitchen sink. "Let him do it."

"He'll make a mess," she argued.

"He'll be fine. Let him do it. He knows how."

She left Nathan to do it by himself.

Nathan's meal contained a cheeseburger, apple slices, and milk. It also had a toy car in it, but Randy wouldn't let him have it until he ate all of his food. Randy handed Nathan a few French fries, which caused Jane to give him a piercing glare. Randy wondered what that evil look was all about.

After they finished eating, Randy pulled Jane aside and asked, "Why'd you give me that look earlier?"

"You gave Nathan French fries."

"So?" he said, not seeing the problem.

"Those are terrible for him. I have a hard enough time letting him eat the burgers from that place. You know how I feel about fried food."

"They're just French fries. What's the big deal?"

"They are loaded with fat and cholesterol. Those are not good for him, Randal."

Randal? She hadn't called him that in a long time, and the last time she did she was mad at him. "They're not good for me either, but you don't stop me from eating them."

"It's your body. If you want to pollute it with crap, knock yourself out, but please don't do that to our son." She scooted into another room.

Concerned now that he had upset her, he said, "Are you mad at me?"

"I would like to instill healthy eating habits in our son. You have him wash his hands all the time. You should be encouraging him to eat healthy foods too."

"A few French fries will not damage the child."

She scowled at him and stormed away.

Randy thought she was totally overreacting. "Jesus, Jane, calm down. He's a little boy. He doesn't get burgers very often and when he does it's okay to let him eat a few French fries. Why do you have to be so anal about these things?"

She turned around and snarled, "You're the one who's germ paranoid and washes his hands a hundred times a day. Yet you say I'm anal?"

"Yes, when it comes to the kids, you are. Sharing an Oreo with Daddy or munching on a French fry once in a while won't hurt him. You're freaking out over something totally insignificant. You have to let Nathan enjoy being a kid."

"You're telling me I shouldn't be concerned about what my son eats?" she questioned.

"I'm not saying that at all. I'm saying you need to quit freaking out every time he eats something you deem bad for him. He takes his vitamins every day, he eats healthy foods and has a balanced diet. He's getting what he needs. Let it go."

"But I worry about him."

"Yes, I know that, and that's fine. You're his mother. That's your job. But you have to choose your battles or you're going to go crazy. Eating a handful of French fries once in a while is not a battle to fight. Throwing them at people is. Refusing to eat or eating with dirty hands is. But the handful of French fries he eats once or twice a year is not." He put his arms on her waist and pulled her close to him. "Honey, look at me."

She lifted her chin but hesitated to look at him.

"I know you ate French fries as a kid. Don't even tell me you didn't."

"Yes, but I want him to be healthy and safe."

"I do too." Randy looked her in the eye. "But you can't shelter him, Babe. You are paranoid over the kids."

"No I'm not," she denied.

"Yes you are. I want our kids to have lots of opportunities to explore. They need to be able to make choices independently and not be afraid to take risks. They need to understand the ways of the world and learn about consequences. But you won't let them because you freak out when Nathan picks up a worm and you immediately jump up every time one of the girls tries to grab something."

"But they might hurt themselves," she tried to justify.

632

"They'll be fine," Randy reassured. "They're just exploring things. That's how they learn. Nathan's developing his curiosity and discovering the world around him. You need to let him be a little boy and play in the dirt, experience nature, and check out the characteristics of worms. And the girls are developing their individual likes and dislikes. We have to encourage that. If the girls try to touch something they might actually hurt themselves with, that's different. By all means, move it out of their reach, but you have to let them be kids."

She sighed heavily.

"I know it's hard for you to see Nathan becoming more independent, but we need to encourage that independence. Childhood doesn't last long. Before we know it our babies will be grown."

In agreement, she nodded. "I know."

"Then let it go."

While the weatherman hesitated, Randy knew the first snowfall of the season would soon be upon them. On a Saturday, in early December, the spiraling, swirling snow made its appearance. The entire city was doused with clean, undisturbed flakes. The ambient light of the overcast skies and the beauty of freshly fallen snow created a peaceful scene throughout the city.

Randy broke out the wools socks, insulated snow boots, North Face jackets, and Gore-Tex gloves. Even though snow tended to make the roads dangerously slippery, Randy was excited about the tender white flakes. Nathan was old enough this year to enjoy the whole snow experience. They built a snowman together in the front yard, and Randy bought a sled and pulled Nathan down the snow-covered street. Driving winds fired huge, dense flakes almost horizontally at them. They were freezing and wet, but sharing this experience with his son was worth it. Nathan's nose and cheeks were pink, but he was giggling so hard and having so much fun that he didn't realize how cold it was.

After sending Nathan inside to warm up, Randy picked up a snow shovel and began shoveling the walkway from the front porch to the driveway, eventually shoveling the driveway and front sidewalk as well. When he was finished, he went inside to get a cup of coffee before he left to put studded snow tires on his car. On the way home, he stopped at his parents' house.

His father was at the kitchen table sipping on a cup of coffee when Randy tromped inside, shaking snow off his boots. "Hey, Dad."

"Hello, Randal," Mark said to his son.

Randy removed his jacket and draped it over the back of a chair. "Nathan had a blast today. He and I built a snowman in the front yard and I took him sledding."

"I bet he enjoyed that."

"He loved it."

"Cherish these times with your son, Randy. He'll grow up right before your eyes."

"Oh, I know." He sat at the table with his father. "The other day I was getting ready to come into the clinic and I turned to see Nathan standing in the bedroom right behind me. He had on my lab coat. The sleeves were way too long and the whole thing was dragging across the floor, but he came up to me with his toy phone attached to his waist and his plastic stethoscope around his neck and told me he wanted to come into the clinic with me and be a doctor like Daddy."

"Sounds like a little boy I once knew."

"He's growing up so fast, and the girls are getting mobile now. It's hard to keep up with two of them scooting around. Jane and I really have to be careful where we leave stuff because both of them love getting into things. And Lauren has expensive taste. She only messes with the most valuable objects she can find."

Mark loved hearing stories about his grandkids. He was proud of the way Randy handled his children. He was such a patient and understanding father, yet firm when he needed to be. Randy and Jane were doing a wonderful job teaching Nathan manners, and they insisted he use them daily. Nathan was a good conversationalist and was exposed to a variety of experiences. Although he had a room full of toys, Randy and Jane weren't spoiling him. He had to earn possessions and could have them taken away just as easily. They were teaching him to always be respectful toward adults and that throwing fits, no matter how badly he wanted to, was not going to get him what he wanted. Randy and Jane were good parents, and Randy was a loving father. Mark was thrilled to see his oldest son take on the role of being a father with such enthusiasm.

Chapter Sixty-Six

The newly fallen snow meant ski season had officially begun. Up on Crystal Mountain, Randy slid to a stop, blasting powder all over the place. He poked his poles into a snow pile and removed his skis, standing them up by his poles. He quickly viewed the scenery, took off his gloves and snow goggles, then went inside the lodge to join Jane. He cupped his hands over his mouth and blew warm air onto his finger to thaw them out. "It's cold up here."

"We're on a mountain in winter with snow on the ground," Jane said, giving him a hard time. "It's supposed to be cold."

"Thank you," he teased. "I didn't realize you were a meteorologist." He leaned in to kiss her then removed his jacket. He draped it over the back of a chair and set his goggles on the table with his gloves. "I need some coffee. You want some cocoa?"

"Sure."

"Alright, save this table. I'll be right back."

Randy and Jane spent a lot of time on the slopes during the winter; they had season passes. Randy was a hardcore skier, tackling the advanced black diamond slopes, jumping chutes, cliffs, and cornices, and dodging trees along the way. The Powder Bowl was his favorite run. About every third run, he would take a more relaxing run on a blue slope so he and Jane could ski together.

Friends and other family members occasionally joined them for weekend day trips on the mountain. Today they were joined by Robby, the Ryan family, and Greg and Raquel Hutchins.

Jim and Sabrina had been diligently hitting the slopes working on snowboarding skills while Jill took the two younger ones to the kids' club to get supervised ski lessons. Jim, Sabrina, and Robby plunged in from shredding on snowboards at about the same time the rest of the clan met at the lodge for lunch. They all gathered around two tables to chow down on huge burgers, sandwiches, and specialty drinks.

Randy looked over at Jim and asked, "How's snowboarding coming along?"

"Gettin' better. Sabrina's really rippin' it up out there." Jim playfully elbowed her.

Sabrina's face flushed at that comment. "Daddy did a really cool grind and spun a 180 off a snowbank."

Randy arched his brows at his best friend. "That's impressive, Dr. Ryan."

After refueling their energy tanks, they all returned to the slopes. Sabrina tried her hand at a few more moves and Jim went on a run to get some speed. At the bottom of the slope, down by the snowdrifts, he saw a teenage boy standing behind Sabrina. He had his hands on her hips, showing her a turn. He made it pretty obvious that he was flirting with her, and she responded by giggling at him. This boy was far too close to her for Jim's comfort. He grunted disapprovingly and headed toward his daughter.

"No, you gotta use some hip action," the boy said. "You'll be throwin' some serious heat and carvin' killer shreds out there."

"Is that right?" Jim interceded.

Sabrina recognized her father's voice and turned around. "Daddy."

He glared at her and asked, "What are you doin'?"

"Justin is showing me how to…"

Before Sabrina could finish her sentence, he snarled at this boy. "Get your hands off my daughter."

The boy stood solid, eyeing Jim.

"Yo, Chump, did you hear me?" Jim reiterated. "I said get your hands off my daughter."

At this point, Sabrina stepped in. "He's a surfer like you, Daddy."

"I don't give a rat's ass if he's a surfer or not. You are not his wahine."

"Dude," the boy said, "I'm just dialin' her in on how to carve so she can score some sweet rides."

"You don't need to touch her to show her that. Get your wave horny hands off my daughter before I go aggro on your ass," Jim warned.

The boy moved his hands away from her.

Sabrina begged her dad to leave this boy alone. "Daddy."

But Jim wouldn't have it. "Go over to the lodge," Jim told his daughter.

"He was just trying to help me," Sabrina argued.

"Go now, Sabrina."

The boy tried to get Jim to calm down. "Hey, chillax, Man."

Jim turned his head to this young man, annoyed that he was interfering. "Yo, Grommet, I wasn't talkin' to you."

Sabrina rolled her eyes and stomped away.

Jim stared this boy down. "Your session with my daughter is dunzo, Dude."

"I wasn't doin' nothin'. I was just helpin' her."

"For a guy who claims he wasn't doin' nothin', you sure initiated a helluva lot of contact."

"Dude, I can't help it. She's frosted."

How dare this young man say that about his daughter. "My daughter is not frosted! She's a 12-year-old girl. Don't you ever touch her again."

This boy's face tightened in fear. "Seriously, Bro? She's only twelve?"

"Yes."

"She don't look twelve." Realizing he had tread on a fellow surfer's turf, this Justin fellow got all apologetic. "Dude, I'm sorry. I did not know."

Jim figured as much. "She shoulda told you. But you still shouldn'ta had your hands all over her."

"Dude, I swear I didn't know. I'm sorry." Justin held his hand out to Jim. "We cool?"

Jim shook his hand and nodded. "No worries."

"I'm peacin'. Lates." And Justin was gone.

Jim returned to the lodge and reprimanded his daughter. "What the hell is wrong with you?"

She cocked an attitude and got sassy with him. "He was only trying to help me. He's a nice guy."

"I don't doubt that. But why didn't you bother to tell him your age?"

She didn't answer.

"Dammit, Sabrina, you have go to be more careful. Just because he's a surfer and seems like a nice guy doesn't mean you can let him touch you like that. You are a child."

"I'm almost thirteen."

Jim's voice escalated. "Being thirteen doesn't mean you can go out with boys whenever you feel like it. You are not old enough to be dating, so you better get that idea outta your head right now, young lady."

Sabrina could see her father was angry. He had never raised his voice at her before. The fact that he had done this made her cry. "I'm sorry, Daddy."

Jim felt like an ass for yelling at her, but he sincerely needed her to understand the seriousness of what she allowed that boy to do. "You're lucky he was a nice boy. Not all boys are." He pulled her close and gave her a hug. "Be more careful, Baby."

She sniffled. "I will. I'm sorry."

He wiped her tears. "C'mon. Lemme see some of that carvin' he was showin' you."

Randy rode a chairlift with Greg, striking up a conversation. "How attached are you to the clinic you're working in?"

Greg took off his ski goggles and replied, "I'm not glued to it. Why?"

"I have a proposition for you."

"What kind of proposition?"

"My dad is retiring the end of June and I need a new partner. I'd like it to be you."

Shocked, yet flattered by this news, Greg didn't know what to say. "Are you serious?"

"Yes. I'm very serious. You'll get hospital privileges at Swedish and have a full clinical staff, complete with lab tech, two nurses, and three clerical personnel. The clinic has a fully implemented EMR system, and you'll have two examination rooms at your disposal that you can organize and decorate any way you want."

"Sounds like a good deal."

Randy tried to entice him further. "We can make our own schedule and tweak it as we need to, to make it work for us. We'll have to share an office, but it has a coffee pot that stays brewing pretty much all day. You'll get thirty days of vacation time throughout the year and two full days off every week with no on-call status. We do have a medical insurance plan, but retirement and malpractice insurance you'll have to cover yourself. You'll make decent money."

"How much?" Greg wondered.

"Last year was a good year. I made around 350,000 dollars." Randy said.

"Over 300K, huh? Not bad."

"I need someone I know I can trust to work with my patients."

"Can I bring some patients with me?" Greg asked. "I have loyal ones."

"Absolutely," Randy agreed. "You interested?"

"I'm definitely interested," Greg replied. "Count me in."

"Good."

"Your dad's retiring?"

Randy sighed. "Yes, and I'm not happy about it."

"I bet not. Practicing with him was all you talked about during residency."

"I know," Randy grumbled. "It will take me a while to adjust. I figured if you came in during his last week to learn the ropes of the clinic, get familiar with the EMR system, and meet the staff and patients, the transition will run a lot smoother."

"That's cool."

They hopped off the ski lift together. "Alright," Randy said. "When we get closer, we'll set up a schedule that will work for both of us. In the meantime, use up whatever vacation time you have. I'm going to take mine before Dad leaves."

"Where you going?"

"Taking Jane to Hawaii for our anniversary. She's never been there and I promised I'd take her someday."

"And you're gonna deliver on that promise."

"Of course," Randy said. "Obstetricians always deliver. See you at the bottom." They raced down the mountain together, kicking up snow on the way down.

Chapter Sixty-Seven

Over the next few months, Randy stayed as busy as possible to get his mind off the fact that his father would soon be retiring. Although Mark and the clinic staff did everything they could to try to ease this transition, it didn't make the situation any easier for Randy.

To clear his head, he often went on walks around the neighborhood, taking Nathan with him. Blades of green grass pushed their way through the soil and daffodils stretched their leaves toward the sun. Trees blossomed all over the Seattle area and a waft of fragrant flowers hung in the air. Robins searched for juicy worms and twittered away in the trees. Honeybees were active with the first pollen.

The lake was full of water fowl—Pied Billed Grebes, green-headed Mallards, beautifully patterned wood ducks, snow geese, and various types of seagulls. Randy took advantage of this and headed over to the nearby lakefront park. At the park, Nathan and Randy saw two bald eagles courting, locking talons and falling hundreds of feet, with the wind whistling in their wings. The racket of song sparrows and chickadees, the arrival of the Rufous hummingbird, the appearance of salmonberry and fuzzy pussywillows—Nathan found it all fascinating.

Following their morning hike and a cup of coffee, Randy worked on trimming hedges and shrubs, mowing the grass, and clipping back extraneous tree branches. To Nathan's amusement, he put out a hummingbird feeder and hung a tray of wild birdseed from the branch of a tree, attracting finches, blue jays, cardinals, and wrens. When the yardwork was complete, Randy washed both cars, with Nathan's help. They both got soaked, but they had a blast playing in the bubbles together.

Lauren and Lacy were both padding around now, which made parenting twins more difficult. Trying to keep two toddlers out of things was next to impossible. Both were developing their vocabulary. They attempted to communicate by babbling in what sounded like short sentences, complete with vocal inflections. And Lauren was funny, her babbling sounded more like singing. Lacy was the more defiant twin. She didn't like to take no for an answer and often toddled away from Randy when he called for her. The girls had two very distinct personalities and different interests, yet they found comfort in each other's presence. Randy read that twins developed their own language, and now that they were older and able to communicate a bit, he was starting to see that this was true.

After lunch and an afternoon nap, Jane and Randy whipped out the stroller and the entire family leisurely strolled to Grandma and Grandpa's house to visit for a while. Randy had been looking over files from his father's patients to get acquainted with the history so he would be ready to take over in a few months. While the kids played in the living room with Grandma, Randy and his father sat at the kitchen table and discussed some of these cases. One particular file caught his eye. "Hmm," he said. "This is odd."

"What's that?" Mark asked him.

"This file. It doesn't make any sense."

"Which file is that?"

Randy showed it to him. "This patient has recurring symptoms. You've treated it several times but it comes back regularly and consistently."

"Yes, she's been having a lot of problems with that."

"Did she mention a pattern?" Randy asked. "What's triggering it?"

"I don't know. When I ask for more details, she's pretty vague. If she'd give me accurate information it would be easier to treat."

"You think it might be an allergic reaction?"

This captured Mark's interest. "Care to elaborate?"

"I read an article recently about how allergic reactions set off by intercourse may be responsible for a significant number of recurring cases of vaginitis. Inflammation of symptoms occurred soon after a woman had sex. The husbands had no noticeable symptoms, but the seminal fluid reacted locally to cause symptoms in the wives. It's possible she could have an allergy to semen. And if that's the case, it could be readily treated simply by using condoms," Randy concluded.

"Yes it could," Mark said, grinning proudly at his son. "Nice job. I will discuss this with her."

Randy closed the file. "Greg's coming in next week to meet the staff and help me work on a schedule."

"I'm glad you're taking the initiative to do that."

"What choice do I have?" Randy shut down his tablet and shoved it in his bag.

"You're still upset about this, aren't you?"

"What difference does it make?" He rose to his feet. "The decision's been made. I'll get over it."

Sensing Randy's scorn, Mark took off his glasses. "Why don't you and I go for a drive. It'll clear your head and help you refocus." He handed Randy the keys to his truck. "Come on. Just you and me. It will give us time to talk."

Reluctantly, Randy took the keys.

The following morning, on his way to the clinic, Randy stopped at Starbucks, where he unexpectedly bumped into Jim. Seeing his friend's cheerful face sitting at a table engrossed in reading the newspaper made Randy's morning brighter. "Hey, Ryan."

Jim folded up the paper and set it down next to him. "Dude, the weirdest shit happened in the ER last night."

Randy pulled up a chair. "When does weird shit not happen in the ER?"

"Duly noted. Anyway, aside from the code blue we had, this dude came in with some kind of sperm collection condom, full clear to the top. The minute I walked into the examination room, he tried to hand it to me."

Although odd, Randy thought this was incredibly funny. "Why?"

"He wanted me to look at it."

"What for?"

"To check for some kind of infection," Jim declared. "He kept sayin' his dick was burnin' and he had some sort of rash. I brought him a specimen cup and told him I wanted a urine sample, but instead of going into the bathroom to provide a sample like any normal person would do, he starts jerkin' off into this cup."

Randy couldn't stop laughing.

Jim continued, "Now at this point I'm starin' at this sick fuck thinkin' he has some kind of fetish for sperm specimens. And as I'm picturing this scenario in my head I'm thinkin' to myself, gee, Dr. Ryan, what do you do in your spare time? I take strange men's ejaculate and I look at their sperm under a microscope."

"Hey, whatever turns you on."

"It doesn't turn me on, Jackass. The guy was a perverted wacko."

Randy chuckled. "I'm glad I ran into you. I noticed you and Jill put in for vacation the same time Jane and I are going on ours. Are you guys actually going somewhere for vacation this year?"

"We want to, we're just not sure where we want to go."

"I have a suggestion," Randy submitted, taking a drink of his coffee. "Jane and I talked about this last night. I was able to get an incredible deal on hotel reservations and can get two free airline tickets with my frequent flier miles. Seeing as you're a surfer and all, and always searching for the ultimate wave, I thought you and Jill might want to tag along with us when we go to Hawaii."

Jim's eyes widened. "You serious?"

"Yes I am. We thought it would be fun to have you guys there with us. You wanna go?"

"The sand and surf of Hawaii? Hell yeah, I wanna go."

"Cool. I'll book your room next to ours."

"Let me know how much I owe ya."

"Don't worry about it. It's on us. But don't forget to bring your surfboard," Randy reminded him.

Forget to bring his surfboard? He was going to Hawaii for crying out loud. "Thanks, Bro. I'm psyched!" Jim replied. "Hawaii is the ultimate surf zone. Look in any international surfing magazine and it will not take long to find a picture of a Hawaiian wave. It's gonna be sweet."

Randy got a chuckle out of Jim's enthusiasm. "And it will give you some time away from the kids to relax and be alone with your wife."

"Totally," Jim said. "He'e nalu, Bro."

Chapter Sixty-Eight

Lying side by side in their bedroom bungalow, Bruce and Mandy were tangled in skin. He leaned forward to kiss her, but before their lips touched, Mandy abruptly jumped out of bed and ran to the bathroom.

Concerned about her, Bruce got up and lightly tapped on the door. "Mandy, you alright?"

He heard her vomit into the toilet. Apparently she was not alright. He left her alone and slipped on a pair of pajama bottoms.

A few minute later, Mandy emerged, face flushed, obviously not feeling well.

"You know," he said as he leaned one shoulder against the doorframe. "Yesterday we had sex and you started to cry. This morning we had sex and you threw up afterwards." He chuckled a little. "You're giving me a complex here."

With a wince on her face, she held her stomach. "I've felt like crap the last few days." She grabbed her robe off the back of the door and slipped it over her shoulders. "I hope I didn't catch that nasty stomach bug that's going around."

Bruce folded his arms across his chest. "Do you think you might be pregnant?" he asked her. "I'm just throwing the possibility out there."

She turned to face him. "It is possible."

Grinning at this prospect, he said, "Why don't we pick up a pregnancy test and find out."

After showering and getting dressed, the two of them ran over to Walgreens. Once the test was administered, they stood in the bathroom staring at the test strip, anxiously awaiting the result. As the indicator window slowly displayed a plus sign, Bruce looked up. A huge smile painted his face. "Guess that explains the crying and vomit fest you had this morning."

Mandy stood in shock as a tear ran down her cheek.

Bruce reached his hand out to her. "Come here."

She fell into his arms.

"I love you, Amanda." He gently kissed the top of her head.

"I love you too."

The following weekend, Mandy and Bruce flew to Seattle to pick up Alyssa and Emily. The two of them checked into a hotel for the night, but first thing in the morning Bruce headed over to Randy's house.

Randy knew Bruce was in town but wasn't expecting to see him this early in the morning. "You're up early. You want some coffee?"

"No, thanks." Bruce came inside and sat on a bar stool at the kitchen island.

Randy pulled a Lakers mug from the cupboard, poured coffee into it, then stirred in creamer and sugar. "Where's Mandy?"

"She's at the hotel. She's feeling a bit run down so I left her there to sleep."

"She been working a lot of hours?"

"No, not really. No more than usual. She just hasn't been feeling well lately."

He gripped his mug and sat on the stool bedside Bruce. "Is she alright?"

"Last week we found out she's pregnant," Bruce said with a grin.

Excited about this news, Randy's lips curved upward. "That's fantastic news. Congratulations."

"Thank you. We told the girls last night."

"I bet they were excited. Emily's going to have a hard time keeping that a secret. It's only a matter of time before Stephanie finds out."

Bruce shrugged. "So? I could care less what Stephanie thinks."

That was the answer Randy wanted to hear. "You hoping for a boy this time?"

"Would be nice. Although in all honesty, I wouldn't mind adding another girl to the family. My girls are my world."

That afternoon, Bruce and Mandy stopped by Stephanie's apartment to pick up the girls. Even though Bruce warned her several times to stop the vile looks and derogatory statements directed toward Mandy, Stephanie ignored his requests. She was always rude to her over the phone, made negative comments about her in front of the girls, and glared at Mandy viscously. To avoid this constant negativity, Bruce sent Mandy out to the car with Emily and Alyssa while he stayed on the porch to talk to Stephanie.

"Last night I overheard you telling Emily something about a baby," Stephanie said. "What were you talking about?"

Bruce took a deep breath and rubbed his chin. "Amanda's pregnant."

Stephanie's jaw dropped. She stumbled for words, not quite sure how to react to this news. "You're having a baby with that woman?"

"That woman is my wife, and the fact that you continuously badmouth her pisses me off."

Stephanie huffed and folded her arms across her chest. "What about our girls?"

"What about them?" Stephanie's irrational and egocentric reasoning never made any sense. She was notorious for blowing things out of proportion and found any excuse she could to pick a fight with him. Bruce stood aside and waited to hear what kind of stupid argument she was going to come up with this time.

"Everything will be about the baby. Our girls won't matter to you anymore."

He immediately contradicted this statement. "That's bullshit and you know it. Having a baby won't change a damn thing as far as Emily and Alyssa are concerned. I love my girls and so does Mandy; there's nothing we wouldn't do for them."

"You're just one big happy family, aren't you? Oozing with a father's love," she said, mocking him. "Oh, that's right. You don't know what that feels like. Your parents never wanted you."

Cut to the core by her callous words, Bruce said, "You are a cold, heartless person, Stephanie." He put his hands in his pockets and stepped off the porch.

She realized she pushed things too far and genuinely hurt him. In a desperate act to redeem herself, Stephanie called out, "Bruce, I'm sorry. I didn't mean that."

Since the day they met, Bruce had never heard Stephanie apologized to him or admit she was wrong. He turned around and stared at her, dull-eyed. "You're sorry?" he declared with a bit of cynicism in his voice. "Wow. I bet that was really hard for you to say." He turned his back and headed to the car to join his wife and daughters.

Chapter Sixty-Nine

The Hansons and Ryans exited the airplane in Honolulu to an abundance of alohas, aromatic flower leis, and the timeless, natural radiance of the islands. Upon arriving in Waikiki, they discovered it was a lively place of pristine white sandy beaches, fine dining, and shopping. Waikiki was truly the playground of the Pacific. It was where all the action was, and with close access to downtown Honolulu, the list of things to do in and around Waikiki Beach was endless. The beach itself languidly curved along the ocean and was flanked by many hotels, including the famous and luxurious Halekulani Resort, which is where Randy, Jane, Jim, and Jill were going to make their home for the next ten days.

Jim wasn't the type of guy to spend money on himself for extravagant accommodations. Needless to say, this resort was far beyond anything he could have possibly imagined. "Holy shit, Dude. This place is fuckin' sweet." Jim peeked over his balcony. "The sand and surf is right outside my window."

"Glad you like it. Unpack, get cozy, and we'll grab some dinner in a couple hours."

After dinner, Jim and Jill sat out on the beach under the moonlight enjoying the peaceful lapping of the waves. "I could live here, with you, in the sand and the surf and die a happy man," Jim said, feeling more relaxed than he had in years.

"You should have been a beach bum," Jill commented.

"Nah, I'd miss medicine too much. The three B's get my blood pumpin' as much as surfing does."

"The three B's?"

"Blood, broken bones, and BP spikes," he replied.

"What about the other three B's?"

"What would those be?"

"Your board, baggies, and the beach."

"Those are nice too," he admitted. "But there's no blood. Well, unless someone falls off their surfboard and totally gashes themselves on a reef cut. Never seen that happen though."

"But if it ever did, your fellow surfers would certainly be glad you were around."

"I'm sure they would."

Jill laid her head on Jim's shoulder, and together they enjoyed the laidback atmosphere, something the two of them, with their work schedules and keeping up with the kids' various activities, rarely did.

While Jim and Jill enjoyed tranquil beach sounds, Jane and Randy were making their own sounds. Sweating, and nearly out of breath, Randy heard Jane cry out in ecstasy right along with him, relieving the intense hunger that had built up. He collapsed in Jane's arms, not moving a muscle; his muscles were too fatigued to move. Panting to catch his breath, he started laughing.

"What is so funny?" Jane asked.

"I was just thinking. Do you remember that time when we first started dating and we went out to that fish and chips place?"

"Yes. You ordered all that fried food." She cringed at the thought of it. "It almost made me gag."

"I tried to get you to eat it, but you wouldn't touch it. You ate a baked potato instead. Wuss."

"You know I don't like fried food."

"I do now. At the time I didn't." He continued, "And then I tried to get the ketchup to come out by shaking the bottle, but when it wouldn't come out, you thought you'd be clever and show me how it was done by tapping on it." He used his fingers as quotation marks to emphasize the word tapping.

"The whole bottle poured out."

"Yeah, all over my food, thank you very much."

"I didn't mean to," she said, embarrassed about this incident. "I thought you were going to be mad because I ruined your food, but you weren't. Instead you gave me this shocked gasp and started laughing at me."

"The look on your face was priceless. You had that guilt-ridden expression like a kid who got caught doing something they weren't supposed to. It was funnier than hell. Nathan gets that same look. At least we know where he gets it from," he teased her.

She playfully whacked his arm.

He chuckled and leaned over to kiss her. "I love you, Mrs. Hanson. You and I have shared some great times together."

"Yes, we have."

"And we will share many more in the years to come." He grabbed her hands and pulled her out of bed. "Now, come on. Get up. Get dressed. The beach is beautiful tonight. Let's check it out."

Waikiki Beach was great for surfing, swimming, snorkeling, or simply people watching. Complete with lifeguards, restrooms, showers, and picnic areas, this beach was a sand lover's paradise. The four friends claimed a prime spot along the strip and spent the day sunbathing, soaking up the magic of Hawaii. Jim embraced the moment and went surfing.

Jim had more edge in his style than Randy had ever seen before. He was more relaxed on the board and aggressively attacked four to twelve foot waves with confidence, surfing with a style ranked up there with the local gurus of Hawaii. Hawaiians called surfing he'e nalu, which literally translated to wave sliding. Sliding the waves and catching a tube ride was what surfers lived for. Jim wasn't any different than the rest of them. Surfing was an exhilarating thrill, a natural high for him. He often told Randy, 'I love the sensation of riding a wave and the feeling I have when I'm out on the ocean.' He referred to surfing as juice, the ultimate joy ride, the one thing that allowed him to leave all of his worries behind and escape from his busy life in the ER.

When it came time to pick themselves up off the golden sand to do some exploring, the Waikiki trolley was a fun way to travel, providing access to the best attractions in Honolulu. With the trolley service, they could forget about figuring out their own way around and spend more time concentrating on having fun. They had an itinerary laden with adventure—visiting historic sites, viewing scenic areas, and sampling a myriad of restaurants. Some stops they made included the Bishop Museum, Sea Life Park, Pearl Harbor, The USS Arizona Memorial, Makapu'u Lookout, and Hanauma Bay.

The hike up the Diamond Head summit provided the best view of the island. The volcanic trail ascended to a 761-foot peak. It was a steep but easy hike, and took an hour and a half to complete. In the afternoon, they viewed nature firsthand by snorkeling through a large, flourishing coral reef barrier. They witnessed an incredibly diverse array of marine life—green sea turtles, manta rays, octopuses, and brightly hued schools of butterfly fish. Several different kinds of eels, invertebrates, and crustaceans were among the reef inhabitants, and they even heard dolphins harmonizing in the backdrop.

They spent a day touring the Waikiki Aquarium, which was located on the shoreline adjacent to a living reef. The vibrant exhibits featured Hawaiian monk seals, sharks, coral reef life, and the mahi-mahi hatchery. Jane and Randy stopped at the gift shop to pick up a postcard book of fish pictures for Nathan and plush baby seals for the girls.

A trip to the Dole Pineapple Plantation merited a visit to the pineapple garden maze. Through bright green hedges, the four friends traversed through twists and turns searching for a way out. Before they left, they picked their own pineapple and enjoyed the succulent fruit as a late night snack.

Besides enjoying the local wildlife, the four friends also took part in the local culture. The Polynesian Cultural Center extended the Hawaiian experience to new heights by offering a day full of musical performances, mystical illusions, palm climbing, and other Hawaiian fare. The evening consisted of a traditional Hawaiian luau. Oahu luau chefs cooked the kalua pig in a traditional imu oven and served it along with chicken long rice and baked sweet potatoes. The all-you-can-eat feast also included a variety of fresh salads and pickled cucumbers. The meal ended with a dessert of coconut cake and fresh pineapple.

Randy got a kick out of participating in the Hukilau, which was a traditional fishing ceremony where fishing nets were pulled from the ocean to the deep sounds of conch shells. As the sun set, the performance began and they were treated to an energetic and fascinating Hawaiian luau show featuring Tahitian hula drum dancers and breathtaking Samoan knife fire dances. The tropical, star-filled sky, warm ocean breeze, and festive island spirit made for a fun cultural experience.

A tour of the Royal Palace offered a glimpse into Hawaii's affluent past. Iolani Palace, the former home of Hawaii's kings and queens, was the only royal palace in the United States. A beautiful black and gold Kamehameha statue, honoring Kamehameha The Great, majestically stood across from the palace. Jim moved closer to the statue and stared at it.

"What are you so fascinated about?" Randy asked him.

"King Kamehameha was said to be a skilled surfer," Jim remarked.

"Really?"

"Yeah. He was the head of a dynasty that ruled the Hawaiian islands for more than a century. Legend has it he was born the same time Haley's comet made its appearance, a sure sign that he would rise to greatness. His remains were hidden with such secrecy, according to ancient custom, that only the stars know his final resting place."

Jim had more worthless information stored in his head than anyone Randy knew. Where he uncovered all of these facts was far beyond comprehension. "And why would anyone care about that?"

"Dude," Jim griped. "Don't let the Hawaiians hear you say that. He's their greatest historical figure. Every year, on June eleventh, they celebrate Kamehameha Day. It's a state holiday. They throw a big ceremony in honor of their king. The statue is draped with leis of flowers and hula dancers from all over the country come to perform. They have a King Kamehameha Celebration Floral Parade where marching bands from all over the world traverse the streets of Honolulu. It's one hell of a party."

"Sounds like it."

Trying to spark Randy's interest, Jim added, "Legend says he was an avid fisherman too."

"Was he?"

"Yup." Jim posed next to the statue. "Take my picture with him."

Randy pulled out his camera and snapped a photo. "I had no idea you knew so much about Hawaiian history."

"Wrote a paper on it once."

"Of course you did," Randy teased.

They spent the next day on the island of Kauai. Since their resort was located on Oahu, they had to take an early morning charter flight out of Honolulu to get there. Eighty-three flights made this trip and back on a daily basis, so booking one was easy. Gate to gate, the flight was about fifty-two minutes.

Once they landed, they rented a car for the day and traveled up to Wailua Falls, which was located on the island's east side, about ten miles northwest of the airport. Surrounded by dense vegetation, this majestic eighty-foot tiered waterfall cascaded powerful water down a sharp cliff into a pool over thirty feet deep. Viewing the falls was best in the morning when the sun shone directly on it, making the water glisten magnificently.

About a quarter mile down the road was a short trail that led to the base of the falls, but it was steep and a bit slippery from the rain shower the island received the night before. Despite the county signs that offered warnings of the steepness and slipperiness of this trail, they decided to brave the short hike anyway.

Jill slipped on a muddy patch. When Jim tried to catch her, his feet buckled underneath him causing both of them to awkwardly fall over each other.

The scene made Randy laugh. "So much for your poise and chivalry, Ryan."

Jim stood up and offered his hand to Jill, helping her get up. "Hey," Jim retorted. "At least she fell on me." Jim had fallen into a puddle and his rear-end was soaked. He tried to glance behind himself as he reached back with his hand to feel for wetness.

"Wish I had the camera out for that one. That was graceful. I thought you were the king of style?" Randy teased him.

"Only on a surfboard, Dude." Jim dusted himself off and held Jill's hand so she wouldn't fall again.

After traversing the Wailua trail and enjoying the view of the waterfall, they took a trip up the Wailua River in a flat bottom boat to Fern Grotto. Fern Grotto was a massive lava rock laden with tropical ferns which grew upside down from the roof.

"This place is gorgeous," Jim said to Randy. "Mark Twain said that Hawaii is the peacefullest, restfullest, balmiest, dreamiest haven of refuge for a worn and weary spirit the surface of the earth can offer."

Randy's forehead crinkled and his brows drew together. "Where the hell do you find all the worthless information you have crammed in your head?"

"You ever read Tom Sawyer or Huckleberry Finn?"

"Yes. I read them both, when I was twelve," Randy declared.

"Mark Twain was a wise man," Jim claimed. "He had life figured out."

"How do you figure that?"

"He knew what it took to get a piece of the pie out of life, Dude. And he knew how to live a long and healthy life. According to his autobiography, there are three kinds of lies: lies, damned lies, and statistics."

"Mark Twain had a sharp tongue, didn't he? I can see why you like him so much."

Jim went on, "And like the mighty King Kamehameha, he too was born when Haley's comet passed by the Earth, but almost eighty years later. Mark Twain also predicted that he would to go out with Haley's comet, and he did, in 1910, one day after the comet's closest approach to Earth."

Randy may have spoken fluent French, but Jim spoke fluent bullshit. "How the hell do you know that?"

"You didn't know that?" Jim mocked.

Randy snorted condescendingly. "No. Why would I?"

"I thought you were the smart one?"

"What the hell does the birth and death of Samuel Clemens have to do with intelligence?"

"Knowledge is intelligence," Jim said. "And knowledge makes the man."

"But the information you have in your head is bullshit. And Mr. I-Know-Everything-There-Is-To-Know-About-Mark-Twain, I don't think he would agree with you. If I'm not mistaken it was Mark Twain who said clothes make the man. Naked people have little or no influence in society."

Jim was clearly impressed. "Oh, so you do know about Mark Twain."

With a smartass smirk on his face, Randy replied, "Who's the man now, Dr. Ryan?"

"Ok, so I was wrong. Guess you know more than I assumed you did."

"I always know more than you think I do, Jim."

Walking hand in hand along the beach outside their hotel, Jane noticed Randy seemed a bit distant. He kept kicking at the sand and staring off into the ocean. "You ok?" she asked him.

Randy turned his head, hearing her voice but not really listening to what she said. "What?"

"Are you ok?"

He shrugged.

She squeezed his hand in loving reassurance. "What's bothering you?"

He took a deep breath and exhaled with a long drawn-out sigh. "I spent nine years in school and four years in residency to practice medicine with my dad. I can't believe, that after only getting the opportunity to work with him for a few years, he's leaving me."

"He's not leaving you, he's leaving the practice," Jane rephrased.

"What the hell's the difference?" Randy scoffed. "I am not ok with this, Jane."

"Did you ever tell him how you felt?"

"Yes, I did, but he's not giving in. My dad said he set up the clinic for me to have a place of my own to practice medicine, and he only intended to stick around long enough for me to establish myself then he was going to retire. Apparently that was his plan all along, but he failed to inform me about this." Randy sat in the sand and poked at the tiny particles. "I worked hard for this. I busted my ass to be the best because I was going to be working with the best doctor I knew. He was my hero, Jane. And now he's leaving. This sucks."

Randy was truly bothered by this. Jane could tell because he was picking rocks from sand and throwing them. He only threw rocks when something was on his mind.

"You need to consider his words, Sweetie."

Not wanting to 'consider' any of this, he said, "About?"

"About the fact that he set up the clinic for you. He did it out of love for his son. You said yourself that you would have done the same for Nathan."

"That's different," Randy insisted.

"No it isn't."

"Yes it is."

She didn't see how he could justify that. "How do you figure that?"

"Because he lied to me."

"No he didn't."

"Yes he did. He said we were partners. Obviously he didn't mean it." Feeling betrayed, he stood up and walked toward the water. Now that he had established a respectable reputation as a physician in Seattle, his partner, his role model, his childhood hero, the man he loved, looked up to, and idolized was leaving him behind. He and his father were supposed to stick together, to be cohorts when it came to medicine, not separate entities going down two different forks in the river of life. This is not how his father said it would be.

Jane had never seen Randy so upset. He always admired his father and spoke very highly of him. Now he seemed horribly distraught and spoke of him harshly. She tried to get him to lighten up. "Randy, I'm sure he has his reasons."

"So he says, but I'm pissed. How can he do this to me? I worked my whole life for the opportunity to work side by side with my father, and he throws it all away like it doesn't mean a damn thing."

"That's not his intention."

"No?" he scoffed. "How the hell do you know what his intentions are?"

"I know he loves working with you. I know he looked forward to the day you joined the practice. Your mother told me that he talked about it for months. He was so excited when you walked into the clinic that morning ready to work by his side. You saw how he went all out to make you feel welcome. He gave you every opportunity to show off your skills and be the prestigious one. He put you in the spotlight every chance he had. He's proud of you and everything you've accomplished."

"If he was so excited about it and so proud of me and loves working with me so much then why is he leaving? Did I piss him off or something? Was I too good? Not good enough?"

For some unknown reason, Randy perceived his father's retirement as a personal attack. Jane didn't understand where this irrational thinking came from. "Your father choosing to retire has nothing to do with you."

"I wish I could believe that."

Randy had tears in his eyes. Feeling sympathy for the pain he felt, she held him in her arms. "Don't take this so hard."

"I hate this," he admitted.

"I know you do."

"I don't know if I can do this without him."

"Yes you can. You love your work, Randy, you always have."

He looked into her pretty eyes. "I'm going to miss having him around."

"He'll still be here. He lives right down the street."

"I know, but it's not the same thing," Randy said. "My dad is at the office every morning, we have coffee together. We share notes and information on patients. We trust each other and depend on each other and read each other like clockwork. He's my partner, Jane."

"I know he is, but now you're going to have a new partner. You and Greg will establish that connection as well. You'll see." Trying to cheer him up, she said, "Raquel told me that Greg is really excited about working with you. He holds you in high regard, you know."

Randy doubted that statement. "He does not."

"Yes he does. Raquel told me he feels honored to have the opportunity to work side by side with you. She said he went on and on about it."

Randy wondered why Greg felt that way. "That doesn't make any sense. Greg has more experience than I do."

"I'm just telling you what Raquel told me. That man respects you." Jane took Randy's hand and they continued their stroll down the beach. "And the good thing is, Greg is your friend."

"Which is why I asked him to do this. I trust him and he's good. I've learned a few things from him over the years."

"I think you two will be a good match and your practice will flourish even more," Jane said.

"I hope so."

Chapter Seventy

With the rugged terrain, glistening water, and warm temperatures, summer in Seattle was the best place in the world to live. Early morning fog meant mist on your face. Sunrise came with white, wispy clouds and the sun's brilliant light reflecting off the lake. The days were busy with barbecues, salmon fishing, and events such as Seafair. Tourists and residents alike enjoyed Pike Place Market, the Seattle Aquarium, and Seattle Center. And the clear view of Mt. Rainier was spectacular.

To commemorate the season, Randy and his dad took Nathan fishing. Floating on the calm waters with the sunrise over the mountains, Randy and his father had little more to do than drink coffee from paper Starbucks cups and munch on warm breakfast sandwiches while they waited for the fish to bite. Randy meticulously packed a few towels and several moist towelettes.

"Why on earth did you bring so many towels, Son?" Mark asked.

"What's the first thing that's going to happen when you get a fish?" Randy replied. "You're gonna spill coffee everywhere."

Mark laughed, knowing one of them always spilled coffee in the boat when they went fishing together. "You have a good point there." It wasn't long before

Mark cried, "Fish on!" He handed his Starbucks cup to his son before rushing to his nodding pole.

As he reeled and yanked, Randy brought out the net. Unfortunately, the fish flopped off the hook into the water. "Fish off," Randy said with a chuckle.

"Damn!" Mark cursed, angry that his fish had gotten away.

Randy had hundreds of fishing experiences with his father, dating way back to when he was a small boy. Fishing and sport crabbing with his father were two things Randy always loved to do. They would fish year-round too, regardless of the weather, catching all kinds of fish, from cutthroat trout and yellow perch to largemouth bass and sockeye salmon. And they'd fish anywhere: lakes, rivers, oceans, and Puget Sound. However at this time of year, between Chinook seasons, they were consigned to keeping only Coho salmon. Randy enjoyed salmon fishing with his father and son, even though deep down the prospect of his father leaving him alone to practice medicine without him was tearing him up inside.

Suddenly Randy got a bite. He reeled in a Coho, reaffirming his worth as a man.

Nathan was thrilled by the catch. "That a big fishie, Daddy."

"It's decent. It's not the monster of the day, but it's a fish. That'll be good eating tonight." As the commotion subsided, Randy snapped a picture of his fish and texted his wife. *Caught one!* He attached the photo to his message and sent it. "Hey Dad, where's your fish?" Randy readjusted his bright yellow spinner lure and cast his line back out. "Still in the water, isn't it?"

"You're about to be, too," Mark replied in retaliation.

By 8:00 A.M. the men hit a dry spell. They had lost or thrown back more fish than they hooked. Out of desperation, Mark proposed the use of hand grenades.

Randy stated, "I don't think that's legal, Dad. But I do have some cured salmon eggs if you wanna give that a shot."

About an hour later, their luck changed. Mark hooked a fish at the same time Nathan's rod started nodding. As Randy reached over and grabbed Nathan's pole, Mark yanked and reeled his. It quickly became clear that he had a worthwhile fish on the line. Randy tried to offer instructions, but the excitement of two hook-ups turned the boat into an instant zoo. Mark reeled his fish in closer to the boat while Randy held the net over the water. As soon as Randy netted it, the men cheered in celebration of a successful catch. "That's a serious fish," Randy said. "Probably weighs at least ten pounds."

When Nathan got a good view of his grandfather's fish, his eyes got huge. "That fishie bigger than Daddy's!" the child boasted.

Mark chuckled at his grandson's enthusiasm. He finally got his fish. All that was left now, the men decided, was for their young fishing apprentice to sully his own hands by catching one. On the next available hook-up, Randy helped Nathan reel in a fair-sized fish that once cleaned, put on ice, marinated overnight in honey, cumin, and soy sauce, baked in foil at 350 degrees for twelve minutes, and served in generous portions for dinner, was an altogether marvelous creature.

As noon approached, it started to warm up considerably and the fish were no longer biting, so the three of them returned to shore and rejoined the urban hubbub with fresh salmon to show for their morning efforts. While examining their catch, Mark offered this summary of the day. "It feels good to do something manly with my son and grandson."

Randy couldn't have agreed more.

Mark Hanson's retirement party was scheduled that night. Randy's neighbor offered to babysit the kids so he and Jane could attend this event.

Randy was extremely edgy and wanted no part of this so-called celebration. "I don't want to do this," he declared, tucking in his shirt.

"He's your father, Randy. You have to go."

"Tell him I'm sick."

She kissed him softly on the lips. "Your dad is expecting you to be there. He'll be crushed if you don't show up."

Randy turned around and glanced in the mirror, trying to knot up his tie. "Why is everyone so happy about this? The hospital, Mom, Stephanie, the clinical staff, and everyone my dad and I know are making this into some kind of neighborhood block party. I don't see how this is such a festive event."

"They want your dad to be happy. He's put many years into his career and the care of his patients. It's his time to take care of himself now."

"Yes, I've heard that line before."

Jane looked at him through the reflection in the mirror. "I don't understand why you're so upset about this."

"Haven't we discussed this already?"

"Yes, but you're still freaking out about it." The doorbell rang. Jane turned her head toward the sound. "That's probably the sitter. I'll meet you downstairs."

The large party room quickly filled with doctors, nurses, medical staff, family members, and friends

Randy and his father knew. Randy was glad there was an open bar. Maybe he could wallow behind a Screwdriver and disappear so he wouldn't have to deal with this.

Ellen Hanson greeted Randy and Jane at the door. "Hello, Honey."

Randy hugged her, not feeling anywhere near as joyful as she was. "Hey, Mom."

Ellen immediately noticed the scowl on her son's face and wondered what was bothering him. "What's wrong?"

"You actually have to ask?"

"Randal, your father has talked to you about this decision."

"Yes, and he claims it wasn't taken lightly and he did all of this for me and he needs some time for himself now...Yes, Mom, I've heard it all before. But that doesn't mean I have to feel good about any of this," Randy declared, displaying a bit of an attitude.

"No, you don't. But you do have to accept it. Be civilized and social and professional for your father," his mother demanded. "He needs you tonight."

"And I need him. But he didn't think about that, did he?" Randy left Jane and his mother and headed toward the bar to get a drink.

Ellen turned to Jane, hoping for an explanation. "Is he ok?"

"He's been upset all week," Jane explained. "He's still hoping he can get Dad to change his mind."

"Why does this bother him so much?"

Jane tried to explain. "Randy worked all those years in med school anticipating practicing medicine with his dad. That's what they always planned. But now that Dad's retiring, he feels betrayed. He thinks Dad turned his back on him and broke his promise of sharing a medical practice together."

Ellen looked over at her oldest son who was ordering a drink from the bar. "That's ridiculous."

"That's what I tried to tell him, but he doesn't see it any other way. He's really been bothered by this and hasn't slept much lately."

Ellen felt pity for her son. She knew how close Randy and Mark were and how much the medical practice meant to both of them. If her husband was aware of how all of this was affecting Randy, he would probably change his mind about retirement. "If Mark knew…"

"Don't tell him. He doesn't need to be upset by that tonight," Jane insisted. She peered over at Randy, who held a drink in his hand staring across the room at his father. "He'll be alright. Give him some time."

As the evening progressed, Randy's mood lightened and he was actually mingling with colleagues and having a good time. He gulped down the remainder of his drink then stepped up to the podium. "Excuse me. May I have your attention please."

All eyes turned to him.

Randy looked at his father and said, "Dad, could you come up here please?"

Mark took his place at the front of the room.

Randy began his speech. "Thirty-five years ago my father began practicing medicine. He was a bright and dedicated doctor fresh out of residency, anxious and eager to take on new patients. And thirty-five years ago, when I was born, he also became a father. Even when I was a small child, he must have caught a glimmer of my desire to truly understand his craft. He helped me build the first bridges I needed to pursue my dreams of following in his footsteps and becoming a doctor. He encouraged my career goals, fed my curiosity about medicine, and led me in the direction I needed to go to get to where I am today. My father is one of the best OB/GYNs in the field, and from him I learned that true medicine is a special partnership between a doctor and his patients. It only works when the physician reaches beyond the outer image, looks into the hearts of his patients, and understands and respects what he sees. I entered this profession dedicated to assisting people who needed medical care, wanting to give back everything my father ever gave me. Right from the start, he was always there to offer support, love, encouragement, and an understanding hand. He's taught me so much, not only about medicine, but also about myself. He's my hero, my inspiration, my mentor, my partner, and my friend. I feel honored that he gave me the best gift he ever could—himself. He shared his energy and his enthusiasm for medicine, taught me to be honest and to respect myself and others, and he showed me love—not only a father's love, but also a physician's love for the wellbeing of his patients. He is the most dedicated man I've ever known—dedicated to his profession, his patients, and his family. On that note, let me introduce to you the man of honor tonight—my father, Dr. Mark Hanson."

The crowd applauded as Randy stepped away from the podium.

"Thank you, Randal, for your wonderful introduction." Mark adjusted the mic slightly. "Have I really been practicing medicine for thirty-five years? That sounds like a long time...about the same length of time as an all-day spell of incoming patients in an ER rotation on a Friday afternoon when the sun is shining. That too can seem to go on and on."

The room filled with laughter; all the doctors present understood completely what a twenty-hour ER rotation felt like.

When the crowd settled, Mark took a sip of water and went on for five minutes about how much medicine and pop culture had changed over thirty-five years. He told everyone what he planned to do during his retirement then thanked a few people for their contributions and support throughout the years.

At the conclusion of his speech, Mark looked directly at his son. Randy knew his father was about to say something sappy. He tightened his jaw and had to fight to contain his emotions.

"I would also like to thank my son, Dr. Randal Hanson, who taught me more about medicine and the human side of patient care than I ever imagined he would. It is with gratitude that I look back on the experiences I shared with my son. I'll never forget the little boy who was fascinated by my medical books and asked for a stethoscope for Christmas when he was eight years old. I'll always remember the many things he accomplished, the awards he won, the speeches he gave, the feeling of pride I felt when I hooded him and escorted him off the stage as Dr. Randal Hanson. The first time my son walked into my clinic as a brand new doctor with a stethoscope draped around his neck, I thought I was the more experienced doctor and my son would learn something from me. How wrong I was. It took a while to understand this, however, for I was a reluctant learner. The conception in those early days between what I thought I needed to teach my son and what he, a new and very gifted doctor, actually needed to learn was misconceived. My son was kind in saying I gave a gift of myself—my energy, enthusiasm, honesty, respect, and love. I want to turn that around, for that is precisely what I feel he has given me. As I leave this profession, I am taking so much of Randy with me, endless memories."

As Randy sat and listened to his father's words, he felt a lump develop in his throat, It was only a matter of time before tears followed.

Looking his son in the eye, Mark said, "Randy, you are so much more than my son. You're my friend, my apprentice, my teacher, and my partner. Thank you for being my traveling companion along a large and important part of my life—medicine. I am forever grateful for your stimulating company, your knowledge and dedication, and the enormous collection of shared experiences we had that are indelibly printed on my mind. You truly are my inspiration."

When Mark stepped away from the podium, the guests in the room stood in ovation. Randy walked up to his father and hugged him. The tears he had fought to hold back all night could no longer be contained. He had kept his feelings hidden inside for months and they were bound to break free at some point. Unfortunately, it happened to be here, tonight, in front of his father and all the medical colleagues they both knew. The retirement of his father was a turning of a page in life and the beginning of a new chapter for both of them.

It was the beginning of a new chapter for Greg Hutchins as well. Monday morning, Greg parked his car in the parking lot of his new clinic, excited about this adventure he was about to partake in. He grinned in delight when he saw the painted glass on the front door of the clinic.

Women's Healthcare Physicians
Obstetrics and Gynecology
J. Randal Hanson, M.D., FACOG

Greg N. Hutchins, M.D., FACOG

Hanson and Hutchins had a nice ring to it.

Randy's sports car was parked outside, as well as several other vehicles. Greg opened the clinic door and stepped inside.

Randy and all the clinic staff stood at the front counter posing in front of a big banner. *Welcome, Dr. Hutchins!* "Good morning," Randy said, sipping on a steaming cup of coffee. "Welcome to your new clinic. Coffee is brewing and patient files await you."

"Thanks," Greg replied.

Randy pointed out the wall where all of his certifications, degrees, and recognitions were hanging. Several spaces, where Mark's framed documents hung for years, were now empty. "There's lots of room for you to hang your certificates, and we had your name painted on the door."

"I saw that. Thank you."

"We have your number set up and ready to go with Swedish, and we've given them the on-call schedule."

Greg was truly overwhelmed by how welcome his new work colleagues made him feel. He couldn't wait to get started. "Cool."

"You ready to start the day?"

"I'm ready. Where's this coffee you mentioned?"

"Come with me. I'll show you." Randy escorted him back to the office where he could get a cup.

Mandy awoke in the middle of the night and ran to the bathroom. Hearing her caused Bruce to stir. "Mandy?"

She hugged the toilet bowl and threw up. Throughout this entire pregnancy she felt overly tired, was sicker than a dog, and had difficulty sleeping. She couldn't get comfortable no matter what she did. She groaned and vomited again. Before she returned to Bruce's side, she grabbed a glass of water and brushed her teeth to get the horrid taste out of her mouth.

As soon as she was snuggled under the covers, Bruce pulled her into his arms. "You alright?"

"Why does being pregnant make me feel so lousy?"

He yawned and groggily replied, "If you don't feel well, you should call in sick today. You won't be much good to your patients if you're ill."

"I'm not ill."

He begged to differ. "You just threw up, didn't you?"

"Yeah."

"Sounds pretty ill to me." He stretched glamorously, fluffed up his pillow, then closed his eyes and tried to go back to sleep.

Bruce got home later than he planned that evening. After placing his stethoscope on the table and setting a stack of mail down, Amanda threw her arms around him, almost knocking him over. He had to grab the back of a dining room chair to keep from falling over. "Whoa," he said as he caught himself with one hand and grabbed her with the other.

She held him tightly and kissed him hard; he could barely breathe. "Mmm," she said when they finally came up for air. "I missed you."

"You saw me this morning."

"So?"

Bruce laughed at the energetic, happy-go-lucky mood she was in. "You almost knocked me over."

Wondering what he found so amusing, she stated, "You're laughing at me."

"A little." He kissed her softly on the lips then put his hand on her pregnant belly. "What did you find out today?"

Mandy reached over to the table and picked up an ultrasound image. "You ready?"

"Yup." In eager anticipation, Bruce took the sonogram in his hand and examined it carefully. A bright smile filled his face. "I knew it." He gently rubbed her tummy. "Another girl."

"Are you happy?"

"Pink bows and pink blankets…I couldn't be happier."

Beach, waves, sand, and surf. Randy lounged in a lawn chair on the beach in Westport soaking up the sun while he watched the seagulls and surfers frolic in the water. He listened to tunes and sipped on the Corona in his hand. He couldn't think of a better way to spend the day than hanging out with his wife, his kids, his best friend, and the rest of the Ryan clan.

Jim came in from a run dressed in black neoprene. He stuffed his surfboard in the sand, unzipped his wetsuit, letting the top dangle down, then sat in the chair next to Randy. Reaching into the cooler for a Corona, Jim asked, "How's Greg workin' out?"

Randy replied, "Going well. He's a good doctor and the clinic staff likes him. He's brought in several new patients too."

"How's the schedule goin' that you two worked on?" Jim slipped his sunglasses on and popped the top off his beer, flicking it with his thumb over to a pile of towels.

"Working out well. He's happy he's not on-call every night, and I'm happy he's reliable and competent.

We make a good team. I can't complain. It's turned out well for all of us in the long run."

"See, and you were worried," Jim replied snidely.

"I still see my dad several times a week. He met me for coffee the other morning and invited us over for dinner last night. He and Mom have been watching the kids while Jane is at work in the afternoon. He gets to play with his grandkids like he wanted."

"That's good."

"Yup. He's stopped by the clinic a few times when he happened to be downtown. We had a big barbecue last weekend and he and I have been taking Nate fishing a lot. We're closer than ever. And the important thing is he's happy," Randy said. "He doesn't have to worry about being on-call and he's able to relax and spend time with Mom. They're going to Europe next month and will be gone for three weeks. They're both looking forward to that."

"I bet."

"I certainly can't complain about the way things turned out. Greg is a hell of a lot happier working with me too. He actually enjoys his job now. For a while he was thinking he got into the wrong specialty."

"That would be a bad thing to figure out after goin' through the hell of residency."

Randy agreed. "No shit."

Jim lounged back in his chair and took a drink from his Corona bottle. "I feel bad that I missed Bruce and Mandy while they were up here. That damn ER shift I was on."

"They were totally cool with it, Jim. Don't fret over it."

"What's goin' on with them?"

"Actually," Randy explained. "They went in for an ultrasound a few days ago and found out that they're having a girl."

Jim rolled on the floor. "Buckman with three girls. Mr. I-Hate-Pink-Frilly-Shit. That's classic." Jim gazed out at the water. The breaking swells were calling his name. He set his beer down in the sand, rose to his feet, and zipped up his wetsuit. "Waves are lookin' pretty stellar, Bro. Surf's up!" Jim tossed his sunglasses onto a towel, grabbed his surfboard, then with his fist held up in a shaka position, ran out toward the water hollering, "Cowabunga, Dude!" He slapped his board on the waves and paddled out.

Randy took another sip of his beer, sat back, and put his feet up. He watched the kids playing in the sand. Nathan was happily building a sand castle and the girls each had a plastic shovel in their hand, scooping up sand and dumping it into a pail. Randy also eyed Jane, who was lounged on a blanket close by, soaking up the sun. She was beautiful in every way. The sun glistened on her sun-tanned skin and her hair blew softly in the summer breeze. Dressed in short denim shorts and a floral bikini top, she turned her head and waved at Randy. He waved back. Then he stared out at the ocean and watched Dr. James Ryan, his best friend, on his surfboard, carving the waves in the sun and surf of the Pacific Northwest Coast. The day couldn't have been much better.

www.ingramcontent.com/pod-product-compliance
Lightning Source LLC
Chambersburg PA
CBHW071328020726
47502CB00001B/12